A MYSTERY BY JOHN PESTA

S0-ARG-248

SAFELY BURIED

— John Pesta

CreateSpace
Charleston, South Carolina
An Amazon.com Company

Cover illustration by Maureen O'Hara Pesta
Cover design by Jesse Pesta

ISBN: 1456344471
ISBN-13: 9781456344474

The Library of Congress has provided the following LCCN for cataloging purposes: 2010918783.

The first edition of this book was printed in paperback by CreateSpace, an Amazon.com company.

Manufactured in the United States of America

For my mother, who loved to read mysteries.

ACKNOWLEDGMENTS

I owe special thanks to several persons who provided professional advice that helped me write this book: David Gohn, a former prosecutor in Jackson County, Indiana; Detective Bob Lucas, crime scene investigator in the Jackson County Sheriff's Department; and Police Chief Steve Scarlett, Jr., of the Brownstown, Indiana, Police Department. Each of them generously shared his time and expertise to answer my questions about procedural matters in criminal cases.

Thanks also to Thomas Hoobler, author or coauthor of scores of books, for his publishing suggestions and encouragement.

And most of all, thanks to my family: my wife, Maureen, who served as my first reader and critic and whose pastel painting on the cover depicts a scene from the novel; my son, Jesse, whose Web site butternoparsnips.com first presented *Safely Buried* in serial form; and my daughter, Abigail, who for many years has urged me to publish my work.

SAFELY BURIED

CHAPTER 1
A Woman in a Cast

IT WAS ten at night. I had just come off I-65, and my high beams lit her up from behind. She was walking along the road between dark, endless cornfields, and her right leg was in a cast. She wore denim shorts and a yellow tank top that didn't quite reach the shorts. Without crutches, she moved as fast as she could on the gravelly shoulder. She would take a long step with her good leg, stiffly swing the cast forward the same distance, and immediately start the next step. Tilting jerkily, she looked as if she would fall with every stride. I crossed the centerline to give her more room to fall. Just as I was about to pass her, she glanced over her shoulder and stuck out a thumb.

I thought her car must have broken down back up the road. But if that was the problem, why hadn't she stayed there instead of striking out for Campbellsville, eight miles away? I was tempted to keep on going—I didn't make a habit of picking up hitchhikers. But there she was, nearly helpless. How could I leave her out here in the middle of nowhere?

I pulled off the road about a hundred yards in front of her and put the car in reverse. The little Civic whirred like a windup toy. She hurried toward me, her cast flailing. I hit the brakes and pushed the door open. I heard her panting, scraping.

She leaned over and peered at me. "Thanks," she said. "I really appreciate this." She was good looking in a tough sort of way. "I don't know if I can fit in there," she said.

A cloud of beer fumes wafted toward me. I should have known she must be either drunk or stoned. All I needed was for her to throw up in the car.

"I can move the seat," I said. I reached down for the lever and slid the seat all the way back.

The corner of her mouth crinkled into a sneer. "That's better, slightly." Without sitting down, she jimmied herself inside by bracing her left leg under the dashboard and pushing herself up against the back of the seat. "Damn it," she muttered under her breath as she struggled to get the cast in. Next a prayer: "There. Made it. Thank God." She slammed the door. "I just hope I can get out again."

She was half sitting, half braced against the seatback. "You don't look very comfortable," I said.

"Hah! That's an understatement if I ever heard one."

She was in her late twenties, maybe early thirties. Her light-brown hair was a mess of tangles, but the breezy look was kind of nice. She had a thin face with sharp features—straight nose, tightly drawn lips.

I waited for a semi to pass, and then I got back on the highway. "Where are you going?" I asked her.

"Not far. I'll show you."

"How come you're hitchhiking? Your car break down?"

She shook her head. "I don't have a car. I thumbed a ride from Indy." She pressed both hands on the seat to support her mostly suspended body.

"What brings you way down here?"

Instead of answering, she made a long yawn, then slapped both sides of her mouth as if apologizing. "I'm going to see some friends of mine. We're almost there. We cross an old iron bridge, and their house is on the other side." She scooted a couple inches closer to me to make more room for the cast.

"I don't think so," I replied. "There's a bridge up ahead, but it's not iron, and we're not almost there."

"Yes we are. You think I'm lying to you?"

She did not sound totally bombed, but she definitely was lost. What had I gotten myself into? She stared straight ahead, as if trying to spot a road that wasn't there. We were in the river bottoms, and it was too dark to see anything except the white lines on the highway. There were no houses, no billboards, no stars. She yawned again.

"Don't fall asleep," I said. "You need to tell me where we're going."

"Don't worry, I won't fall asleep."

"You're half asleep already. By the way, how did you break your leg?"

"Hey, you got anything to drink?"

"Sorry, no. How'd you break your leg?"

"Not even some water? My last ride had a cooler of beer."

"Maybe you should've stayed with him."

She pretended to shiver. "No way. He gave me the creeps." Then I got the answer to my question: "I fell off the roof at my mother's house while I was patching a hole—a tree branch poked a hole through the shingles and decking."

"Really? You fell off the roof? How high was it?"

"Not that high. No more than ten feet, I'd say."

"You're lucky the only thing you broke was your leg."

"Yeah, well, I have a pretty hard head."

From the beery breath and the way she talked, I guessed she worked in a bar. I figured I'd find out for sure pretty soon.

"Who are these friends you're going to visit?"

"We used to be neighbors before they moved to the sticks."

"What's their name?"

"Cheryl and Wayne."

"Cheryl and Wayne what?"

"Garth. Why?"

"I just wondered if I might know them."

She took a deep breath, almost another yawn. "They moved down here because they wanted to have horses."

"And what's your name?"

"Paula."

"Paula what?"

"Henry. And please don't say 'Henry what?'"

"Nice to meet you, Paula. I'm Phil."

With a triumphant laugh she shot back, "Phil what?"

"Larrison."

At least she was still awake.

"Here comes the bridge," I said. "It's not iron, or steel, though. It's concrete."

As soon as we crossed the bridge, the land began rising and scattered houses appeared. Brickton, a small unincorporated village, lay just ahead. I slowed down and said, "Is this where your friends live?"

She did not answer. Her eyes scanned the mostly dark houses.

"So where do they live?" I repeated.

She shook her head slowly. "I'm looking for the street."

Brickton did not have many streets, and there was no iron bridge between here and Campbellsville.

Suddenly she erupted: "There! That's where we go."
She jabbed a finger at the major intersection in Brickton.
"Turn right, turn right!"

I made the turn as ordered and drove at a crawl past
a half dozen old two- and three-story frame houses. "Are
you sure we're in the right place?" I asked her. "Maybe
you got off the interstate at the wrong exit."

She dropped her hand on her lap. "I'm not *that* stupid."

"Well, what do you want me to do now?" I asked her.

She chewed on her lip. Then she turned and looked at
me. "If you want me to, I'll get out here, but if you don't
mind, would you just go out this street a little ways. They
live in the country. Cheryl drove me down here once to
see her place when they first moved in. I know this is the
right street. But it's dark now, and Cheryl brought me
here in the daytime."

"Sure, why not?" I said. "I've got nothing else to do."

So on we went. Give it another half hour or so, I told
myself. After that I could bring her back to Brickton or
drop her off at a motel in Campbellsville. Besides, I really did have nothing else to do. I was on my way
home from the community college where I moonlight-
ed as an adjunct, teaching Journalism 101. At home all
I would do is plop myself in front of the TV and fall
asleep.

We passed a cluster of enormous grain bins and left
the few lights of Brickton behind. Bugs by the hundreds
began splattering the windshield. I made a mental note
of the time: 10:28. Give it till 10:58. Thinking of the time
made my eyelids feel heavy.

Paula must have sensed I was getting tired. She put
her hand on my wrist and said, "Phil, I want you to know
I really appreciate you helping me like this tonight. I know

I'm making you go way out of your way. It's real nice of you." The sudden contriteness in her voice sounded too apologetic. She probably thought I needed a pat on the head to keep driving.

"No problem," I lied. "I just hope we find your friends."

Her hand slid off my wrist. "You and me both."

I slowed down as we came to a Y in the road. I asked which way she wanted to go.

She hesitated a moment, then pointed left. "That way."

Now and then we passed a house or a trailer or a barn as we rolled through the flat farm fields, smashing more bugs. Once a pickup truck tailgated us for more than a mile before shooting past with its radio blaring rap music. Another fifteen minutes passed. We were almost in the knobs. Above us not far ahead were the two radio towers that served Campbellsville and Meridian County. Their lights cast a reddish glow on the underside of the thick mass of clouds.

"Any of this look familiar?" I asked her.

"It might if I could see it," she said. "It's too dark."

"Maybe we should've gone the other way back at that fork."

"No, this is the way. I just forgot how far it was."

My patience was wearing out. This whole thing was nuts. And I was nuts for going along with it.

We drove up a steep hill, followed the ridge briefly, and started down the other side. The forest was filled with the rasp of locusts.

Finally I said, "This isn't working. How about if we go in to town and I drop you off at a motel so you can get a good night's sleep. You can find your friends in the morning."

"I can't afford a motel."

"Don't you have any money on you?"

"Some, but I'm not gonna throw it away on a motel."

"Well, we can't drive around out here all night."

She stiffened. "Okay, then stop the car and let me out. I'll find them by myself." She was silent for a few seconds, then added, "Their place can't be far from here."

"Yeah, right," I said. "Come on, I'll take you to a motel in town. I'll even help you pay for the room—if you'll let me."

"No thanks. I'd rather take my chances out here."

So now I was a threat.

She said, "You can let me out any time now."

I kept going.

The woods ended at the bottom of the hill, and once again we were driving past farms. We went up a short rise onto a one-lane bridge, and Paula whirled toward me: "This is it! This is the bridge I told you about!"

"I thought you meant a *big* bridge."

"I never said it was big. I said it was made of iron, and we just crossed an iron bridge. The house should be coming up soon."

There was a brick ranch home on the left, but she shook her head and said, "Keep going."

A log cabin appeared on the right, then a white mailbox by a gravel road. "Turn there," she commanded.

It was hard to believe we had found the house she was looking for. In fact, I did not believe it. As we started down the gravel lane, there was no house in sight, just a cornfield on one side, a pasture on the other. We clanked over an old cattle guard and came around a bend in the corn, and Paula shouted, "There, there it is, just like I said. And you thought I was making it all up."

A tall farm house that looked at least a hundred years old stood like a white patriarch near the foot of another steep hill. The windows were dark.

"They must be in bed," Paula said. "Blow the horn."

"You want to wake them up?"

"I sure do."

I tapped the horn twice. It sounded like Little Boy Blue's. I hit it again, but no lights came on. "Looks like nobody's home," I told her.

"Damn, where are they?" She fumbled with the handle and flung the door open. She began twisting and squirming to get the cast out. "You need a bigger car," she griped.

I left the motor running with the headlights aimed at the house and got out to help her. By the time I came around to her side, Paula had her cast halfway out of the car. When she got both feet on the ground, I held her hands and pulled her up. She took off at once, hobbling across the overgrown lawn.

"Nobody's home," I called after her. "By now they would have heard us."

She did not answer. Left leg first, she climbed the four steps to the porch one at a time. She knocked on the door. When nothing happened, she banged on the window in the upper half of the door. "Cheryl, it's me—Paula," she yelled. "Are you there?" She banged away again. "Come on, get out of bed. Let me in."

As I started up the steps, the glass shattered. I thought she had broken it by knocking too hard, until she bent over and wiped her bloody elbow on the cast.

"I hope there's nobody sitting in there with a shotgun," I said.

"I gotta use the john," she said.

Thinking ahead this time, she removed her one shoe and used the heel to knock out a jagged piece of glass.

Carefully she reached inside and felt for the lock. The door squealed open.

"Are you coming?" she said.

"Why not? What's a little breaking and entering?"

She found the light switch, and we stepped inside.

The stench was overwhelming.

The house was filled with the smell of death.

CHAPTER 2
Smell of Death

"PEEE-UUUU," Paula said with a cringe and a shiver, "what died in here?"

The rotten smell filled my nose and mouth and seared my eyes. I tried to blow the dirty air out of my mouth before it reached my throat and lungs. I felt as if worms were already inside me.

Paula raised her top over the tip of her nose, exposing her midriff. "I'm going to open the windows," she said. "Leave the front door open too, okay?"

She staggered into the living room, which lay to the right of a wide stairway that led to the second floor. I followed her to the tall windows. The high-ceilinged room contained only a few pieces of furniture, none of which seemed to belong in the old house. In one corner was an L-shaped black sofa with overstuffed seats and back pillows. A reclining chair with cup holders was parked too close to a giant flat-screen TV. A poster of the Grateful Dead hung above the fireplace, and a shaggy muddy green rug covered about a third of the floor, where several empty beer bottles lay amid sections of the *Campbellsville Gleaner,* my employer.

I got one of the windows open and poked my nose against the screen to grab a breath of clean air. Just to be saying something, I said, "Sometimes in these old houses rats and mice die in the walls."

"Yeah, but they don't stink like this," Paula said. She got one window up and left the last one to me. Her steel-heeled cast clonked its way to the dining room on the other side of the entrance hall, and moments later she yelled at me from the kitchen in the back of the house: "Hey, Phil, c'mere. I found your rats."

By the time I reached the kitchen, she was already using a broom to drag a dead cat out of the cabinet under the sink.

"That's a mighty big rat," she said with a sarcastic laugh.

Flies buzzed around the carcass, and carrion beetles crawled on its face. The cat's mouth was open, as if gagging on the beetles. With one hand, Paula used a broom to pull the animal into a cardboard box that she held at an angle with her other hand.

I opened the door to the pantry, where I discovered that the back door of the house was not locked. I called to Paula, "Guess what—you didn't have to break in."

Clonk . . . clonk . . . clonk. "What do you mean?" she said.

"The back door was unlocked."

"Really?"

"Really."

"That's strange." She thought a moment. "They must have went away and forgot to lock it. I hope nothing got stolen." She paused again. "Let's put the cat outside. At least they won't have to put up with the smell when they get back. I wonder why it died. Poor baby. I know. They must have forgot to leave food out for it. But Cheryl would never forget to do that. She loves cats. You know what—I bet they didn't know it got in the house. Its food is probably in the barn. Maybe it got into some mouse poison or something. Yeah, I bet that's it."

"Okay," I said, "let's get rid of it."

I went back to the kitchen and picked up the box. The busy flies buzzed angrily. As I carried the cat through the pantry, Paula held the back door for me and said, "It's a shame I didn't come sooner. The cat looks like it just died a couple days ago."

I laid the box on the ground a few feet from the house and went back inside.

The putrid odor had not left with the cat, and Paula began opening windows in the kitchen and dining room. I picked up a dish towel and used it as a breathing mask. I took short shallow breaths through my mouth as I looked around for something to cover the hole in the broken window. A pair of cloth place mats lay on the kitchen table, and Paula helped me fit them, together with a crumpled-up newspaper, into the hole.

I asked her what she would do now that her friends weren't here.

"I'll stay put till they get back," she said. "Cheryl and Wayne won't mind. I can clean up the place for them. When they get home, I'll replace the glass I didn't need to break."

"Do you have any idea where they went?"

She shook her head slowly. "I don't know. Prob'ly down to Kentucky. That's where their folks live. Hey, you know what—" she made a tinny embarrassed laugh "—I just remembered what I came in here for. I better go do it before I wet myself."

She tottered back to the stairway, grabbed hold of the banister, and tried to climb the steps, but she quickly gave up and sat down on them. Using her hands and her left leg, she boosted herself from one step to the next. She smiled as I watched her. "It's easier this way, she said."

She seemed lighthearted, happy, tipsy. "Don't go anywhere," she said. "I'll fix you a cup of coffee when I come down."

On the wall at the foot of the stairs I spied a pair of switches and flicked them on, lighting up the second-floor hall. I had to go to work in the morning, but coffee sounded good. "Let's drink it on the front porch," I said.

"Sure, that would be nice." Her voice was soft and friendly, tiredly inviting.

At the top of the steps, she hauled herself onto her feet and disappeared. I heard her thumping across the floor.

Then she screamed the loudest scream I had ever heard.

I took the steps two at a time.

She stood shaking in a doorway. "They're dead," she whimpered. "They're both dead." Her voice trembled, *"Oh-h-h-h-h my God . . . oh-h-h-h God . . . Somebody killed them. Oh God. Oh Jesus."*

I peered in beside her. The strength of the stench almost knocked me down. The greenish, blackened body of a naked woman lay twisted on the bathroom floor. A man's body in the same condition hung over the side of the tub, which contained around an inch of bloody water that looked more like mud. So many insects covered the corpses that their skin seemed to move. I could see that the woman's abdomen had ruptured, and the insects had invaded every opening.

Paula swayed back and forth. Her shoulder trembled against my arm. Her mouth hung open as she gazed at her friends. I thought she was going into shock.

"Let's get out of here," I said.

She did not move.

I put an arm around her waist and tried to steer her out of the doorway. "We can't do anything here," I said. "We mustn't touch anything. We've got to call the police."

Her body stiffened. At the top of her voice she screeched in my face, "No! I won't go!" She grabbed hold of the door frame with both hands.

"You can't stay here, Paula. It's not safe. Whoever did this might come back." I pinned her arms and broke her grip.

She freaked out. "I'm not going. You can't make me. They're my friends." She pushed backward, and the two of us nearly went down. "You go yourself," she spluttered at me. She tried to shake me off and squirmed from side to side. "Get offa me. Get the hell out of here. Leave me alone." She gritted her teeth and almost made us fall again. "I told you to leave me alone! I mean it now! Let go of me!"

I gave her a hard slap on the face. I didn't expect it to work, but it did. She stopped struggling. Her breaths came loud and hard.

With my arm around her waist, I guided her toward the stairs. I could only hope she wouldn't start fighting again on the way down. I pictured her slapping and clawing. Maybe that's how this night would end, the two of us on the floor with our necks broken.

As we reached the bottom step, she said, "I still have to use the toilet."

"Not that one," I said. "I'll take you to a gas station. Right now we are out of here."

"Wait." She pulled away. "I have to turn off the lights."

I didn't think the Garths would mind if we left their lights burning, but I let her hobble around while I looked for a phone to call the sheriff's department. I couldn't find one. My BlackBerry was at home on my desk, but it probably would not have worked here anyway because of the knobs.

I went after Paula and found her rifling through a drawer in the kitchen. I half held, half dragged her outside.

The night air was cool. It smelled amazingly fresh and clean. It felt like a blessing.

CHAPTER 3
Call It Fate

WE CROSSED the lawn in the glare of the headlights and the throb of the idling engine. Lightning flickered in the clouds like a fluorescent lamp trying to start, and thunder rumbled through the knobs. Fresh air never tasted so good. In the house I had felt as if I were breathing particles of rotten flesh, but now the cool breeze that rustled through the trees seemed to be cleaning out my lungs.

I opened the car door for Paula.

"What are we going to do now?" she said, twisting herself into the seat.

"We've got to call this in to the police."

"Great," she muttered. "I can see I won't be getting much sleep tonight."

"You're not the only one," I said. I had a lot of work ahead of me. This was going to be a big story for the *Gleaner,* and I had to write it. We didn't have many murders in Meridian County. The last one, which had occurred nearly a year ago, was connected with a meth lab in Nazareth, a small town at the western end of the county. That event was no match for a home invasion and a double murder.

We clanked over the cattle guard and scraped bottom in the gully. A few drops of water spotted the windshield.

Moments later a heavy downpour drummed the roof and sheets of rain swirled in front of us.

Paula said, "I guess maybe you should drop me off at a motel after all."

"I will do that—as soon as we talk to the police."

A long breath pinched her nostrils. Her words came out as she exhaled: "Drop me off first then. I don't like talking to cops. They treat you like dirt."

I laughed. "You're not wanted by the police, are you?"

"No," she snapped as if insulted. "But why can't it wait till morning? I'm tired."

"So am I. But you seem to be forgetting the two bodies you found."

"I'm not forgetting. But what difference would it make? Wayne and Cheryl looked like they were laying there, I don't know, for weeks maybe. We just happened to find them tonight." She puffed out her cheeks and blew. "God, I could use a beer."

"Well, I'm sorry, but we have to call the cops now, not tomorrow. And then I have to write a story for the paper I work for."

She glowered at me. "You're a reporter? Shit. Now I get written up in the paper."

"Call it fate," I said.

I had to get at least a few paragraphs in the morning paper, which meant I'd also have to call the press room and tell them to hold off on printing the first section. They would not be happy about it.

It made no sense to drive all the way to Campbellsville. The county police would come flying back here, and I'd be right behind them. The sensible thing was to stay put. I just had to get to a phone before the presses started rolling. I felt like kicking myself for leaving my cell phone at home.

I swerved onto the county road and headed back the way we had come. The nearby log house was completely dark. My next chance was the brick ranch. I stepped on the gas but hit the brakes almost immediately because the house appeared sooner than I expected and its lights were on.

I pulled into the concrete driveway. A picture window with open drapes provided a wide-angle view of the living room.

I asked Paula if she wanted to go in with me.

"Jeez no, I don't want to talk to *anybody*."

"All right. I won't be long."

I jumped out and made a dash for the house. The porch light came on and the front door opened before I got there. A heavy-set man in a striped polo shirt poked his head out. He doesn't realize what a risk he's taking, I said to myself. He's lucky I'm not the guy who murdered his neighbors.

I took one last running step onto the narrow porch and said, "I'm sorry to bother you, but I need to call the police. May I use your phone?"

"What happened?" he said.

"Your next-door neighbors have been murdered."

"Murdered?" He sounded skeptical and shocked at the same time. "When? Tonight?"

"Please, may I use the phone?"

He yanked the door inward, and I stepped onto a slate floor with a round oriental rug that looked too expensive to wipe my feet on. The living room was as big as my whole apartment.

He pointed. "It's over there."

I crossed the room and punched in the number of the sheriff's department, which I knew by heart. While the phone rang, I introduced myself.

He said, "Nice to meet you, Mr. Larrison. I'm Don Grapevine."

He was slightly taller than I was, which made him about six-feet-one. He had a wide chest and square shoulders. Barely a hint of a paunch bulged against his shirt, whose wide blue and green stripes somehow went with the salmon-pink collar. I guessed he was pushing sixty and trying not to show it. He sported a dark tan that seemed to glaze over the pale blotches on his skin. He had a golden-blond flattop that was perfectly flat and probably dyed.

The phone went on ringing. Where was the dispatcher? What was he doing, playing cards? I hung up and asked Grapevine for a phone book. He went to the kitchen, which was behind the living room, and returned with the directory. I looked up Sheriff Eggemann's home number. I could have called the state police, but the sheriff wouldn't have liked that.

I heard a door open at the other end of the house, and a woman called, "Don, who's there?"

Grapevine didn't reply. I figured he wanted to hear what I was going to say.

The sheriff's slow smooth drawl tickled my ear. After exchanging a few pleasantries—Sheriff Eggemann was never in a hurry—I gave him a capsule account of the night's events.

"Were they shot?" he asked me.

"I couldn't tell," I said. "The bodies are too decomposed. My guess is they've been dead around two or three weeks."

While the sheriff and I were talking, the woman from the other end of the house arrived in a summery cotton robe. She seemed surprised to find a stranger standing in the living room, and as soon as she saw me she pinched the lapels of her robe together. She was decades younger than Grapevine, maybe twenty-seven, twenty-eight, a couple years younger than me. She couldn't be his wife, could she? His daughter? No, she wouldn't have called him Don. His mistress? Let's hope not. Framed in the entrance to the hallway, she stood barefooted, rosy pink from the bathtub or shower, drying her hair with an oversized towel. "What's going on?" she asked Grapevine.

I listened to them with one ear, the sheriff with the other.

"Our neighbors—the Garths—have been murdered," Grapevine said.

Her mouth fell open. She took a few slow steps into the room and stopped beside a grand piano, where she struck a girlish pose, one leg bent, her knee jutting out to the side with her foot perched on its toes.

When I stopped talking for a moment, she silently mouthed the words "Is that true?"

I nodded.

She wandered toward the front window and plopped down on one of two matching sofas that faced each other across a square cocktail table. Her auburn hair glistened next to a lamp. She crossed her arms below her breasts and hugged herself as if she were cold. I realized it was cold in the house. The air conditioner must have been running full blast.

"God, I didn't know them that well, but I did know them," she said to Grapevine. "Cheryl's nice—I mean she *was*. Why would anybody murder them?"

The sheriff said, "You've had a busy night, Phil. I'd like you and your hitchhiker to stay right where you are till I get there. I'll be there as soon as I can."

"We'll be here," I told him.

As soon as I hung up, Grapevine said, "Phil, I'd like you to meet my stepdaughter, Jodie. Jodie, this is Phil Larrison. He's the editor of the *Gleaner*."

"Hi," I said. "I'm sorry I barged in on you like this."

She flicked her wrist. "No problem."

"The sheriff's on his way," I told them. "He wants me to wait here, but I'll get out of your hair. I'll wait in my car."

Jodie said, "I heard you tell the sheriff there's a woman with a broken leg with you. Why don't you bring her in. The two of you can wait here."

"She'll get soaked," I replied. "It takes a while for her to get out of the car in her cast."

"I've got a big umbrella," Grapevine said. "Don't leave her sitting outside by herself. We'll fix you some coffee or tea."

It sounded too good to pass up. "I'll see if she wants to come in," I said, but first I called the press room.

It was still raining when I went outside, but the deluge had been downgraded to a misty drizzle. Frogs peeped in the fields. I expected Paula to cuss me out for making her wait so long. I must have been in there all of ten minutes, fifteen at most. The car windows were fogged up. I saw a runny watery circle where she must have wiped the glass with her hand. I opened the door and began to apologize.

My stomach sank.

She was not there.

Through grinding teeth I mumbled, "Don't do this to me."

I stretched my neck to see if I could spot her somewhere. Come on, God, give me a break, just one break. But it wasn't God's fault she had disappeared. I shouldn't have let her out of my sight. "Paula," I yelled, "come on now."

She could not have gone far. She might be only fifty feet away, taking a pee in the field. Or she could be hobbling down the road, trying to bum another ride. But the most likely explanation was that she was on her way back to the Garth place. She'd hide in the corn for the rest of the night if she had to, till the police were finished. I had found her looking for something in the kitchen—money maybe. She'd go back inside and search the whole house.

I called to her through the rain.

Grapevine came out carrying a red and white beach umbrella, which he opened and held over our heads. "What's going on?" he said.

"She's gone," I said. "She probably went back to the Garths' house. That's where she expected to stay. I'm going to go back and see if I can find her." I felt deflated, limp. "Listen, when the police get here, tell them I'm over there, would you. Thanks. Thanks for your help."

I got in the car and turned on the air conditioner to clear the windows. The sheriff had told me to stay put, but it was more important to find Paula. I knew he didn't want us contaminating the murder scene any more than we already had, but that was the point—we already had. I backed out to the road. Grapevine and Jodie stared at me from the porch. I felt like an idiot for leaving Paula alone in the car.

I probed the edge of the fields with my headlights, weaving from side to side. By now she had to be drenched. How could she get through these fields with her leg in a cast? She might fall and break her other leg. Her cast could get stuck in a groundhog hole.

Darker possibilities took shape. There were packs of coyotes in these hills—they could eat her alive. What if the murderer lived in the log cabin up ahead? Maybe he had followed us to Grapevine's and snatched Paula while I was inside the house. What if he was watching me right now, taking aim as I inched along the road?

Was I still awake? I felt as if I were having one of those early-morning anxiety dreams where I gradually realize I'm dreaming. But how could I have fallen asleep so quickly? I shook myself. My eyes felt stiff, like dried-out meringue. I thought I felt the first faint tickle of a sore throat. My skin seemed coated with greasy dirt. I gripped the steering wheel hard and made a conscious effort to stay on the road, just in case I was still dreaming.

I parked in front of the Garths' house, got out of the car, and looked around. For a split second the scene in the bathroom reappeared. I knew that image would pop into my head for the next twenty years. I had a feeling that Paula was watching me. I called her a couple of times, but she did not answer.

The misty drizzle was now just mist. A thick shelf of mist hung over the corn.

It wasn't long before the flashing lights of two police cars appeared on the ridges of the knobs. They were running silent—no need to wake up the citizenry at this hour. A few minutes later they were in the hollow. They stopped at Grapevine's house for a minute, and then they were on their way over here. Sheriff Eggemann came down the lane in a brown-and-tan SUV, followed by one of his deputies in a brown-and-tan cruiser. Their red and white flashers seemed to bounce back and forth as they lit up the hollow.

The sheriff stepped out of his car and said, "Dangnabbit, Phil, I thought you told me she had a broken leg. How'd you lose her?" He was tall and thin, but not lanky. A decorated veteran of the Vietnam War, he was a popular Democrat who played musical chairs at election time. He was a polite, affable man who looked less like a county sheriff than the county auditor he had been for two terms and the county clerk he had been for two terms before that. He was expected to win his second term as sheriff later this year.

"I left her in the car while I went inside to call you. I came back here to try to find her."

Deputy Jesse Holsapple spat on the ground not far from my feet. "That was real smart," he said.

I had known Holsapple a long time. I had liked him better before he joined the county police, back when he was a full-time carpet installer. He had installed all the carpeting in the house where my ex and I had lived. He had done a nice job, but once he got his deputy's badge he turned into a cocky, no-nonsense kind of guy. He had also become a part-time minister, otherwise known as a half-assed preacher. He served a small church in Shale Creek, where he brought the message to a few folks every Sunday, unless he was on duty.

The sheriff stared at the misty fields. "Well, I reckon she'll turn up sooner or later," he said. "Jesse, get on the horn to the state police and tell them to watch for a female hitchhiker wearing a cast on her leg—that should be enough of a description—just in case she gets back on I-65." Next, he activated the spotlight on the side of his SUV and scanned the surrounding landscape, to no avail.

"Let's take a look inside," he said. "Normally, I'd wait for the state police to get here before going in. That way they can't say we disturbed any evidence, but I'd say it's been pretty well disturbed already, right, Phil?"

"We didn't go in the bathroom," I said.

Holsapple grunted. "At least you done something right."

I shot back, "We found the bodies, didn't we?"

I led the way to the house and showed them the broken glass in the front door. The door had locked itself when we'd left, so the sheriff donned a glove, slipped his hand inside the crumpled-up barrier that Paula and I had made, and unfastened the lock.

"Don't touch anything," he said. He flicked on a small flashlight, and Holsapple did the same.

I followed the sheriff inside with the deputy right behind me.

"It's a little ripe in here," the sheriff said, covering his nose with his sleeve.

The flashlights sent crazy shadows across the walls and ceilings until the sheriff used a gloved knuckle to turn on the living-room lights.

"The motive couldn't have been robbery," Holsapple said. "That TV and stereo wouldn't still be here."

"The bathroom's upstairs," I told them.

As we went up, I had a weird premonition that the bodies would not be there.

I need not have worried.

When he saw them, Holsapple let out a long whistle. "Holy Christ almighty God."

The sheriff stooped down and began scrutinizing the bodies. "I suppose we'd better call the coroner," he said.

"You want me to call him, Sheriff?" Holsapple asked.

"Go ahead, Jesse. He'll want to see what we've got here. He'll hand the case over to the state police, of course. He'd be in way over his head on this one."

The sheriff poked his light under the clawfoot tub. He inspected the two tall windows, both of which were open a couple inches from the top and bottom. The windows were screened, but the insects had found other ways into the bathroom. He looked for shell casings on the floor but did not locate any. When he was finished in the bathroom, we went downstairs, where he stood in the middle of the kitchen and simply looked around.

I told him I had to get back to the office to write my story. I tried to get a few comments out of him—his take on the situation, could he say if they'd been shot?—but he wouldn't commit to anything. "You just sprung this on us," he said. "Give us some time to investigate." In the bright light from the ceiling his face appeared slack and drained. He turned and said, "Phil, you look as tired as I feel. Why don't you go write your story and go to bed. We can talk again tomorrow."

That was exactly what I wanted to do.

As I headed for town, the freshly washed air fanned me through the open windows, the locusts throbbed in the trees, and the red lights on the radio towers watched me like a pair of eyes.

CHAPTER 4
Mackey's Grill

B Y THE time I got to bed that night my eyes were so sore I felt as if someone had scrubbed them with sandpaper. My head felt like a squashed grape. As tired as I was, I had trouble falling asleep. Over and over, my evening with Paula replayed itself in my mind. I'd begin to drop off and something else would pop up in my mind's eye—the bodies in the bathroom with their crawling green and black flesh . . . Paula tottering along on the side of the road . . . Grapevine and Jodie watching me from their porch. . . . I never did seem to fall asleep, yet the alarm clock, my safety valve, startled me when it went off at eight-thirty, an hour and a half later than I usually got up. I showered and shaved, had some coffee and toast, and went to work.

My boss, Edward J. Wylie, owner and publisher of the *Gleaner,* which had been in his family since the late nineteenth century, came out of his office as soon as he saw me.

"Why in God's name did you pick up a floozie like that?" he demanded. "Wait, don't tell me. I don't mean to pry into your personal life." He gave me a big grin and a big laugh.

"You know me," I said, "I always pick up women with broken legs."

He was thickset, broad-shouldered, and nearly bald. His round pink head fringed with silky white hair made him look like Friar Tuck. He was an intense guy, manic at times, especially when the paper had a big scoop.

"I'm glad you do!" he bellowed, leading the way to his office. "And I'm glad the sheriff didn't tell the damn radio stations last night. They came out with the story this morning, of course, but they had to read it in the paper first. At least they gave us credit for once. If they hadn't, I'd have sued their asses off. Did you hear what they had to say about you?"

I shook my head.

"They're calling you the Good Samaritan."

"Success at last—I'm a cliche. Do I get a raise?"

He chortled again. "No, but I'll buy you a cup of coffee. Let's go to Mackey's."

I was always willing to get out of the office for another cup of coffee.

We walked up Main Street past the Courthouse. Another hot day was shaping up. Wispy threads of cloud hung in the bright blue sky with a fingernail moon that looked like another wispy cloud.

Mackey's Grill had four or five customers besides us. Since my wife had moved out, I ate breakfast there three or four times a week, and sometimes lunch, when I didn't skip it. The restaurant was squeezed in between the drugstore on the corner and a law office. Most of its neon sign had burned out years ago, but it had a brand-new glass and aluminum door. A warped poster for the Meridian County Fair leaned against one of the grimy front windows. We sat in our usual booth in the back, next to a 1950s-style jukebox on one side of us and a vinyl-covered swinging door on the other. The door flew at us whenever a waitress burst out of the kitchen with a tray.

A big blonde waitress smacked two glasses of water on the table. "What'll it be today, boys?"

"Two coffees, Harriet," Edward said, "—if it's still fresh."

She whirled away toward the glass pots on the burners. "It's as fresh as it was yesterday, Sweetie," she said over her shoulder.

"I told you not to talk to me like I'm an old man," Edward called after her.

I liked Edward. I couldn't have worked for him so long if I hadn't. He was a glad-hander, a civic booster, a bottom-liner, but he wanted to put out a real newspaper. The news came first, no matter whose toes got stepped on. Once, after the owner of a supermarket pulled his ads because we wouldn't keep his eighteen-year-old son's name out of the paper after he got arrested for driving under the influence, Edward blared, "I'll shut this damn rag down before I kiss that S.O.B.'s ass."

Our coffee arrived, and Edward piped up with, "What do you make of that Paula character, Phil? You think she's still in our neighborhood?"

"I don't know," I said. I dumped a packet of sugar in my cup. "My guess is she hung around the Garth place last night hoping the police would leave. But I bet the sheriff had someone stake out the place in case she showed up."

"Yeah. Maybe they nabbed her. Have you talked to Carl this morning?"

"No, I just got to work when you dragged me over here."

"I thought you might have gone over to the jail before you came to work."

"Why didn't I think of that? I should have known you'd want to come out with an extra edition today."

One side of his mouth twisted into a grinning snarl. "Wiseguy. Yeah, we'll put out an extra—if you find out who committed those murders."

"I'll hold you to that."

His tone turned serious. "You know, the cops may already have snagged her if she got back on the road last night, or this morning."

"I'll find out when I talk to the sheriff."

"Do you think she did it?"

I weighed the idea for half a nanosecond and shrugged. "If she did, she put on a good act. She really went to pieces when she found her friends' bodies."

"Maybe it *was* an act."

"I don't think so."

"Maybe she wanted a witness to see how distraught she'd be when she found them. It would deflect suspicion. Maybe that's why she hitched a ride with you."

"Why would she need to come back and find the bodies?"

"Doesn't the killer always return to the scene of the crime?"

"Right. Sure. Always. But she didn't exactly strike me as a shrewd and calculating person. She was half drunk."

"Maybe that was part of her act." He sat back and stared toward the plate-glass windows at the front of the restaurant. For a moment he seemed lost in thought. Then he leaned forward and said what I didn't need to be told: "I want to milk this thing for all it's worth." He smacked the table, stood up, and dropped a couple dollar bills on it. "Come on, let's get outta here. We've got work to do."

It wasn't that Edward's enthusiasm was infectious. I was accustomed to his fits and starts. But on our way back across the courthouse square, as he blabbered on, I felt something I had not felt in years, a tingle in my belly for my work. My instinct was to resist the tiny quiver of excitement, the way we perversely resist the tug back to life that comes with the spring. But then I saw Paula sitting in my car with her chin down, dazed and lost, staring into the darkness, and I couldn't help feeling sorry for her. I wondered how she had spent the night. I wondered where she was. I wanted to find her.

CHAPTER 5
Snooping Around

As soon as I got back to my office I called the sheriff. I learned that the county coroner, Henry Weir, had seen the bodies last night but was deferring to the state police and had not done a complete examination. "The cause of death is pretty obvious, though," Sheriff Eggemann said. "Both victims had multiple gunshot wounds. The coroner did not want to move the bodies, so at this time we can't tell you how many times they were shot, or where they were shot, but he did say each of them was shot at least once in the back of the head. The condition of the bodies makes it hard to say for sure. They'll probably do an autopsy at the state police lab."

"Would you say they were executed, Sheriff?" I asked.

"No, I would not. In fact, at this point I would rather not say anything at all."

"Maybe the shots in the head were a coup de grace," I said. "Maybe the shooter wanted to make sure they were dead."

"Your guess is as good as mine."

"Have you ruled out robbery as a motive?"

Slowly and patiently he said, "At this point we have not ruled anything out. We do not know why they were killed, and we have no actual suspects. We have identified one person of interest, thanks to you." His breath fluttered in my ear. "It really would help if we could talk to the woman you picked up. I wish you had held on to her."

"What about fingerprints or other evidence? Did you come up with anything last night?"

"Oh, I suspect we'll find lots of prints. A state-police CSI team is working on it as we speak. I imagine we'll find some of yours, Phil. Which reminds me, I'd like you to come over today so we can take a set of your finger-prints—just so we know which ones are yours."

"You're not planning to arrest me, are you, Carl?"

He thought about that, or pretended to. Finally he said, "Well, being as how you're the only one who claims to have seen this Paula Henry person of interest—none of the neighbors that we spoke to saw her—we don't know for sure that she actually exists. So I reckon we might have to lock you up, Phil. Let me think about it for a while."

"No hurry," I said. "By the way, I'd like to take some pictures of the house. Will that be a problem?"

"I expect it will. You'll get in the way of the crime-scene technicians." He tried to stifle a yawn. "But the state police would like to have a talk with you—if they haven't already. Has anyone been in to see you yet?"

"I'll go see them," I said.

"Good. Ask for Detective Lieutenant Bakery."

"Bakery?"

"That's what I said."

Before I went in search of Detective Lieutenant Bakery, I made myself take a deep breath, refocus, and edit a front-page feature that was waiting on my computer. Next I emailed Edward that I would do an update on the mur-ders and get a picture of the Garth house. I was itching to get out there again, but phone calls and other interrup-tions kept me in my chair. Finally I tore myself away.

In the late-morning sun the country air was bright and warm, and the hollow was a picture of serenity. The narrow fields of corn and soybeans stretched to the foot of the steep hills that surrounded them. I wondered who owned this pocket of farmland. Was it Grapevine or someone else? I'd have to find out.

One of the Grapevines' garage doors was up, and a red Miata stood in the driveway. I parked behind the sports car, climbed out of my Civic, and eyeballed the fields around the house. I did not see Paula hiding among the cornstalks, but I could see the roof of the Garth house a few hundred yards away.

A door squealed inside the garage, and a moment later a woman emerged from the shadows. She was lugging a bucket of water with a real sponge poking out of sudsy bubbles. It took me less than a second to realize who she was, but she caught the delay.

"Hello, Mr. Larrison," she said. "I'm Jodie Palladino. We met last night, remember?"

"You're not the woman whose leg was in a cast, are you?"

She gave me an arch smile and set her bucket on the ground. Then she picked up the end of a hose that was lying in the grass, twisted the nozzle, and began spraying the car. She was wearing a white sleeveless top and gray shorts that flared at the sides. She had a nice tan, not too dark, and her skin glistened with sunblock.

"What brings you here?" she said. "As if I don't know." She continued spraying for a moment but suddenly looked at me and said, "It's rude to wash a car when I have a visitor, isn't it?" She twisted the nozzle shut and tossed the hose back on the lawn. Then she hooked her thumbs in the pockets of her shorts and proceeded to give me her full attention.

"So your name is Palladino," I said. Now that I had heard the name, I could see the Italian in her full lips and prominent cheekbones.

"Yes. It was my father's name, of course. He died when I was in kindergarten."

"You can still remember him then."

"Yes. A little bit. He had brain cancer. My mother raised me by herself." Her brown eyes squinted against the sun. "She didn't get married again till a few years ago, after she met Don."

"Its a nice day to wash a car," I said. "How about doing mine."

"Hey, what a great idea! . . . On second thought, I'd better not. I've got too many other things to do today."

"Some other time then?"

"Don't hold your breath."

She took a step to the side and nearly tripped over the bucket of soapy water. "Well, I guess I've been polite long enough. I came out here to wash the car, so I guess I'd better get back to work."

"Me too," I said. "Do you mind if I ask you a few questions about the Garths?"

She wasn't exactly eager to get back to work. Instead of reaching for the sponge or picking up the hose again, she sat against the side of the car, which had already dried. "Ask away," she said.

"How well did you know them? What were they like?"

She sucked in her cheeks, pursed her lips, and thought. "Private. Kept to themselves. I hardly even knew the guy—Wayne—hardly ever saw him. But I'd bump into Cheryl now and then when I went walking. She was always on a horse. One time she asked me if I'd like to ride one of their horses, but I said, 'No thanks, I don't ride.' She dismounted and tied the horse to a fence and walked up the hill with me."

"Sounds like she wanted to make friends."

"I know, but it only happened once. I guess I should have made more of an effort to get to know her better. But she never came over here, and I never went over there." Her voice tapered off as she stared at the ground. Then she looked up and said, "It was my fault. She made the first move, but I never reciprocated."

"How did they make a living? Was this their farm?" I waved my arm at the tall green corn around us.

"Heck no. They weren't farmers. Cheryl told me they wanted to get out of Indianapolis and live in the country, that's all."

"I can see why they liked it here. It's really pretty. Who owns all the land?"

"My mother bought a few acres from a lady in Brickton to build this house. I think most of the land belongs to her."

"Is this where you grew up?"

"No. We used to live in Campbellsville."

"How long have you lived here?"

"Since I graduated from high school. We moved in that summer." She squinted suspiciously. "Just out of curiosity, what has all this got to do with the Garths?"

"Absolutely nothing," I said. "I'm just a snoop. Let's see . . . you were saying you blame yourself for not making friends with Mrs. Garth."

"I'm surprised you still remember." She took a deep breath and went on. "I should have invited Cheryl over for lunch or something. But the thing is, I haven't been back home very long, just the past three months or so.

I had some issues to work out. I wasn't looking to make new friends. But that's another story."

"I like stories," I said. "You want to tell me one?"

"No I don't. I'm trying to forget it."

She pushed herself off the car and walked idly toward the road. The bottom of her shirt had gotten caught in the waist of her shorts, and she reached behind to free it. Abruptly she turned and said, "I heard Mom and Don talking about them once. They were saying how Cheryl and her husband would take off in their RV and be gone for a week or two. Then they'd come back. Then they'd disappear again." She came toward me. "Mom thought they might be doing the flea-market thing—making artsy-craftsy stuff at home, then peddling it at festivals and flea markets. Maybe that's how they made their living."

"Is your mother home?" I said. "I'd like to talk to her, if she is."

She shook her head. "She's in Cincinnati visiting her sister, Anita. She'll be back on Monday." As an after-thought she added, "Don called her this morning and told her about the murders. He read her the story you had in the paper."

"Maybe I can see her sometime next week." I made a mental note to do that. "Do you know if the Garths had any friends around here?"

"I really don't," she answered. "Frankly, I didn't pay much attention to them. I remember one thing though. About a month ago there was a green van parked in their driveway for most of the day. But I have no idea if it was friends, or a serviceman, or what."

"Was it a commercial van?"

"I don't know. I don't think so. All I could see was the back of it as I drove past, and there was no name there."

"Depending on when you saw it—if it was around three or four weeks ago—it may not have been too long before the murders."

She made a little gasp, and her fingers went to her chin. "I never thought of that. There might be a connection."

"Maybe. Maybe not."

"Damn. Now that I think of it, it did seem odd for the truck to be parked out near the county road like that. Boy, if only I had written down the license-plate number—the killer might be in jail already." She laughed. "Now I have a question for you. Do you think the woman with the cast is still around here?"

"I think it's possible," I said, "but if she breaks in to the Garths' house again, the police will nab her. I think they'll be keeping an eye on that place for a while."

"I'm glad to hear that," she said. "It's scary living here all of a sudden, when two people can get murdered like that. It sounded horrible in the paper."

"It was a lot worse than that," I said.

I glanced at my watch. It would have been nice to go on chattering like this, but I had other stops to make. "Well, I'll let you finish your car," I said. "Oh, one other thing—does anyone live in the log cabin across from the Garth house?"

"Glenn Neidig," she said. "He's an old guy with a long beard. He'll talk your leg off if you let him."

"That's good," I said. "It makes my job a lot easier when people talk."

CHAPTER 6
Cloudy Window

M Y NEXT stop was the Garth house. A brown-and-tan police cruiser blocked the entrance to the driveway, and when I stopped in the road, a sheriff's deputy got out. I told him the sheriff had said Lieutenant Bakery wanted to see me.

"You can't drive in," he said, "but you can walk."

He returned to his car and backed up a few yards so I could park in front of him. Then he got on his walkie-talkie and reported that I was coming.

When I came around the bend in the cornfield, I was surprised to see a steep hill so close to the house. Last night I had hardly noticed the hill. A van and four police cars were lined up next to one another facing the house. I took my camera out of my pocket and grabbed some shots. It felt strange to be standing there again, and for a moment I thought I was dreaming. Everything that I had been through last night seemed to have happened long ago.

A man in a short-sleeved white shirt and sharply creased blue slacks crossed the lawn to meet me. He was a few inches shorter than I was, but built more solidly. I might have taken him for a pro football player if it weren't for the ID badge hanging on his belt. Then again, he was probably too old for the NFL. As he came closer, I could see a long scar at the edge of his left eye. It was the only mark on a smooth, closely shaved face whose skin seemed too tight for the bones underneath.

"Mr. Larrison," he said, extending his hand. "Jim Bakery, Indiana State Police." His voice was as sharp and crisp as his pants.

I made an effort to match his grip. "Nice to meet you. Sheriff Eggemann said you wanted to see me."

"That's correct. I appreciate you coming out here. You saved me a trip back to town."

"Don't mention it," I said. "I planned on coming anyway. I'd like to get some pictures for the paper."

"I read your story this morning. You had quite a night last night."

"That's for sure."

"How 'bout telling me about it." He took a small tape recorder out of his shirt pocket. "You don't mind if I use this, do you?"

Leaves of corn rustled in the breeze, and giant white spaniels floated over the knobs. Standing in the sun, I described how I had picked up Paula and how she had led me to the house. The detective did not interrupt until I described how Paula had broken the glass in the door.

"The crime-scene team found some blood on the broken glass," he said. "Did you get any cuts? What I'm getting at is, could any of the blood be yours?"

I held up my elbows. "No cuts."

"Why did you go in with her?" When I didn't answer right away, he added, "You delivered her where she wanted to go. You could have just dropped her off and gone home."

I nodded. "True. I guess I got caught up in the moment. I wanted to make sure she was all right before I left her there by herself."

"Did you have any reason to think she might be in danger?"

"Not really. The house was dark . . . isolated."

He wagged his head slowly from shoulder to shoulder as if weighing my response. "I can understand how you felt, Phil. She was a damsel in distress, and you were—"

"Not a knight in shining armor."

He made a mirthless laugh. "Okay—a nice guy. Were you ever here before last night?"

"No."

"Go on with your story, please."

I told him about everything else: the stench in the house, the dead cat, the bodies in the bathroom, Paula's disappearance—everything up to the arrival of the sheriff and the deputy. At the end of my story I said, "I know it was breaking and entering, but if we hadn't gone into the house, then we wouldn't have found the bodies. Would that make things better?"

Bakery said, "You've got a point," but he didn't seem to mean it.

I asked him if his investigation had turned up any leads, but all he said was he "couldn't comment at this time." I asked if it would be all right if I took some photos in the house, and he said the CSIs weren't quite finished yet. Then he stuck out his hand and gave me a fake smile to signal the conversation had ended. That was fine with me.

I went back to my car and drove across the road. The log cabin had a steep peaked roof like the ones in hillbilly cartoons. The old weathered logs were dusty gray, but a few bands of white chinking looked brand new. A bent stovepipe jutted out from one side of the cabin and rose a couple feet above the roof.

As I hauled myself out of the car again, a pack of hounds began barking and howling in their pens on the right. Between the cabin and the pens was a rickety wooden outhouse, and I noticed a man with a beard standing in front of it and watching me. I hoped he was coming out of the privy rather than going in—I didn't want to hold him up. I raised a hand and called, "Mr. Neidig?"

"That's me."

"Do you mind if I talk to you a little bit?"

"Do I get a choice?" he yelled back. "You're only about the tenth one that's been here today. Jest gimme a minute to duck in here." He snarled at the dogs, "Hey yarrr mutts, knock off that racket," and the racket diminished slightly as he disappeared into the outhouse.

I wondered if he owned any of the farmland that surrounded his cabin and the acre or so of ground on which it stood. I saw no barn, no farm equipment, just an old light-green pickup truck with bulbous fenders that was parked in front of the cabin.

A few minutes later he came out. His narrow shoulders rocked from side to side as he slouched across the crabgrass and dandelions that comprised his lawn.

As Jodie had said, he had a long beard. Thick and gray, it hung down to his sternum. What I could see of his face was dark red from the sun. His eyes looked like thin antique china, but they were as quick as a ferret's. The skin around them was lined and creased like an old leather shoe.

"Howdy," he said. "What can I do fer ya?"

I introduced myself, and we shook hands. We looked straight into each other's eyes. He was short and wiry, somewhere between seventy and ninety years old. A few strands of bluish-white hair stretched across his head.

"Larrison," he said. "You must be the feller that found the bodies over there last night." He pointed a thumb over his shoulder.

"I was in the house, but it was a friend of the murder victims who found them."

"The woman with the broken leg. I read all about it in the paper this mornin'. I picked up a copy at the general store in Hampstead—I needed some bread and milk. I wondered what all that ruckus was last night. I looked out the window and seen the police cars a-comin' and goin'. I had half a mind to go over there and see what the fuss was all about, but I didn't want to get in their way. I asked about it at the store, and they told me there was a story in the paper, so I bought me a copy."

"Have the police been here yet," I asked.

"Have they ever. The sheriff showed up before seven, but I get up around five, so that was all right. Then the state police started comin'—not one car, but four, five of 'em, one after the other, all mornin' long. My tongue's been waggin' so much, it feels like it's gonna fall outta my mouth."

He gave his tongue a rest. A breeze came cascading down the hillside, and an old oak tree on the far side of the cabin began to stir.

The old man said, "I suspect you was the first one I heard drivin' around in there last night. I thought nothin' of it at the time. Thought it was Mr. and Mrs. Garth comin' home from wherever they was at. It's been mighty quiet over there lately—until last night. Now I know why." He wiped his forehead with the back of his hand. "I feel like my head's ready to catch on fire. What say we go set in the shade?"

I had been standing with my hands on my hips, airing my armpits. "Lead the way," I said.

I followed him to the sagging porch on the front of his cabin. A white rocking chair with a seat cushion stood on one side, a heavy metal lawn chair on the other. He took the metal chair, which bent back and forth with a springy rocking motion. I watched the sun flicker in the leaves of the oak tree. It was hypnotic. If I had wanted to, I could have fallen asleep.

"After I seen the police come back, I walked over there," Glenn said. "A couple deputies was there. They looked at me suspicious-like. I told them who I was, and they said they'd want to talk to me later. I hung around awhile, but I stayed outta their way. I would've liked to get a look around inside the house. I reckon them bodies was pretty far gone."

"That's an understatement," I said. To put him in my debt, I gave him a lurid description of the corpses.

He shook his head. "It's terrible. Nowadays there's no tellin' what might happen next. There's too many nuts on the loose."

"Tell me, Glenn, how well did you know the Garths?"

"I got to know 'em some," he replied. "I don't want to speak ill of the dead, but they wasn't real neighborly. I don't mean to say they was hateful or rude, but they didn't go outta their way to be friendly, at least not with me they didn't. Excuse me." He stood up and shouted at the dogs again, which had started barking at the deputy across the road. He sat back down and said, "I'll give you an example of what I mean. One day I was runnin' my dogs on the hill behind their house. I been doin' it for years. I don't hunt no more, but I still like to run my coondogs. They're blueticks. Nice dogs—I'll show you, if you want to see 'em. Well, what happened was they picked up a scent and went tearin' down the hill toward the house, and just where his property line is, he's standin' there, watchin' us. I stopped to have a little talk with him, but the first thing he says to me is, real huffy-like, 'I'd appreciate it if you'd keep your dogs out of these woods.' Now, I'm not the only one that runs dogs around here. Like I told ya, I don't hunt, and they need to run once in a while. There ain't no fences around here. 'Come again,' I says to him. He says, 'I don't want the dogs to scare the deer away.' That made me laugh. There's so many deer in these hills, it's gettin' so you can't go outside without bumpin' into one. I told him so, but he stood his ground, and the next time I was back up in there, above his house, I seen where he had put up a mess of No Huntin' and No Trespassin' signs all around his property. I said to my dogs, 'You fellers better learn how to read.'"

For a man whose tongue was about to fall out, he kept it flapping pretty well. He must have rehashed every conversation he had ever had with Garth and his wife. "She was more friendly than him," he said, "but she kept her distance too. Some time back—I think it was last summer—she was pickin' flowers in the field next to her house—and I asked her what they was buildin' over there—there was a lot of hammerin' goin' on. She said her husband and a friend of his was puttin' some solar panels on the roof to keep their electric bill down. You know what's happened to the price of electricity this past year or two—it's gone clear *through* the roof. The electric company's bleedin' us dry. So they put some of them solar things on the back roof of the house. I said to her, 'Ain't the house too close to the hill? It's in the shade early of an evening.' She said her husband thought it would work jest fine—like it was none of my business. I tried to tell her they'd miss several hours' worth of sunshine every day, but she was one of them people who has an answer for everything—she said they was thinkin' of puttin' up a windmill too. 'To pump water?' I said, and she said no, for electricity—to make up for days when it was too cloudy, or not enough sunshine. They never built the windmill though. I think they was some of them en-vi-ro-ment-a-lists. I got talkin' to the two of them one afternoon. I was sittin' out here, and they come ridin' down the road on their horses—which reminds me, I wonder how them horses are doin' if the owners have been dead for the past few weeks, like your story says. I wonder if there's enough food for two horses in that skimpy little pasture of theirs. I just happened to think of that. Anyway, what I was goin' to say is, they stopped and asked me if I knew anything about an old dump on the other side of the hill from their place. 'Sure,' I said to him, 'it used to be the county landfill, but it's been covered up for years.' He cussed and said he never woulda moved down here if he'd'a known they'd be livin' next to a landfill. 'Our well's prob'ly contaminated,' he says to his wife. I says to him, 'The water ain't harmed me none. If the water was poisoned, I woulda been dead a long time ago.' But they didn't wanna hear nothin' I had to say."

While the old man was talking, the county police cruiser that had been blocking the lane drove off toward Brickton. A minute or two later a small convoy of state-police vehicles pulled out of the Garth place, churning up a long cloud of dust that spread over the cornfield.

Glenn waved at them, and one of the drivers tooted his horn.

I asked Glenn if he knew if either of the Garths had a regular job.

"They must've done some kind of work. They came and went a lot. Usually the two of them went away together, but not always. I asked Mr. Grapevine about them once—him and his wife own that nice house down the road. Now there's a neighborly couple. A real gentleman and a nice lady, well-to-do, but they never act high and mighty, like they're better than you. I remember once—"

"I met him last night. He was very helpful to me," I said. "So you don't know for sure if either of the Garths had a job?"

"I don't think either one had a reg'lar job. I never saw them leavin' in the morning and comin' home for supper at the same time day after day, and I'm right here almost all the time. I can see everything that goes in and out of that driveway. Mr. Grapevine told me he'd heard that Mr. Garth was some kind of salesman that worked out of his home on the telephone or a computer."

I had not seen either a telephone or a computer in the Garth house, but I had not been in every room. Perhaps one of the bedrooms had been used as an office.

Glenn's tongue went on wagging, but I got up and said I had several more things to do that afternoon. I thanked him for the information he had given me, and then I remembered Paula. I asked him to give me a call if he happened to see her.

"I'd be glad to," he said. "But I'll have to call the cops first. They asked me before you did. If she's anywhere in this neck of the woods, I'll spot her."

He followed me down the steps. I thought he was going to tag along with me to the car, but he said, "Don't be a stranger now," and veered off toward the outhouse again.

I made a U-turn in front of the cabin and crossed the road to the Garths' driveway. With the police gone, I had the place to myself. I could look around and take more photos. Maybe we'd run a spread tomorrow. The house looked grim and stark against the green shade of the hill. If Edward didn't want a layout, we could at least run a nice color shot on the front page. Photo captions began running through my head: *House of Horror* . . . *Meridian County Massacre.* . . . Hopefully I could come up with something more clever.

I walked around the left side of the house to the back. The dead cat was gone. I wondered if the police had taken it with them or if some animal had dragged it off. A white propane-gas tank stood about twenty feet behind the house, while out in a field to the right was a dust-gray weather-beaten barn. Not far from the barn was a fenced pasture where two brown horses stood staring at me.

I wondered if Paula had spent the night in the barn. I followed a hard-packed lane toward the big sliding door, only to discover a rusty lock and chain on it. I circled the barn to see if I could find another way in, but there were no missing boards, no spaces large enough to squeeze through.

As I came around the other side of the barn, I noticed the solar panels that Garth had installed on the back of the house. The wide array covered half the roof. The Garths must have had some money if they could afford to buy the house and acreage and install those panels.

One of the horses whinnied at me, so I waded through the weeds to see how they had fared the past few weeks. They began walking toward the fence to meet me. They had a small shelter, and a stream ran through the middle of the pasture. They had chewed the weeds to the ground and looked very thin. Besides food, they needed a good scrubbing and brushing. When I reached the fence, I saw a clear space all around the outside of the pasture that they must have made by poking their heads between the boards to reach the weeds. I rubbed their heads and patted their necks. Then I pulled a few bunches of weeds and held them over the fence. They tore the weeds out of my hand.

Their big eyes looked sad and worried. "I'll get somebody to take care of you," I promised them. Watch it, Larrison, I said to myself—you're getting sentimental.

The shadow of the hill was already spreading up the house. I took a few more photos, and then I wandered around the yard. It was turning into a prairie. I searched for some sign of Paula, perhaps a track she had made dragging her cast. The smell of corn wafted through the air until the breeze died.

A chill ran down the back of my head—once again I had a sense of being watched. I spun around and looked up at the windows on the second floor. For a moment I thought I saw Paula, but it was just my imagination. The windows contained nothing but blue sky and fluffy clouds. But the chill stayed with me as I walked back to the car.

CHAPTER 7
Just Playing

I WAS about a mile from Brickton on an undulating stretch of road through the White River bottoms when a car came flying toward me. It was a red Miata with the top down, and it was doing at least seventy. Just before it reached me I saw Jodie Palladino behind the wheel. I gave her a little wave, but she did not wave back. Had she pretended not to see me? My gut said yes, and I trusted my gut. I'd had only a glimpse of her as she shot by, but her fixed stare and anxious expression told me something had to be wrong.

Another murder? Why not? Anything was possible.

I turned around and went after her. I knew I couldn't catch her, but I took a chance that she would stop somewhere along this road. Maybe she was only going home, but if not, then at least I'd get to see what lay beyond Glenn Neidig's cabin.

The bottomland was so flat I could see her car half a mile ahead of me. I was hitting eighty on the straightaways and gaining on her. She'd have to slow down in the knobs, so I could close the gap even more before I'd get there. Of course, on the other side of the hills, she'd pull away again—unless I drove like a maniac.

My hands sweated as they clutched the wheel. I took the curves as fast as I could as I chased her from ridge to ridge. Either she was a better driver than I was, or she knew the roads better, or both, because the gap between us grew wider and wider.

Down I went into the valley of death. Walls of corn closed in on me at the bottom of the last hill. I slowed down as I approached the Grapevines' house. The Miata was not in the driveway, and both garage doors were open. I stepped on the gas again.

About a mile past the Neidig cabin, the county road angled into a hidden gap between the hills. The road climbed only slightly as it hugged the side of a hill alongside the creek that drained the hollow. I passed a faded green-and-white mobile home whose yard was littered with plastic toys, lawn chairs, and assorted junk. A wheelless carapace, an ancient Hudson, rested on concrete blocks. Half-buried tires that looked something like a humped sea serpent edged an overgrown flower garden.

I passed another trailer and a rundown house before emerging from the knobs near Hampstead. The village had seen better days. A general store occupied the first floor of a peeling three-story building with two antique gas pumps in front. The post office next door had been closed for years. There were no other businesses on the only street, the county road, which twisted and turned past a couple dozen houses and a few trailers. The only signs of prosperity were two well-kept churches, Baptist and Pentecostal.

Jodie's car was nowhere in sight. I figured I had lost her, but on the other side of Hampstead, about a quarter mile past the Pentecostal church, I spotted her car in front of a large Colonial home that stood on a rise about fifty yards off the road. The exterior of the house was gray brick, and four dormer windows studded a high blue-black roof. Surrounded by acres of manicured lawn, the house looked more like a country club. I wondered what the peasantry of Hampstead thought of it.

A pair of monument gateposts that matched the bricks of the house stood at the entrance to a concrete drive-way that curved up toward the house. A brass plaque in the middle of each post displayed the name "Brandon" etched in script. It was an old name in Meridian County. Brandons owned some of the biggest farms, and there were bankers, doctors, lawyers, and teachers named Brandon. Jack "Red" Brandon had served as judge of the Circuit Court for forty-five years before retiring a few years ago. It dawned on me that this must be where he lived. I remembered hearing that he had built a mansion way out in the country on land where his ancestors had settled in the 1820s.

I drove up the long driveway and parked next to Jodie's car. Even before I opened the door I heard voices yelling and screaming. I got out and ran around the house. A child's voice blubbered and cried. A woman whom I did not know was walking back and forth next to a swimming pool. She was soaking wet and pleading with someone in the water.

I ran up and saw a young boy, six or seven years old, tied to a six-foot-long log that was floating in the pool. With him was a much older boy, husky, thick-armed, broad-shouldered, more like a man really. He was methodically rolling the log from side to side, bringing the boy's face to the surface of the water first on one side, then on the other, as if working up the speed to roll the log completely around. A thick rope was wrapped like a cocoon around the boy and the log from his neck to his ankles.

Jodie was standing in the pool, pleading and coaxing: "Scott, stop it! You're scaring Cory. Push him over here. He's afraid. He doesn't want to play this game."

With his big hands around one end of the log, Scott went on rolling it left and right. Gleaming in the sun, his shiny wet shoulders rose and fell in regular rhythm. He seemed content to play the game all day long.

The boy kept screaming. His voice trembled: "Stop-p-p-p-p-i-t-t-t-t! Make him stop-p-p-p-p-p!" Tears and snot ran off his cheeks into the water.

I was ready to pull off my shoes and jump in. Jodie saw me and shook her head with a surprised, disapproving look on her face.

The other woman saw Jodie's reaction and turned and saw me. "Who are *you*?" she asked somewhat hesitantly.

The older boy's head spun around. "Whooooooo's that?" His face turned from me to Jodie to me again. "Whooooooo's that?"

"You're scaring him," the other woman said. "He doesn't know you. You'd better go."

"Yes, please leave," Jodie called. "We can handle this." To the log roller she said, "It's all right, Scott. Don't worry. The man won't hurt you."

"Whoooooooooo's he?"

Jodie took a couple of small steps toward him, and Scott pulled the log toward the deep end of the pool. The boy screamed even louder, if that was possible: "Lemme go! I wanta go home. Lemme go-o-o-o-o!"

Jodie said, "Scott won't hurt you, Cory. He just wants to play."

The other woman sneaked around behind Scott at the far end of the pool. She crawled out on the diving board toward him. I didn't know what she planned to do, but whatever it was, it was not working. Scott saw her out of the corner of his eye, and just as she reached the end of the board, he let go of the log with one hand and grabbed the end of the board. He was a big strong kid, and he began pulling the diving board down. The woman lay flat on her chest and wrapped her arms around the board. Scott pulled it down as far as he could and let go, as if trying to catapult the woman over the house.

Jodie took advantage of the diversion and swam to the log, where the boy was now absolutely terrified. She tried to pull it to the shallow end of the pool, but Scott saw her and went underwater, leaving Jodie to control the log. She kicked at Scott with one leg as she frantically pulled the log. Scott came up underneath her like a whale, lifting her on his shoulders. She screamed at him as she fought to hang on to the log. The other woman dropped into the pool to help steady the log. Scott began laughing. He put both hands on Jodie's head and ducked her. The air crackled with screams and shrieks.

Enough was enough. I pulled off my shoes, grabbed a towel off a chair, and dove in behind Scott. Underwater, I saw him rotate in my direction. I came up behind him and twisted the towel around his neck. He released Jodie and swung his arms backward at me. The water heaved as he tried to pull off the towel and shake me loose. Then he let out a long howl, a deep enraged bellow. He twisted and turned, trying to hit me with his elbows. I felt as if I was wrestling a steer in a rodeo. I stuck a knee against his spine and pulled back hard with the towel. He seemed confused—one moment his hands would go for the towel, the next his elbows would come at my head. Sometimes they found their target.

Coughing and spitting, Jodie made her way to the log, and the two women pushed it to the far end of the pool, where they struggled to untie the boy. I was tempted to duck Scott once or twice to give him a taste of his own medicine, but I didn't want to make the women more upset than they already were. They finally unwound the rope and freed the boy. Crying, coughing, gagging, he clambered out of the pool and ran off toward Hampstead.

Scott finally calmed down, and I untwisted the towel. "There you go," I said, backing away.

As I climbed the ladder out of the pool, Jodie came over and stood in front of me. "What are you doing here?" she demanded.

"Saving your life, evidently."

"You followed me."

"I knew you saw me. Why didn't you wave?"

The other woman said, "Do you two know each other?"

Jodie snapped, "Yes—ever since midnight. He works for the *Gleaner*."

"Oh." She began putting it together.

"I'm Phil," I said. "And you are . . .?"

Uncertainly, she held out her hand. "Lillian Brandon. I'm Jodie's cousin."

We were all dripping into puddles at our feet, but I could already feel the sun drying the back of my shirt.

"Who's Scott?" I said. He was standing in the middle of the pool and running his hands back and forth across the surface of the water.

Jodie said, "I hope you don't put this in the paper."

"It never occurred to me," I said.

"Oh please, you mustn't," Lillian said. "No one was hurt. Scott gets carried away sometimes when he gets excited."

"I noticed that," I said. I wondered if Scott was her son, but I didn't want to say the wrong thing. "Is Scott your brother?" I asked.

Lillian's eyes went to Jodie, then me. "No. He's my cousin—and Jodie's." From her haplessly polite manner I got the idea she thought it might be wise not to irritate the press. She was a plain, slender woman with a slightly wedge-shaped face and a slightly pointed chin. She spoke gently to her hulking cousin: "It's time to come out now, Scott. Let's dry off." He went on sulking in the pool.

"How old is he?" I asked.

"Sixteen," Lillian said.

"He looks older."

"Well, thanks for your help," Jodie said to me. "I imagine you need to get back to work, don't you?"

"I wouldn't mind drying off before I get in the car."

Lillian said, "Would you like me to put your clothes in the dryer for a few minutes? I'll get you a robe to wear while you wait."

Jodie said, "We can dry in the sun."

"That's nice of you," I told Lillian, "but she's right—I have to get back to work."

Jodie said, "You *are* going to put this in the paper, aren't you?"

"No, I'm not. Don't worry about it."

"Scott wasn't trying to drown me," she said.

"He had me fooled."

"Why did you follow me here?"

"Force of habit. Whenever I see a woman driving like she's trying to kill herself, I go after her to get a picture of the wreck."

"Very funny."

I looked straight into her eyes, which at the moment had a golden sheen. "When you went flying past me, you looked as if you'd seen a ghost. I wondered if someone else had been murdered." I added an explanatory note for Lillian: "I was in the area because I'd been talking to some of the neighbors about the couple who were murdered. I was at your cousin's house earlier this afternoon."

"Oh, I see," she said. "I never met them—what was their name—Garth? It's awful what happened to them." She walked over to a short stack of towels and carried it back to us.

Jodie took one to dry her hair, which hugged her ears like seaweed. "Lillian called me to help her with Scott," she said. "I was in Campbellsville shopping." She walked to the edge of the pool and said, "Come on now, Scott. Time to get out of there. Do you think you can handle him, Lill?"

"Sure. He'll be all right now. He'll probably take a nap." Again she tried to coax him out. His head and shoulders rose from the still water like an atoll in a lagoon.

"I hope so," Jodie said.

"Who was the kid he was playing with?" I asked.

Lillian glanced at Jodie. "One of his friends," she said. "He lives in Hampstead."

I said, "Are you worried about what his parents will do when they hear what happened?"

"It'll be all right," Jodie said. "They understand."

"They must be very understanding."

"They are." She gritted her teeth on one side. "It was a difficult situation, but it's over now."

"This is Judge Brandon's house, isn't it?" I asked.

"That's right," Lillian said.

Jodie said, "This wouldn't have happened if he'd been here. Scott always listens to his grandfather."

"Where is the judge?" I asked.

"He and his wife are on a trip to Asia," Lillian said. "Vietnam and Cambodia."

Jodie leaned over the edge of the pool and tried again: "Scott! Out! Now! Papaw wouldn't like how you're behaving." She glanced at Lillian and said, "He's going to look like a prune."

Slowly Scott came pushing through the water toward her.

Jodie straightened up and turned around. "There. Praise the Lord." She raised her eyes and folded her hands in mock prayer.

Lillian hurried over to help Scott up the ladder.

I wondered if he would blow up and come after me as soon as he was out of the pool, but he wasn't hostile. All I got was a dimwitted stare as Lillian led him across the patio toward a bank of French doors.

As she and Scott reached the house, she turned and said, "It was nice meeting you, Phil."

"Nice meeting you, Lillian."

Jodie said, "I'll see you tomorrow, Lill."

I followed Jodie around the house to our cars. Suddenly she turned and faced me, hands on hips. "Promise me you won't put anything in the paper."

"I promise I won't put anything in the paper," I said. "Why won't you believe me? It was a private matter. As long as no one files a police report, there won't be anything in the paper."

Her shoulders relaxed a bit. "My grandfather would die if Scott had to be put in a home. It would break his heart." She began to choke up, and tears welled in her eyes. She turned away and got in her car. She started the engine and shifted into first, but just before she took off she looked up at me and said, "Thanks, Phil. I'm sorry I was so bitchy." Then she roared off.

Her damp, straggly hair blew in the wind as the bright red car raced down the hill.

CHAPTER 8
Blind Horse Hollow

THE NEXT morning I had a call from the sheriff: "Hey, Phil, we're still waiting on those fingerprints."

I went right over to see him.

The jail was a modern new building that looked more like a small prison. In fact, the county made some money by housing inmates from the overcrowded state-prison system. The new structure was an irregular series of modules made of textured concrete block. It was designed so that additional modules could be attached in any direction. Although it looked like a giant set of building blocks, it had some good points. For one, the small neon sign from the old jail still adorned the entrance. It said Meridian County Jail in bright-red letters. For another, no one had escaped from the new facility since it had opened for business five years ago.

"Glad you could make it, Phil," the sheriff said when I showed up at his office.

"I'm sorry, Sheriff. It slipped my mind."

"You working too hard, Phil?"

"That must be it."

His office had two windows, beige walls, and an incessant low hum. His desk was covered with neat piles of paperwork. The only thing that seemed out of place was the big oak desk itself. It was the same one he had used in the courthouse when he was auditor and clerk. Black singe marks along the edge showed where his cigarettes had burned grooves in the wood before he quit smoking.

"Have you found my hitchhiker yet?" I asked.

"Not that I know of," he said, "but let's get your fingers dirty. Then you can ask me some more questions I can't answer."

He led me down the hall and told a female deputy to take my prints. She was a new hire, and he hung around to watch her work. I asked her if it was true that no two persons have identical fingerprints.

Without looking up, she replied, "I suppose we'd have to fingerprint everybody in the world to know for sure, but it's not likely that two people with the same prints would show up at the same crime scene."

I glanced at Carl to show I was impressed.

He told her, "As soon as you're finished, shoot those over to Lieutenant Bakery at the state-police post in Versailles." The name of the town had lost its French pronunciation over the past few centuries. It was now "Versales."

Carl disappeared while I was washing my hands. I tracked him back to his office to find out if there were any developments in the case.

"I haven't heard of anything," he told me, "but you probably ought to talk to Lieutenant Bakery."

"Will he be here today?"

"I don't know. I expect he will."

"Any sign of Paula Henry yet?"

"I haven't heard of any."

I told him I'd had a funny feeling she was watching me when I was out at the Garth house yesterday.

"Maybe she was," he said. "Or maybe it was my deputy."

"The police were gone."

"Travis wasn't."

"I didn't see anyone."

Carl leaned back in his wooden swivel chair and put his hands behind his head. "That was the general idea."

"He must have been parked in the cornfield then."

"Could be."

I got up to leave.

"You got some good pictures in the paper, Phil," he said. "Everybody at Mackey's was talking about the murders this morning. It looked like a tent city the way the papers were poking up over the tables."

"I hope Edward saw it."

"I should have ate breakfast at home. I got hit with the same questions over and over."

"You should have referred them to Lieutenant Bakery."

I went back to the *Gleaner* and held a quick meeting with my staff. Then I had a little talk with our new sportswriter. She was covered up with work because the sports editor had just gone on vacation. I told her I'd help her as much as I could. She was just a few months out of J-school, and she looked hot and stressed. I was afraid she might quit. She knew how to write grammatical sentences, and I didn't want to lose her.

After the meeting I got myself a cup of coffee in the lounge and went back to my keyboard. It was already after twelve, so I decided to skip lunch. While I was batting out a wrapup of Thursday night's action in the Church Softball League, the phone rang and I heard a voice I had not heard in years:

"How's it goin', Phil? This is Chuck Martin."

Martin had held the sheriff's office for one four-year term. He had lost his reelection bid to Carl Eggemann in 2006. A burly, muscular man with wavy gray-white hair, he appeared to be far better equipped—physically—to be sheriff than Eggemann did; however, as Carl had enjoyed pointing out during the campaign, the sheriff's office was an administrative position, not a job for a street brawler. Martin had made another run for sheriff this year, but his campaign came to a screeching halt when he finished third in the Republican primary in May.

We got the pleasantries out of the way, and then Martin said, "I read your story about the two people that were murdered, and it set me to thinking. That house where you found them two bodies—if I'm not mistaken, that's the same place where we found a pretty good-sized crop of marijuana growing back when I was in the sheriff's department."

"Tell me more," I said.

He snickered smugly. "It was a little before your time, but there was a story about it in the paper. We found it growing in a cornfield, in between the rows of corn. The field was full of it. We pulled it out and had a real blaze." He laughed, remembering. "I'm surprised none of the boys got high."

When Chuck Martin was sheriff, we had a lot of stories in the paper about marijuana plants being chopped down and burned. "When was this, Chuck?" I said.

"Well now, let me think. . . ."

I pictured him rubbing his chin and pretending to be trying to recall something he already knew.

"If I remember rightly," he went on, "it was eleven years ago this summer. You can look it up. There was a real nice picture in the paper, right there on page one."

"Are you thinking there's some connection with these murders?"

"I can't say that, Phil. Hell, how would I know? I haven't been sheriff these past four years." He chuckled in a self-deprecating way, but underneath lay contempt for his successor. "No, the people who were killed—Mr. and Mrs. Garth—they weren't living here then, so I don't see how there could be a connection. I just thought I'd mention it to you, in case you might like to remind people what happened out there. Some of your readers might be interested."

"You said it was eleven years ago. You weren't sheriff then, were you?"

"No. I was first deputy."

"I see. All right. I'll look up the article, Chuck. Thanks for calling."

"That's all right, Phil. Keep up the good work."

His last remark was just to butter me up. He was probably hoping I'd mention his marijuana bonfire in the paper and it would make people regret he was out of the sheriff's race.

I hacked out the rest of the sports stuff as fast as I could, and then I took several reels of microfilm out of the vault. We had an old mechanical reader in an alcove off the main office, so I sat there and cranked through back issues of the *Gleaner*. After ten or fifteen minutes I found the article. Under a two-deck headline, "County Police Harvest Marijuana Crop in Blind Horse Hollow," a large photo showed four deputies gawking at the camera in front of a pile of weed going up in smoke. One of them was Chuck Martin. In the distance was the house where the Garths had lived.

Blind Horse Hollow. I had never heard the name till now. Damn, I should have asked Glenn Neidig what the place was called.

The article said the marijuana had an estimated street value of $100,000. The plants had been found growing on a farm owned by Mrs. Esther Dubbs of Brickton. The eighty-one-year-old woman was described as "visibly shaken" when police told her that marijuana had been discovered in her cornfield. "She denied any knowledge of the plants," the story said. "She told police that ever since her husband died in 1995, she has been renting her cropland to another farmer, Clyde Cooper, Brickton Rt. 1." According to the story, Cooper also claimed to know nothing about the illegal plants and was not a suspect in the case. The article concluded, "The sheriff said he believes someone surreptitiously planted the marijuana between the corn rows and was planning to harvest it when it was fully grown."

It did not sound like the best police work or the best newspaper story. Why hadn't the police staked out the cornfield to catch the pot growers when they would return for their weed? I knew what the answer would have been: the tightfisted county council would not appropriate the funds to hire the number of deputies needed to run the sheriff's department the way it ought to be run. And even if they had caught the druggies, the county prosecutor would have plea-bargained the case down to a slap on the wrist. Such attacks helped get Martin elected sheriff in 2002.

The marijuana story gave me an idea. I went across the street to the county surveyor's office in the basement of the courthouse and bought a copy of the plat map of Blind Horse Hollow. Then I went up to the auditor's office to get the names of the current property owners there. It turned out that Glenn Neidig owned 40 acres, Jacqueline Grapevine owned 10, Clyde Cooper owned 86, someone named Walter Boofey owned 23, and Esther Dubbs owned more than 1,100. The rest of the hollow and most of the knobs were part of the Meridian County State Forest, which belonged to the state of Indiana.

The interesting thing was that Boofey's property included the Garth house. Unless these records were not up to date, the Garths themselves had owned nothing in Blind Horse Hollow. They must have been renters.

I wondered if Detective Lieutenant Bakery had also discovered this. Most likely he had, but if not, I could enlighten him. I went back to the office and gave him a call, but he was not at his desk. I left a message for him to call me back.

CHAPTER 9
Car Trouble

BOOFEY
Harrodsburg, KY
I submitted the information to whitepages.com and discovered that no one named Boofey was listed in the Harrodsburg phone book.

Naturally.

Nothing is easy.

I forced myself to write up the rest of the sports stuff that Marcie, the new reporter, had given me. I could see she was hoping I'd ask for more, but I had other things to do. It took me until three o'clock to clear my desk. Then I tried to call Esther Dubbs.

There were two parties named Dubbs in the Campbellsville phone book. Both lived in Brickton, but neither of them was Esther. I phoned both of them to see if I could get a line on Esther, but neither one answered.

I had better luck with Clyde Cooper.

His wife answered the phone and told me he was out in the barn, tinkering with the combine. She told me how to find their farm, which lay east of Brickton: "You go right at that new carpet place before you get to Brickton and then you go till you get to the first road on the left—it's about a mile. Then go left, and then you make another left on the second gravel road you come to. That's our road. Our name's on the mailbox. You can't miss it."

"See you soon," I told her.

It was hot outside. The sign on the bank across from the courthouse said 89°F. It had shot up since noon. My car's air conditioner did not help much when the temperature reached the high eighties.

I found Mr. Cooper lying on his back halfway under a three-row cornpicker. It looked as if a bright-green dinosaur was eating him alive.

"Be with ya in a minute," he called from under the machine. More like ten minutes went by, punctuated by grunts and bangs. Finally he slid out dragging a long wrench after him. "That oughta do 'er," he said.

The upper half of his body was covered with chaff from last year's harvest. He used the long wrench to push himself up. A stout man in his late fifties, he had a jowly face that had not been shaved that day. He straightened up slowly and then reached into his coveralls for a tin of chewing tobacco. He stuck a gob inside his cheek. "What can I do for ya?" he said. Like his movements, his voice was slow.

Pigeons cooed in the rafters while we talked. I told him who I was and explained that I was doing an article about the murders in Blind Horse Hollow. He said he was pleased to make my acquaintance and had seen my stories in the paper. He took down a couple bales of straw for us to sit on. We sat facing each other, with our feet surrounding a dried cow pie. Dust motes glittered in the golden planes of sunlight that penetrated the sides of the barn.

"I understand you rent some farmland from Esther Dubbs," I said.

"Yes, sir, you understand right."

"And did you buy some property from her?"

"I did. She's sold off a few pieces of her land since her husband passed away." He cocked his head and squinted at me. "What's that got to do with them folks that was killed?"

"Since you farm out there, I figured you might be able to tell me something about them."

"Like what?"

"Do you happen to know if they owned the house they were living in?"

"Far as I know, a feller by the name of Boofey owns it—unless he sold it to them."

"Do you know when he bought it?"

"No I don't. I know it was before she sold me the field I was renting from her. It'll be three years ago this fall. I was interested in buying the ground where the house is too, but I had no use for the house." He got up to spit some tobacco into a rusty barrel under the hay loft. Then he started snickering. "You know why I remember Boofey's name? Because it sounds like Goofy. That ain't nice to say, but I can't help it."

I pretended to laugh. "Have you ever met Mr. Boofey?"

"No, sir. I got his name and address from Mrs. Dubbs once because I wanted to get in touch with him and see if he was interested in rentin' his field to me, like Mrs. Dubbs. So I wrote him a letter. I got a note back sayin' he wasn't interested. I didn't really care because it was only twenty acres or thereabouts. But it seemed like a waste of good farmland to me—the woods have started takin' over."

"By the way," I said, "while I think of it—is Mrs. Dubbs's name in the phone book?"

He thought a moment. "I can't rightly say. It was there last time I looked, but that was some time ago. I don't deal with her directly anymore, not since she went in the nursin' home. She's up in years now."

"Who do you deal with?"

"Mrs. Judy Dubbs, her daughter-in-law. She was married to Esther's son, Frank Junior, but he got killed in a car wreck." He shook his head. "It was a real shame. Esther lost her husband and her only son within a year of each other."

"That is a shame." We observed a moment of silence, during which a drop of sweat trickled down my chest. Then I said, "Where does Judy Dubbs live?"

"Over in Brickton."

It was hot in the barn, but a light breeze blew through the open doors now and then. "Getting back to Mr. Boofey," I said, "did he ever live in the house he bought from Mrs. Dubbs?"

His brows furrowed as he tried to recall. "I'm not sure about that. Seems like he may have from time to time, while he worked on the place. I think he came and went. But I'm not over there all that much, so I don't know everything that goes on."

"Did you know the people who were murdered—Mr. and Mrs. Garth?"

He stuck out his bottom lip like a duckbill and shook his head. "Barely. I stopped and talked to him once when I was diskin' the field next to his. I told him I was glad to see somebody was finally puttin' that land to use again—they had horses pastured on it. And before that I seen his wife plantin' wildflowers. She was workin' in weeds up to her waist. I told her to watch out for rattlesnakes, but she just laughed. I said, 'Okay, if you ain't afraid of rattlesnakes, then watch out for chiggers. They itch like crazy.' She seemed like a nice young lady."

"So I've heard," I said. "It's kind of ironic. They leave the big bad city—they were from Indianapolis—for peaceful Meridian County, and they get murdered here."

"It ain't as peaceful as it used to be." He spat into the oil drum and sat down in front of me again. "You know what the problem is—we're lettin' too many of them Mexicans in. They bring their drugs with 'em and take our jobs."

I did not need to hear the usual complaints about Mexican immigrants, but I picked up on one of his points. "Do you think the Garths' deaths may have had something to do with drugs?"

"It wouldn't surprise me none."

"Me neither. I was talking to our former sheriff, Chuck Martin, and he recalled that the sheriff's department, about eleven years ago, found a good-sized crop of marijuana near the house where the Garths lived."

His temperature shot up unexpectedly. "I don't call it a crop. I call it crap. That shit was found on the land I was leasin' from Mrs. Dubbs. I didn't know a thing about it. And I hope you're not sayin' I did."

"No, I'm not."

"Because if that's what you think, then you can get your tail outta here right now." He pushed himself up from the bale of straw and walked around cussing half under his breath. "I'll have nothing to do with drugs. If it was up to me, anybody caught sellin' that shit would be taken out and shot."

Crop/crap, shit/shot—he was something of a poet.

"I'm sorry if I said something to upset you, Mr. Cooper," I told him.

"I farm a lot of ground. That's a mighty isolated place there in the holler. Maybe I should have kept a closer eye on it, but nobody ever done somethin' like that to me before, sowin' marijuana in with my corn." Silhouetted against the bright glare of the doorway, he looked like a walking shadow. "What else do you think I did? You think I murdered them two people while they were naked in the bathroom?"

It was time to go. "Thank you for your time, sir," I said. "Have a nice day."

"Bullcrap."

He wanted to stay mad, so I left him fuming in the barn. The way he had protested his innocence was almost enough to make me think he *was* guilty of something.

Back in the car, I opened the windows and turned on the air conditioner full blast to blow out the hot air. It was too early for supper, and I didn't feel like going back to work. As long as I was here, I might as well pay another visit to the Garth house, on the other side of Brickton. The drive would calm my frazzled brain, and it also occurred to me that it might be a good idea to see what I could see from the top of the hill behind the house. What better time to climb a steep hill than on a humid August afternoon when the temperature was in the nineties?

As the car cooled down a few degrees and I put some miles between myself and Clyde Cooper, my mood improved. In twenty minutes I was winding through the knobs again. I was getting to like it in the knobs. Maybe I'd move out here someday. Retire. Live like a hermit. I could grow persimmons. I could get a goat to take care of the lawn. I could run my dogs.

I parked in front of the house and opened the windows a crack. I locked the car and made sure my BlackBerry was in my pocket in case Lieutenant Bakery called. The phone should work on top of the hill. Thinking, always thinking.

A warm late-afternoon breeze swept down the hillside and flapped the leaves of corn like stiff pieces of paper.

I wondered if one of the sheriff's deputies was still staked out somewhere near the house. If so, I should be able to spot his car from the top of the hill. Then I thought of the horses again. I kept forgetting to find someone to feed them. Maybe I should do it myself.

I walked toward their pasture and was pleased to see them munching on a bale of hay. The horses looked up at me as I approached. Maybe the deputy on stakeout duty had brought them the hay, or it could have been Glenn Neidig. I was glad someone had done it.

The horses did not come over to the fence to get their heads rubbed this time, so I headed for the hill. At the edge of the hill was a nearly dry creek, little more than a trickle of water between puddles, though judging from the smooth, steep banks, it was sometimes a raging torrent. In the woods above me, a committee of crows broke out in raucous squawks as I crossed the creekbed. I grabbed onto exposed tree roots to pull myself up the inner bank.

It was cooler in the woods, but also more humid. Within minutes the back of my head was wet and my shirt was soaked. Tiny flies buzzed my face and tried to get at my eyes. The way I kept flapping my arms at them, I must have looked like a pinwheel. I was tempted to give up the climb, but I kept going. I wanted to see what the hollow looked like from the top of the knobs.

Before I was a third of the way up the hill, I was huffing and puffing. Every few minutes I had to stop to catch my breath. A few years ago I would not have run out of breath so quickly. I was out of shape. For the first time in my life it hit me that I was not a young guy anymore. I made it my challenge to keep climbing.

The hill was a lot higher and steeper than it appeared from below. When I finally made it to the top, my reward was a panoramic view of the surrounding country. I took off my shirt and sat on a flat boulder on the narrow ridge. The breeze fanned my face and chest as I soaked up the scenery.

I wondered how high the hill was. Two hundred, three hundred feet? Maybe even more? I ought to look it up. Now and then a tiny car or truck appeared on the county road. Through openings in the trees I could see Glenn Neidig's cabin and Don Grapevine's ranch home. They looked like miniature houses on an electric-train layout. I tried to find the Garth house, but it was too close to the hill, with too many trees in the way. I also looked for a hidden police cruiser, but I did not see one.

The sky was hazy blue, with wisps of cloud on the horizon. To the north and west was a vista of receding ridges as high as the one I was sitting on. In the opposite direction the land was a flat quilt of forests and farms in various tones of brown and green. As I sat there looking out from the back side of the hill, a black pickup truck came speeding along a dirt road. A small cloud of dust trailed behind it. The truck slowed down to turn onto another dirt road and then moved toward the hill I was on. It disappeared in a stand of trees and emerged on the other side. The feeble sound of its engine began to reach me.

The truck slowed to a crawl. Although the road came to an end, the truck continued across a wide field that looked more like a smooth green lake. As the pickup got closer, I saw that it carried a pile of scrap, but then the trees blocked my view. Moments later the engine stopped.

Two doors slammed. Faint voices came up the hillside. I heard the crash and rattle of junk.

Old man Neidig had said there used to be a county landfill on this side of the hill. Some local yokels must have been using it as their private dump.

I watched the pickup drive away. Then I pushed myself up. Let's go, Larrison. Back to work.

Getting down the hill was almost as hard as climbing up. My legs weren't used to this. I constantly held myself back as I went down so my feet wouldn't go out from under me. It was a tense, stiff descent, and my calves felt sorer by the minute.

By the time I got down, I was so hot, sweaty, and mosquito-bit that I felt like sitting in a puddle in the creek. I splashed some water on my face and resisted the urge to take a drink.

As I pulled myself up out of the creekbed, I heard a car trying to start. I thought it must be the cop who was staking out the place. I angled toward the house. Everything looked the same as yesterday.

The car engine cranked again, and this time it caught. I came around the corner of the house and saw my car turning around on the lawn. I felt my pocket—the keys hadn't gone anywhere, so how could the car be moving? I couldn't see who was driving, but who else could it be? . . .

"Paula!" I yelled.

The wheels churned in the gravel, and a cloud of blue fumes filled the air.

My car disappeared in the corn.

CHAPTER 10
Cellular Hell

I STARTED running after the car, but I gave up after three or four steps. I heard a loud *thump thump thump thump thump*. I thought it was a helicopter directly overhead, but it was the blood pounding in my ears. Dust rose above the cornfield as the car banged and rattled on the gravel lane. I felt naked and alone. I was drenched in sweat.

I heard the car careen onto the county road and take off toward Brickton.

My brain seemed to be working in slow motion. I had to call the police, but I knew my phone wouldn't work in the hollow. I tried anyway. I watched my index finger key in the Sheriff's Department number even though there was no signal. God, you'd think by now somebody would have stuck a tower on top of the knobs. I began running again, this time toward Glenn Neidig's place. Why hadn't I done this already? I would have been halfway there by now. I stopped running. Did I really want to tell the world that Paula had burned me again? I felt like an idiot. And I could not swear it was Paula who had taken the car. Come on, who else would have taken it? But how could she drive with her leg in a cast? How could she even get behind the wheel? The car had automatic transmission, so maybe she could drive it. Maybe she had taken the cast off.

I slammed my brain in gear and ran out to the road. Old man Neidig's truck was nowhere in sight. He was probably not there. It could be a blessing in disguise—I wouldn't have to talk to him and make a fool of myself. And why bother Jodie and her stepfather again? Somebody would come along and give me a ride. Or I could drag myself back up the hill and call the police from there. Then I could call the *Gleaner* and have someone come get me. But time was passing. If I didn't call the police soon, Paula would get away (if it was Paula). Besides, it would take too long to climb the hill again. I wasn't up to it anyway. I set out for town.

I was halfway past the Grapevines' house when the front door opened and Don Grapevine called, "Hey, Phil, is that you? What are you doing?"

I stopped and took a deep breath as I rethought my strategy. "Taking a hike," I yelled back. "To Campbellsville. Somebody stole my car."

"What?" He shut the door behind him and strode toward me across the lawn. "Stole your car? What happened?"

I told him in twenty-five words or less.

"You can use my phone," he said.

"Thanks. I didn't want to bother you again."

"It's not a bother. Let's go inside before you get sunstroke."

I followed him into the house and tried not to drip on anything. I called the jail and asked for Sheriff Eggemann. The dispatcher said he was out of town and would not be back until Monday.

I said, "I want to report a stolen car." I described my blue Civic and gave him the license-plate number. Then I said, "It's possible that a woman named Paula Henry took it, but I can't say for sure. She's wanted for questioning in the Garth murder case. The car is heading toward Brickton right now."

"What direction, sir?"

"Traveling east from the knobs."

"We'll get on it."

Now that I had called the police, I began to relax. The air-conditioning helped too. I turned to Grapevine, who was staring at me with a puzzled and concerned expression.

"That's the woman who was with you the other night, isn't it?" he asked.

"Yes. I hate to accuse her of stealing my car. I didn't actually see her."

He nodded slightly. "Yes, but she's the most likely suspect, if she was still around here."

"To tell the truth," I went on, "it's hard to see how she could do it. The car was locked, and the windows were only open a crack. I had the keys. She would have had to break in to the car, hotwire the ignition, and then drive it with her leg in a cast—unless she had taken the cast off."

"It's not too hard to hotwire a car, if you know what you're doing," Grapevine said. "And perhaps she did take the cast off. That would have probably been harder for her to do by herself than starting the car."

"You think so?"

"I do. Of course, it's also possible that someone helped her remove the cast."

"If she had someone helping her, then why would she need to steal my car?"

He raised his eyebrows. "Good point. It was just an idea."

I looked at my watch. "I've got to get back to the paper. Would you mind if I used the phone to get someone to come and get me?"

"Don't bother," he said. "I can drive you to town."

"That's too much trouble."

"Not at all. Come on."

I followed him through the kitchen and family room to the garage, then out the back door of the garage. A workshop stood off to the side of the house, and a pickup truck was parked in front of it. I was surprised to see a rifle hanging in the rear window. Grapevine did not look like a redneck who rode around with a gun on display. I asked him if he liked to go hunting.

"You bet I do," he said. "Are you a hunter, Phil?"

I shook my head. "I used to go hunting with my father when I was a kid, but somewhere along the line I turned into a pacifist."

"That's too bad," he said with a chuckle. "Maybe you should take it up again." He unlocked the truck and turned toward me. "Tell you what—you come out here sometime this fall, and we'll do some hunting together."

"Thanks," I said. "Maybe I'll take you up on that."

We climbed in the truck and sat in the heat while the engine warmed up. On a day like this it didn't need to warm up, but we sat and waited anyway. A minute later he turned on the air conditioner and we drove around the side of the house on a narrow driveway edged with flowers. The flowers ended where the slab joined the driveway in front of the garage.

As we turned onto the county road, I said, "This is a big truck."

"I like it," he said. "I never owned a Ford before, but when GM took all that bailout cash from the government,

I swore I'd never buy another GM vehicle again. We still have a Suburban—my wife took it to Cincinnati this week—but when we trade that in, it'll be the last General Motors product we ever own."

"I guess I'll have to start thinking about a new car, now that mine's been stolen," I said. I had owned the Civic since 2003, when my parents gave it to me when I graduated from DePauw. "Oh what the heck, at least it's insured," I added. "I doubt if I could get much on a trade-in anyway. It's seven years old and it's got nearly 150,000 miles on it. But it was running fine. I wasn't planning on buying a new car."

"Maybe the police will find it for you. You reported it right away. Maybe they've already found it."

"I won't hold my breath."

"If it's God's will, you'll get it back."

I didn't say so, but I still wouldn't be holding my breath.

We were in the knobs now, and when we reached the first ridge, I turned on my phone to check my calls. I was glad to see that Detective Lieutenant Bakery had tried to get back to me while I was in cellular hell. When I listened to his message, I was even gladder to hear he had left his cell number. No more phone tag, maybe. I wanted to call him back right away, but not with Grapevine sitting next to me.

To change the subject, I said, "Don, I want you to know I really appreciate how you've been helping me the past few days."

He shook his head. "Don't mention it. You'd do the same for me."

I laughed. "I don't know about that."

"Sure you would, just like you went out of your way when you picked up your hitchhiker the other night."

"That was only because I thought she was in a danger-ous situation."

"Makes no difference." He glanced over at me. "You helped her. Now I'm helping you. People should help one another. If I do something for you today, you can pay me back by doing something for somebody else tomorrow. The world would be a better place if more people behaved that way."

"That's a good attitude," I said, hoping I didn't sound patronizing. I had to stifle a yawn. The flickering sunlight and shadows were putting me to sleep.

Don looked at me again. "Do you go to church, Phil?"

Uh-oh, what had I gotten myself into? "I was raised Catholic," I replied, "but I haven't been to Mass in years."

He nodded. "Young people—you're young compared with me—young people often drift away from their reli-gion. My stepdaughter, Jodie, doesn't go to church either. And I'm an elder."

"What church is it?" I asked.

"Campbellsville Presbyterian."

"I went to a wedding there once. It's a beautiful mod-ern church."

"Thank you. If you're ever in the mood to attend a Sunday service, you are certainly welcome. By the way, that reminds me of something. When Mr. and Mrs. Garth first moved in to the old farmhouse, my wife went over to ask them if they'd like to be our guests at Sunday wor-ship. We make it a practice to invite newcomers to worship with us. We never do any arm twisting. It's just our way of welcoming people to our community. Well, when Jackie came home she told me Mr. Garth practically slammed the door in her face. 'We're atheists,' he told her. Now, I ask you, what kind of person tells you flat out, 'We're atheists'? Jackie said Mrs. Garth acted as if she wanted to be friendly, but her husband made it abundantly clear that he did not want us bothering them, so you can be sure we never did."

I said, "Glenn Neidig told me pretty much the same thing—Wayne Garth was unfriendly, but Cheryl seemed like a nice person."

"That about covers it." He limbered up his fingers on the steering wheel. "It takes all kinds, I guess. But it's a tragic shame. They're both dead now. If they were still atheists when they died, you know where they are now."

Yes indeed, I thought. The same place I would be.

CHAPTER 11
The Ex Factor

AFTER GRAPEVINE dropped me off at the paper, the first thing I did was go to the county recorder's office in the courthouse. There I learned that a deed to the house where the Garths had lived had been recorded in Walter Boofey's name in June 2001. I was disappointed that he had not bought it a few years earlier. It might have connected him to the 1999 marijuana harvest that Sheriff Martin had told me about.

Next I checked in with my boss and told him about my latest adventure.

Edward roared with laughter. "So the floozie stole your car." The whole newsroom could hear him.

"I didn't say that, Ed. I didn't see her."

"Right. And it's only 99.99 percent likely that she did it." He roared again.

"Is it all right if I use a company car for a few days?" I said.

"Sure, go ahead. Just do me a favor and don't get it stolen."

I went to my office, plopped down behind the desk, and took a deep breath. I smelled of sweat. I went to the men's room to wash up, ignoring the grinning questions along the way.

Back at my desk, I dealt with the most pressing matters that were waiting for me, and then I called Lieutenant Bakery.

He answered with, "Hey, Phil. I hear your car was stolen." No laughing.

"That was fast," I said. "Did you find it yet?"

"Sorry. Not yet."

"Crap, I thought I'd have my car back by now."

"I'm sorry you're dissatisfied. Excuse me a second." He muffled the phone and said something to someone, then abruptly returned. "I understand you told the sheriff's people you don't know who stole it. Is that correct?"

"Yes. I imagine it was Paula Henry, but I couldn't see her."

"You sure about that?"

"Of course I am."

"The sheriff's department said you told them you saw your car being driven away."

"That's right, but it was too far for me to see who was driving."

"Could you tell if it was a man or a woman?"

"No."

There was a strained silence. Then he said, "She must be the one that took it. We're still looking for her."

"Have you found out where she lives?" I asked.

"I thought you said Indianapolis."

"I mean *where* in Indianapolis. But wait a minute—" I tried to recall exactly what she had told me, and what I had told Sheriff Eggemann. "It just occurred to me that she never actually said she lives in Indianapolis, Lieutenant. What she said was 'I thumbed a ride from Indy,' and that's what I told the sheriff. I don't believe I ever said she lives there. I only know what she told me. But when she was talking about her friends, Cheryl and Wayne Garth, and how they had wanted to get out of Indianapolis and live in the country, she sure sounded as if they all lived in Indianapolis."

Bakery made an exasperated noise that sounded a little bit like a machine gun: "Tu-tu-tu-tu-tu-tu-tu-tu-tu-tu," followed by, "So, for all you know she could live in Tahiti."

"I think we can rule out Tahiti."

"I'm beginning to think we can rule out Indianapolis too," he said. "We found a couple of Paula Henrys in Marion County, but they don't match your Paula Henry." He let me digest this information, then said, "It might not be her real name."

"I hope you're wrong about that," I said.

"I hope so too. But it shouldn't be this hard to track down a woman with a leg in a cast. We're checking with doctors and hospitals now on recent cases."

"I don't buy it," I said. "She had no reason to give me a fake name."

"She probably didn't want her name in the paper."

"That can't be it. When she told me her name, she didn't know I work for a paper. We hadn't found the bodies yet. We hadn't even found the house she was looking for. You're right though—later, when I told her I had to write a story about the murders, she didn't like it that her name might be in it. And she didn't want to talk to the police, which is why she disappeared, I think."

"Yes, you told me that yesterday. Like I said, we'll keep looking for her. We lifted a lot of fresh fingerprints in the house. Some of them must be hers. If she has a record, we'll make a match."

It was time to move on. I asked if autopsies had been performed on the Garths' bodies.

"Yes they have," he said. I heard him flipping through his notes. "Each victim was shot several times with a .45-caliber weapon. Wayne Garth was shot twice in the chest, once in the abdomen, and once in the back of the head. Cheryl Garth was shot once in the left thigh, once in the left breast—which the bullet passed clean through—and once in the top of the head. It was not a professional hit. Too sloppy. The shots in the head were no doubt intended to make sure they were dead."

"Must have been quite a scene," I said. "It sounds as though Cheryl was not mortally wounded until she was shot in the head."

"That's how I see it. She was probably screaming like hell."

"Do you have any suspects?" I asked.

"We have a couple of leads, but I don't want to go there."

"Did you come up with any more information about the Garths?"

"Some. When he was in high school, Wayne Garth was arrested a couple of times for possession of marijuana. That was in Kokomo. Later, in Indianapolis, he was arrested for dealing drugs where he worked. Nothing major. That was almost five years ago, and he's had a clean sheet ever since."

"That's interesting," I said. "Are you aware that back in 1999 a 'crop' of marijuana was found in a cornfield here in Meridian County, not far from the house where the Garths lived? But they didn't live here then, as far as I know."

"I hadn't heard about the marijuana," he replied. "Where'd you get that?"

I told him about my conversation with Sheriff Chuck Martin and the article in the paper. He asked me to fax him a copy as soon as I could.

"And did you know that the house the Garths lived in belongs to a guy named Walter Boofey?"

"Let's see." He went through his notes again. "Right," he said. "Boofey's wife is the former Caroline Dubbs, the daughter of Esther Dubbs, who used to own it. Walter and Caroline got married a year after he bought the property. That's how they met. Look, Phil, I've got to get going."

"Just one more thing, Lieutenant. One of the Garths' neighbors told me they owned an RV. I'm wondering if it was in the barn. Did you see it there?"

"Yes. Why?"

"I'm wondering if Paula—if that's her name—might have been sleeping there the past two nights."

"There is a small RV in the barn, but when I checked it yesterday, it did not appear to have been used for some time. I've got to go now, Phil. Good talking to you. Keep in touch." With that he hung up.

Before I'd forget, I faxed the marijuana article to him. Then I went to the lounge for a cup of coffee and brought it back to my desk. I wanted to write my next story on the Garth case. In fact, that's all I wanted to do. But I still had my day job, and I was half a day behind on my regular work. No dinner at Applebee's for me tonight. I could order a sandwich from Blimpie's later. Or I could skip dinner altogether and lose some weight. I liked that idea better. I needed to get back in shape if I wanted to run up and down the knobs.

I had always worked long days at the *Gleaner*. It did not bother me. It took my mind off other things.

I finished my latest piece on the Garths about 9:30. Then I helped lay out the front page. Since there were no late meetings to worry about on Friday, I managed to get out of the office around 10:15. It was a nice night, so I decided to walk home instead of taking a company car. I wondered if I'd ever see my Civic again. The article I had just written did not mention that it had been stolen. I felt as if I was doing something wrong by withholding information from our readers, but it remained true that I did not know if Paula had taken the car, and if she hadn't, then why would I want to mention her in my story?

I crossed the street and passed the courthouse. Now that I was on my way home, I suddenly felt tired. I had eight more blocks to walk. I crossed Washington Street, went another block on Main, and turned left on Adams. The sidewalk was filled with a noisy crowd of people piling out of the Campbellsville Little Theatre. Some headed for their cars, while others stood around talking with members of the cast who were lined up in front of the theatre. As I picked my way through the mob I came face to face with my ex-wife and her husband.

"Hi, Phil," Vickie said. There was no animosity, no guilt in her voice, only what I always took as mild condescension.

"Hello, Vickie." I looked at her husband. "Hi, Tyler."

"How are you, Phil." It wasn't a question, so I did not answer.

"I've been reading your stories in the paper," Vickie said. "*Very* interesting."

"Thanks."

She tilted her head with a smile, almost a laugh. "But what ever possessed you to pick up that hitchhiker? You always told me not to pick up *anyone*, no matter what."

"I forgot my own advice."

"What if she had a gun or something?"

"She didn't have room for a gun in her cast."

Her eyes popped wide, and with a short burst of laughter, she said, "That's not the only place she could have hidden it."

Her oval face was sensual and smart, with delicate lips that gleamed with silvery gloss under the streetlights. She had a small, pert nose and dark hair that used to be wavy down to her shoulders but was now a short, bouncy perm.

"So how are you doing?" I asked her.

"We're doing great. We just got home from Key West. What a wacky spot. They have chickens running around all over the place." She laughed merrily. "Ty would like to move there, wouldn't you, Ty? But he always talks about moving to the latest place we've been."

Ty was a short-bearded, motorcycle-riding, whitewater-rafting, cross-country-skiing anesthesiologist. At the moment he looked as if he wished his wife and former nurse would get this over with.

"I'm glad you had a good time," I said.

"Thanks, Phil," she replied. "Well, good night."

Her high heels clicked away on the sidewalk. I wished they *would* move to Key West. I always tried to avoid Vickie if I saw her coming. It was usually in a supermarket or drugstore. Conversations like this one depressed me. It would take me a day to get over it.

Why did I have to bump into her tonight? Five minutes ago I had been in a pretty good mood. Tired and worn out, yes, but it was tiredness based on a sense of accomplishing something, a pleasant weariness. I was just starting to feel better about myself. Now, walking the last six blocks to my apartment, I wondered if I was the one who should move. I had been thinking about it for years. Why hadn't I done it? There was nothing holding me here, except inertia. Why did I have to bump into her again? I wished I could get her out of my head once and for all.

On nights like this I generally ended up drinking myself to sleep. I kept a bottle of Johnnie Walker Black Label on hand for just such emergencies.

CHAPTER 12
Dark Hallway

I was in the bathroom shaving when the old land-line phone on my desk rang. I kept it so that tipsters and cranks could find my number in the book. When I answered, a soft, uncertain voice said, "Phil, it's me."

Oh my God, was I dreaming or what? "Paula," I said, "is that you?"

"Uh-huh."

I turned off the radio. "Where are you?"

"In case you don't know already, I'm the one that took your car." Her voice went from low to lower. "I'm sorry. I shouldn't've done it. I'll get it back to you as soon as I can."

"Where are you?"

"Indianapolis."

"Where in Indianapolis?"

"That don't matter."

I heard a woman in the background say, "Tell him we'll bring it back today."

"Who's that?" I said.

"My mom. If she can get off work this afternoon, we'll return your car today. If not, it'll be tomorrow. I could do it today, but she don't want me driving with a broken leg again."

Her mother said, "Tell him we'll fill the tank up."

"Cool it, Mom," Paula said.

"Don't worry about the gas," I said. "Just tell me where you are."

"Why? So you can have me arrested?"

"No, Paula. I just want to talk to you."

"We're talking now."

"I want to see you. You don't have to drive the car back. Your mother doesn't have to miss any work. I'll come and get it."

"You can't drive both cars back by yourself."

"I'll deal with it."

I heard her inhale, hold it, exhale. Then she covered the phone and said something I couldn't catch. But I heard her mother say, "So let him come if he wants to. You owe him that much."

Paula came back on the line and said, "Let me and her talk. I'll call you back in a few minutes."

Click.

Suddenly everything seemed sharper, more vivid. I saw a small reflection of myself in the TV screen across the room. Birds chirped loudly in the trees out front. Bright late-morning sunlight streamed through my grimy windows. I wondered if the two old ladies on the porch across the street could see me standing in my boxer shorts in the middle of the living room.

I went back to the bathroom. Staring at myself in the mirror, I sent a telepathic message: Call back, Paula, call back. I brushed my teeth and gargled some Listerine. While I waited for the phone to ring again, I finished dressing and pulled the sheets off the bed. The "few minutes" turned into half an hour. Then it rang.

"All right," Paula said, "if you want to come, I'll tell you how to get here. But you have to promise me you won't bring the cops."

"That's a deal," I said, "but I'll have to bring someone to drive the other car back."

"Mom can drive it back."

"You said she had to work."

"She traded shifts with somebody. Now here's what you do. You get off I-65 at the Washington Street exit. Go left and then turn right on College Avenue." She gave me an address on College and said, "It's a big blue house."

"I'm on my way."

"Remember—no cops." Her voice was bossy yet pleading.

"How could I forget?"

It was a few minutes past eleven. There'd be less traffic on I-65 today. I should be at Paula's by 12:30.

My apartment was in a one-story brick duplex on Sycamore Street, between Adams and Jefferson. Not until I stepped outside did it occur to me that I had walked home from work last night. I'd have to walk back to the office to get a car. It would add ten minutes to my trip. But I could use the exercise. I walked fast. The bright air felt good in my lungs.

The newsroom was deserted on Saturday. I had my pick of cars, so I took the keys to the newest one, an '09 Ford Focus. Naturally it was low on gas. I drove a few blocks to the Swifty station, where the *Gleaner* had an account, and filled the tank. I figured this was a business trip, and besides, I put in plenty of unpaid overtime. Then I headed for Brickton and I-65.

All the way to Indy I worried that Paula would change her mind and vanish before I got there. It wouldn't surprise me if my car was waiting for me in the street, but no Paula. At least her mother might still be there. I could try to talk her into telling me where Paula had gone.

I occupied myself by dreaming up depressing scenarios like this one. I kept my speed in the low seventies. I did not need another ticket. I already had two within the past two years. I had to stay clean for another four years before they'd both be off my record. I turned on the radio to help me stop thinking depressing thoughts, so what did I get? Glen Campbell singing "By the Time I Get to Phoenix." Was Glen Campbell still alive?

At exactly 12:30 I was on the Washington Street ramp, but I still had another forty or fifty blocks to go on College. That was several miles, with a mess of traffic lights.

Between Lockerbie Square on the south and Broad Ripple on the north, much of College Avenue was in a state of decay, with closed stores and boarded-up houses.

One of the houses had the address that Paula had given me. The three-story frame structure had a bare patch of lawn in front, with concrete steps leading to a wide porch. Except for the slate roof and the slabs of plywood that covered the windows, every inch of the house was painted bright blue. It looked like a giant Easter egg.

I parked across the street. My guess was that Paula and her mother were watching from another house to make sure I had not brought the cops with me. I looked up and down College. Two houses from where I had parked, a black woman with melon-sized breasts and legs like logs sat on the edge of her porch, while two barefooted kids took turns jumping off a tire into a puddle of water to see who could make the biggest splash. I walked down and asked the woman if she knew where Paula Henry lived. She stuck her tongue in her cheek and shook her head.

I dodged a few cars and crossed the street. In the house to the left of the Easter egg, hip-hop seeped out of an upstairs window. A white-haired black man was sitting on a sofa and talking to himself. At the next house down, a pit bull that was tied to a pole bared its teeth and lunged at me. A horn beeped twice. I turned around and saw a woman waving at me from my Civic, which had pulled up behind the Focus. I ran back across the street.

"Phil?" she said.

"That's me."

"Hop in. I'm Paula's mom. I hope you don't mind if I drive."

"Go ahead. Where are we going?"

"Not far."

I went around the car and got in. It felt odd to be on the passenger side of my own car. Paula's mom stuck a hand in front of my chest and said, "It's good to meet you, Phil. I'm Edna Mae Boofey."

"Boofey?" I said as we shook hands. "There's a Walter Boofey who owns the house where Paula's friends were killed."

"I know. He rented them the house. He's my brother-in-law. I married his brother Norval. I was just a kid. It lasted less than a year. He was a real hell-raiser, always getting in fights. Paula was born while we were still together."

"So Walter would be her uncle," I said.

"Yeah, Walter's her uncle. Me and him still get along. I've not seen him for a while though." She turned sideways to add, "I hope you don't think he killed Wayne and Cheryl."

She was in her mid-forties and a little chubby—pleasingly plump was once the phrase. Her wide lips were bright red, and she had large wide-set eyes. She wore white jeans and a sleeveless turquoise top that revealed a

JOHN PESTA

lot of cleavage. Strands of tangerine-red hair blew around her face as she gunned the engine and cut into traffic.

"I have no reason to think he killed them," I said.

"Good."

"What line of work is he in?"

"He drives a truck, a big eighteen-wheeler."

We drove two blocks north and turned right, went three or four blocks, then left, then left again. Edna Mae kept glancing in the rear-view mirror as we zigzagged through the blighted area.

"You don't have to worry," I said. "Nobody's following us."

"I'm just making sure."

"How do you know I'm not wearing a transmitter?"

Her hands tightened on the steering wheel. "Damn, I should have thought of that—I watch enough television. I guess I ought to frisk you." She laughed. "Don't worry. I won't."

The zigzagging stopped, and once again we drove north, parallel to College, which was a few blocks west of where we were. The neighborhood began to improve as we got closer to Broad Ripple.

"So tell me," I said, "how did Paula get the name Henry? Was she married? *Is* she married?"

"No. She's never been married. But she had a boyfriend—Ladainian Henry was his name. A real good-looking black guy. He was in the Marines." She began choking up. "He was killed in Iraq a few years ago. One of those lousy IEDs got him. Paula and him were planning to tie the knot, but he didn't want to get married till he was out of the service. He was afraid he might get killed and leave her with a kid to raise by herself." She sniffled. "He was a good guy, always considerate and respectful. She uses his name to honor his memory." Long tears ran down her cheeks and fell on her chest.

I almost felt like crying myself.

We parked in front of a drab white house with a faded roof that sloped low over the front porch, giving the place a cool, shady look.

Edna Mae handed me the keys to my car, and as we walked to the house, I said, "Tell me something. How'd you know who I was when you picked me up?"

"I was watching for you from the bar on the corner. As soon as you got out of the car, I knew it was you."

I followed her up a few steps to the porch, which looked freshly painted. Two white plastic chairs stood on a blue grasslike all-weather rug. "This is where we live," she said. "It ain't much, but it's home."

The front door opened as we approached, and I saw Paula backing away.

"I got him," Edna Mae announced.

I walked into a delicious aroma of soup. A small air conditioner throbbed in the window. The television was on, but Paula immediately turned it off. The room was neat and clean, but the furniture—a green wingback sofa, a black vinyl recliner, and an oversized rocking chair— looked shabby. A braided rug that was coming apart covered half of the painted hardwood floor. A pair of stereo speakers served as end tables for the sofa, and a lamp whose shade looked like a frilly squaredance skirt was on top of one of the speakers.

Paula stood with her left elbow cupped in her right hand and her left hand patting her right side. She seemed edgy, ready to bolt. She wore a calf-length denim skirt, which hid most of the cast, and a gray cowboy shirt with yellow trim. Without the cast, I would not have recognized her.

Edna Mae said, "Have a seat, Phil," and gestured toward the sofa. She took the rocker in front of the air conditioner. "Paula's real sorry for taking your car, ain't you, baby?" Her eyes went to Paula, then back to me. "We want to give you something. Where's that envelope, Paula?"

"Where you left it—in the kitchen," Paula said.

"Get it for me, please, will you, hon."

Paula made a face and hobbled away.

"I filled up the gas tank this morning," Edna Mae said, but we want to give you something to cover your time and trouble too. I don't want you thinking Paula's a car thief. She doesn't do things like that." She leaned toward me and whispered: "She was scared real bad. That's why she took it. She didn't really steal it."

Paula returned and handed me the envelope, which I held on my lap.

Her mother went on: "Phil, I'm hoping you won't press charges against her."

"I won't," I said. "But it may not be that simple. I believe the prosecutor can still go after her if he wants to."

"See, Mom. I told you!"

"So you reported it stolen already?" Edna Mae said.

"Sure I did. But you'll be happy to hear I didn't accuse Paula of taking it. I saw the car being driven away, but I couldn't see who was driving." I looked at Paula. "I assumed it was you, but I didn't know for certain."

"But now you do," Paula said.

"Uh-huh. Thanks for telling me."

"I should've just drove it back to Campbellsville and left it at Wal-Mart or someplace."

"I'm glad you didn't," I said. "I'd still be looking for you."

Edna Mae said, "She only took it yesterday. It's not even been a day. She ain't damaged it."

"Mom, you're saying dumb things. I'm screwed." She glowered at me. "Why'd you have to leave your car there like that? It was almost like you wanted me to take it."

I had to laugh. "Where were you—in the house?"

"It's all because of you and your damn car," Paula said.

"Sit down, hon," Edna Mae said.

"Shit, if you hadn't given me a ride the other night, then hung around and went inside with me, and if you hadn't left your stupid car there, just begging to get ripped off, I wouldn't be mixed up in any of this. I could've got out of that hell house and nobody would know I'd even been there."

"Right," I said, "it's all my fault."

"Sit down, babe," her mother pleaded. "Don't get yourself excited."

"Oh, Mom, stop telling me to sit down. I've been sitting all day. What else can I do with this damn cast on?" She thumped across the room and stood in front of the air conditioner to cool her chest. "What an ass I am."

"Don't say that. If you and me hadn't got into an argument, you wouldn't have stormed out of the house and went down there like you did."

I tried to calm things down. "Look," I said, "I've got my car back. I don't have to tell the police who took it. I'll just say I went outside and there it was, parked in the street. And that will be the truth, because that's where it will be parked as soon as I get home and park it there."

My Jesuitical training in high school was finally paying off.

Instead of rejoicing at this, Paula went on ranting: "I'm just sick about Cheryl and Wayne. If it wasn't for me, they never would've moved down there to that godforsaken place."

Edna Mae said, "I'm the one that told them about the house, Paula."

"You mentioned it to Cheryl, but I asked you about it first, after they said they wanted to live in the country. I said what about that old house that Uncle Walt owns. Remember?"

"Yes," said Edna Mae, "but it was me that told Wayne how to get in touch with him." Her lips tightened sadly, and she shook her head. "It's not your fault they were killed, Paula. You have to stop blaming yourself."

Paula clomped back across the room to the recliner and finally sat down. She pushed back halfway, raising her cast with the footrest. She left her other leg dangling to the side. She hung her head and rubbed her temples with her fingertips.

I said, "I'd like to talk to your brother-in-law about the Garths. Do you have a phone number for him?"

"It's in my bedroom," Edna Mae said. "I'll get it for you."

A minute later she returned with a slip of paper. "I wrote it down. It's his cell phone."

"Thanks a lot," I said. "What did Wayne and Cheryl do for a living?"

"Cheryl worked in a supermarket," Edna Mae said. "Wayne sold stuff on his computer."

"What kind of stuff?'

"All kinds. Him and Cheryl went to flea markets and yard sales all over the place looking for bargains. Then Wayne resold it on eBay."

Paula put her head back and closed her eyes. She looked as though she wanted to fall asleep and never wake up.

I said, "Paula, I have to tell you something."

Her eyes stayed shut.

"The police want to talk to you."

Her eyes popped open. "You got your car back. Why don't you just take your money and leave us alone."

"Paula!" her mother said, "Phil's just trying to help."

I laid the envelope on the sofa. "They probably would have found you by now if they knew your real name is Boofey."

"As long as it stays that way, I'm safe."

"Why are you afraid of the police?"

She grunted softly. "You wouldn't believe me if I told you."

"Try me." I waited a few seconds. "Your mother's right—I'm trying to help you."

"You just want a story."

"What is your problem? Why won't you trust me?"

She sneered without answering. In the dim light her face had an ashen pallor and her eyes seemed lifeless. She sat very still, staring blankly, with her lips slightly parted. Then her eyes met mine, and a pale fire came into them. She pulled on the arms of the recliner and sat up.

"You want to know why I'm scared?" she said. "Okay, I'll tell you why." She hung fire a moment, seething. "When I was fifteen, I got put in some kind of foster home." As she began her story, her mother made a face, got up, and left the room. Paula waited until we heard a door close, then she went on: "She don't like to hear about it, and I don't blame her. What happened was she got in a fight with my father—they was still together then, more or less—and he ended up in the hospital. I saw it with my own eyes. He had both hands around her neck. He had her down on the bed choking her. I yelled at him to stop. I even tried to pull him off her. She reached out and grabbed the first thing she could get a hand on and hit him on the head with it. It was a heavy metal picture frame, and one corner of it went a half inch deep in his head. They said it could've killed him. He ended up in the hospital, and she ended up in jail. They kept her there for months because she couldn't make bail. The judge turned me over to juvenile protection, and they put me in the damn foster home."

"Where did this happen?" I said.

"Where do you think? Meridian County. We're talking about why I'm afraid of the cops there, remember?"

"I didn't realize you used to live there."

"Do you want to hear what I have to say or not?"

"Sorry. I didn't know I wasn't allowed to talk."

"Christ. Mom sat in jail till her trial came up, and they stuck me in that lousy home all that time. It was a big brick farmhouse that a man and his wife owned. They called themselves our foster parents, but they acted more like jailers. They made the older kids—like me—do all the chores around the house and even work out on the farm. They treated us like slaves. And if we mouthed off about it or cussed or something, we got our mouth washed out with soap. And if that wasn't enough, we got locked in the cellar overnight or we got paddled till our backsides burned. Most of the kids was little. When I was there, I was the oldest one. Kids came and went, but while I was there, there was always five or six of us in the house."

As she told her story, the words came faster and her voice grew bitter. "It was the little kids that had it the worst. Some of them went through hell. They truly went through hell. It took me a while before I figured out what was going on. You prob'ly won't believe it, but I'm not making it up. It's true."

She paused to catch her breath, then pushed on. "Every week or so a cop in a brown uniform would come and pick up one of the kids. He'd take some of the kid's clothes with him. At first I thought the kid was lucky, because I thought he was going home, but most of the time they came back the next day. I remember this one girl— her name was Candy Apple. Who would give their kid a name like that? Maybe it was a nickname, I don't know. She was just six or seven years old. After she came back, she just laid on her bed, curled up sucking her thumb. I told her she was too old to be sucking her thumb, but it was like she was in a trance. I asked her what was the matter, but she just laid there. She wouldn't talk."

A door squeaked open, and Edna Mae came back wiping her eyes.

Staring at the floor, Paula said, "Another kid started having nightmares. I didn't sleep in the boys' room, but I could hear him crying all night long. They just let him cry. The next day I asked our 'foster mother'—Mrs. DeLong was her name—what was wrong with Rickie. The bitch said there was nothing wrong with him and I'd better mind my own business. That night she made me clean up somebody's puke with my bare hands."

It made me shiver. "God, how could you stand it?" I said.

"I don't know. I just did. I can still smell it. I was afraid she was gonna make me eat it. But one thing I did not do was mind my own business. One night when Rickie was having one of his nightmares, I snuck over to his room and tried to calm him down. The old hag and her husband was snoring down the hall. I didn't care what they'd do to me if I got caught. I crawled under the covers with Rickie and started rubbing his back. I told him he had to be big and strong and not be afraid. I told him I'd be his friend. He snuggled up against me. I stayed with him awhile, till he fell asleep and didn't have any more nightmares. I went to him a few more times after that." She paused and looked up at me. "That's how I found out what was going on."

"What was it?" I said.

"The kids was being taken out for sex. Rickie told me he had to play with a big man. They'd play games and watch TV and eat pizza or ice cream, and then the man would take him to his bedroom and they'd 'play' some more in bed. Rickie said the man made him play a game called Lollipops. . . . You get the idea."

"Paula," I said, "was it always the same cop who came for the kids?"

"I can't say for sure. Like I told you, sometimes a kid did get to go home to his family, but usually the cop brought them back the next day. I never knew what was going to happen to this one or that one—they didn't announce it over a loudspeaker. Different cops came to the house. But it seems to me like when some boy came back with that look in his eyes like he'd been through a buzz saw, I think it was always the same cop."

"Do you know his name?" I said.

"You're damn right I do."

Edna Mae said, "Paula, you don't have to talk about that."

"Yes I do, Mom." She raised her head and stared at me. "There was a little plastic name tag on his uniform. One day he took me for a ride. He said it was so I could get out of the home for a while. We went to the state forest, and he parked by the lake. At first he acted nice and sweet. He wanted to know what kind of music I liked, and what was my favorite movie—stuff like that. Then he said I was pretty. He asked me if I had a boyfriend. I said no, and he said, 'A pretty girl like you should have a boyfriend.' I began to get scared. I knew where this was going. He said, 'Want to see something special?' and he unzipped his fly and pulled his junk out. As though I was a little girl, he said, 'This is Herman. Get it? Her man.' I tried to get out of the car, but he grabbed my hand and put it on his prick. It looked as big as a rolling pin to me. He squeezed my hand around it. I told him I knew what he was doing with the little boys. I said if he didn't take me back to the home right away, I'd tell my mom about it. He just laughed. He said nobody would believe me. He called me a feisty little filly. Then he grabbed me by the hair—"

"Paula, stop it now," her mother said. "That's enough."

Paula ignored her. "He grabbed me by my hair and said, 'You look thirsty, honey.' Then he pulled my head down and forced me to open up my mouth."

Tears welled in her eyes, but she did not cry.

Her mother sat on the arm of the recliner and put an arm around her. "Men are pigs," she said. "Present company excepted."

Paula said, "When he was done, he stuck a bottle of water in my mouth and made me rinse out. I was choking and gagging and crying. He told me to knock it off.

He said I was a woman now. Then he examined what I was wearing to see if any of his stuff got on it. I guess he wanted to make sure he didn't leave any evidence behind. While he was checking my clothes and feeling me up, he said—and I remember his exact words—'If you say one fucken word to anybody, I will put a fucken bullet in your pretty little head.' He sounded perfectly calm. Then he smiled and patted me on my leg."

I felt as if bugs were crawling through my veins. "Do you know who he was?" I asked her again.

She spat out the name as if it were poison: "It was Chuck Martin, that's who it was, God-damned fucken Chuck Martin."

CHAPTER 13
Return Trip

T HE ONLY sound in the room came from the air conditioner. Paula was breathing hard, but I could not hear her. It was like watching TV with the sound off. Still sitting on the arm of the recliner, Edna Mae squeezed Paula's shoulder and pressed her cheek against her head. Paula stared fiercely at the floor.

"You went through hell, Paula," I said.

"No shit," she snapped at me.

Edna Mae sniffled loudly. "He ought to be horsewhipped. She still has dreams about it."

"Who wouldn't?" I said. "It was a terrible ordeal."

I had never been a big fan of Chuck Martin. He was a foul-mouthed street brawler, as Carl Eggemann had said, but that was light years away from sodomizing a young girl and threatening to kill her if she talked.

Edna Mae's eyes were red, her lips pinched together. "We would've pressed charges against him, but it was only Paula's word against his, and we didn't have any proof. Who would've believed us anyway? They had me in jail, and Paula was in a foster home." She began to cry again and took a crumpled tissue out of her pocket. "And if Paula talked, I hate to think where she'd be now—in a cemetery."

I wanted to believe Paula's story. I did believe it. Even so, I had to face the possibility that she had made it up, or embellished the facts.

"Paula," I said, "when did this happen?"

"I told you . . . when I was fifteen."

"How old are you now?"

"Twenty-seven. Why?"

She was a little bit younger than I had guessed the other night. "So twelve years ago, 1998."

"Okay."

"I believe Martin was first deputy in the sheriff's department then. He was elected sheriff in 2002, and he held the office until the end of 2006. But he's no longer sheriff of Meridian County."

"Good."

"That means you don't have to be afraid of talking to the police."

"That's what you think. He still has connections."

"Carl Eggemann is sheriff now. He's a good man. Nothing will happen to you if you talk to him. You should tell him your story."

"No thanks."

"I know you're scared. I don't blame you. But—"

"You want me to get my head blown off?"

"Don't you want Martin to pay for what he did to you?"

"He'll never go to jail."

Edna Mae said, "The statute of limitations probably ran out by now."

I shook my head. "Forcible sodomy on a minor . . . threatening her with murder. . . . I don't think so. I'm no lawyer, but I don't think there is a statute of limitations on that. I can ask the prosecutor."

"Paula's scared," Edna Mae said. "You don't just get over the kind of thing she went through. It leaves a scar."

"I know."

"No you don't," Paula said. "You're busy telling me I got nothing to worry about. Jesus Christ! Once I open my mouth, I'm dead. I never should have told you."

"I understand why you're scared," I said. "But sooner or later you'll have to talk to the police. I just want you to know you don't have to be afraid of all of them."

"Forget it!" Paula yelled, waving her hands and twisting out of the chair. "I ain't going to no cops! Chuck Martin is still around. I seen him *yesterday* for Christ's sake! He was at Wayne and Cheryl's, poking around outside. You showed up not long after he left." She gaped at me. "Why the hell do you think I took your car? I had to get out of there before he'd find me." She stood there, angry and rigid, but the way the cast on her leg angled to the side made her seem incongruously relaxed.

"Where were you when you saw him?" I asked.

"Where he couldn't see me."

A longhaired calico cat strolled into the room from the kitchen and stopped and stared at us. Then it moseyed over to the far end of the sofa and began sharpening its claws on it.

"Stop it, Callie," Paula said. She took a couple of Frankenstein steps toward the sofa and nudged the cat away with her plaster-wrapped foot.

"Were you inside the house or out in the barn?" I said.

"Why do you want to know? So you can put it in the paper?"

"I'm just curious," I said. "I can't help admiring how you managed to evade the police."

117

She looked at her mother. "Why'd you have to bring him here?" She turned back to me. "I wasn't in the house, okay? Now let's drop it."

Edna Mae quickly said, "Phil, open the envelope I gave you. See if it's enough."

I wanted to pin Paula down even more. I wondered why she was unwilling to say exactly where she had been hiding. Was she keeping her secret intact in case she returned someday? Why would she ever go back there if she was afraid of getting caught?

I let it drop, for now.

I picked up the envelope, which still lay beside me. I tore off one end and found five twenty-dollar bills inside. "Thanks," I said, "but it's way too much money. You don't have to pay me anything."

"Yes we do," Edna Mae said. "You take the money."

After some wrangling, we settled on twenty bucks and the full tank of gas.

"Would you like some lunch, Phil?" Edna Mae said. "How about a nice bowl of soup?"

"That sounds good," I said, "but first I think I'd better call the bus station and find out when there's a bus from Campbellsville to Indy today. You'll have to catch it if you want to get back here in time to go to work tonight."

I called the terminal in downtown Indianapolis and learned that a bus from Louisville was due in Campbellsville at 3:20 p.m. It was 1:15 now, so we had time for a quick lunch.

We adjourned to the kitchen. Four rickety spindle-back chairs with caned seats stood around an oak pedestal table. I said I liked the chairs, and Edna Mae proudly proclaimed, "They was solid black when we got them, but Paula refinished them. It took her I don't know how long."

I half wished Paula could drive back with me to Campbellsville while her mother drove the other car. I wanted to talk to her some more, but it was better if she stayed at home. I didn't want to take a chance that someone might see us at the bus stop.

While we were eating, I asked Paula how she had broken into my car yesterday and started the engine.

"Piece of cake," she said. "You left the windows open an inch. All I had to do was poke a stick in and push the lock button on the other side."

"Did you hotwire the engine then?"

She leaned over the table and slurped her chicken-vegetable soup. "Sure did."

"Where'd you learn how to do that?"

"On the Internet."

"How many cars have you stolen?"

"Yours is the first. But I never meant to keep it, or strip it. That's the truth."

"Okay," I said. "By the way, do you have a job now, Paula? Can you work with that cast on?"

She shook her head. "Not since I broke my leg. Before that I had a job in a vet's office. I don't know if I'll get it back. Right now I'm on unemployment."

"What kind of work did you do?"

"I washed and groomed the animals."

"Did you like it?"

"It was okay."

I asked Edna Mae what kind of work she did.

"I clerk in a package-liquor store," she said.

"What time must you go in tonight?"

"Seven."

"We'd better get going then."

Edna Mae went looking for her purse, and I said goodbye to Paula. She seemed sullen and edgy. Her eyes looked tired, yet she seemed ready to fly apart like a broken spring. "I hope you get rid of that cast soon," I said.

"You and me both."

"Maybe we'll see each other again one of these days."

"I doubt it."

From somewhere Edna Mae called, "Never say never."

I held out my hand. Paula hesitated, then took it, and we shook. Her hand felt like a little girl's in mine.

I gave Edna Mae a key to the Civic. I figured I ought to drive the Focus. If Edna Mae got in a wreck, it would be hard to explain why she was driving a car that belonged to the *Gleaner*. Whereas if she got in a wreck with my car . . . well, I'd think of something.

She chauffeured me back to College Avenue, where I was happy to see the Focus was still there. I asked her to stay behind me on I-65, but if we got separated we should meet at the rest area south of Edinburgh.

We headed south under long, soft-focus clouds streaming in from the west.

For the first half of the trip I passed the time by plotting where we would leave my car. About halfway home I pulled off the interstate at the rest area. Edna Mae followed, and I told her my plan. She was to leave the Civic in the parking lot of the Frankenmuth Funeral Home, which was one block past the bus stop in Campbellsville.

For the second half of the trip I thought about the foster home where Paula had been sent. Was it still in business? How many kids besides Paula and Rickie had been molested from its doors? What a story it would make, if I could substantiate what she had told me. I wondered how many more stories she could give me.

120

The Greyhound bus stop in Campbellsville was a self-service laundry across from a strip mall. With Edna Mae on my tail, I passed the bus stop and drove another block to the funeral home, a large building that looked like a southern plantation house. I slowed down to make sure Edna Mae did not miss it, but I did not stop. In my rear-view mirror I watched her turn into the parking lot next to the funeral home. She was to leave the car there and take the key with her, then walk to the bus stop. She could mail me the key when she got home. If she'd happen to forget, that would be okay—I had a spare. Sooner or later the undertaker would notice the Civic and call the police. I'd have to practice acting surprised when they would call to say they had recovered my stolen car.

I just hoped Edna Mae would remember not to leave the key in the car. I had told the police my keys were in my pocket when the car was stolen.

Was I breaking the law? Was it a crime not to tell the police that my car had already been returned? Was I obstructing justice? Perhaps. But I could not tell the police about Paula and Edna Mae. I had given my word. Besides, they were confidential sources. I had to protect my sources.

CHAPTER 14
Cranking for Clues

I WOKE to the sound of rain beating on the roof and jangling like a cowbell in the downspout. I lay in bed listening to gurgles and plops. It was Sunday. I didn't have to be at work till 3:30. Pale sunlight filtered through my crummy windows. There was a flicker of lightning, followed by the slow rumble of thunder.

I thought of my car waiting to be found in the parking lot of the Frankenmuth Funeral Home. Had Edna Mae remembered to take the key with her? If not, my ass was fried. I could drive over there and see. It wasn't even seven yet. No one would be there at this hour. Forget it—the Campbellsville Police Department had four patrol cars cruising the streets all night long. "Oh, good morning, Officer, I was on my way to buy some Krispy Kreme doughnuts, and I just happened to see my car here."

I rolled out of bed, stretched, and yawned. I needed a shower, but first I rinsed the old grounds out of my French press, boiled some water, and made a cup of coffee. In yesterday's underwear I sat in the living room with my coffee and listened to the rain. The sound of church bells rode the breeze through the window. What to do, what to do? I could worship with Don Grapevine at the Presbyterian Church. I could try to talk to Walter Boofey, now that Edna Mae had given me his phone number. I could find out which nursing home Esther Dubbs was living in and pay her a visit. Or I could look into the foster home where Paula had stayed.

Once I put my mind to it, the decision was easy: I ate a bowl of Cocoa Puffs and a blueberry muffin while I watched Fox News. Then I showered, shaved, and got dressed. I didn't want to call anyone before nine o'clock on a Sunday, so I paid some bills at my desk.

At nine on the dot I phoned Walter Boofey.

"Yeah what?" he said.

"Is this Mr. Walter Boofey?" I asked.

"Who are you?"

"Phil Larrison. I'm the editor of the paper in Campbellsville, Indiana."

"How'd you get this number?"

"Your sister-in-law, Edna Mae, gave it to me."

"She did, did she?" His voice moved a tenth of a millimeter closer to politeness. "I'm gonna have to get me a new number. You callin' about them two murders up there?"

"As a matter of fact I am."

"I don't know nothin' about it. I'd like to get my hands around the neck of the bastard that did it though."

"Did you know Mr. and Mrs. Garth very well?"

"Not hardly. Edna Mae put them in touch with me. They were lookin' for a place in the country, and she knew I had that old house. They went and looked at it and liked it, so I rented it to 'em. A few months later they asked if I'd sell the place. I said no, my wife grew up there and she's sentimentally attached to it. The only reason I rented it to 'em was so somebody could take care of it for me. I guess I'd better get my butt up there and see what the place looks like. I don't need this garbage."

"Did you ever have any problems with them?"

"No. They paid their rent. That's all I cared about. Look, I can't talk right now. You caught me at a bad time."

"I just have one or two more questions."

"Goodbye."

He hung up.

I paced the apartment from window to window, replaying the curt conversation. Instead of answering my questions, Boofey only added more. Why wouldn't he sell the house to the Garths? Would Esther Dubbs have sold it if her daughter, Caroline, had been attached to it? Why had he even bought it if he couldn't take care of it?

Perhaps fueled by all the sugar in the Cocoa Puffs, my mind raced to imagine possible explanations. Maybe Esther had sold simply because she needed the cash, or because she had moved to Brickton and didn't want to pay for upkeep. Maybe Caroline had not been attached to the place back then. Maybe Boofey had bought it because he once meant to live there. As for his unwillingness to sell to the Garths, well, he didn't have to sell the house if he didn't want to. That line about Caroline's attachment may have been just a polite excuse. When you don't want to do something, one excuse is as good as another. Maybe he was the one who was attached to it. Perhaps he just liked owning a piece of land in the knobs. Lieutenant Bakery had told me that Boofey married Caroline a year after he had bought the place. Maybe it was the real-estate transaction that had brought them together.

Maybe, maybe, maybe. What did it matter anyway?

I had not brought up Chuck Martin's story of the marijuana crop found in Blind Horse Hollow, but what difference did that make either? All Boofey had to say was he didn't know anything about the marijuana, and for all I knew, he'd be telling the truth.

I began to get depressed. My so-called investigation was getting nowhere, and I was spending most of my time on it. On the other hand, only three days had passed since Paula had found the maggoty corpses. Take it easy, I said to myself. Don't beat yourself up. The police haven't solved the murders either.

The pep talk helped. I made another cup of coffee and looked up the two Dubbses in the phone book. There was no listing for a Judy Dubbs, but there was a Frank Jr. I knew that Esther's husband had been named Frank, so it was likely that Frank Jr. was Judy's deceased husband. She may have left the phone in his name for protection, so strangers wouldn't think she lived alone.

A bright cheery voice that made me think of sunshiny water answered on the second ring: "*Hel*-lo."

I introduced myself and asked if she was Judy Dubbs.

"Busted," she said. "What can I do for you?"

"I understand you're related to Esther Dubbs," I said. "I'm trying to reach her. I'd like to talk to her if I can."

"*You* can talk to *her*, but *she* might not talk to *you*. She's got Alzheimer's. She doesn't talk as much as she used to, poor thing. She's in Twin Lakes Health Center—the memory-care unit."

"You're her daughter-in-law, aren't you, Mrs. Dubbs?"

"*That's* right, but *please*, call me Judy."

"Judy, will I be allowed to see her if I go there?"

"What do you want to see her about?"

"I'd like to ask her about a marijuana 'harvest' that took place on her property about eleven years ago."

"You know, she might remember that. That's the kind of thing she still hangs on to. She has her good days and bad days. She's very confused. The wires in her head are crossed."

"I'm sorry to hear that," I said. "But I'd still like to meet her. Maybe I'll get lucky and catch her on a good day."

"You never know. Tell you what—if you go by yourself, you might scare her. She might think you're a dentist. She's afraid of dentists. Or she'll think you're going to steal her sweater or something. Maybe I should be there too."

"I'd appreciate that—but I don't want to put you to a lot of trouble."

"You won't. I go to see her every Thursday anyway. Would next Thursday be okay for you?"

I checked my calendar on the BlackBerry. "That's good for me. Should I meet you there?"

"Yes. Let's make it 12:30. She'll be done with lunch by then. I'll meet you in the lobby outside memory care."

"Sounds good. Thursday at 12:30. See you then, Judy."

"I'm looking forward to meeting you, Phil."

That was different. A friendly voice on the telephone. Maybe I wouldn't have to go on Prozac after all.

As I poured a fresh cup of coffee, what Paula had said about Chuck Martin and the foster home popped into my head. If her story was true, could it be proved? Did I have time to pursue it, or should I turn it over to a reporter? I could look into it first, then decide. I wouldn't want anyone to get the idea that I thought Martin was a sex offender. I'd have to have proof. Personally, I had nothing against the man. The old publicity hound had always been accessible to me. But I didn't owe him anything either. If he had abused Paula or anyone else, the public had a right to know. And he should pay for it.

I envisaged another front-page series. The Associated Press would pick it up. My stories would be in papers all over the state, maybe even the nation. *Dateline* and *48 Hours* would be calling me. . . .

I shook off the vainglory and went to the *Gleaner*. As I entered the building, I heard the press running in the back—probably printing an outside job—but I had the newsroom to myself. I stood at my desk and wondered where to start. The *Gleaner* did not maintain a clip file, so I couldn't go straight to a cabinet and pull out a folder with every story we had ever run on foster homes, and the archives on our Web site went back less than five years. But we did have every issue of the *Gleaner* on microfilm.

In an effort to save time, I called my boss. Luckily I caught him just as he was about to enter his church. I asked him if he could remember if the paper had ever run any stories about a foster home for kids, a big brick farmhouse somewhere in the county.

"Sounds like the Good Shepherd Home," Edward said. "Yeah, we did some stories on it. I think we ran a feature when it opened. Let me think now . . . that would have been back in the early eighties. It shut down when the county built its own group home about ten years ago."

In the background I heard his wife say, "Ed, come on!"

"Who ran the place?" I said.

"Uhhh, you can look it up. I've got to run. The queen's tapping her foot."

At least now I knew I could find something in our back issues. I unlocked the safe and took out every reel of microfilm from 1980 through 2005. I chose this range of dates because Edward had not been precise about when the foster home had opened and closed. It was going to be a tedious job. I had fifty-two reels, two for each year, to look at. If I spent only ten minutes on each reel, it would take more than eight hours to go through all of them. Did I really want to do this? I began to have second thoughts, but the cool, rainy day was tailor-made for research. Rain pelted the windows, and the cubby hole where our ancient microfilm reader stood felt snug and cozy. To move from page to page you had to crank the ancient machine by hand. I sat down and went to work.

Because I was looking for a particular story about the opening of the home, the cranking went fast at first—all I had to check were front pages and feature-fronts. I got through the first two years in fourteen minutes, and on the fifth reel I found it. A front-page story in March 1982 had a photo of the home on a low rise against a backdrop of hills and clouds. A banner headline in 48-point Bodoni blared, "Good Shepherd Home Promises Safe Pasture for Stray Lambs." I gagged. Headlines like that were the work of Miss Maudie Armbruster, the lifelong society editor who was still on the job when I first joined the staff. She was all right when writing about weddings and showers, but her flowery flattering prose should have been banned from the rest of the paper.

I learned from her article that Mr. and Mrs. Hugh DeLong were inviting everyone in Meridian County to join them in celebrating the grand opening of the Good Shepherd Home for the Innocents in the lovely countryside of Clark Township. "This much-needed facility," according to Miss Armbruster, "will provide a caring and disciplined environment for children who, unfortunately, find themselves in need of proper supervision in loco parentis. Mr. and Mrs. DeLong deserve the county's gratitude for unselfishly devoting themselves to shepherding these stray lambs."

God help us. I made a few notes and moved on. I glanced at the headlines and photos on every page to make sure I didn't miss something related to the home. Occasionally, in a summary of courthouse news, I found a couple lines stating that an unidentified juvenile had been placed in the home by Judge Jack Brandon. I cranked and cranked. I began to yawn, but I kept on cranking. In a December 1985 issue I found a photo of members of the Campbellsville Disciples of Christ wrapping Christmas presents for children at the home. In 1986 there was an announcement that the home was planning a fund drive to add a wing on the south side. The *Gleaner* followed the drive for the next two months and eventually reported that more than $60,000 was raised in donations and pledges. The DeLongs then purchased a half-page ad thanking the contributors for their support.

In a 1992 issue I found a photo of Hugh and Grace DeLong receiving a plaque from the Campbellsville Rotary Club in honor of the tenth anniversary of the home. The small photo lacked contrast, which made the couple look as sinister as Paula had described them. Their black hair and clothes merged with the dark background, and their white faces looked like wraiths. Broad-shouldered and big-chested, Mr. DeLong seemed to be sucking in his gut. His wife was a cylindrical matron in a straight black dress.

As noon approached, I thought about going home for lunch, but instead I went to the lounge and bought a Snickers bar and a pack of peanut-butter crackers. After every two or three reels, I got up and walked around the office to work the kinks out of my legs. When the rain stopped and the sun came out, I wished I was outside. Staff members began dribbling in.

In a 1996 reel I found a photo of several children from the home who were touring the old county jail. Deputy Chuck Martin was in the picture, grinning at the camera while two girls and three boys peered into an empty cell. Their names and ages were in the cutline. One of the boys was named Rickie Davidson. I wondered if he was the Rickie that Paula had told me about. I added their names to my notes. I sat back and stared at Deputy Martin's toothy smile. The scene looked like an everyday civics lesson, but I suspected it was more than that. It was probably meant to tell the kids they'd better be good if they wanted to stay out of jail.

In a 2000 reel there was a front-page story about an eight-year-old boy, Barry Wilson, who had run away from the home. The next issue of the paper contained a head shot of the boy when he was six. The *Gleaner* followed the story for several weeks, but the child was never found, despite a statewide alert and an extensive search in Meridian County. The prevailing theory was that the boy had tried to thumb a ride on the highway and someone had picked him up and kidnapped him.

I came across other references to the home, but no stories or photos that provided me with names of other residents.

The county built a modern group home for children in 2001 and hired a professional administrator to run it. Shortly afterward, without fanfare, the Good Shepherd Home closed. I nearly missed a small item on the social pages that said Mr. and Mrs. Hugh DeLong had sold their farm in Meridian County and moved to Florida.

I quit cranking the machine in the middle of the reel for 2003, when I reached the first issue of the *Gleaner* that I had worked on. Since then we had not run anything about the Good Shepherd Home that I could remember. My neck felt stiff and the newsroom was buzzing. It was nearly four o'clock, and I had not yet done a thing for tomorrow's paper, but I could catch up. As I returned the microfilm to the safe, the sliding blur of pages went on running in my head, as if it had been burned into my retinas. I felt nervous and jumpy, but it was a good kind of jumpiness.

CHAPTER 15
The Blue Ghetto

NEXT MORNING I went to Mackey's for an earlier-than-usual breakfast and then to my office. The plan was to spend two or three hours tracking down six former residents of the Good Shepherd Home for the Innocents. They were Candy Apple, the girl whom Paula had identified, and the five kids in the photo that I had found on microfilm.

When the photo had been taken in 1996, the five children ranged in age from eight to thirteen. That was fourteen years ago, so now all of them were adults. Pictured, from left, were Judith Ann Shult, 12; Rickie Davidson, 8; Gary Fromm, 9; Lisa Noe, 12; and Troy Stinson, 13.

I started with the Campbellsville phone book. It listed two parties named Apple, four named Shult, forty-four named Davidson, none named Fromm, two named Noe, and six named Stinson. Of course, the girls could be using married names now, and all six of these former residents of the Good Shepherd Home may have moved as far away from that place as they could get. Or they may have died.

I went to the business manager's desk and borrowed the city directory. In it I found an address for Gary Fromm, but no phone number. The other names I was looking for were not in the directory.

I quickly discerned that this was going to take a long time. I fortified myself with my second cup of coffee of the day, and then, starting with the shortest list of surnames, I began calling people up.

No one answered at the two Apple residences.

A woman named Charlotte Noe told me that Lisa Noe was her sister-in-law and "went out to Texas some years ago."

A man named Joe Noe thought I was trying to sell him a newspaper subscription and hung up.

Two of the four Shults answered the phone, but neither of them knew Judith Ann Shult.

After three calls to people named Stinson, I got Troy Stinson's grandmother, who said he was working at the Campbellsville Training Center. I asked what he did there, and she said, "Whatever they tell him to. He's one of their best workers. He's real careful when it comes to packing boxes and such."

The Training Center employed developmentally challenged persons, as they were now called. To make sure I had located the Troy I was looking for, I asked if he had ever lived at the Good Shepherd Home.

"Yes," she answered with a hint of apology, "a long time ago. His ma ran away, you know. She was a good-for-nothing. And his pa—my son—he had a terrible accident. He worked for the REMC and got electrocuted by a power line. I couldn't keep the boy with me on account of I had to work. . . ."

I stopped listening. I debated whether to go through the motions and talk to Troy, just in case he could tell me something about the home, but I decided to pass.

I waded into the Davidsons. An hour and a half later, on my thirty-ninth call to members of the Davidson clan,

I learned from the wife of one of Rickie's cousins that he had moved to California after getting out of high school and no one in the family ever heard from him again.

I asked the cousin-in-law if Rickie had graduated from high school.

"Oh yes," she said. "He was real smart."

I felt glad for him. "I guess you knew him pretty well then?" I asked.

"Not hardly. I just remember my husband saying that once."

"Do you have a phone number or address for Rickie?"

"No, I sure don't."

"Do you know if your husband does?"

"No. Sorry. You can ask him yourself if you want to call back after five."

"Thank you very much," I said. "I might do that."

I hung up and stood up. My stomach, intestines, pancreas, and gall bladder felt squashed from sitting at the desk. I stretched and yawned. Keyboards clicked loudly in the newsroom. I scratched my forehead, which for some reason felt itchy all of a sudden. Must be dry skin. I went to the men's room and assumed the position of the Thinker.

It occurred to me that I had an address for Gary Fromm. Maybe I could actually talk to one of the people I was looking for. I needed some fresh air, so I decided to try to find him. As I drove through town, I wondered if the police had found my car yet. I was tempted to drive by the funeral home to see if it was still parked there, but I didn't want to take a chance on being recognized. Maybe no one would ever find the car. Maybe it would stay there till I got old and kicked the bucket. Maybe the funeral home would bury me in it.

Gary Fromm lived in the Blue Ghetto, a low-income housing project on the south side of town. There were twelve two-story units in each row of so-called town houses. Their vertical siding, which had originally been bright blue, had been repainted a few years ago and was now bright beige, but no one ever referred to the development as the Beige Ghetto.

I parked in front of Unit G7 and stepped over the shattered toys, cigarette butts, and flattened condoms lying in the parking lot. I rang the bell, which did not ring, and knocked on the door. It was yanked in so fast that I felt as if I was being sucked in with it. A bearded, shirtless man of twenty-three gaped at me with large round eyes and an open mouth.

"Good morning," I said. "I'm looking for Gary Fromm."

"You found him. Who are you?"

Just to be giving him something, I handed him my card, which he read with painstaking slowness. Then he handed it back to me. "I'm doing a story on the old Good Shepherd Home," I said. "I understand you lived there for a while when you were a boy."

"How the fuck d'you know that?"

"I found a picture of you and some other kids from the home in a back issue of the *Gleaner*."

"No shit?" A smile full of broken teeth flashed through his ragged beard.

"That's right. You were nine years old in the picture. I'm looking for people who lived at the home when they were kids. Someone who lived there around the same time as you has told me some interesting stories about the place. I'm trying to get more information."

He stood with one hand on the edge of the door as if barring my way. "Whadaya wanna know?" He shifted his weight from one leg to the other. He looked inside over his shoulder.

I could see this was not going to be a long interview. "Well, for starters, how long did you stay there?"

"Let's see. . . ." He scratched his hairy chest. "I don't know for sure. About a year maybe." He looked past me at someone in the parking lot. He raised his fingers to his mouth, let out a sharp whistle, and yelled, "Hey, Buck, don't forget about tonight."

"Don't *you* forget," Buck yelled back.

I said, "I won't take a lot of your time, Gary. I know you've got things to do. I just have a few more questions."

"So ask 'em."

I took out a pad and pencil. "How did you like living at the Good Shepherd Home? What was it like there?"

"I didn't much care for it," he said.

"Why not?"

"It was too strict. And we had to pray all the time."

"Really? The home wasn't run by a church, was it?"

He glanced over his shoulder again. It was a nervous glance, as if he was afraid someone might be listening to us. "I don't know. Different preachers came in on Sunday. But that's not what I'm talkin' about. Every few hours, every day of the week, it was prayer time."

"What if you didn't want to pray?"

"Ha!" he laughed sarcastically. "You only didn't want to pray once. If you didn't want to pray, or if you just didn't pray along with the others, you got locked in a small room in the cellar for hours with nothin' to eat or drink. And God help you if you took a leak down there."

"It sounds like a dungeon," I said.

"That's what it was, a freaken dungeon."

"The people who ran the home, Mr. and Mrs. DeLong—apart from being strict and making you pray, how did they treat you? Did you feel they were trying to help you?"

"As long as you obeyed their rules, they was all right. They was just too strict is all." He glanced behind him a third time.

"They were supposed to be your foster parents. Did they act like parents who cared about you?"

He fluttered his lips. "Hell no. They was more like drill sergeants. Or slave drivers. They made us do chores around the house and work on the farm. One of my jobs was to clean out the pig pen in the barn. We didn't get paid nothin'. They said we had to earn our keep. When we was in school, we had to get our homework done before we could play games or watch TV. There wasn't much we was allowed to watch on TV."

"Gary," I said, "you might find this hard to believe, but your description of what it was like to live there makes it sound a lot better than what other people have told me."

"I can't help that. I'm just tellin' you what it was like for me."

"I appreciate that. That's exactly what I want you to do. But let me ask you this. Did you ever see a policeman take one of the kids out of the home and then bring him—or her—back the next day? Did that ever happen—"

He cut me off: "No."

"Are you sure? Because—"

"I answered your question." He glanced backward again. "Look, I've got stuff to do. My wife's gonna start bitchin' at me."

"Please. This is important," I said. "Do you know if any of the kids there were ever sexually abused when they were taken out of the home?"

He reared up and shook his head. "No! If somethin' like that ever happened, I never heard nothin' about it."

"I've been told that a sheriff's deputy used to come to the home and take a little boy to some guy's house for 'playtime.' Did you ever hear anything like that from the other kids?"

His lips curled as he bared his broken teeth and struggled to control his voice. "What the shit's wrong with you? Don't you understand English? I said no! Period!"

A young woman in sweatpants and a T-shirt that bulged like a watermelon appeared beside him. She looked as if she was due any minute. "What's goin' on, Gary?" she said. Her eyes met mine for a moment, then fell. She was about eighteen, and she had a pretty face—a lot prettier than her scruffy husband seemed to deserve. Her hair was rumpled from sleep.

"Go back and lay down," he said. "Everything's okay."

"It don't sound okay," she said. "Who are you, mister? Do we owe you money? If we do, you'll get it. We won't cheat you."

"You don't owe me any money," I said. "I'm very sorry if I disturbed you."

"He's sellin' insurance," Gary said. "I told him we don't want none." He gave me a silent snarl and shut the door in my face.

So Gary was ashamed of whatever had happened to him more than half his life ago, so ashamed that he didn't want his own wife to know about it. I wondered if he could be made to testify in court. The way he had carried on made me think a good lawyer would have little trouble getting the truth out of him. On the other hand, he had a certain dullwitted stubbornness that might withstand attack. Time would tell, perhaps.

CHAPTER 16
How Far Can You Go?

Iwas walking to work the next morning when a police car pulled up to the curb beside me on the wrong side of the street. Officer Steve Garret of the city police department stuck his head out the window and said, "Hey, Phil, you won't have to walk anymore. We found your car."

"Great!" I said. "Where was it?"

"The Frankenmuth Funeral Home. It's at the county jail now, being processed. They'll call you when they're done with it. I just wanted to let you know."

"Thanks, Steve. Were you the one who found it?"

"No. The funeral home reported it yesterday afternoon. They said it was left there sometime Saturday." His radio crackled, and he stopped to listen. Then he said, "I'd give you a lift, Phil, but I gotta go. Another fender-bender." He turned on his flashers and sped away.

The plan was working. All I had to do now was wait for a call from the sheriff's department.

The call came after lunch. The county's crime-scene investigator said my car had been recovered and I could pick it up whenever I wanted to. "I hope you have a spare key," he added. "There wasn't any in the car."

Edna Mae had followed instructions.

I found one of the reporters grabbing a smoke out back, and I got him to drive me to the jail. At the front counter I asked for Jim Simpson, the detective who had just called me. Slim Jim, as he was known, had been a CSI only a few months. Previously the county's crime-scene investigations had been handled by the state police, but since the Campbellsville post had been closed for budgetary reasons, the sheriff's department had gotten one of its own men trained. I found Jim and my car in the metal building where he worked behind the jail.

"She's all yours," he said.

I listened as he told me what I had already learned from the city cop. Then I asked if he had come up with anything after going over the car.

"No, nothing," he said. "It was wiped clean—the steering wheel, gear shift, door handles, everything. I checked for fingerprints, swabbed for sweat that could yield some DNA . . . nothing. Whoever took your car did a mighty good job of covering their tracks."

"It sounds like it," I said.

"There was a little damage under the dash, where they got into the wiring to start the car, but not much. You won't even notice unless you look for it."

"Excellent."

"Did you leave any valuables in the car?" he said.

"No."

"Did you have portable GPS or any other electronics that weren't built in?"

"No, sir."

"Well, you're fortunate. It looks like nothing got ripped off."

"There's nothing worth stealing."

"Your registration is still in the glove compartment."

"Is that significant?" I said.

"Sometimes the perpetrator takes it if he means to steal your identity. You didn't have your social security number on anything in the glove box, did you? Any credit cards?"

"No and no."

"Good. You'll have to sign a form, but after that, you're good to go."

He kept talking as we walked back to the jail: "I'll call the city police and tell them to notify the NCIC to delete your car from the national database. That's the National Crime Information Center. It's part of the FBI. It's a computerized database for tracking crimes. When a vehicle is stolen, the agency that receives the report enters the information in the database. Then, when the vehicle is recovered, the agency that recovers it must notify the one that put it in the database to get it deleted."

I was thinking we ought to do a feature on this guy, Meridian County's only CSI. How does his experience compare with what we see on TV?

While I was signing the property-release form, Sheriff Eggemann heard us talking and came out of his office. "Are they taking care of you, Phil?" he said.

"Yes. It's good to get my car back in one piece. Thanks, Sheriff."

"Thank the city police. They found it."

"I'll do that."

"By the way, I reckon you were right in thinking your hitchhiker stole it."

"What makes you say that?"

He started back toward his office, and I tagged along.

"A couple of things," he said. "First, there was no damage to your car, no parts missing. Second, where it was found—a block from the bus stop. I suspect she was hiding out somewhere around the Garths' house, maybe in the barn, and when you left your car to go hill climbing, she saw her chance to get away. But with a broken leg, she didn't want to drive all the way up to Indianapolis, so she came to town and caught the bus. She could have left the car at the bus stop, of course, but she may have been afraid it would be found too soon—like while she was still on the bus." He paused, then added, "The only problem with this scenario is that the clerk at the bus stop didn't remember selling a ticket to a lady with a broken leg. But he said if she wasn't on crutches, he may not have noticed she was wearing a cast."

"Pretty hard not to notice," I said. "Do you have anything else on the Garth case?"

"The latest I heard is the victims' bodies are to be cremated today," he said. "Their families—their parents—want it that way. Lieutenant Bakery can give you the details." He went into the office and sat down.

"Have you talked to the parents?" I said.

He propped his elbows on the arms of his chair and made an A-frame with his fingers, thumbs against chin. "Yes, by phone. I told them they could remove their children's belongings from the house anytime now. I didn't want to rush them, but we're getting sightseers out there. I can't afford to keep a man posted day and night to make sure nobody steals something. We've barricaded the driveway again, but people will go around it if there's no guard."

"Would you mind giving me their phone numbers?"

"That information should come from Lieutenant Bakery. I don't want to step on his toes." He glanced at his watch.

"One other thing, Sheriff—on a different subject—if you've got a minute."

"Now what?"

"Do you know anything about a place called the Good Shepherd Home?"

He nodded. "That was the old foster home. It closed when the county built its own home for kids."

"That's right. I'm wondering if you ever heard any stories about children being abused there?"

"Abused? What kind of abuse?"

"Cruel and unusual punishment. . . . Sexual abuse. . . ."

"Heck no," he said, "Who've you been talking to, Phil?"

"A former resident of the home."

"Got a name?"

"To get the information, I had to promise not to reveal their identity."

"Did he or she claim to have been abused?"

"Yes."

"When?"

"More than ten years ago."

"Ten years. That's a long time." He shook his head. "I wouldn't give it much credence. I know this county pretty well. If there was any truth to it, I think I would have heard about it before now."

"I know," I said. "I'm skeptical too. But I was given some pretty convincing details. It did not sound like a fabrication."

"Don't you have enough on your plate, Phil?" His forehead creased as he leaned on the desk. "Maybe the person who talked to you has a grudge. Some people carry grudges a long time. I wouldn't take it at face value."

"I'm not taking it at face value, Carl. That's why I ran it by you."

He nodded. "If you want the other side of the story, why don't you talk to Grace DeLong? She's the lady who used to run the home."

"She lives in Florida," I said.

"No she doesn't."

"I thought she and her husband moved there after the Good Shepherd Home closed."

He smiled with the satisfaction of someone who knows something you don't. "That's right, but after her husband passed away, she moved back here to be near her family."

"That's good to know," I said. "I'll pay her a visit."

I hurried back to the garage for my car. It felt good to get behind the wheel of the Civic again. Then it was back to the *Gleaner* to find out where Grace DeLong lived. No problem—her name was right there in the phone book. I spent the next hour editing news. That took me to lunchtime. Then I went looking for Mrs. DeLong.

She lived on Periwinkle Avenue, a misnamed street on the south side of town. The avenue was only two blocks long, the beginning of a subdivision that never grew. Small ranch homes with brick wainscoting on the front and vinyl siding everywhere else lined both sides of the street. There were no trees, and most of the small front yards were overgrown. Toys and bicycles lay scattered about, and several for-sale signs sprouted in the grass. Mrs. DeLong's home was one of the few that did not look shabby or unoccupied. I parked in front of her house. As I crossed the lawn, the smell of freshly cut grass hung in the air.

I knocked on the screen door. The inside door was open, and the voice of Elvis Presley singing gospel came from the back of the house. A fairly tall woman with snow-white hair appeared out of the shadows.

"Yes, what is it?" she said, at once impatient and guarded, as if I were about to try to persuade her to pre-pay her funeral or let me blacktop her driveway.

"Mrs. Grace DeLong?" I said.

"Yes."

I introduced myself and said, "I'm working on a story about foster care in Meridian County. I believe you and your husband used to run the Good Shepherd Home."

"We did."

"I'd like to talk with you about the home, if you don't mind." When she did not immediately respond, I said, "If this isn't a good time for you, I can come back some other day."

"I guess it's all right," she said. She unlocked the screen door and held it open.

The living room was stuffed with large, dark wooden furniture. There was barely room to walk. "Have a seat," she said, pointing to an uncomfortable-looking armchair between a curved-glass china cabinet and a long buffet on thin legs. She hurried away to turn off Elvis, returned immediately, and perched on a cameo-back love seat directly in front of me.

When I opened my notepad and took a pencil out of my pocket, she said, "You're using a pencil. I didn't think anybody used pencils anymore."

"I don't like ballpoint," I said. "Too many smears and splotches."

She nodded in approval.

I began the interview with background questions about the Good Shepherd Home. When did they open the home? What led them to establish it? Was it affiliated with a church? What kind of work had they done before starting the home? How many children did they care for over the years? How many employees did they have? Did the county or state subsidize the home? Was it financially successful or a constant struggle? . . .

I had no shortage of questions like these, and after a few minutes, she relaxed and was more forthcoming. When I asked, "What made you and your husband decide to close the home?" she really opened up.

"The county put us out of business," she said. "They built their own home. But they call it a group home, not a foster home. And you know why? Because the people who work there don't act like foster parents. They don't even pretend to try. They're just government employees, that's all they are. But what do I care? Hughie and I were fixing to get out anyway. The two of us were getting too old to deal with the kind of kids they were sending us."

"What kind of kids were they?" I said.

"Kids growing up wild. Their parents never taught them anything. They were poor and uneducated—I'm talking about the parents now. Some of them were drunks or druggies. They didn't care what their kids did. A lot of them were single mothers, living on welfare. The kids had no discipline, no guidance. It got to the point where Hughie and I couldn't take it anymore. I always say those kids drove my husband to an early grave."

"When did your husband die?"

"It's going on three years now since I buried him."

"Is he buried here in Campbellsville?"

"No. Spring Hill, Florida. It was too expensive to bring him back up here. Besides, he always wanted to live in Florida. He's happy there."

"How did you like living there?"

"I liked it fine. But I was all alone after he died."

"Do you have any children?"

She shook her head. "No. I have two brothers. At least I have them. They both live in town here. It was my greatest disappointment that we weren't blessed with children of our own. That was our cross to bear. It was another reason why we started the Good Shepherd Home. We wanted to have children around us. But the job got harder and harder as we got older."

"I bet it did," I said. "Do you feel you were able to help the children who came to the home? Did you manage to turn any of their lives around?"

"I'd like to think so. I hope so. God knows, we tried."

"How did you deal with problem kids? Did you have special training? If a kid did something really bad, how did you handle it?"

"With plain old-fashioned common sense. No fancy theories. You don't need two or three college degrees to know how to raise children. All it takes is knowing how to look after them, give them some love and attention." She held her head high. "I just tried to teach them right from wrong, how to behave properly, how to show respect." There was a proud, boastful twinkle in her eyes.

"Were you very strict with them?"

"Young people need rules to follow. They will test you to see just how far they can go. They want to know exactly how far. Yes. I was strict in insisting they follow the rules."

"Would you say you were a stern disciplinarian?"

"As stern as I had to be. Some children needed more discipline than others. Dealing with children is more of an art than a science. But they all had to follow the same basic rules. It would not have been fair any other way."

"When children broke the rules, how were they punished?"

"I always felt that the punishment should fit the offense. For a little child, often the best punishment is simply being made to sit for half an hour or an hour. I have never been in favor of corporal punishment, but sometimes it is appropriate, I believe. Hugh and I did use a paddle occasionally, when a child stepped way over the line."

"Mrs. DeLong," I said, "I have to tell you that I've spoken to some people who were put in the Good Shepherd Home when they were little. From what they've told me, it sounds as if punishment was sometimes very harsh."

Her mouth fell open. "That's simply not true. What did they tell you?"

"One of them said children were locked in the cellar overnight for refusing to do chores around the house."

"Who in the world told you that?"

"It's not true then?"

"Certainly not."

"You mentioned that you sometimes paddled children. In one case, I was told, the paddling went on so long that it made the kid's backside burn. Could that be true?"

She gaped at me. "If a child does something so bad that paddling becomes necessary, don't you think the paddling should hurt a little bit?"

"So you don't feel the paddling was ever excessive?"

Her chest heaved. "Of course not! Who's been telling you these things? Do you think we would have been allowed to operate the home for twenty years if we had treated children like that? My Lord!"

"I'm sorry," I said, playing the hypocrite. "I just want to give you the opportunity to respond to what I've been told."

With a cold, hard stare she said, "I hope you're not planning to put this in the paper. There's such a thing as libel, you know."

"I will not libel you, Mrs. DeLong."

"I'm glad to hear that."

"I have one more question. I've been told that a policeman would sometimes come and take a child out of the home to some other house, where a man would play games with the child for a while and then take the kid to bed with him. How do you respond to that?"

Her head wagged in super slow motion as her face froze in disbelief. "Is this a joke? What are you trying to do? You're making me out to be a witch. I never heard of such things." She broke into a crazy laugh. "Who have you been talking to? You look old enough to know you can't believe everything you hear. Some of the children we had in the home were not exactly saints. We had all kinds. Some of them were pretty big liars."

"Why would someone make up lies like these, Mrs. DeLong?"

"How should I know? You tell me. Some kids just make things up. I remember one girl telling the other children that her mother was Marilyn Monroe. She said Marilyn put her in the home because she was too busy making movies to raise a kid. It didn't matter that Marilyn Monroe had committed suicide before that girl was even born." This time she laughed triumphantly. "I hope you don't make the mistake of printing those lies in the paper. My husband and I put the best years of our lives into that home. I will not tolerate it if you cause our good reputation to go up in smoke."

"I would never print anything I couldn't prove," I said.

One eye nearly closed as she stared at me. "That's very wise of you. And if you don't believe what I've said, you can ask someone else. Ask Judge Brandon. He's the most respected man in the county. Go talk to him."

CHAPTER 17
Us Brandons Stick Together

THE AFTERNOON was half gone by the time I got back to the office. Several notes lay pinned under my keyboard, but none involved the Garth case, which meant none of them was from Lieutenant Bakery. There was one more thing I wanted to do before getting into my regular work. I called Judge Brandon's house.

Lillian Brandon answered the phone.

I asked her when the judge would be home from Asia.

"Friday evening," she said. "I'm meeting them at the airport in Indianapolis."

"Do you think I could see him Saturday? There's something I'd like to ask him about." I wanted to do what Grace DeLong had said I should.

"I suppose so, as long as it's not too early. His body clock is going to be all mixed up for a while—you know, jet lag. He'll probably sleep in Saturday."

"How about Saturday afternoon?"

"That should work."

I was about to say goodbye, but she quickly added, "Phil . . . I never thanked you properly for your help last week. You went way beyond the call of duty."

"That's okay," I said. "I'm just glad nobody drowned."

"So am I."

"Has Scott been behaving himself?"

"Yes. He's doing fine." She hesitated, then confessed, "I increased his medication. The Judge will throw a fit if he finds out, but I don't care. It needed to be done."

"What's Scott on?"

"Barbiturates. I think he's developed a tolerance though. It takes more than it used to to calm him down. It's a good thing the Judge will be home soon. When his papaw's here, Scott hardly needs any pills at all. He does whatever the Judge tells him. The Judge is like God to him."

"I bet you'll be happy when the Judge gets back."

She made a low sigh. "Yes, in all honesty, I will." Her voice trailed off again, then came back. "Actually, this has been a nice, quiet day for me. Scott's father came and took him to the Kentucky State Fair in Louisville. Scott loves to go on the rides."

"Lillian," I said, "why doesn't Scott live with his parents?"

"Oh," she fretted, "that's a long, unpleasant story. Listen, I know you're probably busy, but I just had a thought. How would you like to come out here for a drink a little later, and maybe something to eat? It would be my way of thanking you for last week."

I was tempted to decline. I still had a full day's work ahead of me. I thought of suggesting tomorrow instead—I was off Wednesdays. But she'd have to take care of Scott tomorrow. What the heck, I had to eat sometime. "Sure," I said, "that sounds good."

"Okay. . . . Super." She sounded surprised. "How about sixish? Is that too late?"

"No, that's good. It gives me time to bat out some work here."

"Okay. . . . I'll see you then."

I edited copy until five o'clock, when I made myself stop. I raced home, took a quick shower, and put on a clean shirt and pants. Then I drove to Hampstead my usual way, through Brickton and Blind Horse Hollow. There was a shorter route, but I wanted to see if the barrier that Sheriff Eggemann had mentioned this afternoon was still in place at the Garth house.

It was. Two sawhorse roadblocks with Keep Out signs on the crossbeams stood end to end at the entrance of the driveway. It wasn't much of a deterrent to a committed sightseer or housebreaker. I decided to move it myself on my way back to town and take another look at the house.

I arrived at the Brandon estate fifteen minutes late. I rang the doorbell and peeked inside through narrow windows on each side of the door. Lillian appeared at the back of the entrance hall and came hurrying toward me. She was wearing a blue and green skirt that looked like a swirly abstract painting and a silk blouse that was a lighter shade of blue.

"Here I am," I said as she opened the door. "Sorry I'm late."

"That's okay," she said with a harried smile. "I didn't give you much notice. Come in. I'll give you a little tour."

I followed her from the hall into a posh living room with oversized sofas and armchairs strategically grouped on plush ivory carpet. A wide archway on the right led to a Queen Anne dining room. Then came the kitchen, where an array of copper utensils hung over a granite island that matched the surrounding countertops. The strains of Bach or Vivaldi or another one of those guys settled on us from small speakers in the ceiling.

Lillian said, "What would you like to drink, Phil?"

"Whatever you're having."

She fixed me a Gibson, the first of my life. Then she led the way down two steps to the family room, which featured a stone fireplace big enough to roast a hog. I stood at the French doors and surveyed the pool and patio, the fields and hills, as if I were lord of the manor.

"You've got a beautiful place here, Lillian—in case you don't know it," I said.

"Thanks. We like it. It's a little bit out of the way though."

"That's okay. The whole county's a little bit out of the way."

"I know. My grandfather wishes it was even more isolated than it is. He wouldn't mind if I-65 was moved a couple of counties away."

"The Chamber of Commerce might mind."

"No kidding."

She sipped her drink and wandered to a sofa facing outside. She settled into the big cushions and tugged her skirt over her knees.

The chitchat continued. Five minutes passed. Ten minutes. I began to regret that I had come. Supper was nowhere in sight, and I still had a ton of work to do. Another five minutes ticked off the clock. When was she planning to feed me? I should have known better than to do this on a work night. I should have said I could come tomorrow, Scott or no Scott.

"Would you like another drink?" she said.

"No thanks. I'd better not."

"How are things going with your murder story?"

I shrugged. "It seems to have stalled out. The police don't have any leads, or if they do, they're not telling. But I haven't talked to the detective in charge of the case today. Maybe I'll try to get ahold of him tonight."

"Tonight? Must you go back to work?"

"Yes, unfortunately. We've got to get tomorrow's paper out."

"Oh, of course. I should have realized." She pushed herself up. "I'd better put the steak on. How long can you stay?"

"Long enough to eat."

"I'm so sorry. I should have thought."

I felt bad for making her feel bad. "Don't worry, Lillian," I said. "We'll get the paper out. We always do."

She took a thick sirloin out of the refrigerator and plopped it on a grill on top of the range. She was a little nervous, rushing. She fixed a large bowl of salad and slid a loaf of French bread wrapped in foil into the oven. I asked if there was anything I could do to help, and she said I could open the wine. I poured us each half a glass. The smoke from the steak billowed up into a large copper hood. She dumped a can of corn into a sauce pan.

Her slightly flaring skirt, which ended a few inches below her knees, was flattering to her straight figure, and her brunette hair, curling inward at chin level, softened her face. She wasn't gorgeous, but she knew how to make the most of what she had.

She took the bread and two baked potatoes out of the oven. We ate in the kitchen under a hanging Tiffany lamp that looked like the real thing. There were no candles on the table, nothing romantic, nothing pretentious, unless you counted the house itself.

"This is delicious," I said.

"Thank you."

She sounded a bit distressed, but once we had some food in our bellies, we both did better. She struck me as a natural, kind, generous person. She had to be generous to have devoted herself to taking care of Scott the way she did. I liked her. But there was no spark.

Halfway through the meal I began quizzing her about her family: "You said Scott's father took him to Louisville. Why does Scott live here instead of with his parents?"

"They're divorced," she said, chewing her steak. "His mother, Marilyn, lives in California. His father, my uncle Frank, is too busy to look after him."

"Why is it your job?"

Her lips squeezed into a frown. She looked at her plate, then at me. "It just worked out that way. The family has always been close. 'Us Brandons Stick Together'—that's our motto." She laughed. "But Marilyn never fit in. She wanted to have Scott put in a home as soon as she learned he had a problem, but Gramps wouldn't hear of it, and Frank came down on his father's side. Marilyn said, 'All right, then you two take care of him,' and away she went."

"But the burden is all on you," I said.

"Not all of it," she said with a shivery shake of her head, "it's not so bad when my grandparents are here. This summer was rather unusual."

"Have you ever thought about getting someone to help you with Scott—a male nurse maybe, someone big enough to handle him."

She nodded slowly. "My grandmother and I have actually talked about that. But it won't happen as long as Gramps is living. He considers it a sacred duty for us to take care of Scott."

"Well," I said, "that's certainly admirable."

"I know. But sometimes I wonder if we did the right thing. Maybe Marilyn was right. Maybe Scott should be in a home where he can get the kind of help he needs to reach his potential." Her eyes glistened. "But the Judge said no. He said he could give Scott what he needed better than anyone else."

"I still think it's asking too much of you."

She stared at her plate and used her fork to fold a piece of lettuce on itself. "I've dealt with it this long," she said. "I can go on dealing with it." Her voice betrayed her discontent.

"What does Frank do that keeps him so busy?"

"Mainly he's a property developer. His latest project is a lake in Washington County. He's got the dam finished. Now he's building a road and waiting for the lake to fill up so he can start selling homesites. He also owns Omega Construction. It does a lot of road paving for the state. And," she went on, rolling her eyes, "he's still in the garbage business with my father."

"What garbage business is that?"

"MWM—Meridian Waste Managers, Inc. The two of them started the company thirty years ago, but they may be getting out of it soon. You can't put this in the paper, because the contracts haven't been signed yet, but they've been negotiating with a national firm that wants to buy them out. Gramps is against the deal. He says the company wants our landfills so they can ship trash here from Pennsylvania and New Jersey."

"How many landfills are we talking about?" Another story was taking shape.

"I'm not really sure. Several."

"I understand there's an old dump on the other side of the hill behind Don Grapevine's house. I guess Don is your uncle too."

"Step-uncle," she said. "That's right, but that land-fill is not one of the ones they're selling. It filled up years ago. It was MWM's first property. My father and uncle bought it and signed a contract with the county. Some people claimed there was a conflict of interest because Gramps was circuit-court judge, but he had nothing to do with awarding contracts. That was up to the county commissioners and county council. Even so, my grandfather insisted that his sons bid as low as they could afford to when dealing with the county. And they always have. No one has ever accused them of bilking the taxpayers."

"I just realized something," I said. "Your father's Ralph Brandon, the president of Campbellsville State Bank, isn't he?"

"Yes. Do you know him?"

"Who doesn't? I didn't know he was in the trash-collection business though."

"It's not something we brag about, but it's a *very* good business. Dad says there's more money in trash than the bank." She began twirling the stem of her wine glass. Then she laughed again. "I'm talking too much. It's your turn. Tell me about yourself. How long have you been with the *Gleaner*?"

"Seven years now."

"Do you like your job?"

"Yes I do. That's why I'm still here."

"Did Ed Wylie hire you to be editor?"

"No. I was just a reporter. It was my first job after college. I planned to stay a year and use it as a stepping stone to a bigger paper, but a few months after I started, the news editor left, and Ed Wylie gave me his job. A year later he made me editor-in-chief."

A big smile broke out on her face. "Wow, you must really be good."

"No. It was the Peter Principle—I was promoted to my level of incompetence."

"I don't think so," she said, sitting back and smiling at me. "You just won't take a compliment, that's all." She had perfect white teeth.

As a rule I did not let my mouth run on about myself. The cocktail and wine must have gone to my head.

"How about some coffee and dessert?" Lillian said.

"No thanks. I'd better get going."

"Can't you stay for dessert? I made a raspberry pie this morning. It's awfully good."

What the heck, I thought. Have some pie. "You talked me into it," I said.

"Good." She hopped up and took the pie out of the refrigerator. As she began slicing it, we heard the front door open. "That'll be Frank and Scott," she said, less than overjoyed. Footsteps and voices approached through the hall.

First to appear was Scott. As soon as he saw me, he stopped and stared.

His father squeezed around him and saw me at the table. "What's this?" he said. "Company, Lill? Sorry to barge in."

He was about five-eleven and slightly on the heavy side, with a ruddy handsome face and a full head of golden-brown hair. It didn't look like a wig. Implants, maybe.

Lillian said, "Uncle Frank, this is Phil Larrison. He's the editor of the *Gleaner*."

"I recognize the name," he said, striding forward to shake hands. "I'm surprised we've never met. Hello, Phil." His grip was firm, tight. His eyes seemed ultra blue, and I realized he was wearing tinted contacts. "Those are some stories you've had in the paper about the murders."

"Thanks," I said. "It's good to meet you."

"Come on in, Scott," Lillian said. "Would you like to have some pie?"

Scott had on a red and yellow T-shirt, and he needed a shave. His broad face seemed even larger than when I had met him in the pool. His lips pouted. His eyes were squeezed nearly shut, as if he were squinting to see me better. "How are you, Scott?" I said.

His expression did not change. He did not move.

Lillian said, "Did you have fun at the fair, Scott?"

"Tell Lill what we did, Scott," his father said.

Scott's eyes slowly widened as he turned toward Lillian. "Un . . . un . . . un . . . un. . . ."

"We had a blast," Frank said. "We went on the double ferris wheel. That was real scary, wasn't it, Scott?"

"Un . . . un . . . un. . . ."

"Sit down, Scott," Lillian said. "Here's a nice piece of pie."

She guided her much larger cousin to the table and sat him on my right. He began rocking slowly back and forth, repeating his syllable. He no longer stared at me. He was focused on the reflection of the lightbulb in the middle of the table.

"Scott's really tired," Frank said. "I wore him out. He'll sleep like a log tonight. Hey, I'll take a slice of that pie too." He sat down across from Scott and waited to be served.

"Frank," I said, "Lillian mentioned that you and your brother own the old county-dump property."

"We prefer to call it a landfill," he replied.

"Do you know it's still being used as a dump?"

The news startled him. "What do you mean?"

I told him I had climbed the hill behind the Garth place the other day and happened to see a pickup truck drive over the filled area and get rid of a load of trash at the bottom of the hill.

"Damn, I guess we're going to have to put a fence around the whole thing. But they'll probably keep dumping there no matter what we do. Once a dump, always a dump." He did not sound upset until he demanded, "What were you doing on top of the hill?" When he realized he had struck the wrong note, he forced a laugh and said, "What were you looking for, more dead bodies?"

"No," I said, "just enjoying the view."

He stuck a forkful of pie in his mouth and said, "How's the murder investigation going? Are the police any closer to solving it?"

"I don't think so," I said.

He shook his head hopelessly and finished gobbling his pie. Then he got up and laid a hand on his son's shoulder. "We had a good time today, didn't we, Scott. You hit the sack now. And listen to Lill." As he left the kitchen he gave me a perfunctory glance and said, "Nice meeting you, Phil."

Lillian followed him to the front door. Their voices echoed softly in the hall as I watched Scott make a mess of his pie.

CHAPTER 18
From Attic to Cellar

I LEFT the Brandon house a few minutes later, after Scott and I had finished our pie. Scott showed how much he enjoyed the pie by rocking faster and faster as he ate, constantly chanting, "Un . . . un . . . un . . . un," a mantra of the misbegotten.

By the time I reached Blind Horse Hollow, the hills at the western end were already casting long shadows across the corn and soybean fields, while the hills at the other end gleamed in the golden sunset.

I felt guilty for spending so much time with Lillian. I still had a job to do. I stepped on the gas, but as soon as the driveway to the Garth house appeared, I saw that the roadblock had been moved and I slammed on the brakes. The pair of sawhorses still blocked the entrance, but now they formed a wide-angle V instead of a straight line.

Someone had gone in there during the past hour or two. Probably that someone had also left, but he could still be there. On the principle that it was wiser to waste a little time checking out a possibility rather than save time and regret not checking, I stopped and dragged one of the sawhorses off to the side and drove in.

As the car bounced and rattled on the washboard lane, the long leaves of corn seemed to reach out to grab me.

Ahead of the car, the high green walls parted continuously, while in the rearview mirror they closed behind me.

The house slid into view around the last bend. I plowed into the overgrown lawn. Faded and peeling, the house looked as if it had been empty for years, but in the thin, gray twilight it stood out boldly, like a stark symbol of fearlessness in the face of the dying light. There was no car around, but recent tracks in the weeds showed where someone had parked and turned around. I wondered who had been there. Sightseers wouldn't have bothered to replace the roadblock. Perhaps the Garths' relatives had come to get some of their things.

I climbed out of the car and waded through the weeds to the porch. The window that Paula had smashed was now covered with plywood. On the off chance that someone was inside, I knocked on the door. No answer. I twisted the doorknob. Locked. I peered through the front windows. Nothing but a dark reflection of myself.

As long as I'm here, I thought, I might as well check out the rest of the place. I went around back, but everything still looked the same. The back door was locked. In the trees on the hillside, the locusts were tuning up.

I did not see the horses in the pasture. They could be lying down, so I crossed the field to get a closer look and check on their hay supply. As it became clear that the pasture was empty, I felt a selfish disappointment. I had not done a thing to help them, yet I was sorry they were gone. The fence was not broken, so they had not escaped. Someone must have taken them away—rustlers maybe.

My next stop was the barn, where I discovered that the rusty lock and chain on the door had been removed. It gave me a chance to get my first look inside. The big door squealed like a pig as I pushed it to the side. A Ticonderoga

RV was parked in the middle of the floor, surrounded by old farm equipment and stacks of straw. I opened the RV's door and looked inside. Like my first encounter with the house, the RV reeked. At least no corpses were lying around. The smell this time was more like a mixture of dirty bedding and old mold. I scrapped the idea that Paula had used the RV for a hiding place, but maybe she had slept on the straw in the barn.

I shut the barn door and followed a little path that meandered past the creek at the base of the hill. About twenty yards from the house, the ground felt spongy. Then it got squishy and wet. It had not rained since Sunday, so how could the ground be this wet? A few feet away, a rivulet of black water seeped out of the ground and trickled toward the dry creek. I caught a whiff of sewage and realized I was standing in the drainage field for a septic tank. Wastewater oozed out of the ground around my shoes. . . .

Someone was in the house.

From where I stood I could see one side and the back of the house. All the windows were dark. I walked fast, nearly running to the front of the house. Even though it was enveloped in the shadow of the hill, not a single light was on inside. I wondered if the electricity had been turned off. But what about the solar panels on the roof? Obviously they would not work in the dark, but wasn't the energy that they captured stored in batteries? There should be some light in the house if someone was there.

I began to have doubts. Was it possible that something other than a toilet or sink or bathtub was responsible for the soggy ground in the field? A sump pump maybe. But a sump pump would not empty into the septic tank, and it wouldn't smell like wastewater. No, it had to be someone in the house.

I went to the front porch and pounded on the door. "Hallo!" I shouted. "Anybody home? Hallo in there."

I went back down the steps and looked up at the second-floor windows. Was it Paula in the house? Was she playing games with me again? No, it couldn't be Paula. It made no sense. More likely it was relatives of the Garths. Maybe they were afraid to open the door. They might be thinking I was the killer.

"Hey! Yo! I know you're in there," I yelled. "I just want to talk. I'm from the local paper. Look—" I took my press card out of my wallet and held it up. "See. . . . I'm with the Campbellsville *Gleaner*. I just want to talk to you."

Still, no one answered.

The sky was now deep blue. The sun would soon disappear behind the hill. On this side it was already getting dark.

I had to do something. I couldn't just turn my back and walk away. I had to find out who was in there. But what if the killer was inside? That was crazy—he, she, or they would have no reason to come back here now, would they? In the weeks that had passed before the bodies were discovered, there had been plenty of time to search the house.

I ran to my car and dug the tire-changing tool out of the trunk. One end of it was an L-shaped lug-nut wrench, while the other end served both as a jack handle and as a pry bar for removing a wheel cover. I ran back to the house and banged on the door again—one last chance for whoever was in there to open up. No one did, and so I jimmied the pry bar under the plywood that now covered the top half of the door. The board practically fell off when I touched it. Only a handful of nails held it in place. I reached inside and unlocked the door. Then I reattached the plywood as it had been.

I opened the door slowly. This was breaking and entering again, but at least I hadn't damaged anything. And I wasn't the first person who had removed the piece of plywood.

I had my tire iron ready in case someone was behind the door. I felt for the light switch. Shadows flew up the stairs.

The living room had been straightened up, slightly. The newspaper sections and beer bottles no longer littered the floor, but the shaggy green rug was still streaked with mud. The Grateful Dead, unsmiling, aloof, stared down at me from the wall. The big-screen TV was gone.

"Anybody home?" I called again, mainly to make my presence known. Belatedly it occurred to me that whoever was there might be a cop. "My name is Phil Larrison," I shouted. "I'm a newspaper reporter. If you're one of Sheriff Eggemann's deputies, I'm not a crook. I'm not here to steal anything. I just want to know who's here." The sound of my voice seemed to twist and turn through the rooms and passageways.

I went from the entrance hall to the dining room to the kitchen, turning on the lights room by room. There was a glass in the sink, a Bedford *Times-Mail* on the table. Beyond the kitchen was a room I had not seen last week, a fairly large laundry room with a washer and dryer, a wooden kitchen table, and an antique pie safe that contained not pies but a jug of Cheer and other laundry products. A brass bird cage with three stained-glass ornaments hanging inside stood in front of a window to catch the light. A plastic basket with a few pairs of panties and bras sat on the table.

The laundry room had two more doorways. One of these opened to the living room, which struck me as odd, but I figured the laundry room must have been used for something else in years past. I expected the other door to be a closet, but instead I found myself staring into a black hole. I twisted the knob of an ancient light switch, and after a brief delay, an incongruous fluorescent bulb lit up above my head and revealed a steep flight of crude wooden steps. It was little more than a ladder, which began right inside the door and led to the cellar. The steps were flimsy and uneven. I was in no hurry to go down there—maybe later, if I didn't find anyone in the rest of the house. Besides, whoever was in the house could get away if I went in the cellar, so it would be a mistake to go down there now.

I took the shortcut I had just discovered and went through the living room back to the front hall. I turned on the lights and started upstairs. Halfway up, I stopped and listened. The house was silent except for the sound of my breath. I had an eerie feeling that someone was behind me. I glanced over my shoulder, but no one was there.

As I neared the top of the stairs, I half expected a psycho with a butcher knife to come rushing out of a bedroom at me. My hand squeezed the tire wrench.

The yellow, crinkly glow that filled the second-floor hall made the walls look like flypaper. I looked in the bathroom first. Less than a week ago, two decaying corpses were lying there. Now it was empty and clean. I wondered if Paula had cleaned it.

The faint odor of urine hung in the air, or at least I thought it did. Maybe it was the lingering smell of death, or the general mustiness of the room. But the tub and sink were dry. Trust your gut, I said to myself. You smelled urine. That means someone used the toilet a few minutes ago.

It was cool in the house, but a clammy sweat broke out on my chest.

I crossed the hall to a bedroom and switched on the light. The room had been used as an office and mail room. A desk and chair stood next to a front window. There was a metal file cabinet, an old sofa, an oak bookcase, and a large dining-room table with Bubble Wrap and other packing materials on top. Priority-mail boxes of different sizes were stacked against the walls. The top of the desk was bare, except for a lamp, a mousepad, a stapler, and a pile of catalogs. The computer and printer that most likely had been there were now gone.

The next room must have been the master bedroom. A king-size bed filled half the floor space. A night table with a red gooseneck lamp stood at the far end of the bed. A chest of drawers and a small armchair completed the furnishings. The closet was crammed with men's and women's clothing on metal and plastic hangers.

I moved on to the room across the hall. Cylindrical stacks of old-fashioned hat boxes nearly touched the ceiling. It looked like a collection. I opened some of them, and a dry, musty odor escaped. They contained either nothing or a few large sheets of colored tissue. I wondered if the boxes were worth something. Perhaps the Garths had sold them on eBay.

The closet in this room was empty, except for a ladder to the attic. There was no way Paula could have climbed it with her leg in a cast. So she couldn't have hidden up there. And the police would have searched the attic. They would have found her . . . unless she had a very good place to hide.

I knew I might get my head knocked off if I poked it up there, but I had to take the chance. This house was going to get searched from top to bottom. No loose ends. I wasn't leaving until I found out who was haunting it.

I went up the ladder and used my jack handle to raise the trapdoor. "Anybody here?" I called through the square hole. "I'm coming up. I just want to talk."

It was hot at the ceiling. I climbed the next two rungs, and as my head cleared the floor, the attic erupted in a blizzard of bats. Hundreds of them flapped and swirled past my head. I lowered the trapdoor until it was barely open an inch. The bats streamed toward the vents at two sides of the house.

As I hung on the ladder, a small brown bat landed on the edge of the trapdoor and stared at me. It hung upside down with its face inches from mine and made a series of rapid clicks. I knew the critters were considered an endangered species, but evidently they were safe in Blind Horse Hollow. I held the door up with one hand and touched the bat with the wrench. He made several angry clicks and took off.

After a minute or so, the flapping died down and I poked my head into the attic again. I expected to see cobwebby boxes and old pieces of furniture, but the attic was empty. It occurred to me that there should be wires from the solar panels on the roof, along with some electrical equipment, but there was nothing of the kind. If the solar panels were hooked up, the wires had probably been run down the outside of the house to the cellar.

I happened to brush the floor with the side of my hand, and then I knew why the attic was empty, except for the bats. Their droppings coated the floor. How could the Garths have put up with it? Why didn't they get rid of the bats and sterilize the place?

A possible explanation came to me. It had not bothered them that hundreds of bats shared their home. They had laid out a welcome mat for the bats. They had tried to help them survive.

I went to the bathroom to wash my hands. A pink towel hung next to the sink. When I pulled it off the rack, it felt damp. For a moment it seemed to prove that someone was in the house with me, but whoever had used the towel may have left by the back door while I was coming in the front. Even so, I pressed on. I looked in the bedrooms again—there were four in all—to make sure no one had slipped into a room after I had searched it. All were still empty.

I started downstairs, and for a moment a faint breeze touched my face. It was as if a door had opened and closed just long enough to let a puff of wind inside. But I didn't hear a door or window open and close. There was no sound of any kind. I ran down the stairs and went from window to window, but I didn't see anyone outside. I hurried back to the laundry room. Everything there was exactly as I had left it.

I opened the cellar door again and peered down the steps. They were old and warped, bowed in the middle. I turned on the light. Jagged shadows pointed the way to a dirt floor.

I wondered if the steps would hold my weight. There was no banister, only a rough clay wall on the left and a post that supported the steps on the right. Just do it, I said to myself, and I started down.

As I took my third step, a pair of hands grabbed my left ankle and pulled it backward between the boards. My right foot was not planted, and I fell forward. The tire wrench that I had carried for protection hit the post and ricocheted against my breastbone. The side of my face scraped the wall as I fell, and my head cracked against the bottom steps.

Flashing circles exploded like stars. Thick leaden slabs moved toward me. Then everything went black.

CHAPTER 19
Fog

COMING TO was like rising to the surface of a sea clogged with gauze. I had a splitting headache. I could hardly move. For a minute or two I wasn't sure where I was, or what had happened. Then I realized I was lying twisted on the floor at the bottom of the steps. One of my legs was still on the steps, bent backward and tingling as if it had fallen asleep. Every other part of me felt stiff and sore. One side of my face burned. It felt wet, a little muddy.

I dragged my bent leg off the steps and rolled onto my back. The leg tingled so much it hurt. A blurry light bulb burned directly overhead. Dazed, slightly dizzy, I stared at it for a while, wishing the fuzziness would go away. How long was I lying here? What time was it? My heart pounded. I remembered taking a nosedive down the steps. . . . Someone had tripped me.

I was tired. . . . My eyes started to close. . . .

Don't fall asleep, I warned myself. You have to go to work.

I used the bottom step to get up on one knee. I waited for a wave of dizziness to pass. Then I shakily got to my feet. I stood on one leg and shook the other one until most of the tingling stopped. I looked at my watch. The hands pointed to 9:20. It seemed much later than that. Maybe the watch had stopped when I hit the ground. No, it was still running. I had been unconscious only a few minutes.

9:20.

Was it morning or night? I had to get to work. My stomach churned in panic. I thought I was going to throw up.

The headache went on pounding, but the pain began to fade. I felt stiff all over. Why was I sore in so many places—my ribs, my ears, the small of my back?

Finally, it began to come back. Someone had tripped me as I came down the steps. Maybe he had worked me over while I was out cold. Was it the same guy who had murdered the Garths? If so, why was I still alive? Why hadn't he killed me too? Was he still in the house?

It was hard to decide what to do. I had trouble focusing. I wanted to look around the cellar, but maybe I should check the house first in case the tripper was still around. What would I do if he was? I should get out of here. Get out while I could.

The left side of my face began throbbing. Without thinking, I rubbed the cheek, which meant I rubbed dirt into the scratches and cuts and made it hurt worse. I remembered scraping the wall as I went flying down. I had to wash the scrape before it got infected. I wondered what I looked like.

I went up to the kitchen. The light was on. There was no mirror, but I could see myself in the window above the sink. It was dark outside. That was good—it must still be Tuesday. My reflection revealed a large brush burn, a network of scratches from cheekbone to chin. Long, thin crimson lines laced the skin under an orange smear of clay. The scratches were still bleeding, though not much. I cupped cold water in my hand and splashed it on the wound to clean it and stop the bleeding. Then I patted my cheek with a paper towel. I hoped the scratches wouldn't leave scars.

To be absolutely sure I was alone in the house I did a quick inspection. As I went from room to room, I thought about my attacker. If it was the same person who had killed the Garths, why hadn't he killed me? I had been unconscious, completely at his mercy. The simple answer was that he had no reason to kill me. This implied that he did have a reason to kill the Garths. This would mean the killings were not random acts of violence. Of course, if someone else murdered them, randomness remained a possibility.

Was it Walter Boofey under the steps? Why blame him? He owned the house. He had a right to be there, not me. He would not have gone away and left me lying in the cellar. He could have had me arrested for breaking in. He might even have thought I was the guy who killed his tenants. Maybe he thought I would kill him too. He had plenty of justification for tripping me on the steps.

How about Chuck Martin? Paula said she had seen him poking around the house. He may have been poking around some more tonight. Perhaps he was trying to solve the murders to show voters they had made a mistake by not reelecting him sheriff. If he was the one who had tripped me, it was probably just to keep me from seeing him in the house. Like me, he must have broken in. He wouldn't want that to come out in the paper. But he wouldn't kill me to keep it out. Or would he?

And, of course, it was possible the tripper was none of the above.

I knew if I had any sense I'd get out of there and go home—or go to the hospital and have my face treated.

But I still wanted to have a look at the cellar. Surely there wouldn't be anyone under the steps again. The bedrooms were empty. No one was sitting on the toilet or taking a bath. I had the house to myself.

I went back to the laundry room and peered down the steps. They looked even more rickety than before, but my skull knew they were solid enough. Get it over with, I said to myself. Check out the cellar and get the hell out of here.

I could feel my adrenaline pump kicking in as soon as I took the first step. All the way down I expected a pair of hands to grab my ankle again, but nothing happened. I touched down safely. Grateful to be alive, I stood under the lone light bulb and looked around.

This was not your finished basement with knotty-pine paneling, pool table, and bar. The cellar was little more than a hole in the ground, more or less square and with uneven walls and floor. It was less than a quarter the size of the floor above it, and I suspected it was excavated years after the house had been built. The ceiling was about a foot higher than those of today's basements, and thick wooden posts supported the first floor.

The first thing that grabbed my attention was an array of electronic equipment with little red lights. I felt as if rats with gleaming eyes were watching me. Several pieces occupied a wide space that had been hewn out of the upper half of part of one wall, about three feet farther into the earth. The expansion resembled a large built-in shelf. Other components stood on concrete blocks below the shelf. Wires crawled down the wall into something called a DC Disconnect, and I realized all this stuff was for the solar panels on the roof.

A few feet away an enormous old furnace hogged up a major portion of the cellar. Next to it, a pair of six-feet-long oil tanks took up even more space. The furnace and tanks also stood on concrete blocks, but these blocks were flush with the ground and decades older than the ones under the electronic components. The oil furnace was no longer in service, having been replaced by a much smaller gas furnace on the other side of the tanks. The gas furnace stood on a pad of poured concrete.

A stack of crumpled boxes, a wooden kitchen table covered with dusty Mason jars and other canning materials, a rust-covered ironing board, a mangle, and other pieces of junk littered the rest of the cellar. I had seen enough. It was time to leave. I turned off the lights and went outside.

The fog took me by surprise. It was so thick that I could not even see my car. Here and there a lightning bug made a blurry glow. It took me a minute to find the car, and then, even with my lights on, it was hard to see where the gravel lane penetrated the cornfield. Visibility was two or three feet. The county road was just as bad. I drove incredibly slowly as I tried to keep the car in the middle of the road.

Halfway up the first hill I rose above the fog, and near the ridge my phone started beeping to let me know I had messages. They would have to wait. A bright gibbous moon made the hollow look like a bowl of mist.

From ridge to ridge I dipped in and out of the fog, and in the river bottoms I was back in the soup again. I thought about going to the emergency room to see if I had a concussion, but I felt okay now. I could also get the scratches on my face treated, but they weren't deep enough to leave scars and would disappear in a couple of days. Besides, I could still help get the *Gleaner* out.

I clutched the wheel, ran the wipers, and strained my eyes to see the road. It took me an hour to get back to the paper. It was almost eleven when I walked into the newsroom, where I was greeted with gasps and astonishment.

"Are you okay, Phil?"

"Were you in a fight or something?"

"What happened to you?"

Edward heard the commotion and came out of his office. He normally wasn't here at this hour, but no doubt he had come in to take my place. "My God, Phil, where have you been?" he said. "I've been trying to call you all night."

"I'm sorry," I said. "I couldn't call in. I was out at the Garth house. I got myself knocked out."

"What? Are you joking? Who knocked you out?"

"I wish I knew." I felt the top of my head. A small lump had swelled up.

"Have you been to the hospital?"

I shook my head. "I'm okay. Where are we here? How's the front page?"

Edward said, "Don't worry about it. You've got to get to the hospital. If you were knocked out—"

"It was just a few minutes. It's just a little bump."

"If you were unconscious, you've got a concussion. You're going to the emergency room. Come on, I'll drive."

One of the women said, "Edward's right, Phil. You look like death warmed over."

"Damn right I'm right," Edward said. "If you don't listen to me, and if you keel over, I'll have Leroy give you mouth-to-mouth."

Leroy was a 280-pound pressman with a bushy black beard that once had got caught in the ink rollers. He was also president of the East Fork Coon Hunters Club.

"You win. I'll go," I said.

Edward yelled, "Mary, how's that zoning story coming? Let Jack see it when it's done."

"I will, Ed," Mary yelled back. "Why don't you take Phil to the hospital."

"Yeah, have his head checked," the sports desk said.

On the way to the emergency room in the fog, I gave Ed a recap of my trip down the steps. "You're lucky you're still alive," he said. "Maybe you shouldn't go out there anymore—at least not by yourself."

"I want to get to the bottom of this," I replied. "I want to know why those people were killed."

"That's fine, as long as you don't get yourself killed too."

CHAPTER 20
Face to Face with the Devil

W<small>HEN</small> I woke up the next day, I felt like an old man with arthritis. I lay in bed in the late-morning heat and waited for my muscles to feel like moving again. I eased myself off the bed and went to the bathroom.

I was afraid to look in the mirror, and when I did I saw a purplish cheek laced with long, thin, scabby lines with whiskers poking through them. I decided to grow a beard until the wound healed. It might make me look more like a professor for my journalism class, which I just remembered I had to teach tonight. One good thing, the lump on my head felt smaller.

I soaked in the tub, made some coffee, and turned on the news. The talking heads were screaming at one another again, and every other story had some kind of celebrity tie-in. I couldn't take it. I zapped the TV and spent the next hour eating breakfast and preparing my class.

At 12:45 I finally got dressed and went to the *Gleaner*. Normally I had off Wednesday, but I went in anyway. I ran a gauntlet of gasps and questions in the front office. I held a brief news meeting to get myself up to the minute. Then I got on the computer.

While I was deleting the nearly 200 emails that had accumulated since yesterday, Detective Lieutenant Bakery knocked on the door frame. When I looked up, he said, "What'd you do to your face?"

"It's what someone else did," I replied. "Come in, Lieutenant. Have a seat."

He took two long strides into my office and sat on the chair alongside my desk. Hunched slightly forward, he was almost in my face. "You look like you got clawed by a cat," he said.

"Thanks." I leaned back and rolled a few inches away from the desk. "It happened at the Garth house last night. I have a confession to make—I sort of broke in."

"You 'sort of' broke in. . . . What does that mean?"

I told him how I discovered someone was in the house, how I banged on the door but no one answered, and how the piece of plywood on the door "practically fell off when I touched it" (a slight exaggeration). I kind of sort of in a way made it sound as though someone had broken in just moments before I did, as if that gave me the right to do the same thing. I told him how I searched the rooms but couldn't find anyone—until I started down the cellar steps.

"Somebody was under the steps," I said. "He grabbed my ankle and yanked it backwards between two of the steps. I went flying head first. I scraped my face on the wall and hit my head. I was out for a while."

With a snarky smile, the detective said, "Do you have a death wish, Larrison?"

"If I do, it's unconscious."

"People get shot breaking into other people's houses."

"I know. That's why I made a racket. I even shouted who I was."

"People don't have to open their door because you shout at them."

"True. But I don't believe anyone lives there right now."

"It could have been the owner, that Boofey guy."

"Then why didn't he answer the door?"

"Maybe he didn't want to. Or maybe he was on the can. If you thought something was wrong, you should have called the police."

"My phone doesn't work in the hollow. I think I told you that."

He made a tinny, sarcastic laugh. "Okay, so you went in thinking it might be the killer. What were you going to do if it was, make a citizen's arrest?"

"Actually, I thought it might be Paula Henry."

"Oh you did, did you?" He stuck his tongue in his cheek, sat back, and patted the arms of his chair with his palms. "That's who I came to talk to you about," he said. "Except her real name is Paula Boofey."

I began to feel nervous. I wondered what was coming next. "Boofey?" I said. "Are you sure?"

"Do you think I'd tell you if I wasn't? We located the clinic where she had her leg set. As soon as I heard the name Paula, I knew who it was. How could two Paulas have broken their right leg around the same time? Not only that, but the description they gave us of her matched your description of Paula Henry."

"Your hunch was right then—she *was* using a fake name. Way to go, Lieutenant."

"Don't congratulate me yet. I still haven't found her."

"Do you know where she lives?"

He nodded. "Indianapolis. She lives with her mother, Edna Boofey. I went to their house, but no one was there. The Indianapolis P.D. is checking it periodically in case one of them shows up, but it looks like they're gone."

My blood pressure went down a point or two. If he hadn't found Edna Mae and Paula yet, he didn't know that I had already found them and kept it to myself.

I continued playing ignorant: "Do you know if Walter Boofey is related to them?"

"Yeah. He's Edna's brother-in-law."

"Did you talk to him?" I said.

"I've tried, but his wife, Caroline, says he's always on the road in his truck. She gave me his cell-phone number, but whenever I call, the phone's not on."

"I see. Well, I appreciate your telling me all this, Lieutenant. It'll keep the story alive in the paper."

"That's what I want," Bakery said. "Put in that anyone who has information related to the case should contact the Indiana State Police or their local police department."

"I will do that. Oh, one other thing. Last week you said you had a couple of leads that you were working on."

"They didn't pan out."

"Do you have a theory on why the Garths were killed?"

He glanced at his watch. "We're treating it as a drug-related homicide," he said quickly. "We found some marijuana hidden in the house—about twenty grams. We brought in a dog, and he sniffed it out under a board in a closet."

"I wish you had let me know," I said. "The dog would have made a good picture."

"Sorry about that. I suspect the pot was for their own use. We've been over the hills and fields with a helicopter, and we didn't see any marijuana growing, but I still think the murders have something to do with drugs. I expected to find a meth lab." He looked at his watch again and stood up. "I'm due in court in Jennings County in twenty minutes. I'd better get going."

I followed him out of my office and watched him rush out to his car. A Campbellsville police cruiser stopped in the street, and Bakery exchanged a few words with the cop at the wheel. Then he took off with his lights flashing.

I was somewhat surprised that Bakery hadn't said anything about the recovery of my car. Maybe he didn't even know it had been stolen. That was fine with me.

I went to the lounge for a cup of coffee. I thought over what Bakery had said about Paula and Edna Mae—how both of them had dropped off the radar screen. Were the two of them in the Garth house? (Maybe.) Was there a secret room? (Maybe.) Was there a second dug-out cellar? (Maybe.) Did one of them trip me down the steps last night? (No.)

I could not believe that either one of them had tripped me. And they certainly wouldn't have worked me over after the trip. But what if someone else had joined them— Walter Boofey, for instance? . . . What the heck, Norval might be there too, and Caroline could be on her way. Maybe the Boofeys were having a family reunion.

I felt like running out to the Garth house right away, but the doctor at the emergency room had said I sustained a grade-three concussion and warned me not to get any more knocks on the head for a while.

Back at my desk, I sat down to write a story with the information Bakery had given me. I had mixed feelings about this one. I was glad I no longer had to conceal the fact that Paula's real name was Boofey, but at the same time I regretted that Chuck Martin would now find out who she was. If what she had told me about him was true, her life was in danger.

I had Edna Mae's phone number, so I tried calling to tell her and Paula that Bakery's report would be in tomorrow's paper. No one answered. I wrote the article, and then I tried calling again. Still no answer. Damn. I had to move on.

I took out my notes on the Good Shepherd Home.

On Monday, when I had tried to locate the six former residents whose names I knew, I was unable to get any information on Candy Apple and Judith Ann Shult. I picked up the phone again.

The phone book listed only two parties named Apple in Meridian County, and neither of them had answered my earlier calls. Today I had better luck.

The first was David Apple, who said he didn't know anyone named Candy.

The second was P. J. Apple, who said he was her brother. "Her name's Gilstrap now," he added. "Her name's in the phone book. Look for Josh."

Josh Gilstrap's address was in the Parkside Trailer Court next to the Campbellsville Airport and Industrial Park. Instead of phoning and possibly getting blown off, I took a chance on finding Candy there and drove to the west end of town.

Lot 81 was occupied by a maroon mobile home with a broad white stripe in the middle. There were no trees in the trailer court, and the brutal mid-day sun beat down as if punishing the inhabitants. The treeless landscape and the low, widely separated factories in the distance resembled a futuristic setting in an old science-fiction movie.

I parked in the street and crossed a mostly bare lawn to the trailer. I knocked on the lower half of the door, waited, and knocked again, this time hard enough to shake the flimsy door. A curtain parted in a window on the left, and a sliver of a face peeked at me.

"Mrs. Gilstrap?" I said.

The window slid up a few inches, and an unexpectedly sweet, musical voice said, "Yes? What is it?"

I introduced myself and asked if she had a few minutes to talk to me.

"I'm busy right now," she said warily. "What do you want?"

Perhaps it was the sight of my face that made her wary. Or maybe it was a function of where she lived. Parkside Trailer Court was not the safest place. Fights and drugs kept the police busy, and a few weeks ago a woman had been raped in her car. I held up my press I.D. "I'm writing an article about the old Good Shepherd Home," I said. "I understand you lived there for a while when you were little. Your name used to be Candy Apple, didn't it?"

"I prefer Candace now."

"Sure. I'd like to ask you a few questions about your memories of the home."

She thought it over. "I guess I can help you with that," she said. "Just a minute."

The window closed, and I heard her running around inside. I started perspiring under the blazing sun. Just as I was beginning to think she wasn't going to let me in, the door squealed open.

She was around twenty, short and stocky, deeply tanned. She had an oval face framed by straight brown hair that fell below her waist. The hair and the long, plain skirt she was wearing marked her as a Pentecostal.

"I'm sorry I took so long," she said. "I was washing up. I had been out in the garden."

I climbed two metal steps into the living room. It was cool inside, thanks to a rattly air conditioner in the wall. Although the exterior of the trailer had a faded, run-down look, the interior was neat and cozy. To the right, an overstuffed sectional sofa wrapped around one corner of the room, which also featured a wooden rocking chair, a gray shag carpet that was spotlessly clean, a small high-definition TV, and a small stereo system. An open Bible lay on a steamer trunk that served as a coffee table. Two trophies for cross-country running were displayed on a shelf, and several graduation and wedding photos hung on the walls.

"Have a seat," she said.

I sat at the kitchen table so I could take notes more easily. She stood with her back against the counter and her arms folded. After some small talk about the heat wave we were suffering through, I asked some safe background questions about when she had stayed at the foster home and how old she had been when she was there. Then I got down to business:

"What was it like there, Candace? Did you like living there? It must have been hard being away from home."

She thought long and hard. I wondered what horrors might be running through her head.

"It's hard for me to answer that question," she said at last. "I know it's a simple question—basic—but it was a difficult time of my life." She stopped and thought some more. She seemed more intelligent, more reflective than I had expected. "Would you like something to drink?" she said. "I have iced tea in the fridge."

"Thanks. That sounds great."

As she poured the tea, she said, "I hate to say anything unkind about other people, so maybe I shouldn't answer your question."

"I understand," I said. "If you want to tell me something off the record, I would go along with that."

"You wouldn't put it in the paper?"

"That's right—as long as we're talking about a private person."

Her doubtful expression suggested she did not like the qualification, but she said, "The therapist I go to tells me it's good for me to talk about what happened. She's a psychiatrist. I could never afford to pay her if I had to. I know she's right—I *should* talk about it. I just don't want to do something that my Lord and Savior, Jesus Christ, would not approve of."

Hypocrite that I was, I nodded.

Candace went on: "I was put in the home after my mother died. She caught meningitis somehow. They said it was a miracle I didn't get it too. She was a single mom, and there was no one else who could take care of me and my older brother. Our grandparents couldn't afford to raise us." She gulped half her glass of iced tea. "Believe it or not, I liked it there, at least at first I did. It was so different from my life at home. Mom loved us, but she had so many problems. We were dirt poor. She drank too much. Men moved in and moved out. She was all messed up. In the foster home we had to be nice to one another. We knelt down and prayed together. Most of the kids hated the discipline, but it didn't bother me. It was like a different world. I started to read. That's where I developed a love of reading. I have to say that getting sent to the Good Shepherd Home changed my life—in most ways for the better."

"That's good to hear," I said. "It's not what some others have told me."

She nodded slowly. "I expect it isn't." She finished drinking her tea. "I try to focus on the good things."

"Do you remember a girl named Paula?"

She shook her head.

"She was only there for a few months," I said. "It was about twelve years ago, when she was fifteen. She told me some bad things happened to some of the kids while she was there."

"Twelve years ago I was only seven," Candace said. "A lot of kids came and went. I don't remember all of them. I didn't get to know them all."

"But Paula remembers you. In fact, she's the one who told me your name."

Candace stared at the floor.

I went on: "She said sometimes a policeman would come and take one of the kids away for a day or two. She told me about a little boy who said he was taken to a big house where another man played games with him and they ate pizza and then the man took him to bed. Paula said after he came back to the Good Shepherd Home, he had terrible nightmares. He would cry all night."

She raised her eyes and gazed at me. "That's true, Mr. Larrison—I mean about the nightmares. I remember the screams."

"Did anything like that ever happen to you, Candace?"

Without hesitating, she said, "One day I was raped. For years I wouldn't talk about it. I tried to pretend it never happened, as if it was all a bad dream. But Dr. Metz helped me learn how to deal with it. When I finally stopped repressing, I felt like a new person. I felt reborn."

She paused, and I watched her mind drift into the past.

"I came face to face with the devil once," she continued. "Some of the kids used to play hide-and-seek in the 'castle' out in the barn. The hay loft was full of heavy bales of straw. They were like giant building blocks, and we made a big castle out of them, with rooms and tunnels. It

192

was fun. I hated when we had to stop playing and go back to the house."

She licked her lips, and her eyes narrowed. "Then one day I was hiding in a little secret room in the castle, and everything got real quiet. The other kids were hiding too. Nobody was moving. It stayed quiet for so long I began to think the others must have snuck out and left me by myself. I began to get scared, then all of a sudden, right in front of my face, a snake stuck its head out of the straw. It was a black snake, and its head came out about six inches and just hung there, real stiff, looking at me. . . . It was the devil. I was so scared I couldn't move. I couldn't even scream. I just knelt there frozen. It flicked its tongue at me. I thought there must be other snakes all around. I seemed to feel one crawling on my legs. . . . Then I heard somebody screaming. The snake was coming out of the straw. The screaming didn't stop, and then somebody was hitting it with a pipe or something and I realized it was me screaming, and I still couldn't stop." She paused as if intentionally heightening the drama. "I did not know it then—I guess I was too young—but later I realized that that was the day I rejected Satan for the first time." She paused again and with a little snort of amazement said, "You know, it's funny. I'm not afraid of snakes anymore. I've watched men handle them in church, and I feel like I could do that too, if they'd let me. My lord and savior Jesus Christ would protect me, just like he protected me in the castle."

This was all very interesting, but it wasn't what I wanted to know. "Candace," I said as gently as I could, "who was the person who raped you?"

"I don't know his name," she said.

"Think back. Could it have been a policeman named Chuck Martin?"

"He wasn't a policeman." She used her thumbs to sweep her hair back from her eyes. She eased away from the counter and released her hair. "The man who raped me was a man who worked on the farm sometimes. He helped Mr. DeLong. He was quiet. He never even talked to me before that day. But one day I was picking daisies in the field, and he did it."

I felt like saying where was your lord and savior then? Instead I said, "Did you tell anyone about it, Candace?"

"No. I should have, but I was too scared. Besides, I thought it was my own fault. We weren't supposed to go anywhere by ourselves."

I said, "The more I hear about the Good Shepherd Home, the more it sounds like a hell hole."

"Satan can appear anywhere, Mr. Larrison. Even inside a church. Think about all those Catholic priests who abuse altar boys. I don't blame the Good Shepherd Home for what happened to me. It wasn't a hell hole, as you put it. Jesus Christ is the Good Shepherd. He said, 'Suffer the little children to come unto me.' I found Jesus there. I saw Satan there too. It wasn't a perfect place, but there is no perfect place in this world, is there?"

"Whatever happens is God's will, right?"

"Absolutely."

"Were the children subjected to any other kinds of abuse?" I said. "Did Mr. and Mrs. DeLong ever paddle the kids?"

"If we did something wrong, I think we deserved to get paddled. Spare the rod, spoil the child."

She sounded self-satisfied, even smug. I felt as if my interview had been hijacked by a religious fanatic. But I didn't want to argue with her. I had quit arguing about religion when I was a freshman in college. It seemed like a futile debate that no one ever won.

On the verge of another dark night of the soul, I went back to the office and made some more phone calls. I spoke to two people named Shult, but neither of them knew a Judith Ann. Then I called Paula and Edna Mae a third time, but still no one answered.

Later that night, driving home from Columbus under a canopy of stars, I fancied the possibility of finding Paula at the Brickton exit again. A full week had now passed since our first encounter, but it seemed more like a month. Maybe I should run out to the Garth house once more tonight. . . .

Be patient, I told myself. Don't try to force it. The truth will out, God willing.

Yeah, sure. Keep telling yourself that.

CHAPTER 21
Memory Care

THE ONLY persons I still wanted to talk to about the Garth murders were Esther and Judy Dubbs. Since learning from Judy that her mother-in-law, Esther, had Alzheimer's, I'd had little hope of learning anything from her, but since my descent into the cellar of the house where Esther once had lived, my hope had revived. Maybe her brain still worked well enough for her to tell me if the house had another small cellar and, if so, how to find it. I felt as if I were in a Hardy Boys mystery, searching for a secret room.

The Twin Lakes Health Center, where I was to meet the two women after lunch today, was located on U.S. 50 about a half mile west of Campbellsville. The long wings of the one-story brick building were surrounded by acres of manicured lawn with winding paths and flower gardens. The only shortcoming was that the so-called lakes were more like ponds and were nearly dry.

The assisted-living/memory-care section of the health center had its own entrance. Half a dozen wooden rocking chairs stood under a high portico. A pleasant-looking, heavyset woman was rocking on one of the chairs and stood up as I approached.

"Mr. Larrison," she said with a bright smile. "It's nice to see you again." She read the lack of recognition in my eyes. "We met at a meeting of the history society you covered last year." She did not mention the scrape on my cheek. Either she was just being polite or it didn't look quite so bad today.

"Oh, that was the dedication of the new museum," I said. We shook hands. "I'm sorry I didn't recognize you."

"Don't worry about it," she replied. "It's easy for me to remember you—you were the only reporter there. But you can't be expected to remember all the people you meet in your line of work."

"Actually I try to," I said. "I just don't do a very good job of it."

She laughed. "Well from now on maybe you'll remember me."

I held the door for her, and we went inside. A young receptionist smiled at us from her desk and said, "How are you today, Mrs. Dubbs?"

"Still kickin'," Judy said. "Hi, Allison. That's a pretty dress you have on. This is Phil Larrison from the *Gleaner*. We're going to visit with Esther for a while."

"Oh, that'll be real nice," said Allison, who looked like a high-school cheerleader.

The spacious, high-ceilinged lobby, with its Corinthian pillars, oversized sofas, flowers, and fireplace, made me feel as if I were in a ritzy hotel instead of a nursing home. Beyond the lobby was a bright sunny dining room where thirty or forty people were eating lunch and Tammy Wynette was singing "Stand by Your Man."

"Have you ever been here before, Phil?" Judy asked.

"No," I said, "but maybe I'll move in. It's very nice."

"If you can afford it. I couldn't. This is the assisted-living section. The other end of the building is intermediate- and skilled-care. Esther is in memory care. That's this way."

I followed her around the receptionist to a pair of large windowless doors, where she punched four numbers into a keypad on the wall. The doors swung open to reveal a wide hallway with rooms on both sides. Halfway down the hall was a common area, which included a pair of desks where a woman in a yellow polo shirt was working, a small dining room where a dozen people, mostly women, were having lunch around a large table, and a lounge where three old men were watching TV, or rather one was watching and two were asleep.

The woman at the desk—her tag said she was a licensed practical nurse—looked up as we approached. Judy said, "Hi, Sharon. How's Esther doing today?"

"Pretty well," the LPN replied. "She wanted to go back to her room."

"Did she eat much today?"

Sharon called over her shoulder to a red-shirted aide: "Hey, Laura, how did Esther do with her lunch?"

"About sixty percent," Laura called back.

"That's par for the course," Sharon said.

On our way to Esther's room, Judy said, "By the way, Phil, Esther doesn't know about the murders. I haven't told her. I was afraid it would upset her. She's so confused, she'd probably get some wacky idea like her husband and his girlfriend were murdered, even though Frank never had another woman." She laughed affectionately. "Poor thing, she's all mixed up. Everything is jumbled together in her mind like a big salad—memories, dreams, TV, real life, her own imagination. I don't think she knows which is which anymore."

"That's too bad," I said. "How long has she been like this?"

"It's a progressive disease, Alzheimer's. I first noticed some problems a few years ago, but looking back, I realize she did some things before then that were probably caused by the Alzheimer's—here we are."

The door to Esther's room stood wide open, as did all the doors in the hall. Judy rapped her knuckles on the door and at the same time said, "Esther, company's here."

Esther was sitting on the end of her bed, about two feet from the TV, with her false teeth halfway out of her mouth.

"Esther, your teeth are sticking out!" Judy exclaimed. "Put them back in your mouth. You look like a monkey."

An old rerun of *Matlock* was on, and Esther burbled something to the TV.

"Here, let me help you," Judy said, reaching for the teeth, which were the uppers. Esther went on talking as Judy gently pulled the plate out of her mouth.

"Those aren't my teeth," Esther said in an unexpectedly firm voice.

"Whose teeth are they?" Judy said.

"How should I know?"

Judy looked at me and rolled her eyes. She went to the bathroom and laid the teeth on the sink. Then she tried to start over. "Esther, you have a special visitor today," she said in a singsong voice. "Look who's here. It's Phil Larrison, from the newspaper, the *Gleaner*. He came to talk to you." She sounded as if she were talking to a little child.

Esther wasn't interested. She went on watching her show and laughed when Matlock, who looked old enough to be in the nursing home with her, got in an argument with a judge.

Judy said, "Did you have a good lunch today, Esther? What did you eat for lunch?" When Esther still did not answer, Judy said, "Let's turn this off, shall we, Esther?" She saw the remote lying on the floor and with some effort picked it up. Then with a deep breath she zapped the TV. "There, that's better, isn't it, Esther? Now we can hear ourselves think."

The white-haired woman in her nineties went on staring at the blank screen. What am I doing here? I asked myself.

Esther Dubbs was a small woman with a sagging face that was creased with wrinkles, though not nearly so many as her wattled neck. I suspected the face had benefitted from plastic surgery sometime during the past quarter century. Her skin had a smattering of brown spots, and purplish veins bulged on the back of her hands. She wore a silky yellow top, gray pants, a white cardigan sweater, and white tennis shoes. A soft, fluffy hairdo proclaimed that she had been to the beauty shop that morning.

Judy said, "Let's sit over here on the love seat so we can talk." She took Esther's hands and helped her onto her feet, then guided her across the room.

"What does he want?" Esther said, looking at me for the first time.

"Phil would like to talk to you about the house you used to live in. You remember the house on the farm, don't you?"

"I don't own it anymore. I got rid of it."

"That's right, you did." Judy shot a wide-eyed glance at me, marveling as if this was our lucky day.

"Does he want to buy it?" Esther said.

"I don't think so," Judy replied. "But why don't you ask him yourself. You're looking straight at him."

"Hello, Esther," I said. "It's nice to meet you."

She seemed a bit mystified. Her eyes had not left my face since she first looked at me. Perhaps the scabby scrape fascinated her.

"I'm Phil," I reminded her. "I'm writing an article for the paper about your old house in Blind Horse Hollow. I'd like to ask you a few questions about it, if you don't mind."

"The horse was named Lug. He belonged to my grandfather."

"Really?" I said. "With a name like that, I bet he was a real workhorse."

She nodded. "He pulled a plow."

"How did he go blind?" I asked her.

"He was born blind."

That's a downer, I thought. You're born blind and you get to pull a plow the rest of your life. "Did you ever ride him, Esther?" I said.

She seemed to try to remember but did not answer.

I came back with, "What color was the horse?"

"Brown."

Judy said, "That's very interesting, Esther. You never told me about Lug before."

"You never asked me about him."

One of the aides rapped on the open door and came into the room. "Excuse me," she said to Judy, "I just wanted to see if she was ready for me to lay her down."

"Not yet," Judy said. "Give us another ten or fifteen minutes, okay?"

"There's no hurry," the girl said. "Whenever you're ready." She bent over Esther and said, "Your hair sure looks pretty today, Hon. I'll come back in a little while, and we'll go to the toitie and take a nap, okay?"

"Yeah, yeah," Esther said.

Judy took advantage of the occasion to tell the girl about Esther's teeth. The girl went to the bathroom and got the plate. "I wish we could put their names on these things," she told Judy. "Sweetie," she said to Esther, "would you open your mouth for me. Let's see if these fit."

"Those aren't my teeth," Esther said. She would not open her mouth again.

I sat there tapping my fingertips together while this was going on, and after the redshirt left, I said, "Esther, would you like to know how I got all these scratches on my face?"

No response. Just the stare.

"I fell down the cellar steps in your old house, and my face scraped the wall."

Judy said, "What did you want down there?"

I wished she would butt out so I could talk to Esther. "I just wanted to see what it's like," I said. "For my article."

Esther said, "We lived in the cellar."

"You did?" I said. "Why?"

"It was nice and cool in the summertime."

"Oh, Esther, you're making that up," Judy said. "You never *lived* down there."

Esther pursed her lips.

"I bet it *was* nice and cool," I said to her. "The floor and walls are bare earth. I bet it was a good place to play when it was hot or rainy outside. I bet you dug holes in the ground, didn't you?" I caught myself treating her like a child and told myself to knock it off.

"We didn't dig any holes," she said as if I had said something stupid. "The floor was made of wood."

"Was it? I didn't realize that."

She nodded emphatically.

Judy said, "They must have used it as a storm cellar." She put a hand on Esther's arm and said, "You went down there when the weather was bad, didn't you, Esther, like during tornado season?"

Esther did not answer.

I leaned forward and said, "The cellar where I fell is like a big room, Esther, but it's much smaller than upstairs. Is there another room like that one under the house?"

Her lips remained pinched together. She stared at the TV.

"Is there another set of cellar steps somewhere?" I said.

Judy laughed and said, "No. She's making it up. You're just funning with us, aren't you, Esther? You have a terrific imagination. You should have been a writer."

Esther ignored her and went on looking miffed.

Judy got up and mumbled to me, "She's in la-la land." She laughed softly and went to the bathroom.

As soon as the door shut, Esther's head swung toward me. She crooked her finger and motioned me closer. I scooted my chair toward her until our knees nearly touched.

"Don't trust her," she whispered.

"Why not?" I said.

"She's no good. She took my husband away from me."

"She did?" I said, acting indignant.

Esther's serious nod reminded me of a little girl. "She takes everything," she whispered. "I have no furniture. She took it. I don't have any money. I can't go shopping.

I can't buy anything. I don't have any jewelry to wear. She took it all. I don't have anything."

I heard Judy tinkling in the bathroom.

"You probably shouldn't keep your jewelry here, Esther," I said. "It might get stolen."

"She *already* stole it."

Water ran in the bathroom sink. "Do you want me to report her to the police?" I said to humor her.

She nodded solemnly.

I lifted my chair backward as the door opened and Judy came out of the bathroom. "We've been having a nice talk," I told her. "Esther says she would like to have her jewelry back so she can wear it once in a while."

"Oh, Esther," Judy said, "we've talked about that a hundred times. You know what would happen. It would get lost, or somebody would take it." To me she said, "I swear, some of the people who work here don't own a pot to pee in."

"Maybe she could have a couple of pieces," I said, "or maybe you could bring her some of her jewelry to wear while you're visiting, and then take it back with you when you leave."

"No!" Esther shouted. "I want my jewelry. It's mine, not hers."

"Now don't get excited," Judy said. "I'll see what I can do." She gave me a cross look and muttered, "Thanks a lot."

Breathing hard, Esther went on fighting: "Where's my furniture? All I have is this junk. I don't even have my own bed."

The girl in the red shirt came scurrying into the room. "What's all the excitement about? You know what,

Esther—I think it's time for a nap, don't you? Shall we go to the bathroom first?"

"Shut up. Get the hell out of here. Leave me alone."

"I have to do my job, Sweetie. You don't want me to get fired, do you?"

"We're going now, Esther," Judy said. "You have a good rest. I'll be back to see you next week. I'll bring your favorite necklace for you to wear, okay?"

"I want my jewelry."

"Goodbye, Esther," I said. "It was nice meeting you."

Sharon, the LPN, entered the room as we were leaving. She and the nurse's aide teamed up to calm Esther down.

Way to go, Larrison, I said to myself. You done good.

The way Esther had clammed up when Judy began correcting her made me wish I had come by myself.

I decided to do that.

CHAPTER 22
A Rude Awakening

A T FIRST I thought somebody was rubbing my back. Then the house started shaking. The walls began coming apart. We were having an earthquake. . . . No, I'm still asleep. I must be dreaming. . . .

"Come on, Phil, look alive."

My eyes popped open. The lights were on. I rolled away from the hand on my back and saw Chuck Martin looming over my bed. I almost swallowed my tongue.

"Hello, Phil," he said.

What the hell? Was I still dreaming? My head felt as tight as a rock. I kept a baseball bat under the bed, but it was on the side where he was standing. I rolled to the other side fast and got up. I was in my shorts. My shirt and pants hung on the doorknob. The clock said 1:44. "What the hell is this?" I said. "What's going on?"

"I gotta talk to you about somethin'," Martin said.

I yelled across the bed: "Are you drunk? What are you doing here? Get out. Go home and sleep it off."

"As soon as we have a little powwow here." His words were slurred.

"You must be crazy. How'd you get in here?"

"The door was open."

"Like hell it was."

"You shouldn't leave your door unlocked. It ain't safe." He laughed at his own joke. "Take it easy, Phil. I just want a few minutes of your time. I got somethin' to say to you. It's for your own good."

"Is that a threat, Chuck?"

"No, a course not, Phil. You an' me—" He hiccupped so hard his head bucked backward. "You an' me are old pals."

"You're soused. Get outta my bedroom."

My throat felt dry, scratchy, raw. My eyes were tight. Beneath the gritty surface of things, I wondered what he planned to do. If he had wanted to cut my throat, he could have done it already. I needed better locks on the doors.

"What'd you do to your face?" he said.

I wondered if he already knew. Maybe he was the one who had tripped me. "I guess you didn't understand me, Chuck," I said. "What I meant was, get your ass out of my apartment. Now."

He gave me a stupid grin.

The former sheriff was wearing a long-sleeved western shirt, chocolate brown with small white fringe. The ceiling light deepened the crevices in his ruggedly handsome face. His thick arms bulged in his shirt, and his midsection was as flat as mine, though I was less than half his age. His thick gray hair looked like sea waves in blue moonlight.

I went to the door for my clothes. He stiffened as if I was about to attack. Then he relaxed as he watched me pull on my pants. His large head seemed only half real, like a statue coming to life. I brushed past him into the living room, where the lights were also on, thanks to the uninvited guest. I put on my shirt and left it unbuttoned as I opened the front door. "Good night, Chuck," I said.

"If you have something you want to talk to me about, call me in the morning."

A cocky grin stayed on his face as he staggered across the room. I thought he was going to leave, but instead he put a hand on my shoulder and said, "Phil, you are not very sociable." With his free hand he grabbed the edge of the door and slammed it shut.

I yanked his hand off my shoulder and shoved him out of my face. He banged into the wall and held up his hands. "Whoa, I didn't come here to get in a fight with you." He hiccupped loudly. "I don't want to hurt you, Phil." Again the grin. Smug. Superior.

I reached for the door, but he did a quickstep and blocked it with his body. "You're rude, Phil. You're not our kind of folks."

"I'm crushed."

"I could crush you if I wanted to, but that's not what I came for." He laughed again, delighted with himself. "You got any coffee, Phil? I could use a cup of coffee." He went on chuckling as he crossed the room to the sofa and sat down. Then he leaned forward with his hands folded between his legs. "You know, Phil," he said, "I'm a guy that believes when somethin' is botherin' you, you shouldn't let it fester. You oughta bring it to a head and lance it. Know what I mean? You ought to get it off your chest."

"Very admirable." I inspected the door for damage, but I didn't find any. Maybe he had come in through the kitchen.

"That's right," he said. "Chuck Martin's a straight shooter. He tells you exactly what he thinks. You always know where you stand with old Chuck."

"He'll even break into your house to tell you."

His eyes began to close, and he tilted forward a few inches before he caught himself and sat up. "I've been hearin' some bad things about you, Phil." Staring down, he pressed his thumbs together above his interwoven fingers. "Things that could get you in trouble." He looked up at me. "I'm gonna give you some friendly advice."

"I don't need your advice. Go home. Or go back to the bar you came from. I'm not going to tell you again."

"Oh. What are you gonna do if I don't go, call your friend, *Sheriff* Eggemann?" The word *Sheriff* was laced with contempt. "Go ahead, call him. I'd like to put my fist down his goddamn throat."

"Why don't you drive over to the jail and check yourself into the drunk tank," I said. "That's where you belong."

"I know you and him are like that." He held up two fingers squeezed together. "You lick each other's ass. Your fucken newspaper is what got him elected." His mood had swung from inebriated glee to drunken rage.

"Gee, I wonder why the paper endorsed Carl Eggemann instead of Chuck Martin," I said.

"Because your boss is a goddamn communist, that's why. One a these days he's gonna get himself tarred and feathered."

"The Klan will ride again, huh?"

"We could use the Klan these days. That bastard Obama—"

"Oh shut up. I've had enough of your crap."

I took two quick steps and grabbed his right arm. As I pulled him off the sofa, he rose on his own. I was expecting a punch or a kick or a bite, and he threw a wild left at my jaw. I ducked away from it, and his fist grazed my chin. I moved in and drove my fist into his midsection. For a moment he looked startled, confused. He began coughing or choking, and then the contents of his stomach spewed out and splattered the coffee table.

I watched the stinking mess drip onto the floor. I felt like rubbing his face in it.

"You prick," he said, spitting the remnants of puke off his lips. "You sucker-punched me."

I was pumped. My fist wanted to pop him again. "You threw the first punch, UpChuck," I said, violating my own rule about not making puns out of people's names. Now I had his vomit to clean up. It was my own stupid fault. I shouldn't have punched the drunk in the stomach.

I pulled him toward the door. I expected another punch to come at me, but none came. His face was white. He looked sleepy and sick. He seemed ready to barf again.

"Outside," I said. "You did enough damage in here."

"You're gonna regret this, you little prick."

"I don't think so." I shoved him out, and he nearly fell off the porch.

"You better watch your back. People are talkin'. They don't like what you're goin' around sayin' about the Good Shepherd Home."

"Shut up. You'll wake up the neighbors."

"I know who you been talkin' to—Paula Boofey. That's what her real name is. It ain't Paula Henry."

"Did you figure that out for yourself, or did you read it in the *Gleaner* yesterday?"

He seemed confused. His eyes almost closed, and he tipped forward. I grabbed his arm and steered him toward the steps.

"You can't believe a damn word she says," he mumbled. "She's a liar. She's nothin' but a lyin' slut."

"And you're a drunken pig. Where's your car?"

He yanked his arm away and teetered down the two steps. He got himself into his car and sat behind the wheel without starting the engine. For several minutes I watched from the porch. It occurred to me that I had never mentioned his name to Grace DeLong. If she had complained to him about me, it showed there was a connection between them and it tended to support Paula's story about what they had done to her at the home.

When the car did not move, I figured he must have fallen asleep. I went inside to deal with the mess he had made.

A half hour later, while I was dipping a barf rag in the toilet, a rock the size of a softball came flying through the front window. The lumpy orange geode showered pieces of glass all over the living room. I ran out front and saw a car with its lights off speeding away under the trees.

CHAPTER 23
Bad Mood

MOTHS, LIGHTNING bugs, mosquitoes, spiders, katy-dids, and even a tree frog poured into the apartment. I spent the rest of the night—what was left of it—sopping up puke, spraying the carpet, taping the shower curtain over the window, whacking bugs, and cussing out Chuck Martin.

I finally got back to bed around 4:30, but I couldn't get a minute's sleep. I kept thinking my old pal Chuck would show up again, this time with a sledgehammer or sawed-off shotgun. Whatever remorse I felt for punching a sixty-year-old man in the gut was canceled out by what he had put me through.

With the dawn of another rotten day in a rotten life I got up again and made a pot of coffee. I tried to stretch the kinks out of my back, and I yawned so hard it hurt my jaw. I felt like going to Swifty for a dozen Krispy Kremes, but with my luck a team of burglars would come through the window and clean out the apartment.

Shit.

What else could I say?

Shit shit shit shit shit.

I turned on the TV. A woman was wailing out of control because a tornado had blown her house away last night.

I turned it off. I didn't want to hear about other people's problems. They might force me to downgrade my own.

I went to the bathroom to take a shower, momentarily forgetting that the shower curtain was covering the front window. I filled the tub instead. The bottom felt gritty. When was the last time I had scrubbed it? The Garths' bathtub looked cleaner than mine. Still, after soaking for twenty minutes, I felt slightly better—until I looked at myself in the mirror.

The beard I was growing wasn't much of a beard. I just looked like I needed a shave. My raked cheek still had a greenish-purple hue that the whiskers did not hide. My eyes seemed to have sunk deeper into my face. Out of habit, I wanted to shave, but I was afraid the razor would slice open the stringy scabs. I needed a haircut too.

To take my eyes off the face, I looked at the rest of me. I had lost more weight. My belly hardly bulged anymore. I wasn't eating as much as I used to. I must be under 175. Not bad for a guy who was almost six-one. If I kept it up, I'd soon be underweight. It wasn't the best body in the world, but it wasn't the worst either. Sexy pectorals, if I did say so myself. Knees not too knobby. Earnest face, but less intense than before . . . less sensitive . . . tougher. . . .

I shouldn't have looked at my face again. The awareness of change came with a sense of loss and regret.

I ate some cereal and had some more coffee. Then I brushed my teeth and left for work.

On the way I debated whether to file a complaint against Chuck Martin and have him arrested. No doubt he'd deny breaking in to my apartment and throwing the rock through the window. There was no sign of a break-in, so he could say I let him in for a talk, and then he got sick because he'd had one too many beers. I even began to feel bad for punching the old drunk in the gut, until I reminded myself of what he had done to Paula. That's what I wanted to send him to jail for, not for breaking in to my apartment. And it wouldn't do me any good if the stupid fight was reported in the paper. What the hell, let it go.

In the stack of mail on my desk was a 9x12 manila envelope addressed in elegant calligraphy. Inside was a handwritten note in the same ornate handwriting, along with a Xeroxed copy of a clipping from an old newspaper. The note said, "We used to live up there in beautiful Meridian County. Saw where Walter Boofey was mentioned a couple of times in The Gleaner. We still take the paper after many years away. Thought you might be interested in the enclosed." The name of Walter A. Boofey was circled in green in the newspaper story. The article had been published six years ago in the *Rockville Palladium-Advertiser*, a small weekly in southeastern Kentucky.

The eight-inch story reported that a special state-police task force had discovered a marijuana crop being cultivated in a field owned by Mr. and Mrs. Boofey. "Mr. Boofey said he did not know the marijuana had been planted on their farm," the article stated, then went on to explain that if police could show that a landowner used his property to grow marijuana, the land could be confiscated. Additional penalties included a minimum five-year prison term under federal law if one hundred or more plants were being grown and a maximum five-year term under state law for more than five plants.

I sat back, rocking slowly and staring at the green blur of leaves that surrounded the courthouse. The story was strikingly similar to the one that Chuck Martin had told me about the marijuana he had taken out of Blind Horse Hollow eleven years ago, when Esther Dubbs owned the land. Was it just a coincidence, or had Boofey planted both crops?

I got the phone number for the *Palladium-Advertiser* out of the Kentucky Press Association directory and called the paper. A woman whose voice sounded like Minnie Mouse buzzed me through to the editor and publisher. His name was Wendell Matthews, and he had a slow, affable drawl. He called to someone to bring him the bound volume from 2004. I gave him the date and page number from the top of my clipping.

"Oh yeah, here it is," Matthews said. "That Boofey fella. It says he lived near Harrodsburg. Let's see what else I can find. . . . Seems to me . . ."

I could hear pages turning.

"Yeahhhh," he said, stretching the word, "here's another item. This ran a few weeks later. He was lucky. He got to stay out of jail and keep his land. The grand jury refused to indict him. That's hard to believe." He laughed cynically. "It must've been our prosecutor's fault. A good prosecutor can get a grand jury to do whatever he wants."

"Maybe a member of the jury was bought off," I said.

"Maybe. It wouldn't be the first time."

"Do you know if Boofey had any other arrests?"

"Not offhand. There's nothing in this article about it. I think I'd remember anything that happened since then."

"Do you believe what he said about the marijuana? Do you think he planted the crop?"

He chuckled softly. "What do *you* think? Sure he knew. That's my opinion. What they do is, these growers, they plant little patches, fifty to a hundred plants, all over the place. Maybe the police'll find some of them. Maybe some won't grow. But plenty of them will. It's a major crop for us."

Relaxed, chatty, he lectured on the local marijuana industry for another five minutes. He said growers often plant the weed in the Daniel Boone National Forest. That way, if the plants are found, no one's land can be confiscated. He said crops were starting to come in right now— the harvest ran from late August into October. "There's lots of money out there," he said. "The big money comes from outside, not here. Local businessmen don't care where it comes from. Most folks in these parts can't afford the stuff, not when it sells for hundreds of dollars an ounce. They grow it to sell. Nowadays the drug of choice around here is meth. It's cheap and easy to make."

"Here too," I said.

"What got you interested in Boofey?" he asked me.

I figured I owed him more than a thirty-second sound bite, so I said, "A couple named Wayne and Cheryl Garth were found murdered in an old farmhouse they were renting from him. The police think drugs were involved, but they don't have much to go on. All they found in the house was a small amount of marijuana. Boofey bought the land in 2001. That was a couple years after the sheriff's department found a good-sized crop of marijuana growing in a cornfield near the house."

"Do they think Boofey's the murderer?"

"No, not from what they've told me."

"I doubt if he would've left the bodies in the house if he killed 'em. It would just draw attention to himself. But on the other hand, maybe he figured if he left the bodies, it would *deflect* suspicion because you wouldn't expect the killer to do that—not when he owned the house they were killed in."

"I went around in circles on that too," I said. "On balance, though, I think if Boofey killed them, it would have made more sense to get rid of the bodies. He could have dumped them anywhere." With a laugh I cracked, "Like maybe down your way—the Daniel Boone National Forest. They might never have been found if he had dumped them there."

"Right. People are always dumping bodies in the forest. Most of them come from Indiana." The Indiana-Kentucky war was still on. "Well, let me know what happens, Phil."

"You bet. I'll send you some articles too."

"Good. Nice talkin' to you."

I hung up and leaned back. I stretched and yawned so hard my arms nearly came out of their sockets and my ears made the ocean sound you hear when you listen to a seashell. I hadn't slept all night. How was I going to make it through the day? To stay awake I went to the lounge for a cup of coffee and drank it while I walked around.

Next, I called my landlord to report the smashed window. All I told him was someone had chucked a rock through it in the middle of the night. "Occupational hazard," I said. He was not thrilled. He said he'd try to take care of it as soon as he could. He owned Tri-County Building Supply, so I didn't think he'd have to try very hard. I asked if his insurance would pay for it, and he muttered something about his deductible.

"I guess you don't know who done it," he said.

"I was in bed." No doubt he'd raise my rent.

I called Lieutenant Bakery and got the usual message to leave a message. I told about the clipping I had received in the mail and said, "It's another indication that Boofey was involved with marijuana. He was charged with growing it, but not indicted." I said I would fax him the clipping.

Then I called Edna Mae's number again. Still no answer.

Where was she? And where was Paula?

Maybe they were back here in Meridian County. Maybe they were involved with Walter Boofey in the drug trade and had joined him in Kentucky. Or maybe Chuck Martin had caught up with them and they were dead. . . .

Except for the news from Kentucky, it was a rotten day.

CHAPTER 24
A Blue and Green Daydream

I WAITED until noon Saturday to call Judge Brandon. I wanted to give him plenty of time to sleep off his jet lag after returning from Asia. The phone rang one time and stopped. I thought I was going to get the answering machine, but then a heavy breath tickled my ear. It sounded like an obscene phone call. A moment later a woman in the background said, "Thank you, Scott. I'll take that." I guessed she was the Judge's wife.

There was a grunt or mutter, followed by the sound of shuffling feet. I pictured a hunchback slouching away under the bells.

"Hello," the woman said. "May I help you?"

I told her who I was and asked if I could talk to Judge Brandon.

"Oh, Mr. Larrison," she said. "I'm Beverly Brandon. Lillian told me about you. She said you might call. I'm not sure it's a good idea to talk to the Judge today though. He's acting like a big crab. We just got home from Vietnam last night."

"I know," I said. "I can call some other time."

A loud, deep voice broke in: "This is the big crab. You come out this afternoon, Phil. I always have time for the press—especially the *Gleaner*."

221

"There's your answer," Beverly said. "Good luck." She hung up.

Jack "Red" Brandon was well into his seventies, but his voice remained strong and authoritative. It conveyed the ready smile and firm handshake of a successful politician. We set a two o'clock time for our meeting.

While I was making myself a sandwich for lunch, Detective Lieutenant Bakery called back.

"I got your fax," he said. "Thanks."

"You're welcome. I thought you probably had that information already, but I sent it just in case you didn't."

"I did not have it." He sounded disgusted. "I did a Triple-I on Boofey, but no arrests showed up."

"What's a Triple-I?"

"A police-record check. If he wasn't indicted, he may have had his arrest expunged, or the agency that arrested him may have removed it automatically. I wish that didn't happen. I think the arrest should stay on the record whether the accused is convicted or not. I think the police should have access to that information."

I wasn't sure I agreed with him, but I didn't say so. Instead I asked if he'd had any luck finding Edna Mae and Paula Boofey.

"Not yet," he said. "Still looking. All I know is they're never at home and Edna Mae Boofey hasn't been at work for the past week."

"What does she do?" I asked, as if I didn't know.

"She works in a package store off of College. But she won't be working there anymore. The manager told me she's been terminated. He said she just stopped coming to work. Didn't quit. Didn't call in sick. Not a word."

"Maybe something happened to her."

"Yeah, and maybe not. These Boofey characters are a pretty slippery bunch." Before I said anything else, he blurted, "Gotta run. Thanks again for the fax."

As I ate my lunch, I wondered why Edna Mae had given up her job so abruptly. From what Bakery had said, it sounded as though she had quit right after driving my car back to Campbellsville last Saturday. Maybe she didn't even work that night. What the heck, maybe she didn't take the bus back to Indianapolis either. All that talk about trading shifts with another clerk may have been nothing but camouflage. Maybe Paula was the one who took a bus ride—from Indianapolis to Campbellsville. . . .

No, none of this made any sense. If they had wanted to return my car and come back to Campbellsville, all they had to do was drive it back together and abandon it somewhere. They did not need to call me up and get me to drive to Indianapolis . . . unless they were using me for something.

Using me for what?

What was the most important thing I had learned by going to Edna Mae's house?

Paula's story about Chuck Martin.

Maybe they were hoping I'd put it in the paper and Martin would get arrested and go to prison and they wouldn't have to worry about him anymore. Or maybe her story wasn't true. Or maybe Alzheimer's was contagious and I had caught it from Esther Dubbs. I felt as if I was going nuts. What was I doing playing detective? I wasn't solving anything. It was just a game I was playing. I was on some kind of ego trip.

I began to feel hot. I turned on the air conditioner and went around closing and locking the windows. I paused to admire the new double-glazed sash in the living room and the new deadbolt locks on the doors. Fast action by the landlord. Try to remember to thank him. Damn, 1:15 already. Better wash up. You're supposed to be at the Judge's house in forty-five minutes. That's Judge with an upper-case J. Get it in gear.

I pulled off my clothes and did a quick washup at the sink. I was in my car at 1:35. Instead of taking the scenic route through Blind Horse Hollow, I took the shorter western route, which bypassed the knobs. I didn't get a speeding ticket, so at 1:59, under a hazy blue sky, I was circling up the driveway toward the Judge's house.

Lillian opened the door and started in surprise. "You're growing a beard!" She was wearing a bright, colorful blouse that had to be a gift from Southeast Asia.

"Did I scare you?" I said.

She laughed. "No, I like it. You look like an artist."

"Not Toulouse-Lautrec, I hope."

She laughed again. "No. Not Van Gogh either,"

She didn't seem to notice my scratches. Maybe the beard was working. "How are you, Lillian?" I said.

"I'm good." She lowered her voice: "My grandfather's mad at me though."

"Why?"

"For increasing Scott's medication."

"Oh, he noticed, did he?"

"Yes, the minute he saw Scott at the airport." She rolled her eyes. "He lowered the dose a little bit this morning. Oh well, at least he's back to help deal with him. Come on in, he's waiting for you."

She showed me into his den, which was on the right, just inside the front door. "Gramps, Phil Larrison's here to see you."

"Hello, Phil," he said, rising from behind an intricately carved desk where he had been sorting a pile of mail. He gave me a firm handshake across the antique desk. Sitting on the floor beside the Judge's chair was Scott, who was looking at a comic book. "Say hello, Scott," the Judge said, but the Buddha did not budge.

"What happened to your cheek?" the Judge said.

So the beard was not working. Lillian lingered to hear my answer. I told them how I was tripped down the steps at the Garth house. The Judge was riveted. He looked deeply concerned, as if the sight of my face hurt his old, oyster-like eyes.

Law books filled the wall behind the desk, and a brown leather sofa and armchair stood in front of three glass-doored bookcases that contained nothing but an extensive collection of small lead soldiers. Plaques, diplomas, photos of the Judge with other politicians, including President Kennedy, covered two walls.

"Lillian tells me you gave her a hand with Scott one day," the Judge said. "I want you to know I appreciate your help, but Scott would not have hurt the boy. He's very careful. Aren't you, Scott?"

"I didn't know what was going on," I replied, "but it looked like Lillian and Jodie were having trouble handling the situation."

"I understand. I wish they had kept their heads instead of getting Scott excited."

He came around the desk and stood with his back to the double windows and his hands clasped behind him. He looked like an elder statesman. Despite a slight teeter in his step, he held himself straight and tall. He had a high, sloping forehead and a sloping chin that disappeared into his neck because of the way he held his head back. His hair was gone on top, but it flowed past his ears like silver flames painted on the sides of cars. He was thinner, much more gaunt than the only other time I had seen him, about six years ago, when he was still on the bench.

He asked me how my boss, "Wild Dog Wylie," was doing, and we chatted about my job for a few minutes. I asked how he had enjoyed his vacation, and he said he had absolutely loved Angkor Wat in Cambodia but he was getting too old to go gallivanting around the globe. "I told my wife no more trips to Asia," he said. "She loves it there, but I'm not up to those long flights anymore. Next time she wants to go to some backward little country where you have to squat to take a crap in a stinking hole in the floor, I'll go to Paris by myself and stay at the Ritz."

I had to endure a travelogue about Hong Kong and Nepal for another ten minutes. Then he went back around his desk and sat down. His silver eyebrows arched as he said, "What is it you want to see me about, Phil, the couple that was murdered in the bathroom? Lillian told us all about it last night on our way home from the airport, and I read some of your stories this morning. I had to get caught up on the news."

"No, actually I came to—"

I wanted to go on, but Scott grabbed the Judge's attention by scratching at the desk and pulling himself up off the floor. His broad forehead rose above the desk, and he stood up and swayed back and forth like a chubby metronome.

"Yes, Scott?" said the Judge. "What is it?"

Scott made a loud, flubbery fart.

"Damn it, Scott, you know you mustn't do that. You do that in the bathroom. Go on. Go to the toilet."

The odor drifted across the room, and Scott plodded through it. I pulled in my feet to give him more space. Lillian took his hand and hurried him away.

The Judge bit his lip and shook his head. "Poor guy. He never does that in front of people. He's not himself. He's been underfoot all day. He's happy we're home. I shouldn't have yelled at him. I hurt his feelings."

"You didn't yell," I said.

"No? Good. I hope not." He stared at the vacant doorway.

I waited a moment and then said, "The reason I'm here, Judge, is to see if you can tell me something about the Good Shepherd Home, the foster home that Hugh and Grace DeLong used to run. I've heard some allegations that some of the children who stayed in the home were physically or sexually abused."

He had been staring blankly out the window until my last few words sank in. "What?" He scowled in disbelief. "Who the hell said that?"

"I'm sorry, Judge. That's confidential."

He made another scowl. "All right. What do your confidential sources say was done to them?"

I related what Paula had told me, omitting no details except names and sexes. The part about a deputy sheriff who took young children to some pedophile's house made the Judge wince and shake his head, either in doubt or disgust. The part about forcible sodomy in a car made him shut his eyes and throw up his hands.

"These are mighty serious charges," he said. "Hard to believe. Hard to believe without proof."

"I know, Judge. That's why I'm here. Grace DeLong told me they're a pack of lies. She said you would back her up."

"And I do. There's not a scintilla of truth in it, as far as I know." His slack cheeks shook emphatically.

"Did you ever hear any complaints or rumors about child abuse at the Good Shepherd Home?"

He stared at me as if I had slapped his face. "If I had, I would have ordered an investigation. My God, Phil, do you think I would have sent children there if I thought there was the remotest possibility they would be abused in any way? I certainly hope not."

"I wasn't suggesting that, Judge. I'm just checking out what I've been told."

He nodded. "I understand. That's your job. No offense taken. But I want you to understand how seriously I would have responded to the slightest hint of such abuse."

"How about the couple who ran the home, Mr. and Mrs. DeLong—did you know them personally?"

"Yes. We weren't close friends, but I knew them."

"What do you know about them? Did they have any training in running a foster home?"

"I never did a background check on them. That wasn't the court's responsibility. Having said that, I do know that the DeLongs were good people. They owned a small farm, and Mr. DeLong drove a school bus."

"I hadn't heard he was a school-bus driver."

"Yes, for many years, I believe. He knew how to deal with children. A school bus can get pretty rowdy. I never heard of any complaints against him. And you know, for many many years I was the only judge in Meridian County, so I believe I would have heard if he was a child molester."

We sat in silence. I tapped my lips with one finger and stared outside.

"Is there a problem?" he said.

I went on tapping. Then I said, "I'm having a problem making sense of it. Almost everyone I've talked to, including some people who were in the home when they were kids, denies that children were abused there. But I don't think my informants were lying. The descriptions of what took place were too detailed—that is, when they finally were willing to talk about it."

"How many informants do you have?"

"Three. But maybe 'informant' is the wrong word for two of them. One person made some very strong accusations. The other two were less willing to talk about what occurred at the home; however, some of the things they told me seemed to jive with the other one's story."

"I see. You said you didn't think any of your—let's call them witnesses—were lying about their experiences. Perhaps 'lying' is the wrong word too. Perhaps they simply exaggerated to get your attention. Or maybe they made up some of the details and then convinced themselves they had really occurred."

"I don't think so," I said.

"People do strange things." He prodded gently: "Just between you and me, Phil, who gave you this information? Were they people I sent to the home?"

"I can't say for sure. I assume they were."

"It's certainly possible. Or it may have been a special judge. I wish you would tell me their names—in strict confidence."

"I'm sorry, Judge."

With a patronizing smile he said, "Well, I admire your discretion."

I stood up to leave, but he raised his hand like a traffic cop. "Tell me, Phil, why all this interest in the Good Shepherd Home. Is it connected with the murders in some way?"

Through the wide windows the manicured lawn seemed to doze under an endless sky. The house was quiet. The air around me seemed to shimmer, as if I were sitting in a bubble. It felt like a languorous daydream. I wished the Judge wasn't there. His words hung in the air like an axe.

"It just came up," I said. "It was serendipity."

"It has no connection to the murders, then?"

"Not that I know of."

"What was the name of the woman you were with when you found the two bodies in the house? I know you had it in the paper, but it's slipped my mind."

"She told me her name was Paula Henry, but the state-police detective in charge of the case said her name is actually Paula Boofey."

"Ah, yes." He sat back, nodding thoughtfully. "I remember a case with a woman named Boofey. It was ten or fifteen years ago, as I recall. Now what was her name? Ellen? Edith? No, Edna. Edna Boofey. She had a daughter named Paula. See, the old brain still works." A sly triumph twinkled in his eyes. "If I had to guess, I'd say Paula is one of the sources of your information on the Good Shepherd Home." Grinning mischievously, he added, "But you don't have to tell me. You have to protect your sources."

My reverie had dissolved. I sat up straight and met his gaze. A fine crazing etched the whites of his eyes. "I still can't confirm it, Judge," I said.

"You don't have to. It's no longer necessary."

"I don't think my informants were deluded," I said. "I don't believe they made it up."

"That's your prerogative. But as for Ms. Boofey, she must have something to hide, or she wouldn't have disappeared the night you found the bodies."

"She was afraid of the police for some reason."

"Yes, so you said in your article. She sounds to me like a clever, gutsy young woman." He got up unexpectedly. "I wouldn't put too much faith in what she says, if I were you." He smiled benevolently and stretched out his hand. "This has been very interesting, Phil." His handshake was even tighter than before.

As we left the den, Lillian came rushing through the hall. "I'm sorry," she said. "I've been on the phone all this time. I was going to ask if you'd like some coffee."

"None for me, Lill," the Judge said. "Nature calls. Good visiting with you, Phil." With a tottering but stately stride, he disappeared into a hallway on the right.

Sunlight dappled the polished floor. Lillian stood on one stiff leg and swayed slightly on her other heel. "We're having a little get-together tomorrow night," she said. "Sort of a welcome-home party for the Judge and Beverly. Would you like to come?"

I didn't think twice about it. "Yes, I would. Thanks." It would give me a chance to meet some more Brandons.

"Good. Around eight. Nothing fancy."

Pots and pans banged and clattered in the kitchen. "Now what?" Lillian said. She hurried around me to open the door. "See you tomorrow then, Phil."

"I'll be here."

I walked out into the blue and green daydream.

CHAPTER 25
The Professor

A NTICIPATE, ANTICIPATE. . . .

Before going to bed that night, I took some steps to fortify my apartment in case Chuck Martin came back. I hammered a nail in the ceiling a few inches inside the front door, bent the nail with a pair of pliers, tied a string around the handle of an old-fashioned brass bell (a souvenir of my marriage), and tied the string to the nail. If someone broke in during the night, the door would hit the bell and wake me up. I rigged up a similar alarm at the kitchen door, but instead of a bell I hung my sauce pan and frying pan from the ceiling. Finally, I moved my baseball bat from under the bed to the top. The Louisville Slugger had accumulated a thick layer of dust and lay beside me like some kind of grotesque sex toy.

I didn't wake up till 9:30 in the morning. The long sleep made me feel like a new man, invigorated, ready to get up and go, but I didn't get up. I stared at the faces in the ceiling and listened to the birds and the church bells. I began to fall asleep again.

The phone in the living room rang. I got out of bed too fast and felt lightheaded for a moment. Probably the concussion, I thought. I answered the phone on the third ring.

An angry, trembly voice said, "You lied to me. I thought I could trust you." It was Paula.

"You can," I said. "What's the matter?"

"You told the cops where we live."

"No I didn't."

"Liar. You put it in the paper. I read it. Our house was even on TV."

"I didn't tell them, Paula. They figured it out on their own. They found the clinic where you went to have your leg set."

She seemed to think about that.

I said, "Are you home now?"

"You think we're stupid?" she shot back. "We got out the back door the minute we saw a police car go by looking at the house."

"Where are you?"

"None of your business. I don't want that in the paper too."

I took a deep breath. "Your real name came out in the paper because the detective in charge of the case released it to the press. I couldn't keep it out of the paper after that." I let it sink in, then added, "You ought to talk to the police, Paula. Stop running and hiding. You're just making them more suspicious."

"We saw Chuck Martin too," she said. "We was at a neighbor's house up the street, and he parked right out in front. He sat there all day watching our house. He never left the car. If he had to take a leak, I guess he used a beer can or something."

"Are you sure it was Chuck Martin?"

"Yes, damn it, I'm *sure!*"

"When did you see him?"

"Right after it was in the *Star*."

"The Indianapolis paper?"

"Yeah. Don't you know what the *Star* is?"

"I didn't know they were following this case." I should have known though. I was slipping. Too much detective work, not enough newspaper.

"Mom's real scared. She thinks we're gonna get killed." She sniffled. "It's my fault. I got her into this mess. But she don't blame me."

"Where's Edna Mae now?" I said.

"With me."

"Are you here in Meridian County?"

"Never mind where I am. I just want you to know one thing. If Mom and me end up in a ditch on the side of the road some night, we had you to thank for it. Thanks a lot."

She slammed the receiver down but missed the cradle. She slammed it even harder and hung up. Par for the course.

I got washed up and inspected myself in the mirror. The bruise on my cheek was nearly invisible, a light purplish splotch that my beard grew through. The lump on my head was gone. To celebrate, I made some coffee and put an English muffin in the toaster.

After breakfast I walked to work to get some exercise. The bells bonged, sending crystal circles through the air. Two old ladies on their way to church smiled at me as if I were one with them in faith.

I had the newsroom to myself. I got another cup of coffee and dug into the stories waiting for me on the computer. Shortly after noon Edward showed up in his go-to-meetin' duds.

"You working Sunday morning again?" he blurted. "You must be bucking for a raise."

"I wouldn't turn it down," I said.

He laughed as if both of us were joking. Then he came into my office and plopped on a chair. "Guess who I had a call from last night," he said.

"Who?"

"I'll give you a hint—the only one-term sheriff in the history of Meridian County."

"Sounds like Chuck Martin."

Edward's cynical grin turned into a scowl as he said, "He had a complaint about you. He wants me to yank on your chain before you do anymore damage to his good name while you're running all over town with your 'wild stories' about the Good Shepherd Home." He squinted with one eye. "I detected the tacit threat of a lawsuit for libel."

Was my chain about to be yanked? I sat back and waited.

Edward continued, "He also said I should fire you for withholding evidence from the police. He said you knew all along that Paula Henry's real name is Paula Boofey, but you kept it quiet until the state police figured it out and you had to put it in the paper. He said, and I quote, 'I can't understand why the paper is protecting someone who may be involved in a double murder.' He wants your head on a pole, Phil."

"First of all," I said, "I didn't know her name was Boofey all along. Second, he doesn't know what I knew and when I knew it. He's just guessing. Third, I had a face-to-face with him yesterday—at two in the morning when he showed up at my apartment."

"What? Two in the morning!"

I gave my boss a censored version of the encounter, omitting the fact that Martin had broken in. When I got to the part about the punch to the solar plexus that made him throw up, Edward laughed in disbelief. "No shit? You belted him? You're lucky he didn't kill you."

"He was drunk."

"All the more reason not to get in a fight with him."

"I was on automatic pilot," I said. "I was half asleep. Then, about a half hour after I got rid of him, a rock came through the front window."

Edward sprang out of his chair and paced swiftly back and forth as if bouncing off the walls. "That guy belongs in jail. You reported it to the police, didn't you?"

"I thought about it," I said.

"What the hell are you waiting for?"

I flipped my hands. "It was pathetic. He acted like a child. And I can't prove he threw the rock."

"Report it! Let the police investigate. It's their job to prove it, not yours. Hell, it shouldn't be hard to prove he was there. His DNA must be everywhere if he barfed all over your living room."

"It's not there now. I cleaned it up."

"You should have called the police right away."

"I didn't want to smell it."

Deep in thought, he strutted back and forth with his hands in his pockets. His suit coat draped behind him like a cape. Then suddenly he veered out of the office and disappeared. A minute later he returned with a .45 automatic in his hand and laid it on my desk.

"This is for you," he said. "It's loaded, and the safety's on."

"You want me to shoot Chuck Martin?"

"I want you to protect yourself, damn it."

"I don't have a license to carry a gun."

"Then get one. Or keep it at home—you don't need a license for that."

I stared at the pistol lying next to my coffee mug. "Okay, Ed. Thanks."

He picked up the gun again and explained how to use it. Then he pointed a long finger at me and said, "Be careful. Don't get yourself killed. I don't want to have to go looking for a new editor. And if you have any sense, you'll report what happened to the police. That moron should be off the streets."

After he left for lunch, I hefted the gun and made sure the safety was on. I didn't want to shoot anybody, but it wasn't a bad idea to have some protection besides my baseball bat.

I put the gun in my desk and got back to work. Around one o'clock, a couple of my reporters came in. While I was in the newsroom talking to them, the front door opened and Gary Fromm walked in. "You open?" he said. "Can I come in?" At first he didn't seem to recognize me, probably because of my beard. Then he said, "Are you Mr. Larrison?"

"Yes. Hello, Gary," I said. "What can I do for you?" I went to the front counter.

He acted nervous and uncomfortable. He looked less scruffy than the day we had met. His hair was combed, his beard was trimmed, and he had a black T-shirt on. "You got a minute?" he asked me.

"Sure, come on in. We can talk in my office."

As he followed me through the newsroom, he said, "I wasn't sure you was open today."

"We're open. We have to get tomorrow's paper out."

"Oh yeah?"

He sat on the chair that Edward had pulled up to my desk, but instead of looking at me, he stared outside at the courthouse.

I sat down and said, "It's good to see you again, Gary. How's your wife? Did the baby come yet?"

"No. We're still waitin'. They wanna do a C-section. The little fart's pretty heavy."

"I bet it's a boy," I said.

"Yeah it is."

"Well, I hope everything goes well. I'm sure it will. They do a lot of C-sections."

"Yeah, but she's still scared. I don't blame her. I wouldn't want 'em cuttin' on me if I was her." He forced himself to look at me. "It's on account of her I'm here. She wanted me to come and see you." He rubbed the bumpy ends of his collarbones with a thumb and index finger.

"What's on your mind, Gary?" I hoped he wasn't about to ask me to publish an appeal for donations to help them pay their hospital bills.

"Remember what you said to me last week?"

"I remember."

"Yeah. Well, I been havin' trouble sleepin' at night ever since. One night my wife woke me up because I was havin' a nightmare. She said I was cryin' in my sleep. I was shakin' all over. My teeth was even chatterin'." His voice began to crack, and he coughed to hide it. "This ain't fucken easy," he said.

"I know it."

"My wife—her name's Stephanie—she wanted to know what I was dreamin' about. I didn't want to say, but my teeth wouldn't stop chatterin'. I couldn't stop 'em. I was scared. I don't scare easy, but I was then. I told her what they done to me—how they took my manhood away. I bawled like a baby when I was tellin' her about it." He began to choke up again and cussed at himself.

I got up and shut the door. "I'm glad you came, Gary. You've done the hardest thing already by talking about it."

He made a derisive snort. "I feel like a freaken baby. And I'm about to have a kid of my own."

"It's good to get it out in the open. You don't want to keep it bottled up inside."

"Yeah. Steph said the same thing."

"She's right," I said. "And it's understandable that you're upset. What you went through was traumatic—it hurt you emotionally. You're coping with it now. You're healing yourself."

"I don't know," he said. "I feel like a piece a shit."

"That's because it's hard to talk about it. It takes courage."

He hung his head and folded his arms on his chest. His mouth hung open, and he breathed hard through his broken front teeth.

"Would you like something to drink?" I said. "Coffee? A Coke? A glass of water?"

"I'll take a Coke," he said softly.

By the time I got back with the soda for him and a cup of coffee for me, he had pulled himself together somewhat. He took a long gulp from the can and belched softly. Then, looking outside or at the floor, he said, "A cop would take me to this guy who had a log cabin in the woods. It was more like a house than a cabin. It was real nice, all fixed up inside. Everything looked perfect. Nothin' was out of place. I never seen so many books before. They covered most of the walls. I guess he was a teacher or somethin' because the cop called him the Professor."

He took another gulp and went on: "The first thing I had to do when I got there was take a bath. He'd watch me get naked, and then he'd watch me while I was in the tub to make sure I scrubbed everything. When I got done, he dried me off himself. He was real slow about it. It took forever. He'd touch me softly with the towel all over. The guy was sick. He liked to hold my balls in his hand." He broke off suddenly and said, "How much of this do you want to hear?"

"Whatever you want to tell me."

Gary's voice acquired a robotic monotone as he described what the Professor had done to him. "Sometimes we went swimmin' in a little pond in front of the cabin, and sometimes we would hike in the woods if it wasn't hot, because the guy didn't like to get sweaty. Mostly we watched movies on TV. First we'd watch a regular movie, like *The Magnificent Seven*, and then somethin' perverted, like men havin' sex with little kids. I never seen stuff like that before. I never knew people done stuff like that. Then he made me do what the kids were doin' in the movie."

"What an animal," I said.

"Thinkin' back on what he done to me makes me wanta go find him and beat his fucken brains out."

"Do you think you could find his cabin?" I said.

"I wish I could. It was pretty far. It took a while to get there."

"More than an hour?"

"Seems like it, but I can't say for sure. It was a long time ago."

"What did this guy look like?"

After a moment's thought, he said, "He wasn't real tall. He was about a foot shorter than the cop that brung me there—I don't know, maybe five-foot-two, somethin' like that. And I remember he talked real fast, like he couldn't wait to get the next word out. He didn't look like no professor to me. He had a flattop, and he smelled like perfume—I guess it was cologne."

"What color was his hair?"

"Blond, real light blond, almost white."

"How old was he?"

"I don't know. Maybe forty or fifty. He had a little flab on him, but he wasn't real fat."

"That's a good description," I said. "Maybe the police can use it to find him."

"I'll never forget what he looked like an' how he smelled."

"What about the cop who brought you there? Was it always the same one?"

"Yeah, a guy named Chuck Martin. He got elected sheriff later on. What a joke."

My heart jumped. "Did he know what the Professor did to you?"

"I think he did, but we never talked about it. I never told him. I didn't want to talk about it." He stood up. "I guess I'd better go. I don't like leavin' my wife by herself right now."

I felt bad for thinking she had sent him to ask for charity. I had forgotten what she had said to me last week. "You've got a good wife, Gary, I told him. "She really cares about you."

"Yeah. I know it."

I watched him rush through the newsroom and out to his truck, a clean but dented pickup. Then I sat down and began making notes of what he had told me while it was fresh in my mind. An edgy thrill ran through me. I finally had someone who backed up Paula's story. I let the ecstasy build, and by the time I finished my notes, I was so euphoric that I couldn't work anymore. Euphoria was dangerous—there was always a letdown—but I let myself enjoy it while it lasted. I walked home to get something to eat.

When I opened the front door, it banged into the school bell and I nearly had a heart attack. But the manic euphoria went on.

CHAPTER 26
Eye Contact

AGAINST THE golden sunset the lights of Judge Brandon's house gleamed like diamonds. A couple dozen cars were parked along the looping driveway with their tires on the lawn. I added mine to the line and walked the rest of the way up the hill.

Laughter and music came from out back. I walked around the garage end of the house, where more cars were parked. The country-club set was standing around the pool and patio, talking and sipping drinks under Japanese lanterns. The women looked like tropical flowers in their summer dresses.

Among the faces that turned in my direction was Lillian's. She was listening to an elderly man with a dust mop of gray hair, but she gave him an apologetic touch and broke away to meet me.

"I like the beard," she said with a big smile. "What can I get you to drink?" She had a new hairstyle with feathery curls and was wearing a striped dress that looked a bit like a sailor's uniform.

"How about a scotch and soda," I replied.

"Can do. I'll be right back."

I didn't see anyone I knew out there, so I followed her inside. In the family room, several kids ranging in age from five to fifteen were lying around watching MTV. The younger ones were on the floor, the others on the furniture. Scott knelt straight up on the floor, jerking back and forth to a music video. Two of the boys were imitating him. Lillian gave them a disapproving, disappointed look, but they went on snickering as if they couldn't help it.

More guests clustered in the kitchen and dining room. Jodie and a woman who bore some resemblance to her formed half of one cluster. Jodie did a double take and waved when she saw me. Then she said something to the guy standing next to her, and I realized they were together. He tilted his head to hear what she was saying, and his eyes came up to look at me. He had spiky blond hair and wore a thick gold chain around his neck and a small gold ring in one ear. I looked away, trying to act as if it didn't matter that he was with Jodie. The island in the middle of the kitchen was covered with fruit, cheese, and small pastries. I helped myself to some sour grapes.

"Where's the guest of honor?" I asked Lillian when she returned with my drink.

"The Judge? He's around somewhere. I saw him talking to my father a while ago."

She began introducing me to people. I got the feeling that some of them were surprised to see Lillian with a man. She took it in stride. She had a relaxed, unassertive manner, long on smiles and nods, short on words. She did not act the least bit proprietary toward me, but I wished I had not followed her inside.

One woman that Lillian introduced me to grabbed my arm and said insistently, "What happened to your face?"

It was not what I wanted to hear. "I tripped and fell and scraped it on a wall," I told her.

She crinkled her pointy nose, baring big teeth and gums that made her look like a donkey and told me about someone she knew who had broken his back by falling off a ladder. He was paralyzed, spent his life in a wheelchair, had his spleen removed, couldn't do anything for himself. . . . She went on and on. . . . The teeth moved closer and closer.

I pried myself away, only to have someone else ask about my face.

"The disguise isn't working," I told Lillian.

"Some people are just too rude," she said. "Come on, I want you to meet my mother."

She found her mother sitting alone in a breakfast nook that jutted into the patio. She was watching the crowd out there and nursing a tall drink.

"What are you doing here all by yourself, Mom?" Lillian said. "Why aren't you mingling?"

She introduced me to Adele Brandon, whose eyes popped up with a sleepy smile. She already seemed a bit tipsy. Thick, wavy blonde hair lay on her back like a rug. She had a friendly, open face, but there was too much makeup on it.

"So you're the man who's been writing all those stories about the murders," Adele said. She began asking questions, and I realized she hadn't read any of the stories in the paper.

While we were chatting, Scott came barreling through the kitchen like a bulldozer. "Papaw, Papaw, Papaw," he said over and over. Guests hung on to their drinks as they dodged out of the way.

"Papaw's busy," Lillian said to him. "What's the matter, Scott?"

"Papaw, Papaw. . . ."

Lillian shrugged helplessly as her cousin bulled his way through the dining room in search of the Judge.

"He should be in a home," Adele said. She raised her tumbler and sighted at me along its moist sides.

"Not as long as his Papaw has anything to say about it," Lillian said.

"Lillian takes care of him," Adele informed me. "She's like his live-in nurse. They take her for granted."

"Now, Mom, don't get started."

"It's true."

There was a crash somewhere beyond the dining room. Lillian made a face and hurried to see what had happened. Her mother shook her head as if resting her case.

I wandered outside. The sky was a soft light blue, and Venus hung low over the fields. I took a turn around the pool. The water looked like smooth, green crystal full of trembling shadows. Citronella candles in netted vases were evenly spaced around the pool and patio. I sat next to one of them on the low wall. The air smelled like orange juice.

Jodie and her friend came out of the house, and someone immediately accosted her. I watched her laugh, sip her drink, nod quickly, say something, laugh again. She had a plain yellow sundress on, no jewelry, nothing fancy. She didn't need anything fancy. I couldn't take my eyes off her. I wondered if there was anything serious between her and the guy with the bling. They didn't look like a match. I got up and moved on before she'd catch me staring.

I went back in the house to get some more grapes, and as I entered the kitchen a stout, elderly woman whom I recognized from photos in the paper, said, "You're Phil, aren't you? Lillian told me about you. I'm Beverly Brandon."

I shook hands with the Judge's wife. "Nice to meet you, Mrs. Brandon," I said.

"Nice to meet you. Lill told me what happened while we were gone. We go away for two weeks, and all hell breaks loose." Tall and busty, she had a merry, outlandish laugh. She struck me as a natural, earthy person, not the type of woman who lived in a place like this.

"How was your trip to Asia?" I said.

"Wonderful! I loved every minute of it. Cambodia—that poor country, what it's been through—it's just incredible. The people are so friendly. Have you ever been to Asia, Phil?"

"No, I've never been anywhere."

Her head tossed back and she laughed a big horsy laugh. "We'll have to take you with us next time we go. You're a newspaperman. You've got to see the world." She laid a hand on my wrist and whispered in my ear, "Thank you for helping with Scott. Lill said they might have had a disaster on their hands without you." She let go of me and stretched out her arms toward the next person waiting to speak with her.

I wondered what had happened to Lillian. Was she gone for the night, taking care of Scott? I squeezed through the crowd and bumped into the coach of the Campbellsville High School football team. He had a beer in one hand, a mini cream puff in the other. Preseason practice was underway in the heat of August. We discussed the team's prospects, which usually were not good. Basketball was the big game around here.

Through a kitchen window I saw Jodie on the edge of the patio. Her golden friend was gone, but now she was talking to a gangly guy who laughed too hard at what she was saying. With each rollicking laugh his nose dipped closer to his cocktail, like the beak of a toy bird. She said something else, and his head bent straight back, howling at the sky. He laid a hand on her shoulder, shaking his head in hilarious delight.

She happened to turn in my direction, and our eyes met as she raised her glass to her lips. This time I waved at her. Our eyes held a moment longer. Then she gave me a wry little smile and looked away.

I carried that look and a second drink into the main hall. No one else was there, but party noise seeped in from adjoining rooms. As if in a museum, I studied the pictures on the walls. The door to the Judge's den was closed, but I thought I heard angry voices arguing inside. I parked myself in front of a large, dark painting by T. C. Steele on the wall next to the den.

Suddenly the door opened and Frank Brandon stormed out. His hair was disheveled, his shirt splotched with sweat. "Do you need something?" he demanded.

"I'm waiting to see the Judge," I said.

He called over his shoulder, "Phil Larrison's hanging around out here. He says he wants to see you, Dad." He gave me a dirty look and left the house by the front door.

I poked my head into the den. The judge was in his swivel chair, and Ralph Brandon, Lillian's father, slouched on the sofa. Scott was sitting on the floor eating a pepperoni pizza out of a box.

"If you're busy, it can wait, Judge," I said. "It's not important."

"Good," he replied. "We're in the middle of a family issue." He looked at Scott as if that explained everything, but I couldn't help thinking something else was going on. "You know my son, Ralph, don't you?" He gestured toward the beagle-faced man with a receding hairline.

"Yes, of course," I said. I knew him from meetings and from Mackey's, that's all. "Good to see you, Ralph."

"How ya doin'?" he said, weary and indifferent.

"Maybe we can talk some later, Phil," the Judge said, "but right now—"

"Sure. Sorry I disturbed you, sir."

"Thank you, Phil. Would you mind closing the door, please."

I loitered in the hall another minute, but the argument had apparently ended with the exit of Frank, so I went back outside. It was beginning to get dark. A few couples were dancing on the patio. I couldn't stick around much longer. I had to get back to the paper.

Don Grapevine, athletic and aristocratic, stood near the pool with a glass of red wine while a large round woman bent his ear. Her bosom was a pair of bowling balls, and a pearl necklace disappeared down her cleavage. Like a saint, or a pastor hoping for a big donation, Grapevine gave her his complete attention.

"*There* you are," Lillian said from behind me. "I was beginning to think you went home." She had a man with her. I hoped it was a boyfriend.

"No, I'm still here," I said, turning. "It's a nice party."

"Thanks. Did you get anything to eat?"

"A little bit. I'm not really hungry."

A mosquito landed on my arm, and Lillian flicked it off. "We need more candles," she said.

"What was that crash earlier?" I asked her. "Did Scott break something?"

"He knocked over a lamp, but it didn't break, fortunately."

"That's good."

She nodded. "He's still out of control. It's my fault for messing with his dosage. Maybe the Judge can settle him down in a few days. I hope so."

"Maybe you should think about what your mother said—put him in a home."

"The Judge will never go along with that."

I felt like saying the Judge must be senile, but I kept my trap shut.

"Phil, she continued, "I'd like you to meet my brother, Doug."

We shook hands. I felt as if he was sizing me up as a possible brother-in-law. He had wide square shoulders, thick arms, and a flabby neck. I asked what business he was in, and he said he worked in the bank, no doubt meaning his father's bank. He asked me how the newspaper business was doing, but as I began to tell him, he saw someone he knew and excused himself. I watched him bear down on a woman in an off-the-shoulders blouse.

"How many brothers and sisters do you have?" I asked Lillian.

"Just Doug."

"He's a big guy."

"Too big. He needs to lose some weight."

We walked like a couple around the pool to the patio. Jodie seemed to watch us with bemused interest. As we approached, she smiled as if we shared a secret and said, "Phil, I want you to meet my mom. Now where is she? There she is." Lillian did not seem pleased.

Jodie hurried through the crowd and came back dragging her mother.

"Mom," she said, "this is Phil Larrison, the editor of the *Gleaner*."

"Oh yes," said Jackie Grapevine, "I know all about you. I see you in the newspaper office sometimes when I drop off Tri-Kappa news, but it's nice to finally meet you."

"Nice to meet you too," I said. "I was in your house last week, but you were in Cincinnati."

"Yes. I went to see my sister."

"Her name's Anita, isn't it?"

"Yes. And I have two brothers, Ralph and Frank. They're both here tonight."

She had Jodie's eyes and hair, but her face was wider and had too many wrinkles for someone probably still in her forties. She had a very dark tan, and I wondered if the wrinkles were caused by years of overdosing on sunshine. She wore a short-sleeved pink top and snug-fitting tan capris that showed off a fairly voluptuous figure.

"Why'd you decide to grow the beard?" Jodie asked me.

"I guess you can't see it in this light," I said, "but I got a big scrape on my cheek." I turned sideways to show them. "The beard's meant to hide it."

Jodie peered at the wound. "Yikes, what happened?"

"I went sneaking around the Garths' house again, and somebody tripped me while I was going down the steps in the cellar."

"Good Lord!" Jackie exclaimed. "Do you know who it was?"

"No, I don't."

Jodie said, "If I were you, I wouldn't go back there anymore. It's too dangerous."

"That's right," her mother said. "Maybe it was the killer who tripped you."

"I doubt it," I said. "I'm still alive."

Lillian chimed in: "And you need to *stay* alive, or one of these days we'll be reading your obituary in the paper."

"I guess I should write it up while I still can."

"You shouldn't joke about things like that," Jackie said.

The Judge appeared at the French doors and scanned the crowd. When he spotted Lillian, he waved at her to come inside.

"Oh shoot," she said, "it's time to get Scott in bed."

"Why does it matter when he goes to bed?" I said.

"We try to keep him on a schedule. Otherwise he gets confused. And you know how excited he can get. I'll be back as soon as I can." She walked quickly toward the Judge.

I felt sorry for her. She was a good person, selfless, kind. But I was not attracted to her. Having spoken to her father a short while ago, I could see an unfortunate resemblance to his slack, doggy-like features. But it wasn't her face that turned me off. It was the way she was. It was her lack of spirit.

Jackie said, "Poor Lillian. I'm going to help her with Scott," and hurried after her niece.

I looked at Jodie. "Are you going too?"

"Uhhh, I don't think so."

"Where's your friend?"

"Which one?"

"The one who looks like he just flew in from the golden West."

She laughed. "You sound jealous."

"Why would I be jealous?"

"I can't imagine," she said with a saucy smirk. "We were friends in high school. That was before he was gay. I bumped into him at the JayC store this week. We got talking, and I invited him to the party, but he wasn't having a very good time, so he left."

"That's too bad," I said.

"Don't take it so hard."

"Is that where you meet guys, at the supermarket?"

"Uh-huh, either there or they show up at the house around midnight to use the phone."

I laughed and came back with "I hate to tell you this, but you're about to get dumped again. I've got to go back to work."

"So you're not having a good time either." She sipped the rest of her drink.

"I'm having a very good time, but I'm supposed to do some work for my paycheck."

"Well, you'd better go where you're needed then."

"I could come back around midnight. How long will this thing last?"

"It will end precisely at 10:30, by order of the court."

"Oh. Well, I could come to your place around midnight with the other guys."

"Sorry. I'll be asleep by then."

"How about tomorrow then?" I said, serious at last. "I'll take you out for lunch."

"I don't think I can. Mom wants me to go shopping with her."

"You can go shopping after lunch. I'll pick you up at ten, okay?"

She acted as if I had presented her with a perplexing problem. Then she laughed and said, "Sure, why not?"

"Great. I love enthusiasm," I said.

We walked around the side of the house to my car. I hadn't asked a woman out since my divorce. I felt the galaxy shift, but you have to take a chance. Life's nothing but chance. If I hadn't picked up Paula on the highway because she happened to be wearing a cast, if we hadn't found a murdered couple in their bathroom, and if I hadn't gone to the neighbors' house to use the phone, I wouldn't be walking next to Jodie Palladino right now on the Judge's driveway under a starry deep-blue sky.

CHAPTER 27
Unfamiliar Roads

A FTER THE Big D, I swore to myself that I would never fall for another woman. I raised my shields, and for several years they had repelled the pheromones swirling around me. But now, lying on my wrinkled sheets as the sun came up, I wished I had Jodie next to me. I would soak up her scent. We would soak up each other. A light breeze brushed my legs. I spread my arms in a kind of fearless vulnerability. I welcomed the feeling. For the first time in years I felt free.

I rolled out of bed and scratched and stretched. As I roamed around the kitchen and living room, my head felt incredibly clear. Everything seemed new. I made some coffee and took a chance on soft-boiled eggs. They turned out nearly okay. Then I shaved, got dressed, and went to work on my car. I had parked under a tree last night, and the Civic was covered with bird crud. I drove to the nearest car wash and went through the automatic wash-and-wax bay. After that, I threw all my junk in the trunk and vacuumed the inside. When finished, the car looked better than it had in at least five years.

Back home, I drank another cup of coffee while admiring the car through the front window. If another bird christened it, I'd get a gun and shoot him. That reminded me of the .45 pistol Edward had given me. I ought to get it out of my desk and bring it home. It was going on nine o'clock. I finished my coffee and brushed my teeth. Then I took a shower and put some better clothes on. At 9:30 I was on my way to Jodie's house.

Jackie Grapevine was trimming rosebushes when I pulled into the driveway. A floppy sunbonnet nearly touched her shoulders, and she was wearing a long-sleeved white shirt and full-length jeans. "Hello again," she said. "Long time no see."

"Right, it must be twelve hours."

"How'd you like the party last night?"

"It was very nice. Your parents have a beautiful place."

"Don't they though?" She laughed as she said, "I'm thinking of moving back in with them. Since our neighbors were murdered, I'm afraid to be here by myself."

"I bet. But at least now you're on your guard."

"Yes, and we have Don's guns all over the house in case somebody breaks in. There's a double-barrelled shotgun standing on my side of the bed."

"Good idea."

"Jodie says I'm paranoid. But I'm not used to living in New York like she is."

I realized she was putting on an act. She seemed self-dramatic, as if craving attention. "You're not really afraid, are you?" I said. "You have Don to protect you."

"Yes, when he's here. But he's back at work now. He took a week's vacation last week, but he's not here during the day anymore."

"Where does Don work?"

"At Cummins, in Columbus. He's an engineer. He's been there—"

"Sorry I'm late," Jodie called, running out of the house. She was in a sleeveless top, a short skirt, and sandals.

Jackie asked where we were going.

Jodie turned to me: "Where are we going?"

"For a ride," I said. "There's a place I want to see at the other end of the county. You can help me find it."

"Don't count on me to find it. What place is it?"

"The old Good Shepherd Home for kids."

Jackie said, "What do you want to see that for? Is it for sale or something?"

"I just want to see what it looks like, and maybe take a picture. We might do an article on foster care in Meridian County."

She shrugged. "Okay, but are you sure you wouldn't rather stay here with me?"

"We're sure, Mom." Jodie gave her a peck on the cheek.

"Okay, have a good time. I'll see you later."

As we walked to the driveway, I felt ashamed of my old Civic, but Jodie showed no sign that it wasn't good enough for her. She hopped in like a young girl and watched me walk around the front of the car. I saw the same bemused expression that I had seen last night when she saw me with Lillian. I thought I knew what it meant last night, but I couldn't tell what it meant this time.

"You look nice," I said as I got behind the wheel.

"Thanks. So do you. The beard suits you." She waved at her mother, who waved back from the rosebushes, and we took off toward Hampstead.

I said, "I plan to shave it off as soon as the cuts and scratches get better."

"Maybe you should think about keeping it. It makes you look older."

"Why would I want to look older?"

"I don't know. Aren't you pretty young to be the editor-in-chief of a newspaper?"

"Maybe the *New York Times*. Not the *Gleaner*."

She gave herself a little slap on each cheek for saying the wrong thing. "I just think the beard makes you look more—I won't say 'experienced,' because I know you're experienced—it makes you look more . . . formidable."

"Well, that's good to know. Would I look even more formidable if I let it grow longer?"

She pretended to weigh the idea. "Uhhh, maybe not. You'd look like the mountain man who lives in the cabin we just passed."

"That's the look I want—South Hoosier redneck."

We drove through the knobs to Hampstead and turned left at the county road. It took us down to U.S. 50, where I turned right. I knew where I was going because the postmaster, a friend of mine, told me how to get there.

Along the way, Jodie asked if the police were any closer to finding out who killed Wayne and Cheryl Garth.

"It doesn't look like it," I told her.

"That doesn't say much for the police, does it?" she complained. "Don—my stepfather—says if you want to get away with murder, you should move to Meridian County."

"The police are trying," I said. "At least the state police figured out the real name of the woman I picked up that night I showed up at your house."

"Yes, it's Boofey. See, I read the *Gleaner*. But they still haven't found her."

"That's true."

"Don thinks she had something to do with the murders."

"Why?"

"He says maybe she came back to burn down the house to hide the fact that they were murdered."

"Why didn't she burn it down right after they were killed?"

"That's what I said. He said it may have been an afterthought."

I took a deep breath and let it out slowly. "Anything is possible. But I doubt she helped kill them. She went nuts when she found the bodies. They were her friends."

Twelve miles west of Campbellsville, we turned left onto County Road 650W, which cut a straight path south through some of the richest farmland in Meridian County. Rolling fields of corn and soybeans, pumpkins and watermelons, and even a little tobacco, stretched to the Muscatatuck River, the county's southern boundary. We passed two green road signs, and I slowed down as we approached the third. I turned right on 185S, a gravel road that bent left almost immediately and underwent a number change to 660W. A quarter mile later the road made a sharp right and became 210S. Dust swirled behind us as we bounced along the washboard road. After another half mile, we went through a patch of woods, and when we came out the other side, I saw the Good Shepherd Home up ahead.

"It looks spooky," Jodie said.

It was a square, three-story house on a low rise. Huge oaks and sycamores surrounded the red brick building. One of the sycamores was dead, its bare white branches reaching into the sky like the ghost of a giant hydra. The tall windows had wide black shutters, and the faded slate roof had been patched with gray shingles in several spots.

Apparently someone lived there. Near the entrance to the lane was a rusty white mailbox that drooped forward on a wooden post like a sombrero on a man taking a siesta, and next to the mailbox was a *Gleaner* newspaper tube. But no one was in sight, and there were no vehicles in front of the house. I drove in to get a closer look.

When we were about halfway up the lane, a spotted dog came charging toward us. I wasn't driving fast, but I slowed down even more to avoid hitting it. Barking, snarling, slobbering, the dog leaped against my side window. I didn't stop, and the dog kept jumping against the side, clawing at the window and snapping at me with bared teeth. It was a pit bull. I blew the horn to scare him off, but that only made him more excited, so I stepped on the gas and gave him a snoutful of dust as he chased us toward the house.

"Nice friendly dog," I said.

"The hound from hell," Jodie said.

I stopped at the front steps and hit the horn again in case someone was inside. No one came out. The lawn was ragged but recently mowed, and an upstairs window had a long, duct-taped crack in it.

"How do you think it felt to a little kid seeing this place for the first time?" I asked Jodie.

"Creepy . . . like a haunted house."

I followed the driveway around back. The dog went on barking and snarling and jumping at the windows. A weather-beaten barn stood behind and below the house, and a small herd of Black Angus cattle grazed in a field. Except for the hell hound that was now lunging at Jodie on her side of the car, it was a peaceful bucolic scene.

Jodie moved away from the window as far as she could. "Isn't this fun?" she said.

"You want me to run him over?"

For a moment she seemed to think I meant it. Then she laughed and said, "No. It's his house. Let's get out of here before he chews through the door."

I drove around to the front and took a picture through the dusty windshield. I didn't run the washer because I didn't want to make brown mud. The dog jumped up on the hood and then the roof. I gunned the engine, and he slid off, clawing at the trunk on the way down. Dust swirled around us as we rattled out the lane. The mutt chased us to the county road and then turned around and went home.

"Well, we got through that alive," I said.

Jodie laughed. "You sure know how to show a girl a good time. What's next?"

"I thought we might take a tour of the wastewater-treatment plant."

She laughed again. "Whatever you say."

I went back to 650W and turned right. A few miles later we crossed the Muscatatuck through a green steel bridge and parked on the Washington County side, where boaters had access to the river. Tall trees on the banks formed an arch, and the river, which was more like a creek, seemed to flow through a tunnel pierced by sunbeams.

We sat on a flat boulder. Jodie pulled off her sandals and dangled her feet in the water. I kept my shoes on—one of my socks had a hole in it.

"It's nice here," she said. "We should have brought a picnic lunch."

"I wish I'd thought of that."

"Or a boat. Wouldn't it be nice to float slowly down the stream?"

"Uh-huh, until we had to row back up."

"That would be your job."

The trees whirred with the sound of locusts. I watched the water sparkle at her feet. Her toenails were a light rosy pink. Her narrow ankles swished back and forth in the clear water. The short skirt rode high above her knees.

"Phil," she said, "do you believe in God?"

The question caught me totally off guard. "I believe in something," I said.

"What do you believe in?"

I remembered what her stepfather had told me: she does not go to church; she had drifted away from religion.

"There might be a God," I said, "but if there is, I don't think it's the one I was brought up with. I don't think he— or she—treats us like little children."

"You're not afraid of going to hell?"

"Are you?"

"I don't believe in hell," she said. "But I worry I might be wrong."

"I think you should just be true to yourself."

She put a hand on my wrist and gave it a little squeeze. "I like that."

Our eyes were inches apart. I put my arm around her waist and kissed her. Her lips pressed back.

"I've been wanting to do that since the night we met," I said.

"I never kissed a guy with a beard before. It's nice."

We sat in the green shade and talked about ourselves. She had moved to New York after college and got a job with MetLife as an actuary. A year and a half ago she began living with a broker who worked at Charles Schwab. His name was Curtis. He was several years older, in his mid-thirties, and separated from his wife. They were supposed to be getting a divorce, but then last Christmas they got back together.

"I was devastated," Jodie said. "We were talking about getting married after the divorce, and then all of a sudden my life goes down in flames."

I said, "I know how it feels," and told her about Vickie.

"I know your ex," she said when I was finished. "We go to the same hair salon."

"It's a small town."

"She hurt you badly, didn't she?"

"It hurt. But guess what—it all went away today."

She squeezed my hand. "Me too."

"You have pretty shoulders," I said.

She drew back and laughed. "Is that all you see that you like?"

"No. Your elbows are nice too. And your knuckles, your eyebrows, your knees. . . ."

"I see where this is going."

We kissed again, longer. I thought about asking her if she'd like to go back to my apartment, but I stopped myself. I hadn't slept with Vickie until our wedding night. It was what she wanted, and I went along with it. I couldn't treat Jodie with less respect.

After a while we drove back to town on unfamiliar country roads. We cruised past farmhouses, cornfields, trailers, churches, cows. Long panatela-shaped clouds hung in the high blue sky like an alien fleet.

We had lunch at Applebee's, across the street from a deserted strip mall that Wal-Mart had nuked. Jodie said, "Look, there's a Big Lots going in over there. They're like pokeweed, a pioneer plant that springs up in a wasteland."

She was bright, quick, and beautiful. I reached across the wide table and held her hand while we waited for our food to come.

CHAPTER 28
The Steps

I STILL wanted to talk to Esther Dubbs one-on-one, so the next morning I went back to the Twin Lakes Health Center. Allison, the receptionist in the assisted-living lobby, told me the code number for the keypad, and I opened the door to the memory-care wing. A little old lady with a walker tried to get out as I entered, but I blocked her way and said, "I think you ought to ask someone to go with you."

A red-shirted aide heard me and came running up the hall. "Where are you going, Frances?" she said. "Let's go back with the others. Would you like something to drink? How about some cranberry juice?"

"No thank you. I'm not thirsty," the woman said as the girl steered her away from the doors. "I must get a few things at the store."

"Not now, dear, maybe the bus will take you later."

I asked the aide where Esther was, and she pointed to the far end of the hall. Esther was sitting at an emergency exit and watching the traffic race by on U.S. 50. I wondered if she, Frances, and the other residents were constantly trying to escape. I pictured half a dozen of them trying to climb out their windows right now.

As I passed the nurses' station, a tall, husky LPN with long blonde hair whirled away from a filing cabinet and said, "May I help you?" She looked like a big, tough roller-derby skater, but she had a winsome smile that seemed on the verge of becoming a laugh. Her name tag read Barb.

I introduced myself and asked if it was okay if I talked to Esther for a few minutes.

"If it's all right with her, it's all right with me," she said with the nearly laughing smile. She came around the desk and peered down the hall. "There she is, straight ahead." She led the way, and I followed in her wake.

"Hey, Esther, you've got a visitor today."

"No," Esther said without turning around.

"Oh yes you do, dear. He's right here."

With an expression both puzzled and indignant, Esther turned and looked up.

I said, "Good morning, Esther. Remember me? I'm Phil. I talked to you last week."

"Of course I remember you. Why wouldn't I?"

Her eyes betrayed her. She had no idea who I was.

"You sure are feisty today, Esther," Barb said. "If a man wanted to see me, I'd put on my happy face."

"Who cares?" Esther said.

"Oh, what a crab you are," Barb said. "Come on. Let's go to your room so you and Phil can talk."

"No."

Barely moving her lips, Barb muttered to me, "Everything's no no no today. She still wants to control her own life. She's a fighter."

"Good for her," I muttered back.

Barb got Esther onto her feet, and Esther tried to shake off her hand. "You'll have to use your walker, if you won't let me help you, dear."

The threat worked—Esther let the nurse hold her arm. I was sad to see her capitulate.

"Is it okay if we sit outside on the rocking chairs?" I said. "It's a beautiful morning."

"You're not going to kidnap her, are you?"

"I hadn't planned on it."

"Would you like to sit outside, Esther?" Barb said.

There was no answer, so it counted as a yes.

"Maybe I should toilet her first," Barb said, "Do you want to go to the bathroom, Esther?"

"No."

Barb was going to walk her all the way out to the portico, but I took over. "I won't let her fall," I promised.

"If she does, I'm in big trouble," Barb said, "so please don't."

She punched in the four-digit code, which I noticed was written on the wall near the keypad. I put Esther's arm through mine and squeezed it against my side as we promenaded through the lobby. She did not try to fight me off. Perhaps she enjoyed being on a man's arm.

We sat in the shade on the left side of the portico. On the other side, an old baldheaded man sat bent over in a wheelchair. He gave us a sideways up-from-under look and said, "Good morning. Nice day, isn't it?" His voice was surprisingly strong.

"Yes," I said. "It's a little bit cooler today."

"Yes it is. Maybe the heat wave is over."

Since he had his wits about him and was outside by himself, I deduced that he lived in the assisted-living section. I thought about joining him, but I didn't want to have to make a lot of small talk. I wanted to grill Esther.

She rocked slowly, barely moving on the large wooden rocker.

"Do you come out here very often, Esther?" I said.

"No. It's too cold."

"You're not cold now, are you?"

She didn't answer.

"Would you rather sit in the lobby?"

She looked straight into my eyes. "I want to go home. Will you take me home?"

"I can't do that. The nurse would think I kidnapped you."

"I don't care what she thinks. I want to go home."

I reached over and touched her hand. "This is a nice place for you to live, Esther. They take good care of you here."

"No they don't," she snapped, quickly frustrated. "I don't have to stay here if I don't want to. They can't keep me here."

Not a good start, I said to myself. I guess we should have stayed inside. I sat back and rocked.

A man pushing a wheelbarrow appeared at the far end of the assisted-living wing and came toward us on the driveway. When he had covered about half the distance, a striking reddish-brown bird with black and white rings around its neck walked out of a flower garden covered with ornamental stones and began screeching loudly. It ran away from the wheelbarrow and then began dragging its wings on the ground.

"Look, Esther," I said, "see that bird? It's a killdeer. She's pretending she's hurt. She must have a nest on those stones."

"I don't like birds," Esther said.

"You don't? Why not?"

No answer.

The man in the wheelchair said, "That bird does that all day long."

"Really?" I said.

"Yep. It makes a lot of noise, but it sure is pretty."

"Oh shut up," Esther said.

I laughed and said, "Why are you so crabby today, Esther?"

"Frank, where have you been?" she said. "Why don't you come to see me anymore?"

"I'm not Frank," I said. "I'm Phil, from the *Gleaner*. I was here last week. You told me about Lug, the horse. I said I'd come back to see you again, remember?"

She seemed perplexed. "Of course I remember."

"Well here I am."

She straightened up, and her nostrils pinched together in a long breath. Then she scrunched up her lips and stared at me as if demanding something.

I said, "Last week you started to tell me about the house where you used to live in Blind Horse Hollow. You said when you were little your family lived in the cellar sometimes because it was cool there during the summer."

I waited for her answer, and finally she said, "That's right." She sounded a tad less hostile.

"I was in the cellar," I told her. "It wasn't as big as I thought it would be. It was about the size of the kitchen, that's all. Was that the whole cellar, Esther, or was it just the furnace room? Was there another room somewhere, another cellar?"

She raised a hand and spread her fingers and thumb.

"What do you mean?" I said. "Five? Do you mean five rooms?"

She grimaced as if frustrated with me.

"How can I get to those rooms, Esther?"

"You go down the steps."

I said, "There was only one room in the cellar when I was there. How do I get to the other rooms? Is there another set of steps somewhere?"

"Don't you remember? You always wanted to play down there when you were a little boy. I wouldn't let you. I was afraid you'd catch a cold it was so drafty."

It was getting too crazy. Her brain was shot. Then I recalled the faint breeze I had felt the last time I was in the Garth house. It came up the stairs as I started down from the second floor. I felt it only for a moment, as if a door had opened and shut. It made me think. . . .

"Esther," I said, "is there a cave under the house?"

She sucked in her lips and stared at me.

My scalp tingled. That was it—a cave. It had to be.

"I've got to go now, Esther," I said. "I must go to work. How about if I take you back to your room?"

"Good, it's too cold out here," she said.

I helped her through the front door and spied a different woman behind Allison's desk. I asked her if she would mind helping Esther get back to her room. I felt ungrateful for passing Esther off like that, but I was dying to get out of there. I said goodbye to Esther and told her I would come again. As the girl led her away, I heard Esther say, "Who was that man?" It made me feel better about dumping her.

I felt antzy all over as I drove across town. I couldn't wait to get out to the Garth house, but first I made a stop at the *Gleaner*. I took the handgun that Edward had given me out of my desk and put it in a plastic bag. Then I raided the printing crew's tool bench in the back shop, where I borrowed a small pry bar and a long, thin file, just so I had a couple of tools in case I needed them. As an afterthought, I sent Edward an email: "possible development in Garth case, will be back asap"

When I set out for the hollow, I thought I was on the verge of cracking the case, but halfway there reality set in. What if I didn't find a cave? Or what if I found it and there was nothing there? My mood swung with the moment, up one minute, down the next, manic-depressive, bipolar, a victim of myself. Don't crash just yet, I told myself. Play it out. Take it one step at a time. Find the freaken cave. Have a little faith. Trust your gut. Maybe I needed a pep pill or something.

I wasn't sure if I should drive right up to the Garth house and knock on the door or if I should ditch my car somewhere—at Jodie's maybe—and then follow the creek to the Garth place and scope it out from the cornstalks. No, too many possible complications. Go in straight up in case somebody's there.

As I slowed down to turn into the Garths' driveway, I saw Glenn Neidig sitting on the bottom steps of his porch. I hadn't talked to him in more than a week, so I stifled my impatience and pulled in to his lane. He was leaning forward, elbows on knees, beard between legs, clipping fingernails onto the ground. The dogs began howling and leaping against their pens as I climbed out of the car and walked across the scrubby grass.

"How do," the old man said as he clipped one last nail.

"How are you, Glenn?"

"Can't complain much, I reckon—not that it would help if I did. What can I do fer ya?"

"I was just wondering what's been going on around here lately?"

"Not much. I'd say we're jest about back to normal."

The dogs were still howling, and Glenn pushed himself off the steps and shuffled to the side of the house, where he let out a roar: "Yarrrrr, knock it off." The din subsided, and he came back and climbed the steps. "Have a seat," he said over his shoulder. "Set a spell."

I followed him up. "Have you been over to the house across the road?" I said.

"Not lately. It gives me the willies thinkin' 'bout what happened there."

"Are the rubber-neckers still going in and out?"

"Not too many of 'em. I reckon most of 'em seen all there is to see by now."

"How about the guy who owns the place—Walter Boofey—have you seen him?"

Glenn twisted one side of his mouth into a snarl and said, "You know somethin', young fella, you mighta found me settin' on the stoop out here, but that don't mean I spend all my time watchin' what goes on across the road. I like to mind my own business."

"Unlike me," I said, laughing. "I know, Glenn, but you've got the best spot to see what goes on over there."

"Sometimes you're better off if you don't see too much."

"Not if you work for a newspaper."

"I'm not so sure about that."

"What about Boofey?" I said. "Has he been around?"

"Yep, I seen him a coupla times. Leastways I think it was him. Drives a big black pickup truck."

"When was the last time you saw him?"

"A couple or three days ago."

"Has he been staying over there?"

"Hard to say."

"Was there anyone with him?"

"Not that I seen."

"Do you know if he's there now?"

"Nope, I sure don't."

I pushed my luck: "Have you seen his truck leave since the last time it went in?"

"Lord a'mighty, what did I jest tell ya? I don't sit here all day watchin' who comes an' goes."

"Sorry," I said. "What about the police—have they been around lately?"

"They came and got their roadblock finally, not that it did much good keepin' people out. It didn't keep you out either, did it? I did see *you* go in one day. Seems like it drawed more people in than it kept out." He took the clipper out of his pocket again and went back to work on his yellow nails. "This used to be a nice, quiet place to live," he went on. "Now cars are a-comin' and a-goin' all the time and people are gettin' killed. It's turnin' into a gol-durned city."

"Let's hope it doesn't," I said. "Good talking to you, Glenn."

"Anytime."

The hounds ignited again as I walked to my car. I backed out to the county road and turned into the lane to the Garths' house. In the rearview mirror I caught a glimpse of Glenn eyeballing me. He might not spend all his time watching what went on across the road, but he certainly was watching me. If I got arrested for breaking in, he'd make a good witness against me. But he wouldn't need to testify. I wouldn't deny it. My excuse, or rather my justification would be that I was 99.9% sure there was a cave connected to the house and that it might reveal why the Garths were killed and who killed them. Finding the cave was worth the risk of going in again.

The house looked deserted. It always did. It was a spook house. Boofey's truck was nowhere in sight. I left my burglar's tools on the seat for the moment and got out of the car. On the porch I was happy to see that the glass in the door had still not been replaced. All I had to do was loosen the plywood again. Piece of cake. But first I pounded on the door in case someone was inside. No answer. On the off chance that someone might be out back, I took a fast walk around the house. Then I added a quick visit to the barn. On the way back I made a point of traipsing through the septic field. It was dry—slightly spongy, but basically dry. My guess was no one had been there for several days.

I got my pry bar out of the car and went back to the porch. From there I had a 180-degree view of the fields, pasture, and hills. I scanned every degree without seeing anyone. I banged on the door a second time and waited. Then I wiggled the flat end of the bar under the wood and worked it loose. I unlocked the door and went in, but this time I hammered the plywood back in place with the side of my fist before I shut the door. If Boofey showed up while I was in his house, he wouldn't know I was there and I'd hear him coming. I'd be ready for him.

What about the car, Larrison? Wake up.

I ran back to the car and drove it around the side of the house. I found an overgrown tractor trail between Grapevine's cornfield and the tangled vines and locust trees along the creek bed. It wasn't the greatest hiding place, but the car would not be seen from the front of the house. I left the pry bar and the file on the seat, but I took the .45 with me.

I made a beeline back to the house. I realized I was sweating—from nervousness as much as from running around. I locked the front door behind me and headed for the laundry room next to the kitchen. Every time the floor squeaked I thought someone would hear it. The door to the cellar was closed. I put my ear against it and listened. No sound came from below. I opened the door as quietly as I could and twisted the light switch. The one fluorescent bulb highlighted the clay wall that had scraped my face. The sensation of tumbling down the steps came back.

I knelt down at the top of the steps and bent over to see if anyone was underneath them. No one was there. Once again, as I started down, I expected a pair of hands to grab my ankle and yank it through the stairs. It's a miracle I didn't break a leg last time, I thought. The worry stayed with me all the way down the steps until both feet were solidly planted on the dirt floor.

Standing in the dimly lighted cellar, I wished I had a flashlight. Why hadn't I thought of bringing one? What a dope I was, rushing around like a nut, remembering the gun but not a flashlight. What did I plan to do if I found the cave, explore it in the dark? It would be as black as hell in there. Larrison, you're an idiot.

My eyes adjusted to the stringy light, and I started looking for some kind of entrance to a cave. The cellar seemed even smaller than I had remembered. The beady red lights on the solar equipment glowed warmly but added no useful illumination. I examined the wall behind the components, including the dug-out section halfway up. There was no cave there, and no way for a person to get inside if there had been.

I inspected the wall next to the steps. More than half the wall was taken up by the ramshackle stairway. The space below the steps, where my tripper had stood, was clear. Behind it was a leaning stack of bulging cardboard boxes that were crushing one another. The corners of the bottom boxes had split open, oozing ancient copies of *Look* and *The Saturday Evening Post*. Other boxes contained dusty dishes, worn boots, blue bottles. . . . If there was a cave behind the leaning tower of junk, which there wasn't, and if the stack of boxes was meant to conceal the entrance, they were too heavy and treacherous to move to get in and out of the cave.

I looked for a trapdoor under the kitchen table that was covered with canning supplies. The floor was solid clay, hard as concrete, no trapdoor.

The rest of the space was occupied by the huge antique furnace, the two long oil tanks that served it, and the much newer gas furnace. A flashlight would have helped me see behind the tanks, but they were so close to the wall and the floor that it was obvious they did not conceal a tunnel.

The two furnaces, one at each end of the tanks, stood a foot or two away from the walls, and so it was easy enough to see there was no cave behind them.

I was ready to throw in the towel down here. Maybe there was another cellar after all. I'd have to find the secret stairway. I'd have to search the whole house, pounding on walls, looking for trapdoors.

Or maybe there was no cave. How could I believe what Esther Dubbs had said? I probably put the idea of a cave in her head and then believed what I wanted to believe she was saying. An idiot listening to a crazy woman. It was time to quit playing detective and forget this nonsense. Maybe the Garths' murders would never be solved. If the cops couldn't solve them, what made me think I could?

It was another moment of despair, and I was at the bottom of the turning wheel when the voice in my head said shape up, doofus. If there's nothing here, why did some other doofus trip you down the steps? It's here. It's right in front of you. Open your eyes.

I stared at the old furnace. It looked like a monster, squatting, waiting. It was big enough to heat the *Gleaner* building. Why did a house this size need such a big furnace? I noticed that it had no air ducts and that its topmost section was gone. A vinyl shower curtain was tied over the opening. I suspected that the furnace had once fed heat directly into the first floor through a large iron grate, but such a register would have been in the middle of the house, not the back. What's more, the old, rough-sawn floor joists passed directly above the furnace. There was no sign that a register had ever been there.

I went over for a closer look. I squeezed behind the fat cylindrical chamber and got a black smear on my shirt and pants. I gave the monster a whack. The metal fabric shook, and a wisp of cool air touched my fingers. The air escaped through a slit where two sheets of curved metal overlapped. I held my palm over the slit and felt the faint rush of air.

I grabbed the side of the furnace and tried to move it, pressing, sliding, shaking, pulling, lifting. . . .

The metal panel rose an inch or so and came free. I gave it a push, and it slid sideways, wrapping around the outside of the furnace to reveal several wooden steps dug into the earth. I could barely see them, but I counted five steps that disappeared into a low tunnel. A steady blast of cool air blew out of the cave, fanning my hot face.

CHAPTER 29
Brains and Muscle

THE "FURNACE" was merely a shell. Its only purpose was to conceal the cave. The inside parts—burner, blower, filters, everything—had been removed. The dug-in concrete blocks on which the furnace stood formed a ragged ring under the cylindrical chamber, and the earth inside the ring had been removed to expand the entrance to the cave. The makeshift steps slanted steeply for the first few feet, and then bare rock tapered downward out of sight.

Did I really want to go down there? I could hardly see the bottom of the black hole. I'd bash my brains out if I tried to feel my way through the cave. I knew I'd have to get a flashlight to explore it, but for now I decided to go as far as I could. The .45 pistol was sticking out of my side pocket, so I put it under my shirt inside the back of my belt, the way they do on TV.

The wooden steps, though resting on solid ground, gave slightly as I went down. My shoes reached the stone floor as my waist passed the rim of the hole. I eased myself lower. With my hands on the clay in front of me and my back slightly bent, I slid slowly down the smooth limestone until the floor leveled off. When I stooped at the bottom of the hole, I spotted a light switch next to my ear. "Thank you, God," I said, "if you exist."

I flicked the switch, and a crooked line of fluorescent bulbs came on. The metal box that held the switch was attached to plastic conduit that pierced the clay from above. A few feet away, the clay gave way to limestone. I figured I was under the back wall of the house. The conduit and light bulbs stretched ahead of me in the upper-righthand corner of the rising and falling passageway.

I had to stoop or walk on all fours to make sure my head did not hit the roof of the cave or the lights. On the ground below nearly every bulb were shards of glass. The limestone cave widened and narrowed, and cool air streamed past my face. Once in a while I could walk almost standing, but sometimes I had to crawl on my hands and knees. I wasn't sure, but I thought I was heading toward the hill behind the house, and when I saw wet spots on the walls, I guessed I was under the creek at the foot of the hill. Erosion channels meandered at my feet, and the smooth walls suggested that the tunnel flooded.

After a hundred feet or so, the passage forked, bending upward toward a vertical oval of bright light and downward into an opening just inches high, where water could escape. I stopped and listened, but there was no sound. I wondered if I had turned on the light up ahead when I flicked the switch back at the steps. I crept on like a hunchback.

At the bright oval I squeezed into a low cavern that was about fifty feet long and half as wide. Its entire length was divided by a curtain of clear plastic sheeting that looked like the Mylar the pressmen used at the *Gleaner*. Several bright lights hung behind the curtain. I parted two of the sheets and stepped through. It was hot behind the curtain—no cool breezes here. Ten high-intensity lamps with aluminum shades hung from the rippled ceiling.

Below them on the tilted, layered floor, where limestone ripples overlapped one another, stood several dozen huge clay pots containing tall, black, wilted plants—marijuana.

Beyond the pots of dead pot were at least a dozen multisection plastic containers with new plants starting in them, maybe two hundred shoots in all. The Garths had probably been cultivating marijuana down here, and when they had been murdered, their crop died with them. But what about the little green shoots—who had planted those? It had to be Walter Boofey, I thought. Who else could it have been? Paula? Maybe, but I didn't want to think so.

I wandered among the stricken plants. It was quite an operation. Literally underground. Far safer than growing the stuff in a field, where the police might spot it from the air. What's more, the police would be unable to detect the heat from these lamps. We had run a feature in the paper on how they used heat sensors to locate marijuana being grown indoors. Their sensors would never penetrate a limestone cave under a hill.

I was also willing to bet that the electricity for the lamps in the cave came from the solar panels on the roof of the house and not from the Meridian County Rural Electric Membership Corporation. It was a way for Garth to hide the amount of electricity he was using. Glenn Neidig had told me that the Garths had also been thinking about erecting a windmill to generate even more power. Perhaps they had plans to expand.

The more I thought about it, the more I was impressed with the criminal mind of Wayne Garth. He could have run electrical conduit to this cave simply by taking it down the steps inside the furnace; however, that could have drawn attention to the furnace, and he didn't want that. So he must have run a wire from the electronic components in the cellar across the ceiling to the back wall of the house, and probably outside, and then dug it down to the tunnel. Wow, all to keep anyone from finding the cave. The guy was good. A details man. He would have made a good editor.

I pushed out through the plastic and studied the rest of the cavern. Spread out on a ledge that was half the height of a table were garden tools, a large box of MiracleGro, a CD player and a pile of CDs, spare light bulbs, a pile of magazines, and a large orange bucket. Several cans of beer stood on a narrower ledge along with a box of Cheez-its and a bag of pretzels that was fastened with a clothespin. Two sleeping bags, an inflated airbed, and a pile of folded blankets lay inside the plastic sheeting, most likely because it was warmer there and sheltered from the constant draft. Paula had probably slept in one of them. Taped to the curved wall, a poster showed a marijuana plant's stages of growth.

Also taped on the wall were several small shots of a good-looking young couple. In one, the man had his arms wrapped around the woman's waist. She laughed as he nuzzled her neck. Other pictures showed the woman on a horse, the man smoking a joint, the woman in a field of daisies. Wayne and Cheryl Garth looked as if they had once been very happy.

I felt as if I were standing in a giant, elongated egg. Around me swirled shades of gray and white, oyster shell and pearl. A guy could get dizzy down here, claustrophobic, what with the ceiling that constantly seemed to be sinking and the walls that kept closing in. Everything was tilted or wavy or curved.

I told myself I ought to go, I had seen enough. But I had to check one more thing. The cave did not end at the far wall. At the far end of the egg there was a mouthlike opening about six feet wide and no more than ten inches high. The cool breeze issued from the arch.

"Who the hell are you?"

The words echoed off the walls as I whirled around. A sawed-off double-barrelled shotgun came marching toward me, pointed at my chest. The man carrying it was a muscular widebody in his mid to late fifties. He had a square, craggy face and ink-black hair combed straight back.

"I'm Phil Larrison from the *Gleaner*," I said. "Are you Walter Boofey?"

His fleshy lips parted, and he ran his tongue around the inside of his cheek. His dark-brown eyes squinted as though he was trying to see me better. His nose had a slight twist, as if it had been broken once and never healed. He stopped six feet away. The end of the gun was two feet closer to my navel. "Yeah, that's me. And you're on my property—again."

"I'm sorry I came in without permission. I knocked on the door. I didn't think anyone was living here."

"So you thought you could walk right in."

"I said I'm sorry."

"That don't cut it."

The shotgun looked like a cannon. His finger twitched on the trigger. I was afraid it would go off by accident. "I was talking to your mother-in-law, Esther, this morning," I said. "She told me something that made me think there might be a cave under her old house. I came to see if I could find it."

"Why?"

"Not many houses have caves under them. I wondered if it might help explain why Wayne and Cheryl Garth were killed."

"Does it?"

"Those marijuana plants over there make me think it does."

I heard women's voices in the tunnel. One of them shouted, "Walter, are you okay? Who're you talking to?" Her words sounded as if they came out of an echo chamber.

Boofey shouted back, "I got a little surprise for you."

The first woman to emerge from the tunnel was a well-built redhead in tight jeans. I thought she must be Boofey's wife, Caroline, but she looked twenty years younger than he did. The second one was Paula. Her cast was gone, and she had cut her hair. She stared at me uncertainly. "Phil?" she said. "Don't tell me it's you again."

"It's me again. Good to see you, Paula."

"Jesus, you can't stay out of trouble."

"Looks that way, doesn't it?"

"Put the gun down, Uncle Walt," Paula said.

The gun went down a couple of inches.

The redhead said, "You're the guy that was here last week—in the cellar."

Up close, she looked older than I had thought. There were crow's feet around her mouth and eyes, and her neck was showing wrinkles. I upped my age estimate to forty-five, but then it occurred to me that she was probably another ten or fifteen years older if she was the daughter of Esther Dubbs, who was in her nineties. She was in terrific shape for fifty-five or sixty.

"You must be Caroline," I said.

"Must I?"

"I think so. I met your husband last week. I believe he accidentally tripped me while I was going down the steps."

Boofey said, "You got that wrong. I'm just the brains of the family. She's the muscle."

"Yeah, I did it," Caroline said. "I thought you were the bastard that murdered our tenants."

Paula said, "You're lucky you're still alive. Caroline was ready to break your neck."

"And she could do it if she wanted to," Boofey said. "She used to be a wrestler and a bodybuilder. She could pick you up and break your back." With a snap of his fingers he added, "Just like that."

"I'm impressed," I said. I almost asked her to strike a pose. "Thanks for not breaking my back."

"You can thank Paula for that," Boofey said.

"Thanks," I said to her.

"That's enough," Caroline said, fed up.

I kept looking at Paula. Her eyes met mine. Silently I mouthed another thank you. She frowned and looked away.

"What do we do with him, Brains?" Caroline said. "We can't just let him walk away this time."

"How's Edna Mae?" I asked Paula.

She rolled her eyes and said nothing.

Caroline said, "I'm getting tired of his squeaky voice."

"We'll tie him up and keep him down here," Boofey said.

"You could dump him in the quicksand," Caroline said.

"Quicksand?" I said. "Are you joking? Where's there quicksand around here?"

Boofey turned to his wife. "We can't risk it. The old geezer across the road might see us. He never sleeps."

I stretched my arms behind me as if flexing my back and went for the gun in my belt. Though he did not appear to be looking in my direction, Boofey took two quick steps and rammed the shotgun into my chest. It made a hollow thud, and it hurt.

"You think I don't know you got a gun, smartass?" he snarled. "Caroline, get it—behind him in his belt."

"God, Walt, what were you waiting for?" She ran behind me, pulled up my shirt, and yanked out the .45. Then she frisked me all over and took my wallet, keys, and cell phone. I felt naked.

"Do it with his gun," she said. "It won't make as big a mess."

Boofey shook his head. "Uh-uh. We need this place a few more days. I don't want his corpse stinkin' it up."

"You're not gonna shoot him!" Paula shrieked.

I began to feel scared. Really scared.

Caroline said, "He can put us all in prison, stupid."

"Do what you said," Paula told her uncle. "Tie him up. Keep him down here till you're done. But you can't shoot him. I won't let you. He helped me. He's my friend."

Caroline said, "You got the hots for him, that's all."

"Shut your face."

"Knock it off, both of you," Boofey shouted. "We're gonna tie him up. Paula, you don't go anywhere near him. You promise me that. Got it?"

Paula didn't answer.

"I don't want you down here unless me or Caroline's here too." He put his hands on Paula's shoulders and made her look him in the face. "I mean it, you hear me?"

"I hear you."

Caroline said, "You can't trust her, Walt. She's a bitch in heat."

Paula screamed at her: "You shut your filthy mouth. You're the only bitch around here." She turned to Boofey. "Don't forget, Walt, it was me that told you about Wayne. You owe me for that."

"Don't listen to her, Walt," said Lady Macbeth. "Shoot him. Get it over with."

"You ain't no murderer, Walter," Paula said.

All this time Boofey's shotgun remained focused on my belly button. I half expected Caroline to take matters into her own hands and blast me with the .45.

"What's the rush?" Boofey said. "Let me think on it for a while."

"Okay, you think," Caroline snapped. She whirled away in a huff and left the cavern. The .45 was still in her hand.

Boofey said, "I guess I'm too softhearted." He turned to me and growled, "Get down on your face. Move!"

"What's your game, Walter?" I said. "Why do you need the cave a few more days?"

"That's for me to know and you not to." He jabbed me with the gun again.

"Paula, what's going on?" I dropped to my knees and then my chest.

"The less you know, the better off you are," Paula said.

"Smart girl," Boofey said. "Now get me that rope over there—the thick one."

She fetched the coiled-up rope and handed it to Boofey. He sat on my rump and twisted my arms behind my back. He took a switchblade out of his pocket and cut the rope in half. He wrapped one piece around my wrists and forearms and tied what felt like a complicated knot.

When he finally got off me, he wound the other piece of rope around my ankles, bent my legs backward at the knees, and forced them down. I screamed in pain, but he just laughed and tied the end of the rope around my already bound arms.

"That oughta hold you." He planted a big hand on my head and pressed my face into the limestone as he pushed himself up. "Don't you go anywhere now."

I felt like a calf at a rodeo, all trussed up while the cowboy preens.

"Come on, Paula," he said. "We got things to do." He started toward the tunnel. When Paula hung back, he gave her a hard stare and his voice darkened. "Let's go, girl."

Her thin lips and gray eyes wavered. I thought she was going to say something to me, but she turned and walked past Boofey. I watched her slip into the tunnel in front of him.

I could hardly move. I felt as if the blood had already stopped flowing in my arms and legs. I wondered if I would ever see Jodie again. Then the lights went off.

CHAPTER 30
In the Dark

THE CAVE was pitch black and, except for the sound of my breathing, utterly quiet. I squirmed this way and that, inching along the tilted plane of limestone, trying to find with my knees or my face a rough spot in the stone to rub my bonds against. The rope was thick. It would take forever to wear it away, but what else did I have to do?

My hands were numb. My crotch itched. I could barely twitch my arms. My legs tingled as if a million tiny pins were jiggling up and down inside. My head began to ache.

I kept squirming. There was no jagged edge. The ancient waters that had carved out the cave had worn the rock smooth. Now and then I almost dozed off, but some pain or itch kept me from falling asleep. And I didn't want to sleep. I had to stay awake. I had to get loose before Boofey and his wife decided it was time to kill me.

Despite the steady breeze, I began to sweat. The cool air fanned the back of my head but did not make the sweating stop. I thought I felt the first tickle of a sore throat. I swallowed it away and rolled on my other side so the wind could blow in my face.

It became harder to breathe. I couldn't complete a deep breath. I opened my mouth in the crazy hope that the wind would blow into my lungs. I felt myself dozing off again, but the thought that I might stop breathing in my sleep kept me awake.

I lost track of time. How long had I been here? An hour? Two hours? Maybe I actually had fallen asleep. The darkness seemed palpable. It covered me like a rug. It crawled over me like an enormous centipede. Hundreds of centipedes were crawling into the cavern. . . .

On the edge of delirium, I remembered the opening at the far end of the cavern. Why hadn't I thought of it sooner? If I could get there, I might be able to find a place to rub through the rope and get loose. There must be another way out. I could follow the wind to its source. I had been wasting time. Suddenly I was in a panic to get in the wind tunnel before the Boofey gang came back. I squirmed like a lizard into the wind.

Because my legs were bent behind me and tied to the rope that was lashed around my arms, I could roll only one way. So I rolled myself 180 degrees in the direction I wanted to go, and then I squirmed on my side until the wind was in my face again and I could repeat the process. It was slow work, and I had no idea how far I was from the end of the cavern. I rolled and twisted again and again, always hoping my next roll would get me there.

The lights came on. I happened to be facing the plastic curtain, and the sudden brightness blinded me. When I shut my eyes, I saw nothing but crimson. I rolled away from the lights. My heart sank when I saw how close I was to the opening. My face was nearly inside the tunnel. I kept squirming.

Someone entered the cavern and came walking toward me. I could not see who it was, but when nothing was said right away, I expected the worst. I rejoiced at the sound of

Paula's voice: "You're lucky Walter and Caroline didn't catch you."

"Paula! Thank God. Help me get loose."

"I brought you something to eat."

"I don't want to eat. I want to get out of here."

"Sorry, Phil. You can't go yet."

"If I don't get out of here, I'm dead."

She came around and stared down at me. She held a small green plate in her hand. "Try not to worry. They won't hurt you."

"Yeah, sure. How you gonna stop them?"

"They're just nervous. They act cool, but they're in this thing over their heads and they're scared. So am I."

"They're crazy, Paula. Why do they need to kill me over a bunch of dead marijuana?"

She tightened her lips and said, "Here, Phil. I fixed you a ham sandwich. I'll help you with it."

She knelt beside me and held a pointed end of half the sandwich in front of my mouth. I caught a whiff of cheap perfume. It made me feel sorry for her, but I hardened my heart. "For Christ's sake, Paula, I'm not in the mood for a sandwich."

"It's all I got." She sat back on her haunches and gazed at me. "You shoulda never came back here. What are you doing here anyway?"

"Looking for you and your mother. Trying to find out what the hell is going on. Trying to figure out why your friends were murdered."

"I'm sorry you stopped and picked me up that night. I got you in a world of trouble."

"If you're sorry, then untie the rope."

She just looked at me.

"Okay," I said, "if you won't untie me, I'll get back to work." I began inching toward the mouth of the tunnel again.

"Uh-uh." She set the plate with the sandwich on the ground and stood up. Her scuffed Keds were inches from my chin. The bottoms of her jeans were thready. She wore a plain white T-shirt under an unbuttoned flannel shirt. "I can't let you leave, Phil." She grabbed the rope that was wound around my ankles and dragged me about ten feet away from the wall.

I said, "Thanks a lot, Paula. You're not being real good to me."

"I'm sorry."

"That's nice to know."

"Do you want your sandwich or not?"

"Give it to Walter. Stuff it down his throat."

"If you're going to act like that, I guess I'll go back upstairs."

"Oh, sorry if I'm acting rude. Maybe if I had some feeling left in my arms and legs, I could be a little bit more sociable."

"Does it hurt bad?" She knelt again and began rubbing my arm. I felt like mouthing off, but instead I let her rub. "Does that help?" she said.

"No."

She rubbed harder.

After a minute or so I said, "Paula, what did you get yourself into here? What's going on? Were Walter and the Garths in business together? Were they selling drugs?"

She stopped massaging and sat back. I saw the struggle in her eyes. "It ain't about drugs," she said. "It's got nothing to do with drugs."

"Those aren't dead roses over there."

"You don't know a thing about it." She gazed at the long plastic curtain. It looked like a gigantic oxygen tent. "Wayne and Cheryl grew a little for themselves, that's all."

"It was more than a little."

"They let their friends have some too, free. They gave me some the last time I saw them."

"They didn't want to make any money. They just loved to grow pot."

"They wasn't dealers."

"Maybe your uncle was paying them to grow it. Maybe that's how they paid their rent."

"No. You think you know everything, but you don't."

"Then talk to me. What don't I know?"

"None of your business."

"It *is* my business. I'm smack in the middle of it." I did not let up on her: "What was your job, Paula? Hauling the stuff up to Indianapolis. What'd you do, carry it in your cast?"

"You don't need to make fun of me," she said.

I felt like an idiot lying on the ground, roped up, arguing with her. "Just tell me what's going on," I said. "What have you got to lose? I can't hurt you. I can't go to the cops."

"You can't now, but later you could."

"Yeah, if I'm still alive."

Her lips tightened to a thin line. Her gray eyes wavered. "You ain't gonna die," she said.

The arm and shoulder I was lying on hurt, so I began to roll over. She pushed me onto my other side, which meant now she was behind me. When I flexed the sore shoulder, she began kneading it with both hands. I stared at a series of smooth steplike ripples that rose past my nose.

"What's the deal, Paula?" I asked again. "Do you know why Wayne and Cheryl were killed? Did they double-cross your uncle?"

She hammered my leg with the bottom of her fist. "No!"

"Who did it then? Do you have any idea?"

"The more you know, the more trouble you're in, so just shut up."

"So you do know who did it."

"I didn't say that."

"Tell me what you know. What difference does it make? Caroline's going to make Walter blow my head off anyway. I'll take the secret to my grave."

She exhaled with a long sigh. Her breath fell on my hair. I thought she was about to relent, but she merely stood up and stepped over me. "I've gotta go," she said. "The sandwich is there if you want it."

"Don't go," I said.

"I got to. They'll be back soon."

"Where'd they go?"

She gave me a little sarcastic laugh. "You never stop with the questions, do you?"

"Did they have an appointment with their psychiatrist?"

"Uh-oh, I better block off that opening before I go."

She went through the sheets of plastic, and I watched her ghostly image moving back and forth as she searched for something to put in front of the hole I had tried to reach. She came out empty-handed and said, "I'm sorry I gotta do this to you." She gripped the rope with both hands and dragged me on my side toward the entrance of the cavern. I jawboned her during the entire trip. Then she retrieved the sandwich and laid it next to my face again.

"I'll be down later," she said.

"Wait. If you know who murdered Wayne and Cheryl, tell me."

"See you later, Phil."

"Don't turn the lights off." It was both a demand and a plea.

She thought a moment and went behind the curtain again. She used a folded rag to loosen all but one of the hot bulbs.

"Thanks," I said as she came out.

She touched me on the shoulder and said, "I'll be back."

As soon as she was gone, I began twisting and turning and craning my neck to find some kind of sharp edge to fray the rope. If I could make it to the clay pots, I could smash one and maybe get a sharp piece. But what good would it do? My hands were useless. I went back to Plan A and started squirming and rolling toward the arched opening again. Call me Sisyphus, I said to myself. I worked at it for a good half hour, and then Paula returned, this time with Boofey.

"What happened to the lights?" he asked her.

"He shouldn't have to lay in the dark," Paula said.

"No lights. I don't want him gettin' loose."

"He can't get loose," Paula said. "Why are we torturing him?"

"We ain't torturin' him. He's tied up is all." He went through the plastic and screwed the bulbs back in.

Paula picked up the plate and uneaten sandwich and hid it behind a box.

When Boofey came back, he said, "I wish I could chain him to the wall."

"I said, "Too bad you don't have an iron maiden and a rack."

"Shut up, funny boy."

"I need to use the bathroom."

"Hold it in or wet yourself."

"Jesus, Walt," Paula said.

"All right. He can piss in the bucket, but you gotta get rid of it."

"Thanks a lot."

Boofey pulled my—or rather Edward's—.45 out of his back pocket and told Paula to untie me. He didn't need the gun. My arms and legs were so stiff and sore that I could hardly move them, much less try to escape. He used the gun to prod me through the plastic, where I got to pee in a rusty bucket. As soon as I zipped up, he put me in a headlock and swung me to the ground. My legs felt like wet noodles, and I went down easily. He sat on me again and began lashing my arms together, just like before.

While I was on my face, I noticed a string of large rocks that had been cleared to the side of the cavern. Some of them were broken and appeared to have fairly sharp edges. I filed the information for later use.

When Boofey was done hog-tying me, he dragged me out through the curtain. Along the way I said, "Hey there, Walt, why'd you kill Wayne and Cheryl?"

"Shut up, Phil!" Paula yelled. "Keep your trap shut!"

Boofey said, "You know something, Paula, I'm beginning to see why you like this guy. He's got spunk. He's an asshole, but he's got spunk. I don't like his manners though." With that, he flung my head and shoulders on the ground and drove his shoe into my ribs.

"You can blame yourself for that, Phil," Paula said.

Boofey chuckled. "I think he likes it."

Despite the pain, I gritted my teeth and said, "Yeah, it feels good. Want me to show you how it feels?"

"See what I mean." He kicked me again.

Paula turned away and left the cavern. Maybe she thought I wouldn't shoot off my mouth if she wasn't there. Or maybe she didn't want to see Uncle Walter work me over anymore.

"Anything else you want to say?" Boofey asked me.

For once I took Paula's advice and shut up. My ribs had taken enough. I pictured a dented fender, a kicked-in birdcage.

"I think you're learning," Boofey said.

He waited a moment to see if I had another comeback for him. Then he followed Paula into the tunnel.

I stared at the rocks behind the plastic curtain. A couple minutes later the lights went out.

CHAPTER 31
You're Dead, Newsboy

THE INSTANT the lights went out, I began wriggling across the floor. I had already plotted a course to the broken rocks behind the plastic curtain, which hung about six feet away from my knees, about ten from my nose. The rocks were another ten feet away. I tried to squirm toward them in a straight line. I didn't do any rolling. I was afraid of rolling in the wrong direction. I didn't know how much time I had before Walter or Caroline would return, but I knew they'd be back. The sleeping bags and rumpled bedding on the airbed indicated that they slept down here instead of up in the house. No doubt they were afraid to use the bedrooms. Whoever had murdered the Garths might surprise them in their sleep.

Despite the pain in my ribs, I inched my way up the shingled layers of stone. I began sweating in the breeze again. It seemed to be taking too long to reach the curtain, and soon I was worrying that I had veered in the wrong direction and was moving parallel to or even away from it. I resisted the urge to move more to my left. I forced myself to believe I was still on the right line. A minute later my forehead made contact with the stiff Mylar.

The heavy plastic reminded me of a burial shroud as it passed over my face. I still had to get through the clay pots. I thought I heard footsteps in the tunnel. I was sure that Boofey would catch me. The lights would come on any minute. This time he'd stomp me to a bloody pulp. I reproached myself for not taking a swing at him when I had my chance a little while ago, when I was taking a leak. What a coward I was. But I could barely stand. My arms were all but dead. Still, I wished I had done something. I could have pissed in his face. If he killed me now, at least I wouldn't die regretting that I hadn't fought back.

Knock it off, Larrison. Don't look back. Stop bellyaching. Look at the bright side—you got this far. Focus on the damn rocks. Save psychic energy. If you get caught, you get caught. You can't control that, so why worry about it?

My heart pounded and my breath heaved as I squirmed between the clay pots. I tried to forget about time. I just shoved and pushed. Shoulder. Upper arm. Hip. Thigh. Knee. The arm felt wet. Was it sweat or blood? I kept hearing footsteps in the tunnel. Belatedly it occurred to me that the lights would come on before anyone came through the tunnel. So I didn't have to worry about footsteps anymore. I forced my head between two large pots rather than go around either of them. I used an ear and cheek to push one aside. I squeezed through and tried to remember how many rows of pots there were. Like a deformed lizard, I wriggled on.

More pots.

Still more pots.

My head hit a rock.

I straightened myself out next to the string of stones and used my face to find a sharp or jagged edge that I could use to cut the rope. I wasn't fussy. The first rough edge I found seemed as good as any. The next challenge was to get myself turned around so that the rock and rope would meet. I did my rollover stunt toward the last row of clay pots and then wriggled and jiggled myself backward to the rocks. I tried to match up the one I had found with the section of rope that stretched from my folded-back legs to my forearms. I began rubbing the rope against what I hoped was the rough edge. I kept tension on the rope by raising my arms and legs as much as I could.

It wasn't easy. Without the wind, I broke out in a hot sweat as I rubbed and rubbed. The rope was thick, and as the minutes passed I began to doubt that I could cut through it. But I put myself in robot mode and kept on rubbing.

Time passed. Ten minutes? Thirty minutes? An hour? . . . I kept rubbing, kept trying to rub the same spot on the rope. I had no feeling in my arms. I wasn't even sure they were moving anymore. . . .

The rope snapped.

For a moment I thought I was dreaming. I emptied my lungs of air that I didn't know was in them. I stretched out my legs. The rope was still coiled tightly around my ankles, but now I could stretch out my legs and work them apart. The more I moved them, the looser the rope became. In a few minutes I had my feet untied. Then I went to work on the rope around my arms. I sat down and rubbed it against a rock behind my back. At the same time I tried to move my arms back and forth, up and down. It didn't take forever, but it took quite a while. Finally I managed to sever it and jiggle my arms free.

My fingers felt like claws, my arms like lead. As I got up, a wave of dizziness made my head swim. I used the low ceiling to steady myself. I tried to shake the stiffness out of my arms one at a time. I rotated my shoulders and flexed my back. I hammered my legs with my fists.

I tried to decide what to do next. My brain seemed to have slowed down. Bright sparkles flashed in my head. I walked into a wilted marijuana stalk and kicked the clay pot. I felt my way through the grove of dead plants to the plastic curtain.

I did not know where I had seen the tools. On a ledge somewhere. I could feel my way along the wall. I needed a hammer or a wrench—some kind of weapon. Or should I head for the hole at the end of the cavern where the wind came from? Where was it coming from? Maybe all I had to do was walk into the wind until I found another way out from under the hill. I needed a flashlight. Maybe there was one with the tools. Or should I go back through the tunnel to the cellar? I'd have to feel my way in the dark. But maybe the Goofeys and Paula were gone. Maybe they went out for supper. I could just walk out the front door. If they were still in the house—if I heard them upstairs—I could turn on the lights and come back to the cavern. It'd be easy to find a hammer or something if the lights were on.

It took an effort of will to make up my mind. I started moving to the right, with my hand on the curtain. I knew it ended near the entrance to the tunnel, but I did not expect my head to bump into the ceiling only a few seconds later. If I had made up my mind sooner, I would have been half-way to the light switch by now.

I felt my way a few steps to the left and squeezed through the narrow opening. With my fingers on the conduit overhead, I walked slowly, bending, stooping, or crawling as the ceiling lowered. My head felt clearer now. The constant breeze blew up my pants legs and fanned the back of my head, pushing me forward. I moved as fast as I dared in the darkness.

Before I knew it I reached the dug-in steps under the furnace. I thought it should have taken much longer. Time must have speeded up. I wanted to think about that, but I made myself focus. I found the light switch and turned it on. The tunnel closed in around me. It seemed more cramped than I remembered. The walls were moving closer. I told myself my senses were out of whack.

Having made it so far so soon, I had a sense of invincibility. I was tempted to go straight up to the cellar and kitchen. Then all I'd have to do is get out the back door. If the Boofeys were there eating supper, I'd take them by surprise and make a dash for the door. Once outside, I could head for the cornfield.

I stopped myself. Too many things could go wrong. The door might be locked. Boofey might have his gun next to him. Caroline could probably outrun me. She was in shape, and I was sore all over. I stuck with my plan and went back to the cavern.

Among the tools scattered on the ledge were a sledgehammer, several screwdrivers, a spade, a maul, a rusty crowbar with a curved end, and an assortment of small gardening tools. There was also a long silver flashlight. I grabbed the crowbar and flashlight and went back through the tunnel. My luck was holding—no one came down to check on me. I poked my head up inside the furnace. The back of it was open. I took this to mean that one or more of the Boofeys were upstairs. I reasoned that they would have shut the furnace if they had planned on leaving the house; otherwise, they'd have left it open so they could get to the cave fast if they had to.

I heard voices in the kitchen. I turned on the flashlight and climbed into the furnace. I moved slowly and carefully to avoid banging the sides. I heard Paula say, "It needs cleaned."

Caroline replied, "So clean it. What else have you got to do?"

"I did it the last time," Paula snapped.

A third woman said, "Don't fight. I'll do it." The voice was soft and low, but I recognized it as Edna Mae's. So the gang's all here, I said to myself.

"It ain't your job," Paula said.

A fist slammed the table and rattled the dishes. "Knock it off," Boofey shouted. "You're gettin' on my nerves."

"Everybody's nervous," Edna Mae said. "Let's just calm down and relax."

The room fell silent, except for the clink of knives and forks.

I panned the cellar with the flashlight. It was too bad there was no outside door—I'd be gone already. If I had a shovel, I could dig my way out. Yeah, right, maybe if I had a week. The clay felt like solid rock. If I could find a place to hide, the next time Boofey went down to the cave, I could make my break. Paula wouldn't try to stop me, and I didn't think her mother would either. I might have to deal with Caroline, but after what she did to me, I wouldn't mind smashing her with the crowbar.

My heart raced. The lights in the cave were still on. As soon as Boofey discovered this, he might realize I was already in the cellar. Or he might think I got loose and turned them on so I could find a light and look for another way out of the cave. But more likely he'd think Paula had turned them on for me. On the other hand, Boofey might not be the first one to return to the cave. Anyone else would think he had left the lights on, not me. . . .

Forget it, Larrison. There's no place to hide in the cellar, so it doesn't matter what Boofey might think. Anyway, hiding's lame. You gotta be proactive.

Edna Mae broke the silence in the kitchen: "So what are you going to do with him?"

No one answered her.

"Well, what?" Edna Mae insisted.

"I say we leave him tied up where he is," Boofey answered. "By the time he gets loose—if he ever does—we'll be long gone."

Caroline said, "It's too big a risk. He knows too much."

"He don't know nothing," Paula said. "He thinks it's all about marijuana."

"You didn't tell him anything, I hope," Boofey said.

"Are you listening to me? I just said he don't know a thing."

"For Christ's sake," Caroline said, "he knows *us!* He can identify us, for Christ's sake."

"So what? It don't matter if they can't find us," Paula said.

"We can't take chances," Boofey said. "If they know who we are, they might track us."

"You said we'd be safe once we got out of the country."

"I said we'd be safe from the police. Not from bounty hunters."

A chair scraped back from the table, and Paula yelled, "You're gonna get us all killed. Before it's over, we'll all be dead."

"Not if we play our cards right," Boofey said.

Caroline said, "If anybody gets us killed, it'll be you. You've got to get over him. Get him out of your head."

"Mind your own business," Paula said.

"She's the weak link," Caroline said.

"Shut your damn face," Paula told her.

Edna Mae said, "Paula, sit down. Eat your supper."

"I ain't hungry," Paula said. "I'm going down to check on Phil."

"No you're not. Leave him be," Boofey ordered.

"See what I mean," Caroline said. "We're at each other's throats because of him. We have got to get rid of him. We're wasting too much time fighting about him. We've got things to do." There was a long pause. Then she said, "Walter! Are you listening? We've got things to do. We can't keep screwing around."

"I'm tryin' to eat," Boofey said.

"All right," Caroline said with false calmness, "you keep trying to eat. I'll take care of our problem right now."

I heard two quick steps and a loud crash. It sounded like the back of a chair and the back of someone's head hitting the floor. Paula must have pulled Caroline's chair backward before she could get up. A flurry of bumps and thumps erupted. Chairs banged the table. Edna Mae screamed, "Stop it, stop it, stop it!" Her words turned to gasps for breath. "Damn it, Walt, help me," she cried.

Boofey laughed. "They're like two alley cats. Let them tear each other's eyes out."

I thought about taking advantage of the melee to make a break for it. If I could open the cellar door and get into the laundry room without being seen, I could use the other door to get into the living room and make a dash for the front door. I started up the steps, but then someone went into the laundry room, and I went back down.

I heard water running in the laundry room. It sounded like a bucket being filled. Heavy footsteps plodded back to the kitchen. "This might cool them off," Boofey said. Paula and Caroline squealed in anger when he emptied the bucket on them. A thin trickle came down through the floor.

Boofey and Edna Mae finally separated the wrestlers.

"Whose side are you on?" Caroline yelled at her husband.

"My side," he replied.

"It's all her fault," Caroline said. "She's the weak link."

"Stinking bitch," Paula yelled at her.

"You better hold on to her, Edna Mae, or I'll break her skull."

"Dry yourselves off," Boofey said.

"She's the weak link," Caroline shouted at him. "She's gonna screw everything up."

Edna Mae said, "Paula is not weak. She's stronger than any of us."

"Bullshit," Caroline said. "Let go of me, Walt. Damn it, let me go."

"No more fightin'," he said.

"Screw you."

Her footsteps slapped through the water as she left the kitchen. Someone began picking up the fallen chairs. A moment later Caroline returned. She hadn't had time to dry off. She walked quickly through the kitchen, and when she reached the laundry room, she said, "I'm going to solve our problem right now." She opened the cellar door.

Paula cried out, "She's got a gun. She's gonna kill him!"

I got under the steps as Caroline started down.

Boofey yelled, "Stay here, hon. I'll do it."

Caroline did not stop. As she took her next step, I hooked the curved end of the crowbar around her ankle and yanked it backward. She pitched forward yelling,

"Walt, it's him!" She came down hard on the bottom steps and moaned in pain, but she did not black out.

I saw the .45 in her hand and made a dash for the furnace. The breeze was in my face. I thought a bullet nicked the heel of my shoe a millionth of a second before I heard the blast.

Walter nearly flew down the steps. "I'll kill you, you bastard, I'll kill you," he yelled, but, gentleman that he was, he stopped to help his wife first.

"Get him," she screamed. "Here, take the gun."

I jumped down into the hole and twisted myself into the tunnel. I crouched and scrambled as fast as I could. I broke light bulbs with the crowbar as I ran, hoping the darkness would slow Boofey down. I heard him crash against the furnace as he came after me. I had to get around the first bend in the tunnel before he'd start shooting. I popped another energy-saving bulb, then another. A shot slammed into the wall in front of me just as I made the turn.

"You ain't goin' nowhere," Boofey yelled. "You're dead, newsboy."

I felt like saying, "We'll see about that, Goofey," but why make him mad?

Breaking the bulbs did slow him down, but when I had to get on all fours, it was hard to crawl with a crowbar in one hand and a flashlight in the other, so I let go of the crowbar. I reached the last bulb in the tunnel and whacked it with the flashlight, but the cavern was all lit up. I thought about waiting for Boofey right here and smashing him in the face with the flashlight when he reached me. But he had a gun. I sprinted toward the low opening at the far end of the cave.

It felt like a surrealist dream as I ran across the slanted ripples through a stretched-out, narrowing egg. The egg seemed to get longer, and I seemed to move slower and slower. I began to panic. I was completely exposed in the cavern. Boofey would have a clear shot at me as soon as he got out of the tunnel. I had made the wrong move. I should have ambushed him. I should have clubbed him with the flashlight.

I glanced back and saw him squeezing out of the tunnel. I was about eight feet from the low opening. It looked like a mouth waiting to slurp me up. I dove at it as Boofey opened fire.

CHAPTER 32
Into the Wind

BULLETS ZINGED off the floor. Boofey's shoes slapped on the limestone as he ran, shooting at my feet as I slid head first through the arched opening. I was in a low passage that was little more than a foot high and angled slightly to the right. Blood pounded in my ears as I slithered as fast as I could, pressed against the side of the cave.

The gun clicked twice. Boofey swore and tossed it away. I stopped crawling and looked back past my shoulder. Boofey's sideways face was staring straight at me. A shiver ran down my spine. I had to convince myself he couldn't see me. I lay still, wondering if he was going to crawl in after me. The ever-present breeze felt cold on the back of my neck.

"Walter!" his wife called from the other end of the cavern. "Did you get him?"

"Does it look like it?" he yelled at her. "He's in there. Get me the flashlight."

His face rose out of sight. I turned around and shimmied backward into the tunnel. The lowering space scraped my rear end. I was afraid I couldn't go much farther. The entire weight of the hill seemed to press down on me. If Caroline had the shotgun with her, I could be dead any moment. With that thought in mind, I forced myself back even more, until most of my body was twisted around the bend in the tunnel. Only my eyes and forehead stuck out past the edge of the wall. I felt as if a snake had swallowed me and I could still see Boofey's shoes through its open mouth.

"Where'd you put the flashlight?" Caroline said.

"I didn't put it anywhere," Boofey yelled angrily.

"I don't see it. It's not here."

"Shit. The asshole must have it."

Caroline's legs appeared next to Boofey's in front of the snake's mouth. "It'll be hard to get down here until we put some new light bulbs in the tunnel. Did he break them?"

"No. *I* broke 'em. Shit! Of course he broke 'em."

"I'll go upstairs and take a few out of the lamps." Her legs disappeared.

"Bring me the shotgun and a box of shells," Boofey said. "And see if you can find another flashlight somewhere."

"I can't carry everything."

"Just get it!"

"All right already. Cool it. It's not my fault he got loose."

I crawled back toward the opening. I thought if Boofey moved away from it, I might be able to crawl out and take him on. I had the flashlight for a weapon. But before Caroline reached the other end of the cavern, Paula and Edna Mae appeared.

"What happened to the lights?" Edna Mae said.

"Her boyfriend busted them," Caroline said.

"Shut up," Paula snapped.

Here we go again, I said to myself.

"Where are you going?" Edna Mae said.

Caroline disappeared into the tunnel.

"Where's Phil?" Paula called to Uncle Walter.

"In there," he said.

I had an odd perspective: Boofey's baggy cuffs and shoes were in the foreground, while the miniature figures of Paula and her mother were far away, as if I were looking at them through the wrong end of a telescope.

"Is he okay?" Paula said, running forward.

Walter did not deign to answer.

"Did you shoot him?" she demanded.

"I don't know. I hope so."

"You bastard," Paula said. "You ain't my uncle no more."

Edna Mae said, "We never signed on for this, Walter. We didn't know there would be any killing."

I moved closer to the opening, but not close enough to be seen.

Boofey growled, "I didn't say I killed him. Caroline went to find a flashlight. Then we'll see if he's dead or alive."

Paula shouted, "Phil! Are you all right?" When I didn't answer, she said, "I'm going in there and find him."

"The hell you are," Boofey said. "You're stayin' right here."

"Take your hand off me," Paula said. When he didn't let go, she slapped him.

Boofey grabbed her by the neck and said, "It's time you learned some respect, girl." He smacked her on the side of the head. She cried in pain as she sprawled on the ground.

Edna Mae ran and knelt down beside her. "Damn it, Walter, what's got into you? This has gone too far. It's not worth it. I don't care how much money we get. Paula and me are leaving right now."

"You leave when I say you can leave, not a damn minute before."

"You can't keep us here," Edna Mae said.

"Oh no?"

"I'm your sister, Walter, not your slave."

He leveled a finger at her. "You're in this till it's over. Got it?"

Paula said, "You can go to hell."

Caroline returned sooner than I expected. "I put a couple bulbs in," she said. At least you can see a little in there now. I couldn't find a flashlight, but here's the gun." She stopped and stared at Paula, who was just getting up. "What happened?"

"She mouthed off once too often," Boofey said.

"Come on, get up, Paula," Edna Mae said. "We're gettin' outta here."

Boofey said, "You listen to me, Edna Mae, and listen good. If I have to, I'll tie the both of you up till this is over with. I mean it." He took the sawed-off shotgun from Caroline and broke it open to see if it was loaded.

Paula screamed. "Phil, run! He's got a shotgun."

She didn't need to tell me. I was already scrambling back to the bend in the tunnel. I squeezed into the thin slit until I could hardly breathe. The two blasts were so loud I thought the roof would come down on me. Buckshot peppered the walls. I clawed my way a foot or two deeper into the darkness while Boofey reloaded. I was afraid he would angle the gun in from the left side of the opening and the buckshot would reach me around the bend on the right. I pushed with my feet to get a few more inches deeper into the tunnel.

The stone that was squashing me came to an end. I raised my head, then my shoulders. Boofey blasted away again, but the pellets sprayed harmlessly behind me. I dragged myself out of the slit and switched on the flashlight. A high chamber, much larger than the marijuana cave, expanded around me. Stalactites hung like thick icicles, and obese stalagmites reached up to join them. I pointed the light this way and that. Shadows fled up the walls or closed around me.

It was an eerie landscape, but I didn't hang around to study it. I started across what looked like a petrified glacier pushing through the left side of the cavern. I had only one way to go, into the wind, and I dashed through the weird landscape before somebody would start shooting again. If someone did, it would be Caroline, because Walter was too thick to fit through the tunnel. But Caroline had no flashlight, so she wouldn't be coming anytime soon.

The cavern narrowed, and the limestone floor cascaded into a vertical pit. The only thing that gave me the nerve to climb down in it was an empty Miller Lite can standing on a rock. Someone had done this before me, so I knew it could be done. Of course I might find the bones of the beer drinker at the bottom of the pit. I went down anyway.

In daylight it would have been an easy descent. With a flashlight it was a major challenge. I took my time, checking with the light before each move. There were lots of good handholds and footholds, and I made it down without breaking any bones. The biggest problem was the wind. It made my hands cold.

At the bottom, the cave was a low, broad, irregular opening that meandered through a field of boulders. Next, it slanted upward at an angle that was only slightly less steep than that of the pit. I stuck the flashlight in my belt to illuminate the face of the rock above me and began climbing. In about ten minutes the tunnel turned into a chute that resembled a waterslide and then leveled off again, more or less.

Other openings appeared as I crawled along. I poked the light inside them, but I stayed in what appeared to be the main tunnel. I didn't want to get lost in a maze, and I figured that as long as I stayed on the main drag, I could always retrace my steps if I had to—unless the batteries in the flashlight died.

Don't think about that, I said to myself. Just move. Faster.

Despite all the twists and turns, the wind still blew through the tunnel. I wondered how far I had come and where I was headed. I wondered if there were tunnels like this all through the knobs. The uneven terrain took a toll on my legs and back. Now and then I was able to stand, but most of the time I had to crouch or crawl. I squeezed between gray, white, creamy boulders and tripped on limestone ripples. The tunnel would drop, angle upward, bend back on itself. I had no sense of direction. I did not know if I was heading toward the far side of the hill or back toward the hollow. But the bias was definitely downward.

I stooped. I crawled. I squeezed through tight spaces. I climbed over rocks. I worried about the flashlight. What would I do if the batteries died? I would feel my way in the dark—what else could I do? I'd fall in a pit and break my skull. Without the light, I'd be dead in no time. I may have had a better chance of surviving if I had gone after Boofey and his wife in the marijuana cave. I should have waited for them to leave the cavern. I could have ambushed them in the cave or the cellar. At least then I would have had a chance. It was stupid to come in here. It was a deathtrap.

I ought to turn around right now and go back, while the flashlight was still working.

The tunnel forked. It was purely a guess which way I should go. Maybe someone had blazed a trail. I searched the walls for a mark, a scratch. Nothing. I chose the passage on the right and scraped an arrow in the stone in case I had to backtrack, or if the tunnel looped around on itself without my realizing it.

I had a single-minded mission now: keep moving, and move fast, before the light quit. It was still bright, but how long would it last? Wherever I pointed it, a black shape seemed to duck behind a rock. Another fork divided in front of me. I made a guess and scratched an arrow on the wall. What difference did it make which way I went?

Suddenly I felt tired, as if the adrenaline that had been pumping through my veins just gave out. The strength drained out of my legs. I pressed ahead as if I had a deadline to make, but it got harder and harder to move. Then it occurred to me that I could stop if I wanted to. I could rest as long as I wanted, because I had nothing else to do. The Boofeys weren't coming after me. I could switch off the flashlight and go to sleep. It would save the batteries. It was a simple realization, but it felt like a major discovery. I lay down and turned off the light. Absolute darkness covered me like a shroud. There was nothing but darkness. I reached up and touched the top of the tunnel to make sure it was still there. The smooth limestone felt like the lid of a coffin.

I did not think I'd be able to sleep, but a half-awake dream began playing. I was crawling through a rocky tunnel that came to a dead end, but when I turned around I saw another tunnel feeding into it. Then there were several tunnels feeding in, with others feeding into them. . . .

I jerked awake. I felt as though I had been asleep just a few minutes, but I was drenched in sweat and I had another headache. My arms were stiff. The bones in my legs felt brittle. I tried to flex my fingers and toes. The joints were stiff, frozen, arthritic. I tried to raise my knees, but my ribs rebelled in pain. I felt as if I were slowly being pulled apart, stretched on a rack in utter darkness. I was still dreaming.

Were my eyes open or closed? I made a conscious effort to open them, to close them. It made no difference. Either way I saw nothing but nothingness. But I could feel. My back was sore. It was something. I hurt, therefore I am. The wind streamed past my ears. . . .

I felt for the flashlight, found it, felt for the switch. Had I fallen asleep again? Was I really awake? I was able to move. My head still ached. I turned on the light. I was still alive. Where there's light, there's life. I felt a burst of energy. At the same time I was hungry, starving. I felt as if I hadn't eaten in days.

I did not know which way to go. I remembered the arrows I had etched in the wall. There was one right next to me, pointing in what seemed like the wrong direction, but it was my arrow. I had to trust it. I began crawling again.

If I had been traveling in a straight line, I would have reached the other side of the hill by now. The distance from one side to the other was not great. I knew this from having climbed the hill. It was steep on both sides. The ridge was barely as wide as a one-lane road. But I had not traveled in a straight line. I had gone up and down and in every direction. All I could do was keep moving. Eventually, if I lived long enough, I'd cover every inch of the cave system. If there was another way out, I'd find it.

It was a good thing I was on my hands and knees. Had I been on my feet, in another second I might have fallen into the hole where the wind came from. Air rushed up from deep in the earth. I heard water falling far below, but all I could see with the flashlight were the smooth sides of a limestone shaft that was impossible for me to climb down.

I dropped a rock into the shaft, but the sound of the wind beating on my eardrums kept me from hearing it hit bottom. I dropped several more rocks. I tried covering one ear and holding my head out of the wind, but nothing worked. When I finally grasped that the wind was not going to be my ticket out of the cave, I was tempted to play a little poker and go all in by jumping into the shaft. If I got lucky and hit deep-enough water, maybe an underground river would carry me out of the cave. But more likely I'd break every bone in my body or end up drowning in the Meridian County aquifer.

Weirdly, as my hope of escape faded, I thought of Jodie. That hope too was fading. I stared into the hole. All I had to do was let myself go and the misery would end. I felt myself tipping forward. . . .

I pulled back. I was shaking all over. I couldn't do it. Why not? What difference did it make if I died a quick death now or a slow one by starvation? It does make a difference, I said to myself. You've got to play the game out. Why? You just have to.

When I stopped shaking, I crawled around the edge of the shaft. The ledge was only a foot or so wide. Wouldn't it be wonderfully ironic if I fell into the hole now that I had performed my puny existential act? It wasn't to be. I made it to the other side of the shaft and kept on crawling. I felt like an insignificant bug in a meaningless universe.

The wind was gone. It was no longer in my face, and it was not at my back. I assumed it meant there was no outlet for the wind in this direction. Did the Garth house draw it the other way? Did the wind stop blowing whenever the furnace was closed? No, that was ridiculous. There must be another outlet somewhere back that way. I had been going the wrong way. I should have been moving with the wind at my back. There must be a place where it branches off.

I was about to turn around, but just then the flashlight picked up something shiny ahead of me. I scrabbled over loose rocks and found a wrapper from an Almond Joy bar. It was enough to keep me going.

The tunnel got smaller. I slithered on my belly. I was tearing my clothes to shreds. After a few yards I was able to crawl on all fours again. There were more forks, more dead ends. I scratched my arrows on the walls, and on one occasion it paid off when the tunnel I had chosen circled into itself and I found myself facing the arrow I had drawn a few minutes earlier.

Hours passed. I rested again, this time sitting with my back against a wall that was curved like a beach chair. In case I fell asleep again, I made a mental note to go left when I'd wake up. I did fall asleep, and this time I had no nightmares. When I woke up, I went left.

Some of the crevices were so narrow that I could barely squeeze through them. Other times they grew into small caverns, all curves and ripples like the marijuana cave. I wondered if anyone else knew about these caves. Wayne and Cheryl Garth probably had. Spelunkers would have a field day in here. If I ever got out, I'd have to write a feature about them. I'd have to get some photos of those stalactites and stalagmites. . . .

I was on my hands and knees. The roof of the tunnel sloped downward. I thought I might run out of room in this branch. It got so tight that I was afraid I might get wedged between the rocks. But the tunnel appeared to widen ahead, so I kept squeezing through. Then I caught a faint whiff of something bad. A dead animal? A dead litterbug?

The flashlight glimmered on something bright. I expected to find another beer can. I lay my head sideways and held the light in front of it. A noxious odor hit me in the face.

Several yards away I saw the bottom rims of several large yellow drums. I wondered if I was hallucinating. I squiggled through the opening. The drums stood close to the wall. If they had been any closer, I wouldn't have been able to get into the cavern. I stood up and walked behind them, holding my breath. The cavern sloped upward and around a bend. It was filled with fifty-five-gallon drums, hundreds of them, at least. The cavern was longer and wider than Boofey's torture chamber, and the drums disappeared like a river around the bend.

Most of the drums were gray or black. Some had stencilled markings on them. Others had labels. At a glance, they all looked rusty. The air reeked of chemicals. On one of the yellow drums near me, I saw the words Polychlorinated Biphenyls.

I was in a cave full of toxic chemicals—PCBs—and the drums were leaking.

CHAPTER 33
A Handful of Stars

I couldn't breathe. I was afraid to. "I gotta get outta here," I said. My voice bounced off the walls. "So move your ass already." I pulled my shirt up over my nose and zigzagged up the low grade through the drums. I felt contaminated. My eyes stung as they do when someone near you has a major case of body odor.

I had to watch where I stepped. Here and there a ribbon of liquid oozed from a drum and meandered across the floor as if searching for a crack. Halfway through the cavern, the limestone gave way to clay, which absorbed the chemicals. Some of the stacked drums were leaking onto those below, creating pools on the lids and flowing over the rims. Some of the drums that I passed had bills of lading in clear envelopes taped to the sides. I peeled one off. It showed that the drum had been shipped to Meridian Waste Managers from a company in Bloomington. So I was on MWM property. I had made it to the far side of the hill. The cave was probably connected to the old county landfill.

When I couldn't hold my breath any longer, I raised the top of my shirt and used it as a face mask again. I breathed through my mouth in a futile effort to avoid smelling the chemicals. My eyes were on fire. I blinked constantly, trying to make tears to wash the fumes away.

I wondered if Wayne Garth had discovered the drums just as I had. Glenn Neidig had called him an environmentalist. The old man said Garth was concerned that runoff from the closed landfill might get into his well. But Glenn hadn't said anything about drums of chemicals. He would have if he had known about them.

The wheels were turning.

Maybe Garth had threatened to report the leaking chemicals to the EPA. Maybe that's why he and his wife were killed. Didn't Paula say marijuana had nothing to do with it? But if the Garths were murdered to keep them from exposing the fact that the chemicals had been disposed of improperly, it meant the prime suspects were the owners of the landfill—the Brandons. So maybe the Garths had tried to blackmail the Brandons. Maybe that's what got them killed.

I didn't want to believe it. There had to be another explanation.

I let myself take a deep breath through the shirt. The more I thought about it, the more likely it seemed that someone in the Brandon family was behind the murders. The PCBs were leaking into the ground. It was a mind-blowing situation. Cleanup costs could run into the millions—many, many millions. Lillian Brandon had said her father and her uncle were negotiating to sell MWM. If word got out that their company had hundreds of leaking barrels of PCBs stashed in a cave, no one in his right mind would buy their company. Even more damning, Lillian had said the former county dump was not one of the landfills that were up for sale. Why not? Perhaps because the Brandons did not want to take the chance that a new owner would discover the drums and come after them for the cleanup costs.

And what about Boofey and his wife—how did they fit in? They were the ones who were acting like killers. I did an about-face: maybe the Brandons had not killed the Garths; maybe the Garths told Boofey about the PCBs and he saw an opportunity to cash in; maybe he got rid of Wayne and Cheryl before they decided to expose the chemical cave; maybe the Boofeys, not the Garths, were blackmailing the Brandons. I had heard Edna Mae tell Walter the whole thing wasn't worth it, no matter how much money they got. The blackmail plan might be going down right now.

Something else Paula said came back to me. "Don't forget," she had reminded Boofey, "it was me that told you about Wayne. You owe me for that." Perhaps she wasn't demanding credit for telling him about Wayne Garth as a possible tenant for the old house. Maybe she meant she had told him that Garth had been trying to blackmail the Brandons. Maybe she had somehow found out about the PCBs after disappearing from my car outside the Grapevines' house.

The flashlight sent a pale yellow beam across the drums. A sickly hole spread through my chest—the light was beginning to fade.

The herd of drums ended around the bend at the upper end of the cavern. Perhaps because the slanted floor carried the leaking chemicals away from me, the odor was less acrid where I now stood. About fifty feet away, the tunnel was filled with trash. The pile tapered toward me like a tongue sticking out of an eyeless face. Gouges on the walls and ceiling indicated that the cavern had been enlarged, but I could not tell how far I'd have to dig to get out. Was the entrance only a few yards away, or would I have to slog through a mile-long tunnel of rotten garbage?

I leaned the flashlight on a rock, pulled a short board out of the trash, and waded into the heap. The top of the cave was about seven feet high at this point. I knelt in the trash near the top of the pile and dug into it with the board. It took about ten seconds for me to learn that this was not going to be easy. I was not dealing with a pile of loose, everyday kitchen trash. I was dealing with tons of junk. Half buried around me were a baby's car seat, a grocery cart, a wading pool, a sofa, a box spring, a vacuum-cleaner bag, bricks, insulation, termite-riddled wood, rubber boots, a lawn mower, newspaper pages, dried-out garbage, brown diapers, a washing machine, an ironing board, an artificial Christmas tree, a woman's wig—you name it. And worst of all, everything was crushed and mixed in with dirt. I had wanted to use my little board as an oar and paddle my way through the trash, but it was nearly impossible to make any headway.

By the time I cleared a space about three feet long, my arms were already giving out. I gave them a rest and caught my breath. I had sunk several inches into the pile. I wondered if there was another entrance to the cave. "If you want to find it, garbage man," I said aloud again, "you'd better get going before the light goes out." I knew it was going to die sooner or later. If I had to, I could work on the trash pile in the dark.

I hauled myself out of the pile. One of my socks felt wet. I pulled up my pants leg and saw a glob of black grease on my ankle. I used a can to scrape off as much as I could.

The roof of the cavern sloped into a low tunnel. I didn't feel like crawling again, but I decided to give the tunnel a try, at least for a few minutes, in case a limousine was waiting for me at the other end.

I crawled into the tunnel. It did not look favorable. One more tight squeeze. I went about twenty feet and found another low passage on the right, which was the wrong way, back into the hill. I passed on it and came to a rocky drop, a slope I could get down on my behind. This tunnel angled toward the outer hillside, and my hopes began to rise. I climbed a low, craggy wall and entered another passage. The floor was rugged, stony, hard on the knees, but at least I was on my knees instead of my chest. The tunnel ended in a shallow pit shaped like a saucer.

I jerked back as the acid in my stomach rose to my throat. I felt hot and cold at the same time. My skin began to crawl.

In front of my face lay the skeletal remains of a child. Its head hung to the side at a ninety-degree angle. It was no more than four feet long. It wore a once-white T-shirt, ragged jeans, and black-and-white basketball shoes that looked like old-fashioned sneakers, the kind a boy would wear. A brown membrane of mummified skin clung to some of the bones in the hands and face. The eye sockets were empty, but a stretched tent of skin covered part of the skull, where a small patch of short, spindly hairs sprouted like dried-out grass.

The boy had died years ago, at least five, maybe even ten, but how the hell would I know? The cool temperature in the cave may have helped to preserve the remains, and evidently no animals, other than insects, had found the bones, even though they were exposed. The skeleton lay on its back. Perhaps the kid had been exploring the cave and had fallen and broken his neck. But there was nothing to climb in here—he could not have fallen very far. So how could he have broken his neck so severely? And if he was exploring, he must have had a flashlight or something.

I scanned the area with mine. Unless the skeleton was lying on it, there was no flashlight, lantern, or any other kind of light on the ground. Maybe a second kid had been with him. Maybe that kid took the light and went for help but got lost in the cave. There might be another skeleton lying somewhere. Or maybe the other kid was responsible for the boy's death and never reported it. Maybe they got in a fight. . . .

Come on, Larrison, how likely was that?

If a little kid disappeared, a massive search would have been launched. I remembered the *Gleaner* articles about the boy who had run away from the Good Shepherd Home and was never found. Maybe he had hidden in the cave. The entrance from the dump may not have been blocked by trash at the time. But he could not have gotten this far without a light. Again, of course, the skeleton might be covering it, but I wasn't about to move the bones to find out. Besides, the other problem remained: how could he have broken his neck so badly?

There was a simpler explanation. Perhaps the boy had not been exploring the cave or hiding in it. Perhaps someone had killed him somewhere else and dumped the body here.

Simple was good, but it wasn't quite that simple. If the entrance from the dump had not been blocked by trash, then all kinds of critters—dogs, rats, raccoons, coyotes, possums—would have found the body and ripped it apart. Everything but the clothing would be gone by now, and the clothing would be in shreds. Unless . . . unless the entrance had been blocked up with trash immediately after the body had been dumped.

My flashlight was now just a crinkly yellow glow. I had to get back to the trash heap before it died altogether.

I wasn't going to find another way out of the cave. My only hope was to dig my way out through the trash. I felt a new sense of urgency. I had to get out. I had to report what I had found to the police. I had stories to write.

I crawled as fast as I could. I felt as if the boy's skeleton was nipping at my heels. Usually the return trip seems to go faster, but the trip back to the trash pile seemed to take me twice as long. When I finally got there, I had trouble finding the board I had been using as a scoop. I was in a panic until I spotted it at the bottom of the pile. I must have dropped it there without thinking.

I climbed back up to the tunnel I had started and tore into the trash again. I felt stronger. I was charged, driven. I found some plastic Wal-Mart bags and wrapped them around my hands to cut down on nicks and cuts. I raked the little board through the dirt and loose bits of junk. I pulled out the larger pieces and flung them behind me. I raked, dug, pulled, and dragged as fast as I could while I still had a glimmer of light. It was tedious, disgusting work, but I made some progress. I told myself it was not an endless pile of trash. If I kept at it long enough, eventually I would get through. It was not infinite. Assorted junk and filth piled up behind me in the tunnel I was digging. Soon I was closed in, surrounded by trash. My little space was like a capsule moving through the trash.

I began to worry about running out of air. I worried that I'd run into some immovable barrier such as buried trees or slabs of concrete. Just dig, I said to myself. Worry about it if and when you have to. Think about something else.

I thought about the children at the Good Shepherd Home who had been taken to some pervert's house. I thought about Gary Fromm and the Professor. Did one of the kids get killed, accidentally or otherwise? Did one of them drown in the Professor's pond? Did Chuck Martin dump the body in the cave? No. Dumb idea. It violated my working hypothesis that the entrance was blocked right after the body was dumped. Martin could not have arranged that. But one of the Brandons—or someone who had worked for them—could.

The flashlight went out. I shook it to get every last photon out of it that I could. Then I tossed it behind me. The darkness was as black as pitch. It felt impenetrable. I had psyched myself up for this moment, but even so I began to feel depressed. I worked more slowly, feeling for a spot where I could jab the board. Now that I was in the dark, I gouged my hands constantly despite the plastic bags. I struggled to pull larger items past me. Like a blind galley slave, I plunged my oar into the sea of trash and swept it behind me. My arms, my shoulders, the back of my neck began to ache. Every minute or so I stopped to flex them.

I had no idea how wide the entrance to the cave was. I couldn't tell if I was digging in a straight line or if I had veered to one side or the other. I did know I was still at the top of the pile, because the roof of the cave was only an inch or two above my head. And I was nearly certain that my veer had not become a U-turn. In other words, I was not heading back where I had started. So I dug to the right until I reached the side of the tunnel, and then I made a left and hugged the wall. It meant extra digging, but at least I felt I was heading in the right direction.

One good thing happened: I found a curved piece of metal. It felt like a bicycle fender, and it penetrated the trash pile better than the board I'd been using. I went a little bit faster, but I had to stop and rest more often, and as I got more tired, I got more depressed. Sweat ran off me. My shirt stuck to my back, but I was afraid to take it off. It gave me a millimeter of protection against sharp-edged junk. At times I came to as if I had been digging in my sleep. My throat was dry and raw. If I had found a bottle with some liquid in it, I would have swallowed it no matter what it was.

You know, the voice said, you're not going to dig your way out of here. The entrance is blocked. It has to be. Boulders. Railroad ties. Concrete. Whoever hauled in those drums and whoever got rid of the boy's body didn't want them to be found. The entrance is sealed. Your only way out is to go back the way you came, and without a flashlight, that's impossible. You're dead, Larrison. You're dead.

Was I really dead? Maybe so. Maybe this was my hell. I'd dig on forever through light years of trash until I reached the barrier at the end of the tunnel and had to turn around and dig the other way. I should be grateful I wasn't digging through a cesspool for all eternity. But at least then I'd have something to drink.

I couldn't go any farther. I stuck the bike fender in the wall of trash so I'd know where to start digging again, and then I lay on a piece of linoleum and closed my eyes. I wondered why I closed my eyes. What did it matter if they were open or shut. Everything was black. But not solid black . . . shades of black . . . very slight gradations that seemed to pulse or jitter. . . .

I slept fitfully, waking often, always too tired to start digging again. I thought about Jodie, or rather half-thought, half-dreamed about her. Her feet splashed in the river. I kissed her again, but this time her face receded, becoming smaller and smaller, fading to an infinitely small point. I felt my arms moving, slashing through trash. Was

I awake or asleep? I woke myself up to see if I had been asleep. I smelled like garbage, or thought I did—I wasn't sure. I was part of the trash heap, indistinguishable from it, one with it. . . .

I pushed myself up. My back hurt from lying on something hard. I felt my way back into the hole I was carving out. I found the bicycle fender and began digging again. I chopped at the trash. I grabbed hunks of it and threw it behind me, over my shoulder, smack in my face. I started laughing. Don't laugh, I warned myself. I dug fiercely, frantically. Slow down. Pace yourself. I began talking out loud. I sang the few songs I knew. The more I dug, the more I despaired.

In a trance, I began to pray: Blessed be God. Blessed be His holy name. . . . I snapped out of it. It was hypocritical to pray. If I died and went to hell, it was where I deserved to go. It was wrong to try to save my soul with a deathbed confession, a coward in a heap of trash, a piece of shit. Blessed be darkness. Blessed be nothingness.

I dug.

I slept.

I came to a fork in the trash. Both tunnels were crammed with trash. I picked the wrong one. It spiraled downward. . . .

I woke up drowning in sweat. I felt for the wall. It was still there. I dug in blind compulsion, neither awake nor asleep.

I was dying of thirst. That was a good thing, wasn't it? It meant I was still alive.

I tried to gauge how far I had come. Fifty feet? A hundred? I had been digging for hours, maybe a day. It was impossible to tell. How long had I slept?

Don't think. Just dig. Don't think. Just dig. Don't think. Just—

A ton of dirt fell on me. I pressed my face into a crushed cardboard box and sucked for air. My arms and shoulders were pinned, but my legs were free. I used them to work my hips and chest from side to side. Dirt flowed into my ears. I pressed my arms into the trash and wiggled them as hard as I could in an effort to open crevices for the dirt to fall through, off of me.

I could hardly breathe. I thought I was drowning in dirt. My lungs were bursting. I forced my head into the trash and dirt.

I heard a loud, raspy noise. Locusts. I raised my head and saw a handful of stars through a hole in the clouds.

CHAPTER 34
Red Eyes

I DRAGGED myself out of the ground as if I were clawing my way out of my grave. The sky was a mass of low clouds with breaks here and there edged with silver moonlight. At ground level, the old landfill was a lumpy flatland that was struggling to become a forest again. The scrawny trees that had sprung up looked as though they had grown from garbage rather than seeds.

I devoured lungful after lungful of cool, clean air. I sat in the weeds and leaned back, listening to the locusts and watching the holes in the sky drift past the stars. An owl hooted in the woods above me. In the distance the glow of Campbellsville cast an orange glow against the bottom of the clouds.

It may have been a giddy delusion caused by the joy of being free, but I felt strength flowing into my limbs. I stood up and stretched. I felt the pleasant pain of flexing the stiffness out of my arms. Then I started up the hill. My brain seemed to be working in slow motion. I wasn't sure what to do first. Get to a phone. Call the cops. Report the boy's bones and the PCBs. My phone was gone. Caroline Boofey had confiscated it. I could drop in on Jodie and make the call. I could bum a ride to town.

The forest was filled with little skittering sounds on the ground and the incessant two-part chorus of the locusts in the trees. Occasionally a slightly lopsided moon appeared and helped me tack from side to side through the tangle of greenbriar. In the steepest places, I had to use branches and tree trunks to pull myself up. Every few minutes one of the thorn bushes snagged my clothes or beard. Mosquitoes whined in my ears. I didn't mind the scratches and bites. I was out of the cave. I was free. I was still alive. I did not let myself think about what I should do next. I could start thinking again when I reached the top of the hill. And then I'd play it by ear.

What with twisting and turning back and forth and stopping to catch my breath, it seemed to take an hour to reach the top of the hill. I expected to be directly above the Garth house, but the lights of what could only be Glenn Neidig's cabin and the Grapevines' house were way off to the right, much farther away than I thought they should be. I walked toward them along the narrow ridge.

I didn't realize it at first, but I was having trouble seeing things. Things seemed to disappear. A tree directly in front of me wasn't there unless I turned my head a little to one side. Then I realized a migraine was starting up. I sat on a boulder that bulged a foot or so out of the ground. I closed my eyes and waited, hoping to fend off the headache. A string of tiny silver boxes flickered in the dark. Then a line of bright triangles began pulsing. I lay on the rock and watched them pulse and slide. The whirr of locusts filled the night. Down in the hollow a dog began barking. Half a dozen others joined in, yelping and howling.

After twenty minutes or so, the migraine went away. I congratulated myself for fighting it off. The secret was to lie down and close your eyes as soon as the vision thing got going. But now it was time to do something. That's what must have caused the headache—I was stressed because I wasn't sure what I wanted to do. Should I call the police, or should I go to the *Gleaner* and write my story first? What time was it? The paper might be off the press by now. I decided to see what was going on at the Garth house before I did anything else. I pushed myself up off the rock and got moving. Across the knobs, the red eyes gleamed at me as I walked along the ridge.

When I was almost directly above Glenn Neidig's cabin and therefore the Garth house, a bite-sized car or truck appeared on the road coming from the direction of Hampstead. I didn't think anything of it until it slowed to a crawl. It passed the cabin and the lane that led to the house and continued crawling along until it reached a spot where it could turn around. Then it slowly retraced its route until it nosed into a field some distance beyond the cabin. The headlights went out.

I started down the hill as fast as I could. The slope was so steep that I had to grab onto tree trunks or low branches to keep from falling. The moon broke through the clouds, and the sudden brightness helped me plot a course around the thorn bushes. I exhaled the words, "Thank you, moon." I also thanked the locusts and crickets, two owls, and a whippoorwill for covering the noise I was making on the leaves and sticks.

There was little if any doubt in my mind that whoever had pulled off the road was heading for the Garth house. I was in a race to get there first. Halfway down, I could see a light in a side window, probably the living room. I wondered what time it was. At the foot of the hill, I held onto a thick vine and eased myself down the high inner bank of the dry creek. I crouched behind the opposite bank. From there I could see the lighted window.

The silhouettes of three men appeared between the house and the horse pasture. As they moved closer, I could see that at least two of them were carrying handguns. The third man had a long log in his hands. They paused for a brief conference, and then the one with the log and one with a gun crept toward the front of the house, while the third man, a big, heavyset guy, went to the rear. I watched him sneak up to the back door and try to open it, but it was locked. He placed the point of his gun against the lock and waited.

A woman inside screamed, "Somebody's on the porch!" and the light went out. A loud smash and the sound of breaking glass came from out front. It sounded like the log was used as a battering ram. At the same time, the guy in front of me blasted the lock with his gun and kicked in the door, but instead of charging inside, he crawled into the pantry like a marine on the beach. I heard the kitchen door hit the wall, followed immediately by a shotgun blast. The marine fired two more shots, and Caroline Boofey cried out in pain, "Walter . . . Wally." A chair fell over, and a moment later there was a heavy plop on the floor.

On the second floor, a window near the left end of the house opened, and Paula's head poked out. Without hesitating, she came climbing out the window. I got out of the creek and ran to the house. Hanging from the sill, she lowered herself about a third of the way down the wall and let go. I caught her around her legs and broke her fall. She gasped and flailed her elbows as we tumbled on the ground.

"Paula," I hissed in her hair, "it's me—Phil."

She went on battling for a moment, then twisted her neck to see me. Her mouth spread wide in a clownish look that went from shock to disbelief to joy in half a second, "Oh Jesus, you're alive!"

"Not for long if we don't move. Let's go."

We scrambled apart and got up. I grabbed her hand and pulled her toward the creek. I nearly dove over the bank, dragging her with me.

A second shotgun blast erupted in the house.

Breathing hard, Paula said, "How'd you get out?"

"Tell you later. Where's Edna Mae?"

"I don't know. I was upstairs when she yelled."

"There are three of them," I said, "two in the front and one in the back. It looks like they mean to wipe out the Boofeys just like the Garths."

"I knew this would happen." Her voice trembled. "I tried to tell Walter, but he wouldn't listen. We're all gonna get killed."

"We're not dead yet." I had a weird sense of power. It was as if, having survived my trek through the caves, having inhaled PCBs, having dug through an acre of trash, having caught Paula jumping out a window, nothing could stop me.

She tried to climb out of the creek, but I grabbed the bottom of her shirt and held her back. "Stay here," I said.

"I gotta help my mom."

"You'll get killed, Paula. Edna Mae's smart. She probably went down to the cave."

"How do *you* know?"

"We can't go in there. We don't even have a gun."

"You don't have to go with me."

I clutched her shoulder and gave her a shake. "Use your head, Paula."

She crinkled her nose and said, "Peee-uuu! You smell."

"Thanks."

She gave me a little shove and tried to get out of the creek again, but another shotgun blast inside the house stopped her.

There was a loud crash. Someone yelled, "Oh shit!" Boofey must have got one of them. Guns fired like crazy, and things began breaking, falling, smashing—dishes, glasses, a china cabinet maybe. "You damn piece a shit!" the voice yelled again. It sounded like Frank Brandon.

A light in the dining room came on, and a second later a window shattered. Paula and I ran a few yards through the creek and saw Walter Boofey hung up in a window screen. The long screen, now attached only to the window-sill, encircled his neck like a huge collar as he thrashed to get loose.

"Those bastards," Paula cried.

"Come on," I whispered. I took her hand and led her through the creek to the back of the cornfield. From there, hidden among the tall thick stalks, we had a clear view of the side of the house.

Someone else in the dining room shouted, "We've had enough of you, pal." When he stepped up behind Boofey, I recognized Lillian's brother Doug from the Judge's party.

"Go to hell," Boofey snarled.

"You first, shitface."

Boofey struggled to pull his head out of the screen. A shot was fired, and he squealed in agony. Paula gasped and stiffened. Boofey cursed again.

Seconds later Doug Brandon bent over him, and Boofey made a long deep straining moan that sounded as though he was struggling not to scream. There was another shot, and his entire body lurched sideways. Boofey's quavery voice went on cursing.

"Finish him off," Frank said.

"I will when I'm good and ready." Doug paused a moment. "He killed my dad."

"I know. We need to get your dad out of here."

Doug shot Boofey again to hear him scream.

Paula covered her ears and sank to the ground. I felt her shaking against the side of my leg.

Finally Doug put his gun against the screen and said, "Bye-bye, pig." He shot Boofey twice in the head.

Frank and Doug Brandon left Boofey hanging out the window. There were several bumps and scrapes, as if furniture was being shoved around. Then the dining-room light went off, but the lights in the hallway came on and cast a faint glow in the background. Noise came around the front side of the house from the porch. I left Paula where she was and ran between the cornrows. I saw Frank and Doug carrying Ralph Brandon's body out of the house.

I ran back to Paula. "I want to follow them," I told her. "Do you know where my car keys are?"

"Your car ain't here," she said.

"Where is it?"

"Walter got rid of it."

"Where? How?"

"He sank it in quicksand."

I took a long, slow breath.

Paula explained: "When you didn't come out of the cave you went in, him and Caroline blocked it up with big rocks. He thought you either got shot or you'd get yourself killed in there some other way. He got rid of your car so nobody would know you was here."

"What about *his* car—or Caroline's? Where is it?"

"They're both in the barn—his truck and her car."

"Where are the keys?"

"Hanging in the kitchen, unless they still got them on them."

"Come on."

She got up and ran with me toward the house, but on the way she said, "I ain't leaving. I gotta find Mom."

"Okay, you do that," I said. "But I need those keys."

I led the way in carefully, afraid to make a sound the Brandons might hear, even though they were out in the field. "Is there a light on the stove?" I said.

"Yeah there is," Paula said.

"Turn it on, but don't turn on any other lights."

She switched on the stove light and jumped back with a shriek. Caroline Boofey sat in a pool of blood on the floor with her back against the side of the refrigerator. Her head hung to one side like a broken puppet's. Her eyes stared blankly, and her mouth hung open with a dumb expression. A large red splotch that resembled the continent of Africa covered her chest.

"Where are the keys?" I said.

Paula had frozen. She gazed at Caroline.

I spun her around. "Paula, where are the keys?"

From the laundry room, Edna Mae said, "They're on the hook by the door."

"Mom!" Paula ran to her with open arms. "Thank God, oh thank God, thank God," she said, fast and shrill. They squeezed each other tightly, both of them in tears.

Edna Mae did not see Caroline until she nearly tripped over her legs. Her wide mouth gaped, and her chin trembled. She turned away and leaned on the table with both hands. Paula helped her sit down.

"Walter's dead too," Paula said.

Edna Mae's eyes swam in pools of tears. "I knew this would happen," she said. "I knew it from the start."

"We need to get out of here," I said.

Paula leaned over behind her mother with her arms wrapped around her neck and shoulders. She kissed the top of her head.

"Come on, ladies, it's not safe here," I said.

"I never wanted nothing to do with blackmail," Edna Mae said. "It was all Caroline's idea."

"It's my fault," Paula said. "I gave Walt that letter I found."

My skin was jumping so much, it felt like it was coming off the bones. I thought the Brandons might come back and burn the house down. I had to call the police. Where was my phone? I couldn't focus. "What letter?" I said.

Neither of them answered.

"I saw barrels of toxic chemicals in the cave," I said. "They're leaking. Is that what the letter was about?"

Still no answer.

"Damn it!" I yelled. "Tell me!"

"Okay, okay," Edna Mae said. "Wayne threatened to report them unless they cleaned up the dump."

"So the Garths were killed to shut them up, and Walter and Caroline took over the blackmail attempt."

"No!" Paula shouted. "It wasn't like that. Wayne and Cheryl wasn't into blackmail. They just wanted the chemicals got rid of."

"That's true," her mother said, nodding.

I pulled the keys off the hook. "Look, we've got to go. Now!"

Paula said, "I ain't going nowhere near them killers again. If you want to go after them, go yourself."

"I'm not going after them," I said. "I'm going to call the police." I remembered my BlackBerry. "Do you know where my phone is?" I asked her. "Caroline took it. And my wallet and keys, and the gun."

"The gun's empty," Paula said.

"I still want it."

Edna Mae said, "Your stuff's downstairs in the cave. I'll go get it for you."

As I listened to her go down the steps to the cellar, I suddenly felt very tired. I got myself a glass of water at the sink.

Behind me, Paula said, "I'm glad you're all right." For once her voice was soft, almost tender.

"Thanks," I said. "I'm glad you are too."

She scrunched up her lips, and we stared at each other over Caroline's body.

CHAPTER 35
The Scoop

W HEN EDNA Mae returned with my things, I said, "We've got to report this to the police right away. Is there a phone that works in the house—a land line?"

She shook her head. "Just Walter's cell phone, but you have to go up on top of the hill for it to work."

I turned on my BlackBerry. There was no signal, but at least it wasn't broken. "I can use mine," I said. "Let's go."

"Where to?" Paula said.

I wasn't sure. My head was buzzing. Behind my eyeballs was a gritty weariness, but my nervous system felt ridiculously supercharged. It was hard to think. I had to call the police, but I had a story to write too. I ought to phone Edward and tell him to hold the press. "What time is it?" I said.

Edna Mae glanced at her watch. "Going on 1:30."

What about Frank and Doug Brandon? They were getting away. Where would they go? The Judge's house maybe. They had come from the direction of Hampstead, but if they went back that way, they could make a turn at Hampstead and take the short way to Campbellsville. No, Frank would run to the Judge. I felt an irrepressible urge to get there as fast as possible. You must be nuts, I said to myself. If that's where they went, you could get your head blown off. But I needed to strike while the iron was hot. I wanted to get the Judge's reaction to Ralph's death. I wanted to hear what he'd say about the PCBs and the skeleton in the cave. I wanted to find out how much he knew about all this. I wanted to quote him. If he wouldn't talk to me, at least I could say I had given him the chance.

What should I do with Paula and Edna Mae? I could take them to the Grapevines' house, but Jackie Grapevine was a Brandon, and she might not like playing hostess to two women who could help put her brother and nephew in prison. I could put them up in my apartment, but I didn't want to drive all the way to Campbellsville and then back out to the boonies. And I shouldn't let them out of my sight. What if they disappeared again? Maybe I should call Sheriff Eggemann and ask him if they could stay at his house for the night, but this too meant a trip to Campbellsville, and Carl would want a statement from me. There wasn't time for that.

Come on, Larrison, make up your mind. Do something!

"Do you know the old guy across the road?" I said.

"No," Edna Mae said, "but I seen him snooping around a couple of times."

"I'm going to ask him to let you stay at his place for a few hours. You'll be okay there."

Paula said, "Why? Where are *you* going?"

"There's someone I've got to see."

"Who? The cops?"

"No, not yet."

"How 'bout you take us to the bus station."

I almost laughed. "You can't just walk away from this, Paula. Three people were shot to death tonight. We have to talk to the police. But not now."

"We can stay down in the cave," she said.

"That's too dangerous. Those guys might come back. I wouldn't be surprised if they burned this place down. You don't want to be in the cave if they do."

"Phil's right," Edna Mae said. "We can't stay here. I don't *want* to stay here. Not with Caroline and Walter's bodies. Where is Walter anyway?"

"You don't want to see him, Mom."

"Come on, we're wasting time." I turned off the stove light and ushered them through the pantry. We stepped outside into the cool night air. The clouds were gone, and a thousand stars filled the sky. The scent of corn hung heavy in the air.

As we walked to the barn, I thought they had acquiesced too easily. They probably figured they'd have less trouble getting away from Glenn Neidig than from me—not that they'd ever had much trouble getting away from me. A car came down the road from the direction of Hampstead, and I worried that it might be Frank and Doug, but it didn't slow down. Edna Mae pushed the barn door to the side, and I went to the vehicle standing just inside the door. It was a fairly new Ford Taurus, which I assumed was Caroline's. I told Paula and Edna Mae to get in, and then I pulled out of the barn and drove slowly past the pale-white house.

We crossed the county road, and Glenn's dogs started howling. The living-room and porch lights came on as if the howls had activated them. When the three of us got out of the car, the cabin door opened and Glenn stuck his head out. "Howdy, folks," he called. "You lost? What can I do fer ya?"

I said, "It's Phil Larrison, Glenn. I need some help."

"Whadaya need?" He stepped outside in jeans, a T-shirt, and socks.

I led Paula and Edna Mae to the foot of the steps and told him who they were. Then I asked if he had heard the shooting across the road a little while ago.

"What shootin'?" he said, taken aback. "No, I never heard a thing. I was fast asleep on the couch with the TV goin'."

"Three people were shot and killed," I said. "Two of them were the owners of the house, Walter Boofey and his wife."

Edna Mae interjected, "My brother and sister-in-law."

The dogs howled even louder when they heard her voice.

"The other one was one of three men who came to kill them," I explained. "My guess is they're the same guys who killed the Garths. They took their partner's body with them, but I'm afraid they'll be back. Edna Mae and Paula need a safe place to stay for a few hours, just in case they show up again."

"Well, if that don't beat all. This used to be a nice quiet little valley. Now it's like the wild frontier. Sure, they can stay here. I'll look after 'em for ya." He came down the steps and shook hands with the women. "The name's Glenn," he said. "Let's git inside before they come back and see us standin' out here gabbin'." To me he said, "What about you? Where're you goin'?"

"Thanks, Glenn," I said. "I'll be back as soon as I can."

"He's going after the murderers," Paula said.

"I reckon you called the police?" Glenn asked me.

"I will," I said.

"Yeah . . . okay." He wagged a hand at Paula and Edna Mae and said, "You can go on inside, ladies."

As they went in, I whispered to Glenn, "They might try to go back to the house, or ask you to take them somewhere. Try to keep them here. They're key witnesses."

He nodded. "I'll let the dogs outta their pens. I'll tell your lady friends they're coydogs and they had better stay indoors if they don't wanta git eaten alive."

"I hope that works."

I hurried to the car and backed onto the road. I saw Paula and Edna Mae watching me from the doorway. I stuck my arm out the window and waved at them over the roof as I took off for Hampstead.

The Taurus felt like a big car to me, loose and bouncy compared with my Civic, which Boofey had allegedly drowned in quicksand. Where the hell was the quicksand anyway?

I passed the spot where I had seen the Brandons park when I was up on the hill. It was a patch of gravel in front of a rusty gate. I wondered again which way they had gone, and again I decided that the Judge's house was my best bet.

When I was about halfway through the gap in the knobs, my BlackBerry began chirping out a list of messages. I punched in Lieutenant Bakery's number. There was no answer. I began to leave a message in his voice mail, but then he picked up.

"Yeah, Phil, what's going on?" He sounded scraggly from sleep.

"Three people died tonight in a gunfight in the house where Wayne and Cheryl Garth were killed," I said. "Two of the bodies are still there—Walter and Caroline Boofey's. Three guys came after them, and one of them got killed. The other two took his body with them. They're probably the same guys who killed the Garths. It's all about blackmail. The Boofeys were trying to blackmail the owners of an old dump where toxic chemicals were improperly disposed of in a cave between—"

"Slow down, Larrison. Where are you?"

I caught my breath. "I'll talk to you later, Lieutenant. I'm in the middle of something right now."

"Wait! Don't hang up!"

"You're breaking up, Lieutenant." I turned off the phone.

There, I had made a report to the officer in charge. It wasn't a very complete report, but it was enough to keep him busy. I didn't want to tell him where I was going. I didn't want the cops to show up while I was talking to the Judge. They'd shut me down. And I didn't want to spend the rest of the night giving a statement to the police. I wanted to write my story. I wanted to get it in today's *Gleaner*.

I called my boss. His phone rang four times before he answered, groggily.

"Edward," I said, "we've got to redo the front page."

He was speechless for a second, stunned, then suddenly alert. "Where the hell have you been?" he blurted out.

"In a cave with toxic chemicals and a skeleton. Listen, Ralph Brandon's dead. He was shot and killed tonight in a gun battle in the house where the Garths were murdered. The couple that owned the house, Walter and Caroline Boofey, were killed too—for trying to blackmail the Brandons over the chemicals, which are leaking out of their barrels into the ground. Ralph's son, Doug, shot them both. Frank Brandon was shooting too."

"Are you shitting me?"

I heard Ed's wife say, "Who is it?" in a soft, sleepy voice.

"I've got the story, Ed. I'll be in to write it up as soon as I can."

"Do you know what time it is? The paper came off the press over an hour ago."

"Don't put it out, Ed. Take it out of the box out front. We've got to get a story in this issue, or everybody else will beat us. Right now, it's all ours."

"It'll cost me thousands."

"Send me the bill."

"I'll do that." He sounded ticked-off but immediately changed tone: "Okay, I'll get the press crew back in."

"You won't need them for at least a couple hours. There's something I've still got to do. Then I have to write it up." I paused to build suspense. Then I said, "Ed, I've got it all. I spent the past two or three days—I don't know how long it was—in a maze of caves under the hill behind the Garth house. I found hundreds of barrels of PCBs in there. And I found the skeleton of a little kid in the cave."

"Jesus. You're not gonna write something that'll get us sued, are you?"

"I hope not, Ed. Hey, by the way, what day is it?"

"He wants to know what day it is," Edward told his wife. To me he said, "It's Friday. Get your ass in to the office."

"Be happy, Ed," I told him. "You're gonna love me. You're gonna want to give me a raise."

CHAPTER 36
There Was an Accident

THE BRANDON house glowed like an amethyst in the moonlight. Half the rooms were lit up. I turned into the driveway between the oversized gateposts. A dreary, desolate feeling lodged in my chest as I drove up toward the house. A white Cadillac Escalade was parked at a crazy angle in front of the garage doors. I parked beside it and got out.

The sky seemed thin and fragile, perforated with stars. It reminded me of an overused sheet of carbon paper. My shirttail was hanging out. I tucked it in. I reeked of sweat, and for a moment I thought I must have befouled my pants in the cave without knowing it, but then I realized it was fertilizer from a nearby field that I smelled. I glanced inside the SUV. Ralph Brandon's body lay on its side on the back seat.

I crossed the lawn in front of the Judge's den, giving his windows a wide berth even though the drapes were drawn. The room was quiet, and I thought no one was there until the Judge shouted, "Damn it, Frank! Damn it! What the hell got into you?"

I peeked through one of the narrow panels along-side the door and saw Lillian coming down the stairs in a robe and slippers. When she got closer, I tapped softly on the glass and showed my face. She was startled to see me. She stopped and seemed to debate whether to let me in. Then she hurried past the den and opened the door a crack.

"Phil, what are you doing here this time of night?" she whispered.

The Judge bellowed, "Lillian, who's there?"

I said, "I have to see the Judge." I pushed the door open slowly but firmly and stepped into the hall.

"What happened to you?" Lillian exclaimed. "What's going on?"

"Sorry, Lillian," I said, brushing past.

"Who's there?" the Judge roared again.

"It's Phil Larrison," Lillian called back.

The Judge's wife appeared in a long nightgown at the head of the stairs, her hair a fluffy cloud around her face. She stopped in the middle of a yawn and stared down at me.

I went into the den. Frank Brandon was standing in the middle of the room, glaring at me with a baffled and fierce expression. He looked like a train wreck. His shirt was bloody, his hair disheveled, his tanned face slick with sweat. Doug Brandon was slumped on the leather sofa with his head back, staring at the ceiling. He jerked upright as I entered. Judge Brandon sat at his desk in a red silk robe over his pajamas. Coils of gray hair sprouted on his chest. His forearms lay flat on the blotter pad, and his brows wrinkled as he peered at me. His large, startled eyes made him look like a fish that had just been pulled out of a pond.

Frank blurted, "What the hell are you doing here?" He looked at Lillian as if she must be to blame.

"Sorry to barge in on you, Judge," I said. "I guess you know what happened tonight."

From behind me, Lillian said, "What? What happened?" She squeezed past me into the den.

The Judge stared at her miserably.

Doug said, "I'll take care of this," and started to get up to take care of me.

The Judge raised a hand. "Sit down, Doug, and keep your mouth shut."

Lillian raised her voice: "Would someone please tell me what's going on?"

"Why don't you tell her?" I said to Frank.

"You bastard," he muttered. His left jaw clenched hard, puckering the cheek.

I heard Beverly Brandon coming through the hall. I moved out of her way as she entered the room. "What's wrong, Jack?" she said softly.

"Sit down, Bev," her husband replied. "You too, Lillian. Please. Sit down." He gestured toward the sofa and chairs.

The women sat next to Doug on the sofa.

With a grim frown, the Judge rubbed the heels of his hands into his eyes. When he stopped rubbing, he seemed to have woken from a bad dream. "I'm sorry to tell the two of you this," he said to Beverly and Lillian, "but Frank says Ralph is dead."

Beverly gasped. "Oh dear God, no." She clutched Lillian's arm. "What happened?"

Lillian stared at the Judge. His eyes shrank from hers. She whirled toward her uncle, who said, "That damn Boofey killed him."

Lillian hardly moved. Her head made a barely perceptible shudder. Her eyes burned into Frank Brandon's haggard face.

"He killed him with a shotgun," Frank added.

Beverly's mouth fell open, and a low moan came out. Stunned, she began to waver back and forth. Lillian put an arm around her grandmother's broad shoulders and squeezed her tightly. The touch seemed to release Beverly's tears. She began sobbing and gasping for air.

Lillian cast a disgusted glance at Frank. "It's all your fault my father's dead."

"Like hell," Frank shot back. "Blame Boofey. Boofey killed him."

I tossed my two cents' worth in: "Yeah, Boofey killed him, but you failed to mention that the three of you broke into his house. It's too bad the Boofeys weren't in the bathroom. You could have given them the same treatment you gave Wayne and Cheryl Garth."

"You shut your damn mouth," Frank yelled.

Doug made a little snort, almost a laugh. "He's asking for it."

"Shut up, Doug," Lillian said. "You're as bad as he is. I hope you both rot in hell."

"I'm sorry about your dad," Frank said. "We did what we had to do."

The Judge roused himself from a stupor. "That's enough!" He shook his head. "Ralph never should have gone with you tonight. None of you should have gone there. Boofey's a career criminal. What did you expect to happen?"

"Boofey's dead, and so's his wife," Doug said with a cocky sneer. "Like Frank says, they shot first. They got what they deserved."

The Judge glared at Frank. "Is that true? They're both dead?"

Doug said, "I got both of them. It was self-defense."

"It was self-defense all right," I said, "but it was the Boofeys who were defending themselves. The three of you broke into their house. You were armed with high-caliber handguns. It was supposed to be another execution, just like the Garths."

"How the hell—where were you?" Frank demanded.

"Outside. In the yard. I wasn't alone either."

The Judge hung his head.

Doug stared at me, his eyes a dark threat. The tip of his tongue slid from side to side between his lips. The Judge gripped the front of his chair between his legs and rocked slowly back and forth. "Do you know what Boofey and his wife were up to?" he asked me. He searched my face as if feeling me out, hoping for understanding or sympathy.

"Yes I do," I told him.

"You know he was a blackmailer?" He uttered the word with contempt. His eyes went on searching.

"Yes," I said. "He learned about the PCBs after the Garths were murdered. Wayne Garth found them in the cave where they were hidden. I doubt if Boofey ever saw the drums. But he did know about them, and he saw a copy of a letter Garth wrote demanding that the chemicals be cleaned up. That's where Boofey got the idea to blackmail the owners of the old county dump."

"He knows," Frank said, pacing again. He came toward me with fists clenched and stopped inches away from my face. "You bastard, sneaking around here all the time, sucking up to Lillian. You're as rotten as Boofey."

"Ralph is gone," Beverly said, no longer crying. "Jack, our son is gone." Forlorn, shell-shocked, she gazed at him across the room.

"Yes, Bev," the Judge said.

Lillian pressed her cheek against the side of her grandmother's head.

With a long, loud breath, Doug stood up and said, "I need a beer."

"You do not need a beer," the Judge snapped. "This is not a party."

"Dad," Frank said, "we did the right thing. There's only one way to deal with a blackmailer." When the Judge did not answer, he went on, "If we'd given him the money he wanted, someday he would have come back for more. You know that. He had to be stopped. We did what we had to do."

Judge Brandon lapsed into thought, and the room fell silent. For a minute or so no one said a word. Then the Judge proclaimed, "Mistakes have been made," using the passive voice to minimize responsibility. "Big mistakes. My sons never should have gone into the hazardous-waste business." He glared at Frank. "They lacked expertise." I suddenly realized it was not a soliloquy. He was talking to me. "But no one appreciated the seriousness of the problem back then," he continued. "No one knew how difficult and how expensive it was to dispose of toxic chemicals. My sons thought if they stored the drums in the cave, out of the weather, they would be all right. The drums stood on solid rock, so even if they leaked, the liquids would be contained."

"That's what you think," I said. I knew I sounded snarky even as the words were still in my mouth, but I could not stop myself.

The Judge was not accustomed to having his opinions treated with disrespect. Flaring, he said, "You are correct. That is what I think. But those barrels have not harmed anyone. They've been safely buried in the cave for years."

"Keep telling yourself that, Judge," I said. "But what about Wayne and Cheryl Garth? They weren't blackmailers, but they were murdered."

The Judge said, "That was another mistake. The chemicals should have been cleaned up, as they wanted."

Frank nearly shrieked, "We couldn't afford that. It would have bankrupted all of us. It would have cost millions to clean it up, tens of millions."

"Nevertheless. . . ."

Frank said, "They *were* blackmailers. It was just a different kind of blackmail."

I looked at him and said, "It was cheaper to kill them than pay for the cleanup, huh?"

"They were dirt," he said. "Pot-smoking drifters."

The Judge seemed to drift away.

"They were nothing but scum," Frank said.

"At least they didn't murder anyone," I said.

Frank looked straight into my eyes. "No one would have got hurt if they had minded their own business."

"Is that a threat? Am I next?" I said. "The truth is no one would have got hurt if you had disposed of the chemicals properly."

A soft, lilting moan escaped Beverly's lips.

The Judge said, "Lillian, take your grandmother upstairs."

"No," Beverly said. "No."

There was a tense silence. When no one else spoke, I said, "Who murdered the Garths, Frank? Was it you, Ralph, and Doug, or just one or two of you?"

"You bastard," Frank said. "We didn't 'murder' anybody. Like Doug said, it was self-defense. We were under attack. They were trying to destroy us. We had to do something."

Doug spoke up again: "What proof is there that any-one in this room 'murdered' somebody? It could be argued that the Garths were killed by someone in their line of work. The police think their deaths were drug-related."

"What about the Boofeys?" I said.

"If they shot first, it certainly sounds like self-defense," said the Judge.

"The woman shot first," Doug said. "Then I shot back."

"Be quiet please, Doug," the Judge said, less harshly this time. To me he said, "With regard to what happened tonight, you claim to be an eyewitness, but you say you were outside the house when the Boofeys were killed. If Ralph and Frank were the victims of a blackmail attempt, it is conceivable that they thought they could scare the blackmailers off with a show of force and the situation spiraled out of control when the Boofeys began shooting."

"We covered this already," I said. "My question was 'Who murdered the Garths?' Remember?"

Lillian, who had maintained a stiff silence, finally broke down. "Tell him, Frank," she blurted out. "And don't try to blame it on my father, now that he's dead. Tell him who murdered the Garths. Tell him it was you and Doug. *Tell him!*" Her last two words, deep and hoarse, sounded as if they had been ripped out of the flesh in her throat.

Frank barked, "Shut up."

It was Beverly's turn to comfort Lillian, whose body was being convulsed with sobs that made no sound.

A sorrowful grimace passed over the Judge's face. "Mistakes were made," he muttered somberly. He stared into space as if lost in thought. "I take responsibility. We never meant to harm innocent people. We thought we had a perfect place to store the drums. We believed the landfill cave was secure. But now you say the chemicals are leaking into the earth. We did not anticipate that. We should have, but we didn't. That was our mistake. But it's an error that can be rectified. We can still get rid of the drums—I mean dispose of them properly. Four blackmailers have died, the Garths and the Boofeys, but—"

"Judge," I cut in, "I said this before, but I'll say it again. I don't believe the Garths were blackmailing you."

"They were not good people. You know that, Phil." He leaned forward on his desk, reasoning, not quite pleading. His skin seemed translucent, a sheet of waxed paper over a brown and purple map.

I said, "All they wanted, as I understand it, was for the chemicals to be cleaned up."

Beverly Brandon sniffled and stared at me with a hapless frown. She looked as if she had aged ten years in the last ten minutes.

The Judge said, "You know, Phil, if you put these things in your paper, you destroy the good name of a family that has done many beneficial things for this county and this part of the state. Think about that. We made mistakes, but I think it's fair to say that over the years the Brandon family has helped many many people. We've always tried to help people who were less fortunate than ourselves."

I shifted my weight from one leg to the other and rolled my shoulders slightly. "What are you asking?"

"Just that you think about what I said."

I sensed a tacit hint that I would not regret it if I did what he asked. "What about the skeleton in the cave? I said. "Am I supposed to think about that too?"

Beverly moaned. "Oh dear God." Judge Brandon recoiled indignantly, as if I had insulted him. His nose became sharp and flinty. Frank swung around toward him as if asking for permission to break my neck. Doug's face was fire-engine red. Lillian's eyes stared at me in fear. I wondered if all of them knew about the dead boy.

"It's a child's skeleton," I continued. "It's in another cave, some distance from where the chemicals are. My guess is—and I think it's a pretty good guess—it's what's left of a boy who supposedly ran away from the Good Shepherd Home."

Hunched over in his chair, Frank began nodding slowly. "I get it now," he explained to the others. "He was in the caves, just like Garth." Without turning around, he asked, "How'd you get in?"

"You can read about it in the paper," I said. "Right now I'm interested in whose bones are in that cave."

A cloud of hopelessness engulfed the room. I went on without mercy: "I've been told that Chuck Martin used to take kids from the so-called Good Shepherd Home to other places, including a pedophile professor's house. I'm wondering if he ever brought any of the kids here as well."

The Judge smacked his open hand on the desk and glowered at me. "Are you calling me a pedophile now, Mr. Larrison?"

"What was his name?" I said. "Was it Barry Wilson, the boy who 'ran away' from the home?" I paused a moment and looked at Judge Brandon. "No, sir, I'm not calling you a pedophile," I said. "I wouldn't be surprised, though, if Chuck Martin brought some kids here to play with someone else, Scott maybe. Did Scott kill the boy?"

Beverly sat bolt upright. "Stop it," she begged.

"I'm sorry, Mrs. Brandon," I said, "but this has got to come out. The police should be able to identify the remains, either through dental records or DNA. I don't know if they'll be able to prove the boy was ever brought here, but I have a hunch someone will talk."

"It's not true," Beverly wailed, pounding her fists on her lap. "How can you say such awful things?"

Frank turned and shouted, "You won't get away with this. You think you can walk in here and say anything you please, even call us perverts. You're nothin' but a two-bit reporter for a two-bit paper. What does Wylie pay you for the shit you dish out—twenty thousand? You're not even worth that. Look at you. You look like a pig. You stink."

"Let me take him outside," Doug said.

The Judge slumped in his chair. The folds in his old skin looked like wax dripping from a candle. His head drooped, and his arms lay on the chair as if he were about to be electrocuted. "We wanted to help the children," he said. He seemed hypnotized. "We thought it would be good for them to spend some time in a nicer place. Most of them were poor kids from the wrong side of the tracks. When we lived in town, Chuck Martin would pick them up at the Good Shepherd Home and bring them to our house so they could play with Scott. Scott needed someone to play with. We thought it would be good for him as well as them." There was a long pause. I thought he had finished speaking. Then he added, "But one day there was an accident."

"Dad, don't go there," Frank said.

"What kind of accident?" I asked the Judge.

"One of those terrible things that happen sometimes." He paused. "I've been quiet for too long," he said as if still in a trance. He paused again. Then, in a feeble voice that I could barely hear, he said, "Scott and his friend were watching a cowboy movie on television, and then they went down to the basement to play." His chin began trembling. "It was just an accident, a terrible, terrible accident." His eyes brimmed with tears, and he coughed to keep from crying.

Beverly said, "They were only playing, Mr. Larrison. Scott didn't mean to hurt him."

Lillian, whose face was a gray mask, squeezed her grandmother's hands.

Beverly went on: "Scott was so big for his age. We should have known better than to let him play with such a small boy. But they were the same age."

"Scott's still playing with small boys," I said. "I've seen the kind of games he plays. What happened?"

Frank said, "What's the matter with the two of you? You want this in the paper?"

"Was he drowned in the pool?" I asked Beverly.

She shook her head. "We didn't have a pool at our old house. He was—"

The Judge completed the sentence for her: "—hanged by the neck."

I said, "If it was an accident, why didn't you report it to the police instead of putting out the story that the kid ran away from the home?"

"That's what we should have done," the Judge said. "But I was afraid Scott would be put away for the rest of his life. It was my fault, no one else's."

"You had Scott's best interest at heart, Dad," Frank said. "The mistake was letting him see the light of day. I should have put a pillow over his head the day he was born."

"Don't talk like that," Judge Brandon said. "He's your son. He's a Brandon. He's one of us. And he has a right to live as full a life as possible." He looked at me and opened his hands, as if for understanding. "We tried to make it up to the boy's parents. They were dirt poor, and they had three or four other kids. They went along with the story that the boy ran away. He actually had done that a couple of other times."

"After playing with Scott?" I asked.

He gave me an angry glance but tolerated my question. "I don't know. I don't think so. In any case, the story was that he had run away and was never found. We helped the parents as much as we could, but the father was a drunk. He was in jail more than he was out. But I got him a job with the county highway department."

Beverly said, "We did our best."

"They didn't care," Frank said. "The father's a drunken thief, and the mother's a whore."

"So you feel it didn't really matter if they had one less kid?" I said.

"It didn't seem to," Frank snapped.

The Judge swiveled sideways and stared at his reflection in the window. "All I ever wanted to do was work for the public good . . . make Meridian County a better place . . . keep my family together. . . . I never wanted to hurt anyone. But I made mistakes."

His fingers jittered against the edge of the desk, and his head shook. He pulled open the middle drawer, dug through some papers, and brought out a gun.

Beverly yelled, "Jack! No!"

My insides sank. I thought he was going to kill me, but in one continuous motion he raised the .38 revolver to his temple and pulled the trigger.

The loud report shattered the air. The Judge slumped in his chair. His arm fell to his side, and the gun thumped on the floor. A crimson stream of blood ran down his cheek onto his robe.

Beverly ran screaming to his side and wrapped her arms around his head as if trying to stop the bleeding. The Judge's mouth hung open. His crazed eyes stared blankly.

Lillian buried her face in her hands.

Frank looked at me and said, "You damn bastard, you did this."

"You killed him," Doug said to me. "You as good as murdered him."

A roar came from the doorway. "Papaw!" Scott charged into the den like a bull. "Papaw hurt!" He knocked Beverly aside with his shoulder and grabbed the Judge's arm. "Papaw!" He tried to make the Judge stand up.

Beverly said, "He can't get up, Scott." She tried to pull her grandson away.

"Uppp," Scott bellowed. "Uppppp."

Frank Brandon sat rubbing his forehead, squeezing the skin to the middle. Doug Brandon stared at me with the eyes of a rattlesnake ready to strike.

I watched the dismal scene for a couple of minutes. Then I went outside and called Sheriff Eggemann. I felt as dry and crumbly inside as a hollow tree. Through the window I could hear Scott howling.

While waiting for the police to arrive, I called in the story to the *Gleaner*.

CHAPTER 37
You Was Real Nice to Me

THE PARAMEDICS were wheeling the Judge's body out of the house when Sheriff Eggemann arrived. "Looks like you had another busy night, Phil," he said as he climbed out of his car. His uniform looked crisp and smooth, but his hair was curled up on one side from sleep. He left the lights on his cruiser flashing.

"I'm afraid so, Carl," I said.

He stopped the gurney to take a look at the Judge, and then I followed him inside. Beverly Brandon was alone in the den, gazing at her husband's empty chair. Carl leaned over and held her hands. "I'm real sorry for your loss, Bev," he said.

She swallowed hard, nodding. She fell to pieces again when she said, "I miss him already. I miss him so much it hurts."

Carl gave her a few more words of comfort, patted her on the hands, and straightened up. In the hall he said, "Do you have anything to do, Phil?"

"I'm doing it."

"You go home and get some sleep. I'll talk to you in the morning."

I told him where I had left Paula and Edna Mae. "They were not involved in the killings," I said.

"You're sure about that, are you?"

"Absolutely."

JOHN PESTA

"I'll keep it in mind."

I drove home the long way, through Blind Horse Hollow. I slowed down as I passed Glenn Neidig's cabin. Only the porch light was on, and three hounds sat there like sentinels watching me. I figured Paula and Edna Mae were trapped inside.

At the Grapevines' house all the lights were burning. No doubt they had learned Judge Brandon and Ralph were dead. One of the other Brandons had probably called Jackie. I was tempted to stop, but I looked and smelled like an ogre and I didn't want to act like one.

On top of the knobs it hit me that the whole thing was over. In the weeks ahead I'd have a slew of stories to write, but my life would be normal again. I felt a twinge of regret. More than a twinge.

About a half hour after I got back to my apartment, Glenn called. "I thought you'd wanta know the state police jest arrested your lady friends," he said.

"I thought that would happen," I said. "How'd it go?"

"Real quick. The police handcuffed 'em and took 'em outta here before they knew what hit 'em. They looked real scared, especially the younger one."

"Did they say where they were taking them?" I asked.

"The county jail, I reckon, but no, they didn't tell me nothin'."

"Thanks, Glenn. I appreciate your letting me know."

"So what the hay happened tonight?"

I was too tired to talk, but I owed him something, so I gave him a quickie version of my story that would appear in the morning paper.

"That's too bad about Jack Brandon," he said. "He was a good man, but I reckon even a good man can do some

370

bad things once in a while. But I wish he hadn't've took his own life. I always thought suicide was the coward's way out." It had slipped my mind what a talker Glenn was until he rattled on: "But that son of his, Frank, I never knew anybody that had much good to say about him. Ralph, the banker, he was all right, just a little standoffish, snooty like. The Judge was a man of the people, but not his two boys. Frank was here a few days ago. He was wantin' to know if anythin' was goin' on across the road. I told him I seen the property owners—Walter Boofey and his wife—a-goin' or a-comin' a coupla times. Maybe I shouldn't've told him. They might still be alive if I'd kept my mouth shut."

He could be right, I thought. I listened to him yak on a few more minutes before I said I needed to get some sleep. Then I poured myself a half inch of Scotch and went to bed.

I slept till 6:30, when I woke up with a headache. I made a cup of coffee, my first in days, and then I took a much-much-much-needed shower and drove to work in the Boofeys' Taurus. Since they had drowned my car in quicksand somewhere, I felt justified in using theirs. Around a dozen people were lined up at the newspaper box in front of the *Gleaner* building. The paper was selling like hotcakes. Edward would be thrilled. He'd probably raise ad rates.

I went in the back way and picked up a copy of the front section that was lying on the floor. A two-deck banner headline in 60-point type read:

Judge Jack 'Red' Brandon Kills Self after Toxic Chemicals, Child's Skeleton Found in Caves

A 24-point subhead in the middle four columns said:

*Ralph Brandon, Two Boofeys Die in Shootout Over
Bribery Scheme; Suspects in Garth Murders Held*

The story was pretty much as I had dictated it off the
top of my head last night on the phone. It was not my best
piece of writing, but all the major facts were there. The
front section of the paper had been reprinted. A pressman
who was still cleaning ink rollers told me the night shift
also had to pull out Section B and the ad inserts from the
original front section and then recollate everything.

"I guess they hate my guts," I said.

He opened one side of his mouth and nodded slowly.

At 8:00 I went to the jail. Sheriff Eggemann was still
there. Tired and irritable, he told me Frank Brandon and
Doug Brandon had been arrested and charged with the
murders of Wayne and Cheryl Garth. The shootout with
the Boofeys was still under investigation, with more
charges pending. I asked if he had notified federal and
state agencies about the leaking PCBs, and he testily
replied that it was only eight o'clock and he doubted if
he could raise any of them this early. I asked when he
thought the entrance to the cave at the landfill would be
cleared so the child's skeleton could be examined, but all
he said was, "Give me a break, Phil," and stood up.

"What about Paula and Edna Mae Boofey?" I said.

"What about them?"

"Where are they?"

"In a nice, cozy cell. I put them up for the night at tax-
payer expense."

"That was big of you, Carl. May I see them?"

"No. They're in the women's wing."

"When then?" I said.

"When they're ready to go."

"So they haven't been charged with anything?"

"Didn't you tell me they were innocent?"

"I didn't know I had so much influence."

He finally cracked a grin. "You don't."

I did not tell him Paula had told Walter Boofey about Garth's discovery of the PCBs, which led to the blackmail scheme. Why complicate things?

Carl asked a female deputy to check on Paula and Edna Mae. A few minutes later the three of them came down the hall toward the front desk. They had washed up, so their faces looked fresh, but their clothes were wrinkled and soiled, Paula's especially. I expected her to be mad at me, but she didn't mouth off.

"Good morning, Phil," Edna Mae said. "They say we can leave."

"I know," I said.

She whispered, "I'll be glad to get out of here."

Paula said, "You and me both."

"So what are we waiting for?" I said.

I led the way out front to the parking lot. I offered to buy them breakfast, but Edna Mae said, "We already ate."

I told them about Judge Brandon's suicide and the two arrests. Then I described what I had gone through after taking refuge in the cave.

"We thought you was dead for sure," Paula said.

"Maybe I am," I said. "It all seems like a dream."

Edna Mae pinched my arm and laughed. "Nope. You're alive."

I walked them to the Taurus and handed Edna Mae the keys.

"I was wondering how we were going to get home," she said.

"You probably won't be able to get your clothes and things out of the Garths' place until the police are finished with their investigation," I said.

Paula said, "I don't ever want to see that place again."

"Do you need a ride?" Edna Mae asked me.

I shook my head. "I'm okay."

"Then we're outta here." She gave me a big hug.

Paula was staring at me. I saw what looked like the beginning of a tear in her eye. Suddenly she stepped forward and put her arms around me. "You was real nice to me," she said in my ear. "Thanks."

I gave her a little squeeze and patted her on the back. She hopped in the car, and I watched them drive away. Edna Mae tooted the horn at me from the highway.

Later that day I called Jackie Grapevine and Jodie to express my sympathy on the deaths of Judge Brandon and his son Ralph.

"I'm sorry about your father and brother," I said to Jackie.

"Thank you," she replied curtly, as if I didn't really mean it, and turned the phone over to Jodie.

"Hi," I said. "I'm very sorry about your grandfather and your uncle. How are you? You doing okay?"

She did not answer right away, and I thought she was going to hang up, but then she said, "I can't talk about it right now. I'm too upset."

"I understand."

There was another long pause. Then she said, "Our family's been destroyed." Her voice cracked on the last word.

"Would you like me to come out there, Jodie?"

"No. No. I need to be alone for a while." Her breath whispered through the line. "Goodbye, Phil."

I did not like the sound of that goodbye.

The events in Blind Horse Hollow provided news fodder for months. An army of investigators from the Environmental Protection Agency descended on the county. The drums of PCBs were removed from the cave, and studies got underway. Ground and water samples were collected throughout the cave system, and test wells were drilled all around the knobs to determine PCB levels. People, especially those living near the knobs, were outraged, not only with the Brandons but also with the government. Those who had wells feared their water had been poisoned. Environmental groups wanted the government to excavate the caves and remove all traces of PCBs. Opponents considered this an impossible task and cited the costs involved. Stories of hearings filled our news hole, and angry letters covered the editorial pages.

During the time before his trial, while out of jail on a five-million-dollar property bond, Frank Brandon tried to take Meridian Waste Managers, Inc., into bankruptcy, but the government blocked the move.

At the trial of Frank and Doug Brandon, Paula testified that Walter and Caroline Boofey had tried to extort a million dollars from Frank and Ralph Brandon, the owners of the former county landfill. She said the Boofeys also blamed the Brandons for killing Wayne and Cheryl Garth. "The blackmail was mostly Caroline's doing," Paula said. "She talked Uncle Walter into it. They said if they got the million dollars, they wouldn't tell the police about the chemicals in the cave and who done the murders."

According to Paula, the Brandons agreed to pay but stalled for time. "Uncle Walt wanted the money in cash, and they said it would take a while for them to get that much cash together," she said. "But they was lying. They found out we was staying at the house, and then they tried to kill us just like they killed Wayne and Cheryl."

"Why did you stay in the house?" the prosecutor asked.

"It was stupid. We thought we was safe down in the cave," Paula said. "And we thought they would never expect us to be there. But somebody prob'ly seen us and told them."

The police investigation revealed that the Garths had been shot with the same gun that had killed Walter Boofey. Though Doug Brandon had killed him, the weapon belonged to Frank Brandon. It tied him to the murder of the Garths.

Forensic evidence also showed that the skeleton I had found in the cave was that of Barry Wilson. Chuck Martin admitted helping the Brandons cover up the boy's death at the hands of Scott. At his trial Martin broke down in tears and said it was the worst mistake of his life. "I did it for Judge Brandon," he said. "Judge Brandon loved his grandson. You can't imagine how he loved that poor kid. He didn't want Scott to be taken away. He felt it was his duty to take care of him. What I did I did for him."

Martin also admitted to transporting children from the home to people he described as mentors and big brothers, but he insisted it was always at Judge Brandon's orders. Grace DeLong backed him up. Of course, it served her own interest to do so.

The strategy of blaming the Judge worked for Martin. The jury was not swayed by Gary Fromm's story of the Professor. Martin's lawyer persuaded them that the Judge had in fact ordered him to take the boy there, and so the jury did not hold Martin responsible for the abuse Gary suffered. Even more important, Gary's story could not be corroborated, because the Professor could not be found.

As for Paula's claim that Martin had sodomized her when she was fifteen, there was no proof of that crime either. As with Gary Fromm, it would have been her word against the ex-sheriff's. Her connection to Walter and Caroline Boofey was another strike against her. As a result, the prosecuting attorney did not subpoena her to testify against Martin.

Most people thought Paula and her mother were as deeply involved in the blackmail attempt as Walter and Caroline were. I did not tell the police and the prosecutor everything I had heard while I was in the cavern. "Walter and Caroline were the blackmailers," I said. "Paula and Edna Mae were against it. I heard Paula say it would get them all killed. And I heard her mother say she and Paula wanted to leave. Walter Boofey would not let them go." This was true, as far as it went, though based on what I had heard, Edna Mae and Paula had gone along with the blackmail attempt at the start.

I did not have the heart to implicate them. After all, they backed out of the blackmail scheme in the end, and I told myself that if it hadn't been for Paula, the truth probably would never have come out. What's more, she had saved my life twice. No charges were brought against them.

Jodie would not go out with me again until three weeks after Judge Brandon's funeral. We went to Zwanzig'z in Columbus for pizza. She was moody and quiet, and it was a struggle for her to hold up her end of the conversation.

Afterward, as we drove through the knobs on the way back to Blind Horse Hollow, she asked me to stop the car somewhere. I pulled into an overlook where there was a bench and a picnic table, and we got out and sat on the bench. As we gazed down at the farms and the silver ribbon that was White River, she said, "I have something to tell you. I got my job back. I'm going back to New York."

My heart sank. "When?" I said.

"Tomorrow. I'm all packed."

"I don't want you to go."

She stood up and walked to the edge of the hill. "I can't live here anymore. Everything's changed."

"Sure. I know. But give it a little more time."

"I've tried. I can't. I see how people stare at me. It's like 'Brandon' has become a dirty word."

"Don't go, Jodie," I said.

She looked at me sadly. "I'm sorry, Phil. I know how you feel, but I wouldn't be good for you. I'm all messed up."

"You'll get through it."

She shook her head. "Someday maybe, but not if I stay here." She began to cry. "I think you'd better take me home."

Later that night, lying in bed alone, I tried to tell myself it was just another meaningless episode in a meaningless life. One thing leads to another in a series of random events, and nothing matters. But if that's true, I said to myself, why does it hurt so much?

Made in the USA
San Bernardino, CA
06 November 2013